CHATURANGA

ANDREW C. KATEN

Inner Compass Publishing
Lexington, Kentucky

Published by:
Inner Compass Publishing

Inner Compass Publishing
Lexington, Kentucky
innercompasspublishing@gmail.com

Printed in the United States of America

ISBN-13:
978-0692586181 (Inner Compass)

ISBN-10:
0692586180

Praise for *Chaturanga*

"[Katen] makes learning fun, he boils down very complex issues, geopolitics, ancient and modern history, international corporate strategy and more in a very digestible manner. Told through the eyes of his young protagonist, it is full of wanderlust and adventure, one that Marco Polo himself would have recognized and enjoyed. The genius in it for me is his use of oil as the linchpin of his book. Once trade goods such as silk, spices and precious gems animated the Silkroad; today oil is the lubricant reanimating that ancient route and is the Axis Mundi upon which the whole world now turns!"

>   – Francis O'Donnell, Artist, Author, Explorer & Emmy
>   Nominated filmmaker of the PBS Documentary "In the
>   Footsteps of Marco Polo"

"What a great story. And what a great way to encourage the interest of teenagers in history, politics, current events, geography, and economics."

>   – Larry Eubanks, Ph.D., Associate Professor of
>   Economics, University of Colorado at Colorado Springs

"This novel tells an exciting story through a historical, cultural, political and contemporary narrative that will captivate, educate and stimulate young adults. The writing is fluid, informed, and imaginative."

>   – Hussein A. Amery, Ph.D. Division of Liberal Arts and
>   International Studies, Colorado School of Mines

"...an entertaining, heartwarming, hair-rasing, inspirational and educational journey into the world of energy exploration and intriguing geopolitics. Well done! I did not want it to end."

>   – Stephen Doyle, President, BtuBaron LLC

"...a delightful romp, an epic adventure. Engrossing, imaginative, and beautifully wrought, it is a tale of legend, lore and discovery that, like the best of books, will educate, fascinate, and resonate. Katen's book is one that you will keep, share, and one day, want your own children to read."

>   – Troy Matthew Carnes, teacher and author of
>   *Rasputin's Legacy*

To my beautiful family.

CONTENTS

PART I: THE OPENING

PART II: THE MIDDLEGAME

PART III: THE ENDGAME

PART IV: THE OPENING

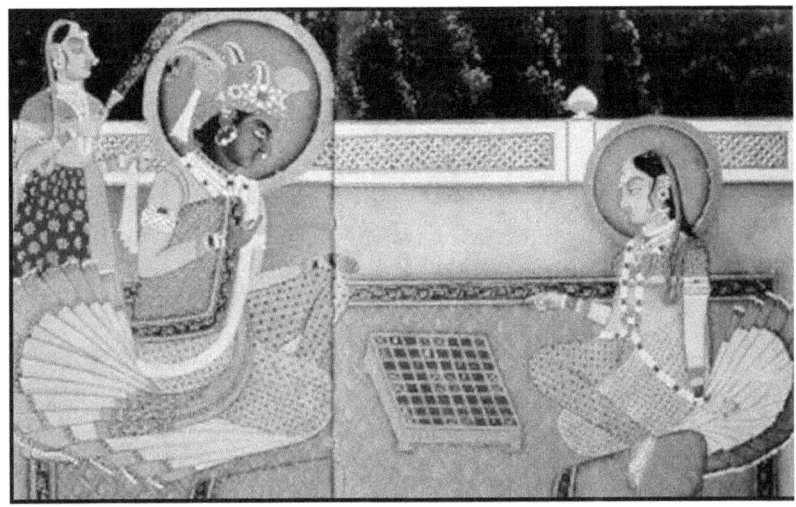

Chaturanga is an ancient strategy game that originated in India in the fifth century. Meaning "four divisions" in Sanskrit, the earliest version of the game likely involved four players. The exact rules – even the meaning of its ornately decorated board – are not well known.

From India, Chaturanga spread along the Silk Road, where it became popular among all classes of society – merchants, soldiers, and rulers. Over time and across thousands of miles, the game continued to evolve. Eventually, it reached Europe, where it is known today as chess.

Numerous versions of Chaturanga endure, though the rules and strategies depend on where and by whom they are played.

PART I: THE OPENING

1 KHAN'S GAMBIT

"Pearls don't lie on the seashore.
If you want one, you must dive for it."
– Chinese proverb

The Silk Road
Central Asia
1290 A.D.

Howling winds wrapped the caravan in a shroud of sand, obscuring the men and their animals from the outside world. Heads down, eyes and lips drawn tight against the onslaught, the travelers forged ahead into the storm. No sign of life, no prospect of salvation was anywhere to be seen. Wordlessly, as if resigned to their fate – or perhaps indifferent to it – the convoy pressed on.

There were ten men in all – eight on horses and the other two crewing an ox-drawn wooden cart. The men wore conical metal hats with woolen earflaps, tattered silk scarves and leather armor. Gripping the reins in one hand, the riders clasped their spears in the other, points doggedly fixed skyward in defiance of whatever mayhem the gods might throw at them. Atop the spear of the lead rider fluttered the threadbare remains of a regimental banner, its color drained long ago by the friction of nature and combat. Maintaining their formation in spite of the sandstorm, this unit of ten displayed the proud and disciplined bearing of professional soldiers.

In fact, they were much more than just common soldiers. They had been hand-chosen by the regional khan of all western lands for a mission of extraordinary importance. The cargo which they carried was vital to the empire's survival, and their orders were to deliver it east to the Great Khan's capital in Beijing. Each soldier had accepted his assignment with the knowledge that he might perish along the way. But to these men, death was nothing to fear. They were the best and bravest warriors of the largest empire in all of history – they belonged to the elite Imperial Guard of the Mongol Horde.

Approaching what appeared to be a dusty river bed, the lead rider raised a gloved fist as his unit took up a defensive ring around their commander. They had to be getting close, he thought, squinting in the direction he hoped was south. It had been a week since departing the security of the oasis-city at the foot of the Mountains of Heaven, and three months since they broke camp on the shore of the Oxus River. But of all their travels, no place had proven more difficult than this final stretch of unforgiving desert. If they could just get across, the remainder of their journey to Beijing would be child's play.

Seeing no sign of danger, the commander barked an order to his men and spurred his horse forward into the squall. Despite the faltering steps of his mare, the commander did not realize his mistake until the rest of his unit was stirrup-deep in the current. What had seemed to be a dry river bed in the fog of blowing sand was in fact a fast-flowing river.

The commander yanked back his reins and shouted at his men to turn around, but they simply stared at his silent warnings, not comprehending the danger which bore down on them. By the time they realized their predicament, it was too late. The commander's horse lost its footing – both rider and beast toppled into the water and were immediately dragged away in a torrent of mud and debris. The other riders soon followed, their arms and heads momentarily bobbing above the surface before disappearing downstream in the fog of sand.

For what seemed like several minutes, the ox cart remained upright, grounded on a gravel bar, as the drivers desperately cracked their whips and shouted orders to the paralyzed animals. Then a surge of turbulent water lifted one side of the cart, momentarily balancing it atop the waves, before flipping passengers and cargo into the raging vortex below. Within seconds, the entire caravan was gone, swallowed by the river as if it had never been. A chorus of ghostly screams filled the air as the lost souls of centuries past welcomed their new companions in eternal slumber. Nothing but the wind remained.

2 THE MOST BORING SUMMER EVER

"The regular course was Reeling and Writhing, of course, to begin
with; and then the different branches of Arithmetic – Ambition,
Distraction, Uglification, and Derision."
– The Mock Turtle,
"Alice in Wonderland" (Lewis Carroll)

Fairview Middle School
United States of America
May 25, 2015 A.D.

Patrick looked up at the clock on the wall, its big hand
tracing a slow arc while its little hand seemed frozen. It felt like it
had been 2:40 for the past twenty minutes.   Mr. Blackburn
continued his lecture about Genghis Khan to a classroom of forty
distracted eighth graders, some of whom had their eyes glued to
the clock like Patrick, while the rest stared at their books, or desks,
or the wall. It was the last day of school before summer vacation.

Patrick sighed and looked back at the clock – 2:43.
Resisting the urge to bang his head on his desk in agony, he instead
relaxed his mind enough to reflect on who he might invite to
Candace Jenson's fourteenth birthday party in two weeks.
Whomever he took was not really as important as making certain
that he did not go alone. He'd made that mistake last year, when
he and his best friend, Ryan, had stood in the corner for an hour
watching other kids dance and trying to screw up the courage to
ask a girl and join the ridiculous affair.

One reason the party was such a big deal was because the rest of the summer, well... wasn't. Wasn't a big deal, that is. Patrick's mother had recently decided to return to work as a lawyer and wouldn't be able to stay home with him. After years of doing laundry and cooking meals, she convinced his father that it was finally time to use the law degree she'd spent three years earning. His dad would be gone over the summer on another business trip. He worked for an oil and gas company, and it seemed like he was always away on business to some place or another.

This summer, Patrick would be staying with his grandfather in Springdale. Not that he minded spending time with Grandpa – far from it, in fact. Grandpa was his favorite family member and they got along tremendously. He told the most incredible stories and maintained a virtual history museum in his cabin.

But hanging out with Grandpa all summer was not quite the same as playing baseball and video games with Ryan, loafing at the pool, or riding the roller coasters at Taylor Park. Springdale had no movie theaters, no pool, and no internet. And there were no other kids there – only old people and weird artists. A fourteen-year-old could only read so many books, listen to so many stories, solve so many of Grandpa's codes and riddles, jump off the dock so many times, and...

The school bell screamed at him like a fire alarm. Startled out of his daydream, Patrick's hand slipped out from under his chin, which finally slammed down onto his desk after making it through 152 days of Mr. Blackburn's history class. Rubbing his jaw, he watched his classmates climb over each other to reach the door.

Ryan slapped his back and grinned. "Come on buddy, it's summer! We're high schoolers now. Let's get out of here!" Patrick slung his bag over his shoulder, took one last glance around Mr. Blackburn's classroom, and hurried out the door to begin what was sure to be the most boring summer ever.

His mother was on the phone when Patrick walked into the kitchen and tossed his book bag onto the counter.

"Yes, okay," she said. "So what's that mean?" She hesitated for a few minutes. "Uh-huh. For how long?"

Her eyes met Patrick's, and then she jotted some notes down on the list she was making. As he listened, Patrick realized she was talking with his dad.

"All right, you stay there. We'll fix a snack and be there as soon as we can." She nodded again, smiled, and said, "I love you, too. We'll see you in an hour."

When she hung up the phone, she looked at Patrick for what seemed like an entire minute. Patrick looked back. Neither spoke. Then she walked over and wrapped her arms around him, squeezing him and kissing his hair. Hugs can be awkward for fourteen-year-old boys, and Patrick usually squirmed or pushed away.

But today, he didn't move.

"Grandpa had a heart attack," she finally said, trying to keep her voice from cracking. "He's at the hospital with Dad. We're going to get packed and go see him, too."

The news stunned him. A lump began to form in his throat and he tried swallowing, but it only seemed to grow larger. As if reading his mind, Mom spoke again.

"Grandpa is in stable condition and seems to be doing okay for now. Dad is doing okay, too, but you and I need to go keep him company." Patrick nodded again, still unable to look up.

She spoke more softly. "Patrick, I know this is hard for you. But Grandpa's tough, and so is your Dad." After a few seconds, she added, more slowly, "And so are we. We can be scared and tough at the same time."

Patrick looked up at her and nodded. He tried to smile back with confidence – to show her he could be tough, too. But he started to cry like he hadn't since he was a little boy. And just like then, he didn't try to push her away.

Once they had left the house and were on their way to the hospital, Patrick felt a little better. It was time to be strong for his dad and Grandpa.

Poor Grandpa, all alone in his old age. Patrick's grandmother had passed away when he was five, so he remembered her only vaguely. She and Grandpa had met at the beach when they were teenagers. He was a surfer and she was finishing high school. They'd married soon after and rarely left each other's side over the next half-century.

Trying to picture Grandpa as a young man, let alone a surfer, was not easy for Patrick. To Patrick, it seemed Grandpa had always had thin gray hair and bad hearing. The warm and caring old man that he knew – the one who still listened to his record player and habitually fell asleep in his reading chair before dinner – could hardly be the same handsome nineteen-year-old with a surfboard under one arm and a tan, bikinied Grandma under the other in the framed photo by Grandpa's bed.

Then again, perhaps the photographs were forgeries. The possibility was not far-fetched, really. Aside from his proficiency with magic and codes, Grandpa was an infamous prankster. Countless small-time mischiefs kept the mood light and the family on their toes when Grandpa came to visit. But the magic, riddles, and pranks aside, Patrick loved his Grandfather most of all for what his other family seemed to appreciate least.

Grandpa was an amazing story-teller. He recounted fantastic tales of his travels across the world with Grandma. A six -month motorcycle trek through South America, climbing the Andes Mountains, surfing off the coast of Chile, and spending three months aboard a sailboat that rounded the Cape of Hope were just a few of the adventures that they had enjoyed together.

Of all Grandpa's stories, however, the ones that really captivated Patrick's imagination were those of Grandpa's own father (and Patrick's great-grandfather), Thomas Eaton. On those special nights when they visited the cabin in Springdale, Grandpa would light his pipe and rock back in his chair as he and Patrick sat around the fireplace in his sitting room. These were magical nights for a young boy.

Remembering Grandpa like this, Patrick regretted how he had felt during Mr. Blackburn's class earlier today. To think he had actually *complained* about having to spend an entire summer with Grandpa – eight weeks of exciting stories, games, and conversations with the person he loved more than anyone else in the world. Patrick rolled towards the window and closed his eyes tightly. As the windshield wipers swished a slow and steady beat, his mind drifted to the last story Grandpa had told him about his great-grandfather.

3 FROM PAPERBOY TO REPORTER

"I'm the twinkle in my Grandpa's eye..."
– Author Unknown

Patrick's great-grandfather traveled the world searching for buried treasure, ancient art, and lost civilizations. During the first half of the twentieth century, Thomas Eaton lived the kind of adventures that most people today could only imagine in books or movies. Born in 1902, he spent much of his boyhood in the mountains surrounding his family's ranch in Montana – fishing, hunting, horseback riding, and studying the plants, animals, and rocks of his remote world. When he wasn't wandering the back-country, tracking grizzly bears or testing his courage running rapids, he was on horseback delivering errands for various businesses around town.

By the time he was Patrick's age, Thomas earned a decent wage selling newspapers for the local tribune. Despite his youth, he soon became knowledgeable about local politics and the influence of the press. He developed a special talent for blending into crowds and making friends wherever he was, and he became a keen observer of his fellow humans. These skills not only helped him sell papers, but they also provided him with fascinating leads that he fed his grateful editors.

While delivering papers and collecting payment, he often found himself in the doorways of barbershops, dark corners of bars, and back alleys of gambling houses. Frequently overlooked for his youth, Thomas witnessed the town's most interesting – and often its darkest – secrets. His boyhood activities would no doubt

9

horrify most mothers today – and certainly his own, as well, had she any idea of where and how he spent his days. Anyone who knew Thomas back then would have described him as having a boundless appetite for adventure and extraordinary knack for survival.

So it was that Thomas went from selling stories on the streets of his town to writing them. As a senior in high school, he worked forty hours a week as an investigative journalist for the paper he'd once peddled for a nickel. His nose for tracking down a lead – combined with his talent for loosening the tightest lips – quickly earned him fame throughout the state as a tenacious and heroic reporter. It came as no surprise when, a few years later, he accepted a full scholarship from a small western college, where he earned a journalism degree in half the time required by most students. Months before graduation he'd been recruited to write for the largest newspaper in San Francisco, a city of growing international importance, and where he would launch his journalistic career.

Within six shorts months, Thomas had attained celebrity status in the booming city on the coast. However, just six months later, his luck began to turn. He'd focused all his energy and talent on exposing the city's most dangerous gangsters and corrupt politicians. Now, sinister forces began to stir in certain parlors, back offices, dark basements and alleys. There were consequences for upsetting the status quo.

Following warnings from friends and trusted contacts, and then several suspicious near-accidents, Thomas realized his spotlight had gotten too hot. A well-tuned antenna for danger told him it was time for a change of scenery. Thomas's editor agreed, and they decided to find a new place for Thomas to write his stories, far away from the vengeful reach of local troublemakers.

And so, at the fresh age of twenty-two and without a single friendly face on the other side of the ocean to welcome him, Thomas boarded a steamship from San Francisco to China, carrying everything he owned on his back. As the ship passed under the Golden Gate Bridge, its passengers gathered on the stern to bid farewell to the United States. On the far end of the ship, standing alone on the bow, Thomas looked west towards Asia in eager anticipation of adventure, exploration, and world-class news stories.

Over the years, Patrick had listened to this story, as well as many others of his great-grandfather's exploits. In fact, he had become the sole heir to them. At one time or another they had been shared with Patrick's cousins or uncles, too. But as family members grew less interested, Grandpa decided to reserve these tales for Patrick only. This special status warmed Patrick's heart. He enjoyed the satisfaction – and not a little pride – knowing he would be the lone caretaker of Thomas Eaton's life and escapades. Just as his relationship with Grandpa was strong, Patrick was confident that he and his great-grandfather would have been best of companions, as well. Perhaps the three of them would have had daring and fantastic adventures together.

Grandfathers and grandsons are known to share uniquely special relationships, and this was the case for the Eatons, as well. Grandpa treated Patrick with love, respect, and acceptance that he didn't get from anyone else. Of course, Patrick did not doubt for a moment that his mom and dad loved him, too, and very much at that. In fact, compared to many of the boys he knew from school Patrick felt he had little to complain about.

But regardless of his privileged life at home, Patrick was most at peace when he was at the cabin with Grandpa, listening to stories, playing chess, working to crack one of Grandpa's invented codes or riddles, or reading side-by-side in the sitting room. Grandpa spoke to him as an old friend, asked his ideas and perspectives, and never lectured about what Patrick should or should not do. He didn't make sarcastic remarks about Patrick's newest hairstyle or clothes, or remind him that he could do better in school, or even reprimand him for day dreaming. Grandpa didn't get mad when Patrick accidentally tracked mud and leaves in from outside, or when he forgot to put a coaster under his drink. Grandpa hadn't once criticized Patrick for missing a ground ball in a baseball game, poor handwriting, or forgetting to do something he was supposed to do.

It seemed Grandpa was only capable of smiling and nodding approval at Patrick's doodling and wandering imagination. He waited patiently for Patrick to finish a book chapter or drawing before asking his attention. He listened kindly to Patrick's dreams of growing up to be a photojournalist, an inventor, or an astronaut (depending on whichever required the least amount of school). The old man pointed out the tremendous benefits of forgetting to wash one's ears – namely that ear wax is an excellent protectant against sand and dirt. When Patrick slept in, Grandpa explained that kids need more sleep than anyone because their brains get so tired thinking up great ideas all day long. And if Patrick was in a bad mood and didn't feel like talking – or snapped at him – Grandpa only patted his shoulder and returned to his reading.

With Grandpa, Patrick knew he was a good person. He was unique and talented. And it was possible for Patrick to do anything he desired with his life.

4 WORLDS APART

"One father is more than a hundred Schoolmasters."
– George Herbert, 1640

The one-hour drive to the hospital near Springdale ended up taking closer to two hours due to rain and traffic. But Patrick welcomed the additional time – it gave him a chance to do some thinking about Grandpa and talk over the situation with Mom. The optimistic news from Dad merged with boyhood memories from the cabin to lighten Patrick's mood.

Walking through the sterile, polished hallways of the hospital, Patrick couldn't help but reflect on how different it was from Grandpa's lake house. The warmth of the cabin – cluttered with books, maps, artifacts, and souvenirs from distant corners of the world – was a far cry from the beige cinderblock walls and the monotonous beeping hum of the hospital equipment.

At the far end of the hall, Patrick saw his dad reading a book in an otherwise empty waiting room. Patrick was startled by how tired, and how much older, his dad looked. Mom went straight to him for a hug, while Patrick hung back and watched. He wanted to embrace his father and wasn't sure why he did not. Before he could give the issue further thought his dad hugged him. For the second time today Patrick felt like crying, though he managed to hold back this time.

"Grandpa's going to be okay," Dad said. "They've finished treating him and think he'll recover just fine, but he won't be running marathons anytime in the next few days." With those few words from his father, Patrick breathed a quiet sigh of relief and drifted to a nearby chair. He thumbed through a magazine while his parents talked and the weather channel purred on the television in the background.

It was strange to see his father like this – with puffy eyes, wrinkled shirt, and messy hair. Dad was normally a giant, full of energy and action, always certain about what needed to be done and how to do it. But tonight, talking to Mom by the water fountain, Dad looked like Patrick felt – apprehensive and uncertain. Patrick lowered his eyes and returned to the magazine.

Although Dad spent most of his days working in an office, he'd once been a field geologist who trekked through deserts and jungles, far from the comforts of civilization, in order to study rocks and fossils or discover veins of precious metals and hidden reservoirs of oil. In the old picture on Mom's nightstand, Dad looked very much like the man Mom described from her early memories – strong, rugged, and sure of himself, sporting a suntan and bleached beard, with a boyish grin and twinkle in his eye. As with his grandfather, however, Patrick found it difficult to reconcile the young man in the photos with the gray-haired adult with whom he lived. Dad may have carried a rock hammer and hand lens at one time, but now he wore a suit and shiny shoes to work.

Yet it seemed these different personalities actually belonged to the same man. If true, then the spirit of adventure may run in Patrick's blood, as well. But here in the twenty-first century, he was doubtful whether he could pick up the torch carried around the globe by previous generations of Eaton explorers.

Regardless how much Patrick wished, the world seemed too small a place now. In school he had been taught that the rainforests were shrinking, and the world was endangered by overpopulation. With too many people came the disappearance of frontiers. No longer was the west full of outlaws and bandits, the ocean floor unmapped, or the source of the Nile legendary. Even Mt. Everest – the tallest mountain on earth – had become a tourist attraction that was visited and climbed by hundreds of people every year. No question about it, the days of the explorers were over and done with. The frontier had vanished. After all, what could possibly be left to discover?

Flipping through the magazine, too distracted by his thoughts to read, Patrick finally took notice of the story open before him. Underneath its title, "From Alexander to America: Afghanistan's Struggle with Empire," was a large color photograph of an old man standing next to a mud wall. He looked at least ninety years old, with dark, leathery skin and a long beard, full-length robe, sandals, and turban. His face offered no expression.

And yet the man's eyes seemed to pierce the surface of the page, as if seeing Patrick across distance and time. The caption described him as a villager from Balkh (a city in northern Afghanistan), who had endured years of occupation during his life – first by the Soviet Union in the 1980s, then the Taliban in the 1990s, and finally forces led by the United States after the September eleventh attacks. The man's family had lived in their valley for hundreds of years. They were all fervently religious, and they made their living raising animals and crops and trading with other valleys. The biggest threat they faced was not crowds or concrete, but rather their country's endless wars and violence. The man's life was so different from Patrick's that it was hard to believe they lived in the same century.

Patrick looked up from his magazine to study his father, who was sitting with his hands in his lap, quietly staring out at the rainy night. Patrick couldn't remember if his dad had visited Afghanistan to study its rocks or mountains. It seemed like he had, but keeping track of who did what, and where, could be tough in the Eaton family.

As much as Patrick wanted to add his own chapter to the Eaton saga, the prospect seemed unlikely. Even if the world was still big enough to explore, he was only fourteen years old. By the time he was old enough to have his own adventures, the frontiers really would be gone. Even Afghanistan would have shopping malls and theme parks by then. It seemed like Patrick had come along a couple of generations too late.

But even if he would never have his own adventures in faraway lands, at least Patrick could savor the stories that Grandpa told him of his great-grandfather. Reassured by this thought, he put down the magazine and leaned back in his chair. As he closed his eyes, his thoughts floated away from the hospital, his grandpa, and the everyday life of a fourteen-year-old boy in this too-small world. Drifting off to sleep, he found himself traveling side-by-side with Thomas Eaton as he embarked on his first journey through Asia nearly a century ago.

5 GO WEST, YOUNG MAN

"Where there is an open mind there will always be a frontier."
– Charles F. Kettering

When Patrick's great-grandfather stepped off the boat in Shanghai (Shang-HI) in the summer of 1924, he was instantly enchanted by the sounds, smells, tastes, and sights of China. Thomas Eaton knew at once that he had entered a land and culture vastly different from the rural mountains and small towns of Montana. Even San Francisco, with its population of half a million, seemed insignificant compared to the three million people living in this metropolis. Situated where the Yangtze (Yang-ZEE) River flows into the Pacific Ocean, Shanghai – the "Paris of the East" – was the center of trade and commerce for all of Asia.

Thousands of European, American, and Russian businessmen made the western part of Shanghai their home. As settlers in a foreign land – many of whom had brought their families with them – they tried to recreate a way of life that was familiar to them. Inside gated communities they built homes, gardens, and parks like those found back in London, New York, or Moscow. Nevertheless, just a few miles away, on the other side of Shanghai, and in the vast lands beyond, lurked ancient China – exotic, mysterious and, all too often, dangerous.

Despite knowing almost nothing of China when he arrived, Thomas swiftly put to use his talent for making friends and gathering information. He hired a local boy as an interpreter and began wandering the city's streets and alleys, mingling with natives and foreigners, tasting local foods, and jotting notes in his journal. From marketplace to theater, temple to government building, and slums to the luxurious homes of politicians, Thomas befriended and interviewed everyone he met. Within just a few weeks, his face became known and welcomed wherever he went. And, although he had yet to send a single story to his editor back in San Francisco, Thomas had already amassed an enormous collection of sources and potential leads.

Thomas also learned that he had arrived in China at a very interesting time. After more than two thousand years of rule by emperors, the last imperial dynasty had finally been overthrown just a dozen years ago in 1912. In its place, the Republic of China had been created. However, there remained a great deal of argument about who should rule the second-largest country on earth. Throughout the northern, southern, and western provinces, local leaders continued to fight each other for power. Consequently, this period of Chinese history has become known as the "Warlord Era."

In addition, a group calling itself the "Communist Party of China" had recently formed in Shanghai, where it was attracting support from local workers. Nobody seemed to know much about them – or what they planned to do if they gained control of the country. But something told Thomas that he would hear more of them in the future.

Meanwhile, Thomas was soon drawn back into the shadowy world of politics, corruption, and crime. Although he had left San Francisco to escape retaliation from criminals and dirty politicians, here in the Far East his nose for a good story put him at risk once again. Within a few months of his arrival in Shanghai, Thomas published a series of shocking and revealing newspaper articles about the most powerful official in the city. This man was a police detective whose job was to investigate illegal gambling and the drug trade. As it turned out, he also happened to be associated with some of the very people that he was supposed to arrest and put behind bars.

When Thomas's articles appeared on the front pages of newspapers around the world, certain people in high and powerful places became embarrassed and angry at having their secret ties to this detective revealed. While the stories delighted his editor in San Francisco – who published one account after the next for the fascinated readers back home – Thomas discovered that his own spotlight had once again become too hot. It was time for another change of scenery.

So it was that on a moonless night in the late summer of 1924, Thomas again found himself alone on the front of a boat looking west. But this time, rather than on the deck of a world-class steamship, he chugged up the Yangtze River in a grimy, sputtering tugboat. He left behind the crowds, familiar faces, and celebrity-like status he had enjoyed in Shanghai and entered China's remote and mysterious interior as a pale stranger from the outside world. From now on, he could no longer rely upon friends or fame to keep him safe. Here, he would be known only as *gweilo* – "foreign devil."

It took Thomas four months to complete the 3,000-mile journey to the isolated outpost of Kashgar (KOSH-gar) in the westernmost province of China. After leaving Shanghai in August, he had gone up the Yangtze River as far as Chongqing (Chong-CHING), where he'd hired a local guide and team of mules for the trip north. However, he soon grew to suspect that his guide intended to double-cross and rob him. Thinking quickly, he had sent the man on an errand to a local town and then made a hasty getaway in his absence.

Driving his mules hard – and constantly looking over his shoulder for any sign of pursuit – Thomas skirted the Altun Shan (ALL-toon Shawn) Mountains and reached Lanzhou (lan-CHOW) by the middle of October. From Lanzhou, he bought camels and retraced the ancient Silk Road west, around the Taklamakan

(TAK-la-ma-CON) Desert, and eventually to Kashgar. Arriving in December, tired and weak, he was relieved to find sanctuary with local British diplomats. For the first time since leaving Shanghai, he could finally let his guard down.

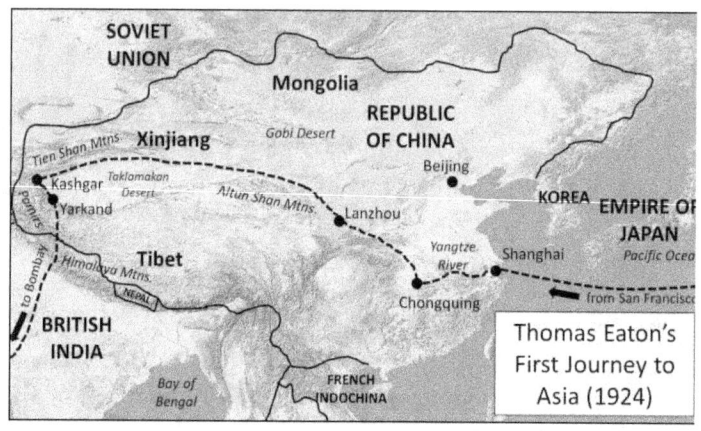

Thomas Eaton's First Journey to Asia (1924)

Thomas looked like a different man upon reaching Kashgar. During his expedition, he had dodged bandits, bribed warlords, and at one point even disguised himself as a Buddhist monk to avoid capture. Two of his mules had died from exhaustion along the way. He was virtually unrecognizable from the young, clean-shaven reporter who had left Shanghai months earlier. His skin, which had been pale and smooth when he started out, was now deeply tanned and cracked, and his beard and hair long and sun-bleached. Whereas his talents for making friends and blending into crowds in Shanghai had merely gotten him good stories, in the rugged backcountry of China these skills had kept him alive.

But despite his weather-beaten appearance and numerous close calls with thieves, frostbite, and dehydration, Thomas did not regret the expedition for a minute. Along the way he had learned about the geography and history of China. He had also made many friends and developed a deep respect for the diverse culture and character of China's many ethnic groups. And, perhaps most importantly, he had learned a great deal about himself and what he was capable of.

Thomas had come to view life as a journey towards enlightenment, believing firmly that every person has a basic choice when faced with difficulties: to quit or go on. From Montana to San Francisco, and Shanghai to Kashgar, he had always set his sights on what he wanted, and he never stopped until he reached them. He had always done what he thought was right and just, even when his life was threatened by corrupt politicians or highway bandits. Crossing China from east to west had been the most demanding challenge of his young life but, through thick and thin, Thomas had always chosen to go on. He never quit, and he never looked back.

The stories of his great-grandfather captivated Patrick. He visualized the breathtaking scenery that Thomas had witnessed along the way: the sun rising over terraced green rice fields to the east, beating down on the still silence of an empty desert, and settling behind snow-capped mountains to the west. Patrick imagined how Thomas must have felt alone in a strange land, danger lurking around every tree or rock, and knowing each day might be his last. Patrick often dreamed he was traveling by his great-grandfather's side, studying the horizon through binoculars or sharing rice stew by the camp fire under a cold, star-filled sky.

By comparison, Patrick's life seemed easy and uneventful. He could hardly fathom the courage and grit that Thomas must have possessed. Patrick had never weighed the risks of crossing a desert, decided whether to bribe a bandit or try to outrun him, or agonized over when to drink the last drops of his water. Patrick had never been on a steamship or tugboat, or packed or ridden a mule, let alone eaten one. His daily problems were confined to homework, getting to baseball practice on time, or deciding which girl to take to Candace Jenson's birthday party. Whenever Grandpa finished a story, Patrick wondered if he actually possessed the kind of bravery and determination that seemed to be a condition for calling oneself an Eaton.

Since Patrick only visited Grandpa on weekends, it took nearly all of last summer to hear the full story of Thomas's journey across China. During their days together Grandpa would show Patrick some of the souvenirs from Thomas's travels. Patrick carefully examined a talisman of green jade worn by a Chinese warrior centuries ago. He scratched his head at the cryptic language of an ancient Buddhist scroll which Thomas had found in the ruins of a monastery. For hours at a time, he flipped through photo albums, intently studying the black and white images of Thomas in a heavy coat, boots and hat lined with the wool of yak, and the "fu manchu" that he had grown in an effort to blend in with the locals. Most intriguing was a bejeweled dagger given to Thomas by a fellow traveler, and which he had carried under his coat for protection.

After lunch, Patrick and Grandpa would play chess or devise a code. The old man was an expert at creating secret ciphers and encryptions. Apparently, Thomas had used them from time to time during his travels, and he had taught them to Grandpa as a boy. Three-quarters of a century later, Grandpa passed this knowledge on to Patrick. He showed Patrick how to write with invisible ink and then how to make it reappear. They toyed with transposition ciphers that involved switching letters, and substitution ciphers that made use of numbers and symbols. They made up brilliant key words based on information only the two of them knew. Each weekend, after he'd left the cabin and returned home, he and Grandpa would mail coded letters to each other. Reunited again the following weekend, they would laugh at the silly messages they'd sent.

Sitting in the hospital waiting room, Patrick felt a new, and much deeper, appreciation for his time with Grandpa. It sounded like Grandpa was going to be okay, after all. In a way, Patrick felt he was being given a second chance. If so, he did not intend to waste it. He promised himself, then and there, that he would never again turn down an opportunity to be with Grandpa. In light of his new outlook, the idea of spending an entire summer at the cabin made Patrick smile in anticipation. What enthralling discussions they would share! What tricky codes and riddles he would solve! What incredible artifacts and photos they would investigate!

Best of all, this summer he would learn more about his great-grandfather's incredible adventures. Indeed, China had only been the beginning of Thomas Eaton's escapades through the Old World.

6 GO EAST, YOUNG MAN

"Man cannot discover new oceans unless he
has the courage to lose sight of the shore."
– Aristophanes

"When can I see Grandpa?" Patrick asked his mom. She had just come out of the recovery room.

"In a few minutes, honey," she smiled, patting his shoulder. "Let Dad talk with him a bit longer, and then you can see him briefly. He needs his rest, so we can't make it a long visit."

Patrick nodded. He realized his grandfather was not exactly in shape to run a marathon, but just the same he wanted to share his excitement about their upcoming summer together. Besides, if the thought had cheered him up, he figured it might do the same for his grandfather. So, his mom's next words took him by complete shock.

"Patrick, honey, I need to tell you something. I realize you were looking forward to spending this summer with Grandpa. But this—" She waved her hands to imply the hospital and entire crazy day. "This changes things. Grandpa will be okay, but it's going to take time. He's going to need to rest this summer. He would absolutely love to take care of you, but he's just not going to be strong enough yet." She paused to look at him, her eyes full of sympathy.

Anger welled up in Patrick. "No! I have to stay with him this summer, Mom! You don't understand. We made plans! We have stories to tell…"

24

His mother didn't argue with him. She sat upright, hands clasped tightly in her lap, and looked at Patrick without saying a word. Her eyes moistened as she nodded her understanding.

"Last summer, Grandpa told me all about his dad..." Patrick pleaded. "... how he traveled through China, the way he outsmarted bandits, and how he almost ran out of water in the desert. And Grandpa promised to tell me more this summer! I have to stay with him!" Mom listened, but did not move or speak.

"Mom..." he started again, this time beginning to cry. "Please! I have to stay with Grandpa. Today, I didn't think I would ever see him again..."

At this, his mom got up and came over to him. She knelt down, wrapped her arms around him once more, and whispered, "I know, sweetheart. I know... I know you're scared because Grandpa's old, and you want to appreciate every minute you have together. I know..."

They might have stayed like that for hours – Mom kneeling by Patrick, his head on her shoulder and her arms around him, as he cried. But after a few minutes, they were interrupted by his father. He had come out of Grandpa's room unnoticed, and now he spoke to Patrick.

"Son..." He rubbed Patrick's back. "Buddy... Grandpa wants to see you now. He's awake and he's asking for his favorite adventurer."

Grandpa looked lifeless on the white-sheeted hospital bed. He had hoses and wires attached to his nose and arms, and several machines next to his head ticked and beeped. The window curtains were open, and Patrick could see the rain beating silently against the glass.

Dad steered Patrick over to a chair next to the bed. Patrick sat down cautiously, unable to take his eyes off Grandpa. Dad pulled up another chair and they sat for a moment together, neither saying a word. Then Dad reached over, gently put his hand on the back of Patrick's neck, and said," You can talk to him, buddy. He can still hear you, even if his eyes are closed."

Patrick nodded, but all he could muster was, "Hey, Grandpa." He rubbed his hands together and looked back at his dad, who smiled and nodded reassuringly.

"Hello, my friend." The voice came very softly. Patrick had not seen Grandpa's lips move, and he wasn't certain whether he'd really heard the words or just imagined them. He looked at Dad, raising his eyebrows, and then turned back at Grandpa who was now smiling.

"How are you, Grandpa?" Patrick asked, immediately feeling silly for asking such an obvious question. "I mean, it's good to see you." He stopped talking, afraid of what ridiculous words he might utter next.

"I'm okay, Patrick." This time, Grandpa's voice seemed a bit stronger, though his eyes remained shut. "Just a little tired, but I'll be fine. Tell me... how are you?"

Without a sound Dad stood, patted Patrick's back, and left the room. The two old friends were alone with each other.

"I'm okay, I guess. Just worried about you, Grandpa. Dad said you're going to be okay."

Grandpa smiled again. "Yes, Patrick. I'm not as young as I used to be, but I'm not going anywhere, either. I'm happy to see you. Tell me more... how is school?"

Under the circumstances, Patrick felt embarrassed at sharing news as trivial as school. But he humored Grandpa anyway, explaining that he'd had an okay year. He admitted his grades would not be as good as his parents hoped, which seemed to make Grandpa smile again. He talked a little about some of his teachers, then switched topics to share a funny tale about Ryan. He briefly mentioned Candace's party, too, but his voice trailed off... His eyes moistened again.

"All day, I've been thinking about our summer together," he blurted out. "I was so excited! I was remembering Thomas's time in China, and how you said you'd tell me about his other adventures." Patrick's teary eyes beamed with love for his grandfather.

Grandpa listened with his eyes closed. His hand searched for Patrick's, and he patted it when he found it.

"Yes, my dad had many other adventures," Grandpa said softly. "China was only his first. But I think we'll have to wait. There's been a change in plans and –"

"I know, Grandpa," Patrick interrupted, wanting to shield his grandfather from the pain of having to explain bad news which Patrick already knew. "Mom told me. It's okay. We'll still visit on weekends, like last summer. It'll be great anyway!"

Grandpa turned his head towards Patrick and opened his eyes again. They seemed suddenly clear and full of life. When he spoke his voice was strong, just like the man Patrick remembered so well.

"Don't you worry, my friend. I promised that you would learn about your great-grandfather this summer, and so you shall. But it will not be with me. The universe has conspired to deliver you a very special gift. This summer, you will go with your dad to the Old World."

Patrick's body stiffened at the news. He was stunned. His mom had said nothing of this. Patrick had just assumed she would wait to go back to work until after school started again in the fall. He'd never traveled alone with his dad, let alone on a trip to the far side of the world.

"Your mom has done a very good job raising you," Grandpa continued firmly, locking eyes with Patrick. "She is an amazing mother. Now it is time for her to be an amazing lawyer, too. You have been a good boy, Patrick, and have made her proud. You are also becoming a young man with the heart of an explorer. It's time for you to follow your dreams. And your dad..."

Grandpa's voice lingered for a few moments. "Your dad is a hard worker. He is also a passionate geologist, father, and son. Sometimes it's good to remember all of these things."

He paused for a moment, as if catching his breath. Then he said, "This summer, I think you will all learn something about yourselves."

Patrick still said nothing. He just stared at his grandfather – unbelieving, scared, and excited at once.

"You and your dad are going to Azerbaijan (AZ-ər-bye-JAHN) next week. It just so happens that your great-grandfather passed that way as he began his second voyage through Asia. You will discover far more about Thomas Eaton in the footsteps of his travels than you ever could with me." He paused, as if to let these words sink in. "But before you go, I must tell you what happened after your great-grandfather reached Kashgar."

7 IN AND OUT OF ASIA

"There are no foreign lands. It is the traveler only who is foreign."
– Robert Louis Stephenson

From the plane window Patrick could not make out exactly where they were. The ground below was a patchwork of mountains, rivers, cities and roads. At times, clouds veiled the landscape and their plane seemed to float on an endless white sea of cotton. For a pilot flying this route seventy-five years earlier, it must have been difficult to keep one's bearings and avoid getting lost.

Fortunately, technology had come a long way since then. Patrick shifted his attention from the window to a large television monitor in the front of the cabin. The screen displayed an electronic map of the world so that passengers could follow the plane's progress from Germany to Azerbaijan as a dotted red line. Based on the length of the line – which seemed to stretch about halfway between the two countries – Patrick estimated they had another few hours before they reached their destination.

It had already been a long and tiring day. After a grueling eight-hour flight from the United States, Patrick and his dad had landed in Germany, where they welcomed the brief layover as a chance to stretch their legs. But sitting in the airport lounge chair with his head propped against his coat, Patrick had begun to feel the first effects of jet lag. While it felt like midnight to Patrick – long past his normal bedtime – it was already eight o'clock in the morning in Germany. His body's internal clock was out of sorts. He had tried to take a nap in the terminal, but the sights and sounds of the international airport were too alluring for a fourteen-year-old boy to be bothered with sleep.

As a hub for travelers from all over the world, the airport's assortment of exotic languages, colorful clothing, and mouth-watering restaurant aromas had dazzled Patrick. He had sat quietly observing the hundreds of people who passed back and forth in front of him on their way to far corners of the world. From time to time, he had entertained himself by assigning made-up identities to the more interesting-looking individuals.

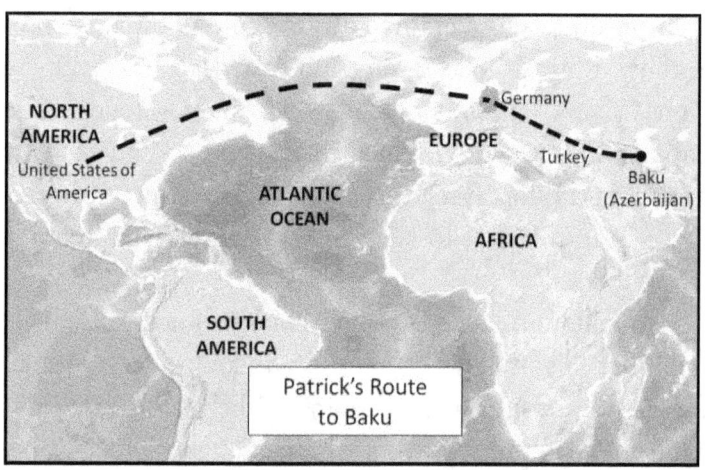

Patrick's Route
to Baku

For instance, he might imagine one person as a father on his way home to a family, another as an engineer off to build a bridge, and a third – the man with the curled mustache and heavy coat – as a spy looking to make a secret "drop." He would barely begin to study this person's leather bag or moccasin shoes, or take note of that person's beautiful jewelry or striking facial features – and then make up a fitting story – before they disappeared into the crowd and were replaced with someone equally intriguing. All the while, in the background, an endless throng of busy travelers – hurrying this way and that – twisted and turned like the body of a huge snake.

At last, unable to keep his eyes open any longer, Patrick had fallen asleep against his dad's shoulder. But after what seemed like only a couple minutes, he was awakened by the call to board their plane for the last leg of their trip to Azerbaijan. Now he sat in a cramped plane seat, tired but unable to sleep, staring out a tiny window at the scenery far below.

Throughout the day, Patrick had been too busy to think much about his conversation with Grandpa a week ago. Between playing video games, talking with Dad, and people-watching at the airport, he'd been completely distracted. But now, with the battery of his video game dead and his dad working on his computer, Patrick's mind returned to his grandfather.

It was hard to believe that only five days had passed since they had visited the old man at the hospital. Since then, Grandpa had continued to feel better and had returned home to his cabin. Patrick and his dad had driven up to Springdale yesterday to check on him and bid farewell for the summer. As they were headed out the door to return home, Patrick had gone over to hug Grandpa in his chair by the fire. The old man surprised him by slipping Patrick a fist-sized package wrapped in plastic. When Patrick drew back to examine it, Grandpa gestured to put it in his pocket.

"Take it with you on your adventure and read it as you go," he had said with a wink.

On the ride home last night, Patrick was nearly overcome with excitement. He peeled away the plastic slightly – just enough to detect what appeared to be an old book, its yellowed pages tightly bound in a worn leather cover. Despite his overwhelming curiosity, Patrick managed to control the urge to tear away the remaining plastic. He wanted to honor Grandpa's instructions and wait until his adventure began. So, when he got home he stowed the package in his luggage, fully intending to read it the next day during his long flight to Germany.

But with all the excitement this morning – calling Ryan to say goodbye, rushing to get the car packed, and satisfying Mom's endless pleas for hugs and kisses – Patrick forgot all about the package. He didn't remember it again until after he had already checked his luggage at the airport. Consequently, his mystery gift sat in the underbelly of the plane, packed in with all the other suitcases. He'd have to wait until Azerbaijan to explore its secrets.

Patrick peered down at the landscape of Europe, which crept slowly past his window far below. In the distance the sun glinted off what looked like a large body of water. Looking up at the television screen, he could see that they were about to fly over the Black Sea. It wouldn't be much longer before they entered Turkey's airspace.

He turned back to the window. As clouds once again obscured the view below, his mind drifted back to his bedside talk with Grandpa one week ago.

As it turned out, Kashgar had been Thomas Eaton's home for five months. One reason was simply that he could not leave. After a long and arduous journey across China, Patrick's great-grandfather was too tired and weak to undertake another long expedition. Over the previous four months he had shed almost thirty pounds and suffered various ailments from insect bites, malnourishment, and drinking unclean water. While he expected to quickly recover his health, he was nevertheless confronted by a much larger problem, and one that ultimately forced him to stay put – geography.

According to many who have been there, Kashgar lies farther from the ocean than any other city in the world. Notwithstanding its actual distance from the Pacific or Indian Oceans, the natural barriers that surround it have made the city an oasis for most of history. To Kashgar's north, west, and south lie some of the world's tallest mountains. While a few narrow paths wind over and between these peaks, they are nearly impenetrable for much of the year due to heavy snowfall, avalanches, and flooding from monsoon rains. To Kashgar's east stretches one of the world's most desolate and forbidding deserts – the Taklamakan. Travelers courageous enough to enter it must endure temperatures ranging from below freezing in the winter to over 120 degrees in summer. But perhaps more terrifying than its extreme cold or heat are the Taklamakan's epic sandstorms, which are said to have trapped – and even buried – entire caravans of unlucky voyagers.

Considering that winter had only just begun, Thomas's hosts in Kashgar insisted he remain as their guests until at least spring, when the frozen mountain passes would finally begin to thaw. In light of his condition, Thomas could hardly object. Looking up at the intimidating snow-capped peaks, he was not especially anxious to get on the road right away. Besides, he greatly enjoyed the warm reception given to him by the British consulate. After countless nights sleeping on the cold ground, eating plain soup and rice, and unable to let down his guard even for a moment, Thomas was grateful for a bed, nutritious food, and the protection of the consulate walls.

Consulates are diplomatic offices that one country establishes within the borders of another country. While similar to embassies, they are usually smaller. They are designed to help fellow citizens who are visiting or working in that foreign country, as well as to maintain friendly relationships with the local government. Consulates can assist travelers with obtaining visas (permissions to enter a country), help expatriates (citizens that live and work abroad), and assist migrants and refugees.

Since the 1800s, the British consulate in Kashgar did all of these things and more – and not just for British citizens. It was known far and wide as a safe haven in an otherwise harsh and dangerous Central Asia. Weather-beaten trekkers from all countries and walks of life could depend on a warm meal, soft bed, and friendly conversation in Kashgar. The consulate was also a jumping-off point for treasure-hunters who undertook expeditions into Tibet and western China in search of buried artifacts. Finally, it was no great secret that the consulate was a listening post for British spies who kept tabs on their giant neighbor and rival to the north – Russia.

As an American, Thomas was somewhat of an enigma in Kashgar. Of course, he was not the first person from the United States to visit. But none shared his reputation as a world-famous journalist. The British were familiar with his newspaper stories from Shanghai, and they begged for one account after the next as to how he had out-witted and exposed that city's corrupt underbelly and yet managed to escape with his life.

His new friends were also interested to learn what Thomas knew about the rising Communist Party of China, the group that had formed in Shanghai while Thomas was there. Just a few years before, in 1917, another communist group known as the Bolsheviks (BOL-sheh-viks) had overthrown Russia's Tsar and established a new government, the Soviet Union. Since then, communism had begun to spread its tentacles into Europe and Asia.

Britain suspected that the Soviet Union was encouraging uprisings and revolutions in other countries. If so, then both communism and the new Soviet Union posed a serious threat to Britain. What would happen if the Soviet Union managed to replace the governments of China, India, Afghanistan, or Persia with communist systems? Would this cost Britain its colony in India? Might Britain be driven out of Asia entirely?

In 1924, these were big and important questions for those who worked at the consulate. For weeks, Thomas was plied with food and drink in return for entertaining and informing the lonely gatekeepers of this distant outpost. They never seemed to grow tired of this fascinating character from America. He told exciting tales and brought them valuable information – all with a larger-than-life personality and charming accent that could only belong to a man from Montana.

Over the next several months, Thomas also became friends with fellow travelers and locals. He even managed to get an invitation to dinner at the Soviet consulate down the road, whose chief was an arch-rival of the British Consul-General and understandably suspicious of travelers from Europe or America. As he had done many times before, Thomas loosened lips, gathered information, and brought smiles to the faces of all he met and wherever he went.

At some point during his stay in Kashgar, Thomas also developed an interest in archaeology. Perhaps the stories of buried towns and caravans had captured his imagination and thirst for treasure. Or, more likely, the rich history, culture, and art of Central Asia sparked an intellectual passion for discovery and understanding that he could not put to rest. In any case, events had transpired in Kashgar that were to forever change the course of his life.

The following April, at the first hint of melting snow, Thomas had tossed his pack onto his shoulders, bade farewell to his friends, and set off with a guide and team of yaks. His destination was south to the city of Yarkand (YAR-canned), and from there over the mighty Karakoram (CARE-uh-CORE-um) Pass – a well-known but perilous route to India that, at times, surpasses 19,000 feet in elevation. Over the centuries, countless locals, explorers, tourists and spies had perished trying to navigate the boulder-strewn crevasses and cliffs of this legendary route.

As Thomas stood atop the pass – straddling the border with India and high above all the world – perhaps he paused to look back at China and contemplate all he had seen and done there. More likely, however, he had only flashed a smile before hastily turning south towards his next adventure. Asia had gripped his heart and mind, and whatever his immediate plans, there was little doubt that he would soon find a reason to return.

8 LAND OF FIRE

"Geography determines the course of history."
– Herodotus

After arriving at their hotel in Baku (Bah-COO), the capital city of Azerbaijan, Patrick slept for nearly five hours. Although he managed to keep his eyes open during the taxi ride from the airport, his body collapsed as soon as it touched the satin sheets of the hotel bed. When he awoke later that evening, his dad was sitting at a table by the window with his laptop computer open and talking to someone on the phone – probably his boss. On the television, a soccer match between two European countries was narrated in a strange language.

Patrick threw back the covers and sat up, still in his traveling clothes. Even after his long nap he felt exhausted. He wandered groggily over to the window next to his dad and peered out at the bright lights of the city. He could have easily been looking at Chicago or Atlanta.

"Feeling better?" his dad asked when he hung up. Patrick shook his head and rubbed his eyes. "What do you say we go downstairs for a bite to eat? That might help. There are some folks we need to meet, anyway." Patrick yawned and nodded. His belly grumbled agreement.

The elevator doors opened to a lavishly decorated lobby. A vast mosaic marble floor spread out before them, surrounded by gold-trimmed pillars that reached the ceiling. Far above the lobby, a massive dome of brightly colored glass mirrored the patterns on the floor. A pristine, white grand piano stood by itself in the far corner of the lobby.

Patrick and his dad hustled past the busy hotel attendants to a crowded restaurant on the other side of the lobby. They stood for a moment at the entrance as his dad's eyes searched the tables for a familiar face. Out of the crowd emerged a grinning, middle-aged man in a gray suit, his frosted hair combed neatly to one side, and a hand outstretched.

"Good to see you, Dan!" the man said loudly over the noise of the crowd.

Smiling in return, Patrick's dad shook his hand and replied just as loudly, "How are you, Roger? It's been what – a year?"

"Sounds about right. Things have been busy here. Lots of progress, as you may have heard. You'll probably see some things around town that make you think you've been gone longer. Baku continues to grow and grow." He stepped closer and lowered his voice, still smiling. "Behind me are the folks from British Oil and Gas, and over there is one of the Chinese companies." He paused, scanning the room. "There are the Iranians. Oh yeah, and the Russians are way in the back... as usual."

"Looks like everyone's at the party," Dad replied, nodding. "Roger, this is my son, Patrick. He's helping me out this summer. His mom's gone back to work and... well, he's along to keep me out of trouble."

"Terrific!" Roger beamed, turning to Patrick. "I'm Roger Neilson, U.S. State Department. I work here in Baku. When folks like your dad come into town, I like to meet with them, help out with paperwork and so forth, and fill them in on the situation here. What a great opportunity you have to see life on this side of the world!"

Patrick smiled and shook his hand. He recalled his conversation with Grandpa from the previous week. "Do you work at the consulate?" he asked.

Roger looked surprised for a moment, and then said matter-of-factly, "Nope, an embassy. Baku is too big a city for a consulate. But you clearly know your stuff, don't you?" Patrick nodded proudly.

"I got us a table in the corner," Roger continued, pointing to the back. "Skip hasn't arrived yet?" Skip was Dad's boss. "Well, it'll just be the three of us then. You'll meet your interpreter tomorrow." He looked at Patrick, adding, "Unless you happen to speak Azeri." Patrick shook his head. "No? What about Turkish? Hmm. Russian?" He chuckled as he led them over to the table where he had been sitting.

"Actually," he continued once they had been seated, "You'll be surprised to find that many people here – especially the younger ones – speak English, as well as French, German, and several other languages. Baku has become quite cosmopolitan over the past twenty-five years." He hesitated, looking rather amused. "Although, I guess you could say it has always been a place of great diversity…"

The quizzical look on Patrick's face encouraged Roger to continue.

"Azerbaijan has continually attracted foreigners. Over the past two thousand years it has been ruled by one empire after the next – the Greeks, Persians, Mongols, you name it... In the early 1800s, it was Russia's turn."

Roger paused to check his cell phone, and then took a sip of water. Seeing the interest in Patrick's eyes, the diplomat continued.

"Azerbaijan's geography has been valuable to the strategies of many empires. Think about it: the country lies directly between Europe and Asia. It borders the Caspian Sea, and literally sits right in the middle of Russia, Turkey, and Iran (Persia). Armies have crisscrossed the region time and again."

Patrick tried to recall any mention of Azerbaijan in his world history class, but he drew a blank. He'd heard of the

38

Russian Empire of course, and the Persian and Ottoman empires, too. Roger carried on with the history lesson, obviously relishing Patrick's interest.

"Azerbaijan was part of the Russian Empire for a hundred years until it finally declared independence in 1918. However, its freedom was short-lived. The Russians returned less than two years later – this time as the newly formed Soviet Union. They came for Baku's oil, but eventually conquered the entire country. It was a very bloody and tragic affair for the Azerbaijani people. In the end, Azerbaijan became another cog in the Soviet machine. It wasn't until 1991 – when the Soviet Union was collapsing – that Azerbaijan finally became independent again."

Patrick recalled the Soviet Union from Grandpa's story last week. Centered in Moscow, the government was communist and sometimes encouraged rebellions in other countries in the hope that they, too, would embrace communism and fight against the capitalist West.

"But aside from geography, oil and gas are what continue to attract the world's attention. Even Azerbaijan's name comes from a Persian word *azar*, meaning *fire*. The name probably originated with the ancient Zoroastrians, who burned oil in their fire-temples. I believe Marco Polo even referred to Azerbaijan's oil way back in the thirteenth century, as well. But it wasn't until the invention of the internal combustion engine (in the 1800s) that Baku really grew. That was the beginning of its oil boom. All the world's oil companies came here, and soon Baku's population was growing faster than that of London, New York, or Paris. By 1900, this little city was producing half the world's oil!"

Patrick's dad nodded along. He must have heard this lecture before. Patrick sipped his water, riveted to Roger's explanation. It was incredible that a place he'd never heard of before last week actually seemed to be one of the most important cities in the world.

"And guess what? It's no different today." Roger tapped his empty water glass on the table to emphasize his point. "It's still Baku's oil and gas that gets the world's attention. The Soviets had this place locked down for half a century, but since the 1990s it has been, well... open for business. And the economy has boomed as a result." Roger gestured at the room of well-dressed business people. "No more communism. Azerbaijan is a constitutional republic now."

Just then their waiter arrived with their food. Patrick had gone with a safe bet – a hamburger – which he was rather surprised to find on a menu so far from home.

"Are all these people here for oil?" Patrick asked when the waiter had left.

"Not quite," Roger answered. "Azerbaijan is becoming quite the tourist attraction, too. Although, it still has a lot of work to do in that arena..." He took a bite of his rice dish and dabbed his mouth with a napkin. "Actually, that brings me to the reason for our dinner. I need to brief you and your dad on the current situation here."

Roger straightened up and laced his fingers together on the table in front of him, temporarily forgetting about his meal. He launched into another talk – this time about modern Baku. As he spoke, his eyes frequently darted from Patrick and his dad to scan the room, cataloguing all who entered or left the restaurant.

"As I said, this city has grown tremendously. It's a virtual metropolis. There are museums, galleries, malls, bowling alleys, cinemas, and fast food. The amount of wealth this city is attracting is astonishing. But it can still be dicey for travelers, so you should stay on your toes."

Roger pointed out the dangers of exploring the city alone at night. He explained that the roads and traffic were inconvenient at best – and hazardous at worst – and recommended using the city's metro instead. Above all, he insisted Patrick and his dad stay within city limits, as the regions surrounding Baku are exceptionally risky, especially for Westerners. "Not that you plan to leave the city... but if you do, I can't guarantee your safety."

Roger spoke for a good ten minutes and then, as if to let his words sink in, returned to his dinner. A few bites later, though, he added a final point.

"Keep your passports and visas on you at all times – you may be asked by the authorities to show them. And you don't want to risk having them stolen out of your hotel room. There have been reports of thieves posing as hotel room service or maintenance workers."

With that, he leaned back in his chair and sipped coffee, satisfied his briefing was complete.

9 INTERESTS

"Few are those who see with their own
eyes and feel with their own hearts."
– Albert Einstein

After they bade farewell to Roger and returned to their room, Patrick and his dad called Mom to let her know how their day went. Then Patrick stretched out on his bed and flipped through channels on the television while Dad took a shower. Only a few were in English, but Patrick wasn't really listening anyway. He was pondering Roger's dinner talk.

Roger Neilson seemed to be a walking encyclopedia of Azerbaijan. He'd answered every question Patrick had asked without so much as glancing at a book, map, or the internet. According to Dad, Roger had worked in this region for many years. He spoke several languages and had even adopted some of the local customs. For instance, when they were leaving the restaurant Roger had shown Patrick the traditional method by which men greet other men in Azerbaijan. He shook Patrick's hand, kissed his cheek, and said "salaam" (sa-LAHM), which in Arabic means both "peace" and "hello." The display of affection caught Patrick by surprise, and he blushed. Roger laughed and assured him that this greeting was very common throughout the Muslim world.

According to Dad, he and Roger had become friends during many trips to Azerbaijan. Dad explained that Americans who work overseas tend to stick together. And they often get to know their embassy officials, too – especially in countries with paperwork hassles or security problems.   Roger had a good relationship with the oil and gas company Dad worked for, and he always did his best to smooth out any diplomatic wrinkles for its employees. But he was also available to assist any Americans who stepped on Azerbaijan's soil and asked his help.

Patrick was able to grasp most of what Roger shared with them about the relationship between the governments of the United States and Azerbaijan. On one hand, it made sense that the United States supported democracy here. In school he learned that the United States promoted democracy throughout the world. And it seemed logical, too, that the United States wanted to help Azerbaijan's free market economy grow. No longer suffocated by communism, the country could now sell oil to the world, which meant that the Azerbaijani people had more jobs and more money. These all seemed like good reasons for the United States to be involved in Azerbaijan.

But Patrick was a bit confused by some of the other things Roger said. For example, Roger kept referring to the United States' "strategic interests" in Azerbaijan. Patrick wasn't really sure what was meant by "interest." Roger had also repeatedly used terms like "regional cooperation" and "energy security." Patrick had heard these terms in the news back home, but he was unclear exactly what they meant, too. His teachers said that the United States' role was to keep the world free and safe – an explanation that had always seemed reasonable enough.

But now, sitting in a hotel room in Baku, he wondered if these U.S. "interests" had less to do with freedom and democracy, and more to do with geography and energy. After all, Roger had emphasized over and over that it was Azerbaijan's location on the map and its oil and gas – not its freedom or democracy – that had made it so valuable to empires throughout history. Patrick decided he would try to learn more.

"Find anything to watch?" his dad asked, drying his hair with a towel. Patrick shook his head. "Well, there will be plenty of other stuff to do here. Tomorrow we'll meet our interpreter, and maybe even take a stroll around town." Patrick nodded in reply.

His dad sat down on his own bed, facing Patrick. "You haven't said much today. Are you all right?"

"Yeah, Dad, I'm fine. Just tired." He stared at the television for a while. "How long are we going to be in Baku?"

"For a couple months. But like I said on the plane, we might take a trip over to Turkmenistan at some point. It's still up in the air. But if we go, I think you'll find that place very interesting."

"Turkey?" Patrick asked, this time looking at his dad. He knew where Turkey was from the large map he'd seen on the airplane.

"No – Turkmenistan. Different country altogether. It's on the other side of the Caspian Sea – east of here. In the meantime, I need to spend the next few days at our local office. You can hang out here at the hotel. Between television, your video games and the pool, you ought to stay entertained."

"Can't I go to the office with you?" Patrick asked, hopefully.

"Maybe we can take a tour some day later this week, but the office here isn't really much of a place for kids. Just a bunch of people discussing where to put drill rigs and pipelines. I doubt you'd find it very interesting." He smiled. "Hardly the stuff of a fourteen-year-old boy's imagination."

"But I thought geologists did cool stuff outside, like look for gold or gemstones. Isn't that what you used to do?"

His dad had started to get up, but now he hesitated and looked over at the television for a few seconds. Then he turned back to Patrick.

"Yeah, at one time I did. But that was long ago. Field geology is a young man's game. I probably could have stuck with it, but that would have meant being gone all the time. When you were born, I made the decision to work in an office, instead, so that I could be home with you and Mom."

"But you're never home, anyway. You're always at the office," said Patrick glumly, looking back at the television. "If you're going to be at work, shouldn't you just do what you love?"

His Dad watched his son for several seconds, as if trying to find his words. Patrick pretended to be engrossed in a Turkish game show.

"I *do* love my job, Patrick. But I love you and Mom more. I try my best to give you both a good life. I realize it's not always a perfect arrangement. Believe me, there are times that I wish I could be out in the desert looking for gemstones…" His voice trailed off, as if he sensed he had gone too far. "It won't be as bad as you think, buddy. We'll have some fun, too – starting tomorrow."

He went to brush his teeth.

Patrick rolled over and closed his eyes. Two months in Baku, sitting in a hotel room and watching television. What an adventure, he thought cynically. He could hardly wait to tell Grandpa of his wild summer. Gee, Grandpa, I learned so much about Thomas's adventures in Asia while swimming laps in the hotel pool! Boy, it sure is exciting being an Eaton – what thrilling television shows we get to watch!

Frustrated, his thoughts turned back to his great-grandfather. Grandpa had explained that, after crossing the Karakorum Pass, Thomas trekked south through India to the coastal city of Bombay, now known as Mumbai (moom-BYE). From there, he had boarded an ocean liner back to the United States. He was only a year older than when he'd left San Francisco, but he now possessed what amounted to a millennium of wisdom.

His new passion for the ancient history and art of Central Asia led Thomas back to college, where he earned a graduate degree in archaeology. His research focused on the Silk Road, its geography and importance to world empires, and the various goods that were traded by caravans between China, Rome, and Persia. Mostly, though, he became fascinated with Silk Road money: the gold, silver, and bronze coins that could be found strewn from one side of Asia to the other.

Thomas pored over the discoveries of other archaeologists who had searched the Taklamakan Desert decades earlier. Some of these pioneers had uncovered coins and jewelry, as well as paintings, sculptures, and texts that told the history of Western China. Many had stayed at the same consulate in Kashgar as Thomas. Nearly all were scorned by the Chinese government, which viewed them as irresponsible treasure hunters who had robbed China of its cultural wealth.

Thomas hungered to return to Central Asia and pursue the coins and other artifacts that still lay beneath its sands. Along the way, he also hoped to improve the reputation of archaeologists. Perhaps he would finally help dispel the label, *gweilo*, by which he and so many other Western travelers were known in China.

That was where the story of Thomas Eaton had ended. Grandpa explained that it was up to Patrick to learn what happened next. To do this, all that was required was for Patrick to keep his eyes open and his heart true. The secret gift that Grandpa had given him would serve as a guide. Keep it close, Grandpa said, but don't rely upon it completely. Many years have passed – and much had undoubtedly changed – since Thomas visited Asia.

Hugging him on their final night together, Grandpa had said, "You are an Eaton, Patrick, which means you must think and see for yourself. You come from a long line of explorers, but you must never forget that you are your own man."

With that, Patrick smiled. Tomorrow, he would investigate Grandpa's gift. And, somehow – some way – he would make this summer about more than just an air-conditioned hotel room. The universe had conspired to bring him here, his Grandpa had told him. The rest was up to Patrick.

10 IN POLO'S FOOTSTEPS

"The world is a book and those who
do not travel read only one page."
– St. Augustine

The next morning Patrick awoke early. His body was still struggling with jet lag – the tiring effects of traveling from one time zone to another. Dad had said it would take several days at least before his body would adjust.

Patrick crept across the dark room to the window and, peeling back a curtain, realized it was still dark outside. He sighed and rubbed his eyes, unsure what to do next. The clock by their beds showed 5:20. Dad was still asleep and Patrick didn't want to wake him by turning on a light or the television.

He stumbled back to his side of the room where his suitcase lay open near his bed. Groping around the clothes inside, his hands discovered the plastic wrapping of Grandpa's gift. Quietly, he retrieved it and made his way to the bathroom. After shutting the door, he turned on the light and looked down at the mysterious package.

Grandpa had told Patrick to open the gift once his adventure had begun. Well, according to his dad, sitting in a hotel room was about as much adventure as Patrick could expect this summer. So, he might as well have a look now.

He started peeling back the plastic where he'd left off a couple nights before. Within a few seconds he was left holding a well-worn, leather-bound book. Imprinted on the front cover, in faded gold lettering, were these words:

JOURNAL OF
THOMAS PATRICK EATON,
A SILK ROADS EXPEDITION, 1928-

Patrick sat and stared at the cover for several minutes. He couldn't believe what he was seeing – his great-grandfather's journal! His pulse quickened and his hands began to sweat. Gingerly, he peeled back the cover to look inside. On the first page were the same words as on the cover, this time printed in dark lettering. Beneath the text was a hand-written message scrawled in ink:

For my son (born 10/23/1927) –
May the road rise up to meet you.
May the wind always be at your back.
May the sun shine warm upon your face,
and rains fall soft upon your fields.

Patrick recalled seeing these words somewhere else. Then it occurred to him they were framed in a picture at Grandpa's house in Springdale. These were the first lines of an old Irish prayer, his Grandpa had once told him. Patrick couldn't remember how the rest of the prayer went.

He continued to ponder the inscription. Something about the date grabbed his attention – 1927. If Grandpa was born in 1927, that would mean he was almost ninety years old. But that couldn't be right, could it? Patrick strained to remember Grandpa's age – it seemed like he was born during the Great Depression which, as best as Patrick could remember, took place during the 1930s. If so, then Grandpa couldn't be older than eighty or so. Patrick shook his head in exasperation – he always had a hard time doing math in his head. He would have to remember to ask his dad later.

The next several pages were filled with his great-grandfather's handwriting. He had used pencil, and in some places letters were smeared. But Patrick could make out most of the words if he read slowly. They began like this:

April 25, 1928· It has been three days since arriving in Istanbul [is-tan-BOOL]· *This old city lies on the western shore of Anatolia* [anna-TOLL-ia: the traditional name for the region of Turkey], *the crossroads of the world· For thousands of years, Istanbul – known in ancient times as Byzantium and then Constantinople – has stood guard over the land bridge between Europe and Asia, as well as the waterway that connects the Mediterranean and Black Seas· It has served as the capital of many empires and watched countless others pass by – both on foot and by ship – on their way to conquer distant lands·*

Stepping off the boat, my feet were as light as feathers, as if rejoicing in their return to the Old World and the splendid quest that lies ahead· Although Istanbul is nearly 5,000 miles from Shanghai – precisely on the opposite side of the continent from where my previous journey began more than four years ago – I believe it is the ideal place to begin my second trek across Asia·

For one thing, Anatolia is the western starting place of the legendary Silk Road. From here, trade and culture spread east across mountains and deserts all the way to China, and back again. And this same city welcomed the great explorer Marco Polo when he returned from China over 600 years ago.

Anatolia is also the birthplace of coins. As early as the seventh century B.C., the people of Lydia minted coins made of "electrum," an alloy of silver and gold found naturally in the pebbles of the Pactolus River, just south of here. Over the centuries, Greek and Roman coins passed through Anatolia on their way to China, as well as to and from Mesopotamia to the south.

My goal over the next year is to follow the legendary Silk Road from one side of the continent to the other. I aim to retrace the footsteps of the traders and pilgrims who carried not only coins, but also goods, ideas, customs, religions, art, technology, and language across the world. I plan to experience for myself the tastes and sounds of Central and Eastern Asia, which in so many places have hardly changed over the past two thousand years. I hope to discover evidence of lost oasis towns and caravans, many of which were already buried and gone by the time Polo visited. With a bit of luck, I might also unearth some of their treasures and artifacts, which have been locked away for so long.

50

My mission will almost certainly call upon all the knowledge I acquired during my studies at university. It may also depend on my skills as a journalist, and the perspectives I gained during my other travels. But, without a doubt, the coming months will test all my courage, determination, and endurance. For now, I bid farewell to the safety and familiarity of the Western world, and once more enter Asia.

Awed by his great-grandfather's goals, Patrick put down the journal to reflect on what he had read. He heard his dad rustling about in the room, but after a few moments, all was quiet again. His dad was still asleep. Patrick smiled to himself. Some people just aren't cut out for life on the road!

He opened the journal again. The next several pages contained a lengthy "to-do" list of preparations for Thomas's journey. For example, there were supplies to be purchased and paperwork to be filled out and approved by local officials. A chart showed food items that he would need to buy – rice, flour, dried meat and fish – as well as cookware and containers for drinking water. He had brought with him from the United States all the items he would need for his archaeological research – a compass, field tools, maps, and various books.

On a following page, a map showed the route that Thomas intended to follow to China. First he would take another boat ride – this time north from Istanbul through the Bosporus (BOSS-pore-us) Straits, into the Black Sea, and then east along the northern shore of Turkey. Thomas planned to go ashore at Trabzon (trab-ZONE), another old Silk Road city, to meet his guide. He would purchase the majority of his equipment and food there, as well as a crew of several locals and at least a dozen horses. From Trabzon, he would then head south over land. This route was one of many that led from Istanbul (Constantinople) to the Silk Roads' southern destination, Persia (modern-day Iran). It was also the path taken by Marco Polo.

Patrick used his finger to trace the course his great-grandfather planned to take. According to a note which Thomas had scribbled at the bottom of the map, his trek from Istanbul to Persia would cover some fifteen hundred miles. While his boat ride across the Black Sea might be relatively easy, from Trabzon he would have to navigate a difficult mountain range before finally reaching the flat floodplains of Mesopotamia.

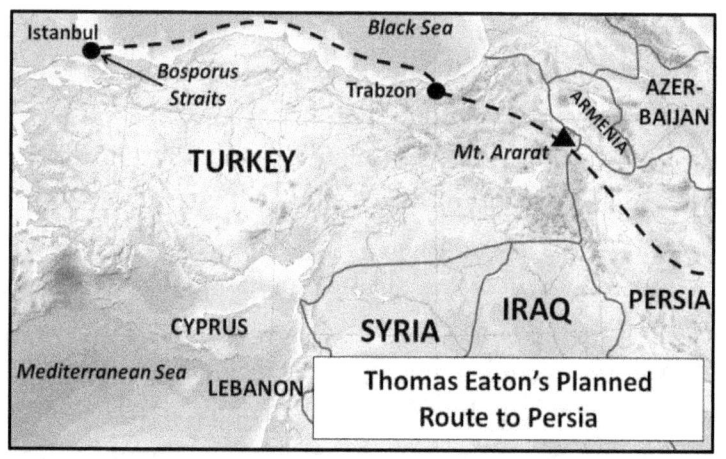

Along the way, Thomas planned a brief "side trip" east to Mt. Ararat in Armenia. In his journal he wrote:

Marco Polo stopped here, too, and described its natural springs and baths, which he believed were among the best in the world. However, I am drawn particularly to Mt. Ararat for its own historical importance. According to the Bible, this snow-capped mountain is the final resting spot of Noah's Ark. The region was also important in the development of coins –

its metalworkers fashioned various metals into currency and other items over two thousand years ago. I plan to discover whatever I can during my visit.

Patrick again heard his dad stirring. He closed the journal and opened the bathroom door. The curtains were open and the light from the window bathed their room in a soft orange glow.

"Well, look who's the early bird!" said his dad, grinning. "What have you been up doing?"

Patrick shrugged casually and flipped on the television. "Nothing much. Are you going to the office today?"

"Nope. Today you and I will have a little fun around town. First, we need to meet our interpreter. Then, I thought we'd take the metro over to Old City and have a look around."

"Old City?" Patrick asked.

"Yep. Old City is the historical center of Baku. Lots of interesting sights there. Then, I think we'll meet Roger and Skip for lunch. After that, who knows?" Dad's boss was a big, gregarious Texan whom Patrick had liked from the first time they'd met.

Patrick pulled on his clothes and grabbed his backpack. Slouching in a chair, he watched a Turkish soap opera while his dad shaved and got dressed. There was something Patrick had meant to ask him, but now he couldn't remember what it was. Ten minutes later Dad was ready, and they left the room in search of breakfast.

Just before the door closed, however, it occurred to Patrick that he'd forgotten his passport in the room. Remembering Roger's advice about thieves, he hurried back inside to grab it. Seeing the journal by his pillow, he decided to bring it, as well. Stuffing the items in his backpack while they walked to the elevator, Patrick found himself wondering which of the two he could least do without.

11 OLD CITY

"Think, in this batter'd Caravanserai Whose
Portals are alternate Night and Day, How
Sultn after Sultn with his Pomp Abode his
destined Hour, and went his way."
– Omar Khayyam

Their interpreter was waiting for them in the hotel lobby
after breakfast. A somewhat pudgy man in a baggy brown suit, he
sat in a chair near the hotel entrance, sipping coffee and looking
uncomfortable. He seemed to recognize Patrick's dad and stood
up awkwardly – nearly spilling his drink – and extended his hand
in greeting.

"Ah, Bey Eaton, so nice to meet you. My name is Ahmed
Batuk [ŎHK-med ba-TOOK] – interpreter at your service." He
smiled enthusiastically.

"Greetings, Ahmed. I'm Dan Eaton and this is my son,
Patrick." He placed his hand on Patrick's shoulder.

Ahmed bowed slightly to shake his hand. "It is a pleasure
to meet you, Patrick." Patrick smiled back and, following Roger's
example from the night before, blurted out "Salaam."

Ahmed's face showed surprise at first, and then softened
into a grin. "Wa alaykum," he replied in Arabic. Translating to
English, he added, "And peace be upon you."

Turning back to Patrick's father, Ahmed continued, "Mr.
Neilson has asked that I assist you in any way possible. I also have
a car and will take you wherever you please."

Dad looked at Patrick and grinned. "Well, I guess we'll have to risk Baku's roads, after all, won't we? No metro for us today." To Ahmed he said, "We would like to see Old City this morning. My son is quite a student of history." Patrick blushed, unsure why his dad said this.

"Yes, of course, Bey Eaton. Old City is an excellent place to see the history of Baku. I am happy to take you there." He escorted them through the hotel doors out to the busy street, where his taxi was parked nearby.

The ride to the Old City was terrifying. Ahmed could have been a world champion race-car driver anywhere else in the world. He accelerated quickly, swerved violently between cars and potholes, honked his horn relentlessly, slowed down only by slamming on his brakes – and always at the last second – and he did all this while speaking casually about Baku, as if he were simply sitting on a park bench sipping coffee and chatting with old friends.

Perched on the edge of the back seat, Patrick's eyes bulged and his knuckles whitened from clenching the headrest of the seat in front of him. His body swayed with each hair-raising swerve or two-wheeled roundabout, and if it hadn't been for his seatbelt he undoubtedly would have had a bruised forehead. During several close-calls, Patrick glanced at his dad sitting next to him, whose face wore a grin and seemed to be on the verge of laughter. Dad appeared to be thoroughly enjoying this crazy roller coaster ride! How could this be the same man that Patrick knew from home – the businessman and stickler for rules?

When his eyes weren't focused on the traffic, Patrick glimpsed from his window a blur of high-rise buildings, richly decorated houses and shops, tree-lined boulevards, and sidewalks crowded with pedestrians. He could not recall visiting a city as large as Baku. Every so often, he caught sight of three colossal blue skyscrapers shaped like flames in the distance. He recalled Roger's comment about the origin of Azerbaijan's name – from *azar*, meaning *fire* in Persian.   Wow, Patrick thought, even its architecture reflects the importance of oil and gas to Azerbaijan.

"Yes," Ahmed continued talking to Patrick's father, "Baku continues to grow. Two million people now! The problem is the roads, as you can see.   Very busy, very dangerous!   The government has built walkways under them to keep pedestrians away.   But every year many people are hurt, or worse, in traffic accidents." He swerved to narrowly miss a car that was changing lanes.

"And what about you?" Patrick's dad asked.   "Are you from Baku?"

"Me? No, no! I am from the countryside to the west. I came to Baku many years ago, just before the Soviets left..." He pointed out his window to an enormous, drab concrete building covered in square windows, arches, and pinnacles on the roof. Surrounding it was an equally massive and monotonous wall. "Speaking of the Soviets, that is their former palace. Now it's our House of Government.   Most Soviet landmarks were torn down after 1991 to make room for all this." With his other hand, he swept the modern architecture that pierced the skyline. "Even the Lenin Museum – once dedicated to the Soviet Premier – is now a museum for carpets and rugs!" He chuckled.

"I assume you speak Russian, too?" asked Dad.

"Yes, I am fluent in Russian. Most Azerbaijanis speak at least a little Russian. I also speak Azeri and Turkish. And English of course! What do you think?" He looked at them in the rearview window, eyebrows raised optimistically.

"Your English is good." Dad replied. "Much better than my Azeri!" Ahmed laughed.

Through the front windshield Patrick could see they were approaching what looked to be a gigantic castle.   "Is that a fortress?" he asked to no one in particular.

"Yes, indeed," Ahmed replied. "Welcome to Old City, or Inner City as it is sometimes called. It was built in medieval times

– the twelfth century or so – although some say it is older. Very beautiful. Look over there." He pointed again, his eyes seemingly never watching the road. Patrick found it amazing they had not hit anything yet. "That is the Maiden tower. Very old – fifteenth century perhaps. We Azerbaijanis are proud of that monument – her image is on our coins and paper money."

"Why is it called the 'Maiden Tower?'" Patrick inquired, peering at the tall, cylinder-shaped stone structure.

"Good question!" Ahmed seemed delighted that his guests were taking such interest in his culture. "Many stories exist. One is that the king – the Khan of Baku – forced his daughter to marry. She was so unhappy that she leapt from the tower into the Caspian Sea rather than live a life she couldn't choose for herself. Another story says her brother locked her up, and she jumped to avoid a life of imprisonment. Yet another suggests that, because the fortress was never taken by force…"

Ahmed was interrupted by another driver who tried to cut him off. He shouted a stream of insults and abuses from his window, honking his horn and gesturing wildly with his hands. An instant later, he was calm and smiling again, and continued as if nothing had happened.

"Yes, many stories. But who knows?"

They parked on the street outside the fortress. Ahmed pointed out that they would have to pay a hefty fee to drive inside Old City. Besides, he said, they would be able to see more by walking.

As they strode through the thick stone entrance to the walled city, it seemed to Patrick they had been transported a thousand years into the past. The ultramodern buildings, sleek automobiles, and electric pulse of their taxi ride were gone. Here, the air was clear and calm, carrying only the echoes of their footsteps from the traditional stone structures, courtyards, and ornate fountains.

The three of them strolled down the main road, Dad and Ahmed talking while Patrick peered wide-eyed down narrow cobblestone alleys that curved out of view. On his right they passed a group of old men sitting at tables off the road, playing chess, drinking tea, and smoking cigarettes. To his left was a small stone building whose exterior was covered with hanging carpets and rugs. A smiling man sat on the doorstep and shouted to them as they passed, "Beautiful rugs. The best you will find! Very cheap!"

Ahead, they approached a massive square courtyard surrounded by a long, low-lying building with several small arched openings.

"Old City's caravanserai [kara-VAN-sir-AYE]," Ahmed announced, halting to let them absorb the view. "In the thirteenth and fourteenth centuries, Silk Road caravans from all over – Anatolia, Persia, China, and India – came here to trade their goods. Attendants watered and fed camels here in the courtyard while their owners rested inside after their long journeys."

"Sort of like a roadside inn?" Patrick's dad asked.

"Yes, that is a good way to think of the caravanserai. Traders might stay for days or weeks, selling their merchandise, buying other goods to take home, catching up with old friends, and sharing news from distant lands."

Patrick scanned the empty courtyard, trying to imagine it full of bleating camels and shouting attendants working busily to unload cargo and feed the animals. It must have been a lively place in its heyday. Now it stood eerily still, and Ahmed's voice echoed off the distant stone walls as he continued with its history.

"You see, this was a sanctuary for travelers in old times. There were many other places like this along the Silk Road – usually every fifty miles or so. Rulers agreed to protect the caravanserais that lay within their kingdoms. It benefited each of them to preserve the flow of commerce and knowledge through their lands. Many of these rulers also sent spies along the Silk

Road to gather information about other kingdoms – so they wanted to keep these roads open and safe not only for other travelers, but for their own secret agents as well."

They lingered for a while without speaking. Patrick was struck by the contrast between old and new – between the empty caravanserai and the flame-shaped skyscrapers he could see in the distance. The two structures had been built nearly 800 years apart, yet stood within plain view of each other.

It was amazing to think that this city – known far and wide during the early Middle Ages as a hub of international trade – was still important to the world's economy. Just as Baku had once attracted caravans from faraway places, today visitors like Patrick and his dad continued to visit, if for slightly different reasons. It seemed strange to Patrick that this courtyard had buzzed with world culture at a time when America had not yet been discovered by Europeans.

His thoughts were interrupted by his dad's voice. "Hey, Patrick!" He looked up to see Ahmed and his father by one of the small openings in the building that surrounded the square. "How about we get something to eat?" Patrick nodded and hurried to catch up.

Patrick savored the cool, sweet taste of the pomegranate fruit drink, which soothed his taste buds after each bite of spicy *pilaf* – a traditional Azeri meal of rice, vegetables, and chicken. Drinking slowly, his eyes took in his surroundings.

He had followed Ahmed and his dad through a small wooden door in the building that surrounded the courtyard. Given the door's plain appearance, Patrick had expected to enter an equally unremarkable room. Instead, the entryway opened into a high-ceilinged dining hall furnished with dark wood furniture, tiled mosaic wall art, ornate ironwork, and white-clothed tables. A stone fireplace in one corner glowed red, and the caravanserai

59

reeked of wood smoke and history. Several diners sat at tables, while a handful of old men rested on rugs on the floor, smoking cigarettes and sipping their tea.

"Can you imagine what this place was like centuries ago?" Patrick's dad whispered, looking around the room. "The stories that these walls have heard..."

They were shown to a table where Ahmed translated the menu. When their food came Ahmed devoured his eagerly, but never missed an opportunity to describe yet another aspect of Baku's history.

"All this was built by local Muslim rulers," he said as he chomped away. "Baku was conquered by the Persians, and later the Ottomans. Finally, the Russians came. They built many of the buildings and roads surrounding Old City, or Inner City. So, the area just outside the walls is called Outer City."

Patrick had heard all this from Roger's lecture the previous night. "You must be tired of other people coming here and telling you what to do," he said frankly, taking another sip of his drink.

Ahmed looked at him with eyes that seemed to soften, even in the dim light of the caravanserai. "We Azerbaijanis are both blessed and cursed by our geography. We are a small country in the middle of great powers. And we have oil, which all the world wants. We desire only friendship and peace. But sometimes our friends decide they want to be our parents, instead. Do you know what I mean?"

Patrick nodded yes, though he wasn't sure he did understand. This was a perspective to revisit with Dad or Roger.

"So you're from the countryside to the west?" his dad asked Ahmed. "I think that's what you said on the ride here..."

Ahmed looked wary all of a sudden, and he lowered his eyes as he scanned the room. Speaking quietly – almost mumbling – he replied, "Ah, yes, to the west... from the countryside. But, like I said, I have been in Baku for many years. I am an Azerbaijani from my head to my toes!"

"Where in the west?" Patrick asked. "Like on a farm?"

Ahmed looked at the both of them for several moments. He tapped his finger on the side of his tea cup, as if trying to decide whether to go on or change the subject. Finally, he sighed and said quietly, "I am from a region in western Azerbaijan whose fate is...how do I put it, *uncertain*... My family is Armenian. For the past hundred years, Azerbaijan and Armenia have been fighting each other, especially over this little piece of land where I spent my childhood. In fact, this conflict has been going on for longer than any other in the world today, except perhaps the dispute between Israel and Palestine."

The waiter returned with a plate of sticky pastries covered in nuts. The conversation paused while the waiter cleared their finished plates.

"Pahklava!" Ahmed exclaimed, his voice once again boisterous. "My favorite dessert! Very good – you must try this." Again, he attacked the dish with gusto.

After a few minutes of silence, he cleared his throat anxiously, and then continued from before. "So, as I said, Armenia and Azerbaijan do not exactly see eye-to-eye. It is a very complex issue. Basically, the Russian Empire used to control this whole area. But when the Russians left in 1919, the Armenians and Azerbaijanis began to fight over this little region to the west. It is known as Nagorno-Karabakh [Na-GOR-no Car-a-BOK]."

Ahmed took a sip of his tea. "Then the Soviets came. They had bigger fish to fry, so they made us stop fighting for a while. But when the Soviet Union collapsed, we were back to our old ways again. It doesn't help that Armenians are Christians, and Azerbaijanis are Muslims."

"You're Christian?" Dad asked.

"No." Ahmed almost spit his drink out. "That's what is so ironic. I'm Muslim. But I'm also Armenian." He smiled and shook his head at the paradox. However, seeing their puzzled expressions, he added simply, "It's complicated."

"Why does everybody want the Naguro… Kara… Kara –"

"Nagorno-Karabakh," Ahmed repeated.

"Yeah. Why does everyone want that area so badly?" Patrick asked. "Why doesn't one side just give it up so that everybody can live in peace?"

"Ah, good question, Patrick. But it's not so simple." Ahmed licked the pastry's sticky residue from his pudgy fingers. "For one thing, the region is home to many people. Some want to be part of Armenia, some want to be part of Azerbaijan, and some want their own country." Looking at Patrick's dad, he added, "Plus, there is the very important matter of oil and politics. But that is a conversation you should have with Mr. Neilson." He wiped his mouth and looked around for their waiter.

With that, it was obvious Ahmed did not want to discuss the issue any longer. They paid for their meal and stepped back into the hot, bright sunshine of the courtyard. As Patrick stretched his arms and yawned, Dad looked at his watch and asked, "Back to our hotel for a nap?" Patrick nodded in agreement, and the three strolled out of the ancient walled city, returning to the hustle and bustle of modern Baku.

12 MISHA

"History is the consensus of survivors in authority.
Reality is the weighted mean of individual perceptions."
– Author Unknown

Although Patrick was tired when they returned to their room, he was unable to take a nap. The combination of jet lag and another hair-raising taxi ride left him too jittery to sleep. Plus, the air-conditioned hotel room managed to recharge some of the energy drained by the hot Baku sun earlier this morning.

Dad opened his laptop and started to do some work. "We'll meet Roger and Skip this afternoon," he said. "Why don't you go for a swim? There's an amazing pool downstairs."

Patrick grinned. He had brought his swim trunks for this very reason. After a quick change of clothes, he grabbed his backpack and headed out the door.

The pool was on the bottom level of the hotel – twelve floors below their room. As the elevator silently ticked past each floor on its way down, Patrick reflected on his morning with Dad and Ahmed. He had never experienced anything quite like the Old City and its caravanserai. The historic stonework, colorful languages and artwork, and exotic smells and tastes fascinated him. This part of the world really was ancient – a place where architecture and traditions could go unchanged for centuries, and memories and feuds often hang on from one generation to the next. As both Roger and Ahmed had pointed out, Azerbaijan was no stranger to the international spotlight. Patrick shook his head, again wondering why he had never heard of this country in any of his classes.

The elevator dinged and its doors opened to reveal the most incredible pool Patrick had ever seen. It was enormous – virtually twice the size of his middle-school gym. Every inch was bathed in pastels: a cool blue glow reflected from under the water, while a warm orange radiated from lanterns that flickered on rows of floor-to-ceiling pillars. The pool itself was laid out as a long rectangle crowned on both ends by half-circles – it must have been at least 200 feet long. In the middle of the rectangle, two gigantic side-pools bulged out in the shape of oriental fans. On the mosaic tile floor surrounding the water, lined up neatly, were numerous cloth-covered beds.

Stunned by the magnificent view, Patrick wandered over to the nearest bed and stood there, unsure what to do next. His eyes returned to the breathtaking view. The entire arrangement was so flawless that he was afraid to take off his sandals or put down his backpack out of fear he would spoil it. Surely, the Khan of Baku's baths could have been no more extravagant than this masterpiece!

"May I help you, sir?" Patrick startled at the voice. He turned around to see a well-groomed man in an elegant hotel uniform and white towel over one arm. "I am the pool attendant. Can I get you anything?"

"Um, I, uh…" Patrick sputtered, unsure how to answer. "I just wanted to go swimming." He stared at the man, whose face softened into a polite smile.

"Yes, sir. Please – have a seat on the deck chair." He pointed to what Patrick had assumed to be a bed. "Your towels are here, and magazines there. Would you like something to drink? Perhaps a…" He looked Patrick up and down, guessing the young American's age. "…water?"

Regaining his composure, Patrick replied, "Pomegranate juice, please."

The man raised his eyebrows in surprise. "Excellent choice, sir." He hurried off to fill Patrick's request.

Patrick looked around again. He had the whole pool to himself! Grinning suddenly, he dropped his bag on the deck chair, kicked of his sandals, and tore off his shirt. Running towards the water he leaped high into the air, grabbed both knees, and splashed down the biggest "cannon ball" this side of the Atlantic Ocean.

Half an hour later, Patrick reclined lazily in his pool chair, ankles crossed, sipping his favorite new drink while examining Thomas's journal. After the morning in an Old City caravanserai, and now a swim in a royal Azeri bathhouse, Patrick was beginning to feel like quite the world traveler. Of course, he had not even been in the country a full day yet. For that matter, he had not really given up any of the comforts of the modern world. Their luxurious hotel was practically a resort, and even Ahmed's taxi was hardly an example of "roughing it."

Even so, Patrick realized he had stepped outside of his normal ordinary life. He wasn't exactly climbing the Himalayas or riding a camel across a desert, but on the other hand he wasn't sitting around playing video games at home with Ryan, either. While it had only been one day, he was beginning to sense the mystical and powerful charm of the Old World. It occurred to him that this same feeling may also have captivated his great-grandfather three-quarters of a century ago. With that thought, Patrick opened the journal and continued reading.

From Trabzon in northern Turkey, Thomas had traveled by horse southeast to Mt. Ararat, a distance of some two hundred and fifty miles. The trip took two weeks – at a pace of only twenty miles a day – but Thomas enjoyed the convoy's slow progress.

For one thing, it gave him an opportunity to test out his new guide. Thomas needed someone who knew the land, spoke Turkish and English, and could shoulder the responsibility for managing a convoy of attendants, horses, and baggage. Furthermore, he was looking for a loyal and trusted companion – someone upon whom he could rely for advice and assistance if suddenly he found himself in a tight spot. When it came right down to it, he needed someone he could trust with his life. Thomas had already been betrayed by a guide once before in China. This time he planned to be more careful.

As it turned out, his British friends in Kashgar recommended someone to him. Before leaving the United States, Thomas had written to let them know he was planning a return to Kashgar – this time from the west rather than the east. Upon discovering that he would begin his journey from Istanbul, the consulate suggested Thomas contact a man named Misha (MEE-sha), who had also been of service to Her Majesty's Government in the past.

In fact, Misha, came very highly recommended. He descended from a long line of Turkic ancestors who had lived in Anatolia for centuries as fishermen by the Black Sea or as animal herders who wandered the Turkish Plateau. Misha did not know when, or from where, his ancestors had first arrived, but they had been in Anatolia long enough to survive the Mongol invasion in the thirteenth century.

Misha had fought in the (First) World War as a soldier in the Ottoman (Turkish) army, where he was distinguished twice for bravery. Following the defeat of the Ottoman Empire and her allies, he returned to his village near Trabzon, and again took up the life of a farmer. However, just a few years later a group of British officers were on a tour of eastern Anatolia and needed a local interpreter. Misha volunteered, and within a short period of time his ability, courage, and loyalty had earned their deep respect. Although Thomas had known him for only a couple weeks, he was impressed with what he had seen so far.

A second reason Thomas was in no hurry to reach Mt. Ararat was that he wanted to learn more about eastern Anatolian culture and history. Naturally, he had studied this ancient region in his archaeology classes at university. But it was while on the back of a horse or in front of the camp fire that Thomas truly learned about Anatolia from the mouths of its people.

Each day of their pilgrimage to Mt. Ararat, Misha would share with Thomas an additional chapter from the long history of this region. He sometimes began the day's lecture on horseback next to Thomas, although this was typically interrupted as he rode off to scold a careless crew member or galloped away from the caravan to scout ahead. He would continue after lunch while he and Thomas sat in the shade of a tree, taking refuge from the blistering midday sun. However, even then Misha was typically too busy making sure the horses were properly cared for, measuring their progress on a map, or inspecting the status of the convoy's food and water. Only at night by the fire, after camp was set up and the day's numerous tasks completed, could Thomas expect Misha to finally relax and finish that day's narrative. While the crew spread out around the camp – their conversation and laughter gradually dying out as one after the next fell asleep – the archaeologist and his guide would sit on rugs, drink their tea, and talk.

Misha told Thomas about the region through which they were traveling, known as the Armenian Highlands (among its many other names). It includes eastern Anatolia, as well as the present-day countries of Armenia, western Azerbaijan, southern Georgia, and northwestern Iran. In 1928, when Thomas passed through, the region served as the border of three great powers: Turkey, the Soviet Union, and Persia (Iran). Long before that, however, the Armenian Highlands occupied a prominent role in history. In fact, today the area is referred to by many archaeologists and historians as "the epicenter of the Iron Age" because metallurgy (the art of metal-working) is thought to have begun here. Over thousands of years the region has been fought over by the Byzantines, Persians, Ottomans, and many others.

Of the region's entire history, however, perhaps its darkest chapter was written only a few years before Thomas arrived.

On our thirteenth day together – a day before reaching Mt. Ararat – Misha shared with me his memory of a horrifying incident that had happened here not long ago. He began his story with great reluctance, and I was soon to understand why. It seems that in the year 1915, the government of Turkey established a new policy for its eastern lands. This area, which includes our present location, had been occupied for centuries by Armenians, as well as Assyrians and Ottoman Greeks. The Turkish government decided to claim eastern Anatolia for Turks only, and it set about removing – or eliminating – all non-Turks from the region. The tragic result was that hundreds of thousands of people – perhaps millions – perished in this government-sponsored genocide. Many others were marched to Syria or elsewhere and told never to return.

It seems this monstrous act occurred during the (First) World War. Apparently, Misha did not learn of it until after leaving the army in 1918. When he returned home, some of his non-Turkish friends had already been expelled from the country. He told me that he was – and still is – ashamed of his government's actions. While he swears to me he had nothing to do with the ghastly affair, he nevertheless asked me to forgive him and his people. He emphasized that Turks are by nature a very warm and thoughtful people, and he feels this incident will be a permanent scar upon their honor.

As he spoke, Misha shed tears of shame and regret – the first and only hint of emotion I have seen from him since beginning our journey together. I was unsure what to say, and so I merely offered my opinion that governments rarely act on behalf of the people they claim to represent. He is no more to blame for the actions of the Republic of Turkey than I am to blame for the United States' massacre of the Native Americans or enslavement of Africans. In any case, I am of the opinion that my guide is a good man, and I will maintain this faith in him unless he gives me reason to believe otherwise.

Understandably, that was a long and restless night for me. I lay awake for many hours thinking about Misha's heartbreaking story. As an archaeologist, I have studied numerous massacres carried out under the auspices of empire. But practically all of them occurred very long ago – usually hundreds or thousands of years. This has perhaps caused me to overlook the fact that those ancient people had families, friends, and dreams, too.

In contrast, the Armenian genocide that Misha described occurred just fifteen years ago. It remains fresh in his memory, and most certainly in the minds

69

and hearts of the Armenians, as well· While I had hoped the morning sun would chase away these melancholy thoughts, I was distressed to find they were very much still with me when I awoke· As we approached Mt· Ararat, I was considerably less cheery than when we had begun our journey· What had begun as a grand adventure now seemed more like a funeral procession·

Patrick closed the journal and gazed across the pool. He sat silently for several minutes, contemplating his great-grandfather's words. During the past day he had been so focused on the excitement and old-world charm of Azerbaijan that he had not considered the less glamorous aspects of the region's history. He recalled Ahmed's story from lunch. Here was a man who, even in the twenty-first century, was afraid to admit out loud that he was Armenian.

Once again, it occurred to Patrick that, despite all its evidence of modernization, Azerbaijan was at its heart an ancient place with a very long memory. Even with Baku's skyscrapers, luxurious hotels, and fast-food restaurants, this region of the world was still very much defined by its geography and history.

13 CHANGE OF PLANS

"BOUNDARY, n. In political geography, an imaginary line
between two nations, separating the imaginary rights of
one from the imaginary rights of the other."
                                    – Ambrose Bierce

Patrick fell asleep when he returned to their room. The
swim had relaxed his muscles, and the background noise of the
television temporarily drowned out his excitement about Central
Asia.

When he awoke in late afternoon, his dad was talking on
the phone. Noticing Patrick stirring, he put the phone on his
shoulder. "Hey buddy, do you want to say hi to Grandpa?"

Patrick threw back the covers and rubbed his eyes, still
trying to adjust to his new sleep schedule. He smiled groggily and
reached for the phone.

"Hey, Grandpa!"

"Hello, my friend!" Despite the long-distance connection,
the old man's voice sounded strong. "Are you enjoying your
adventure so far?"

Patrick glanced at his dad. "Yeah, it's pretty cool. We
visited a caravanserai this morning – sort of like a roadside inn for
the old Silk Road caravans – and then I went swimming in the
most amazing pool. You would love it!"

His grandfather laughed. Patrick imagined him sitting on
his porch looking out over the lake. It seemed so strange that he
was on the other side of the world at the very house where Patrick
had first learned about Asia.

"As nice as swimming in the lake?" he asked.

"Um, well, not better – just different," Patrick replied.

"I'm just giving you a hard time," his grandfather chuckled. "Yes, I'll bet it is very different. That's the beauty of traveling – you get to see it first-hand instead of just hearing about it through stories. Speaking of stories, what do you think about the package I sent with you?"

"Awesome!" Patrick replied, cupping the phone with his other hand. "I accidentally packed it on the plane, so I didn't even get to look at it until we got here. But I've been reading it ever since." He saw his dad's forehead furrow and Patrick changed the subject. For some reason, Patrick hadn't felt like telling his dad about the journal. They spoke for a few more minutes before Patrick handed the phone back to his dad, who hung up a short time later.

"Well then," his dad began, leaning back in his chair. "We're meeting Roger and Skip for dinner downstairs in an hour. Hungry yet?" Patrick nodded. "Good. We can talk some more about our plans. I've got a lot to get done in the next few days. But I thought you might come to the office with me later in the week."

Patrick looked up and managed an "okay."

"Sounds like Grandpa has gotten you started on some sort of a project..." Dad looked at Patrick out of the corner of his eyes while he put away his laptop. "Think you'll be able to stay busy for the next few days?"

"Yeah, I guess. Can we go see some more stuff around Baku? That was fun!"

"Of course we can, but probably not until the weekend. There's just too much I have to get done before then. Hang in there buddy. Things will pick up – I promise."

He patted Patrick's shoulder and headed off to shower.

Dad's boss, Skip, was waiting for them at the entrance to the restaurant, which was once again noisy with travelers from around the world. Skip was a decade or so older than Dad – and was another geologist who had "hung up his boots" long ago. Now he was in charge of the company's Caspian Sea division. Dad's company drilled for oil and gas all around the world, and the Caspian Sea was just one of the company's many projects. Patrick had met the man on several occasions and really liked him. A native Texan, Skip sported jeans, cowboy boots, a handlebar mustache and perpetual grin. He talked a lot, and loudly – frequently telling jokes that Patrick didn't always understand, but which put everyone else in stitches.

With ruddy cheeks and gleaming eyes, Skip shook his dad's hand and high-fived Patrick. "I can't tell you how glad I am that you're with us on this one, partner," he boomed at Patrick. "Last time we were in Baku, I told your dad he'd better bring his assistant on the next trip. Now you get to see where the oil business really began. Although, I always point out that we Texans did oil bigger and better than anyone else!" His laugh roared high above the noise of the restaurant crowd.

Roger had called to say he was running late, so the three of them went ahead and ordered their food. Patrick's eyes lingered on the menu's hamburger option, but after a few seconds they settled on the rice dish Roger had tried the night before. He also requested a large pomegranate juice.

Throughout the meal, Skip and Dad chatted about work – contracts to be signed, wells that needed replacing, budgets and costs, and geology. The details were mostly beyond Patrick's comprehension, but he knew his Dad's company drilled for oil and natural gas throughout the region – both on land and over water. Modern technology allowed them to continually find and extract new energy resources from regions where the "easy" oil was already gone. At the moment, Skip was griping about politics – by far the biggest challenge to drilling for oil.

73

"Let me break it down for you, Patrick," Skip said, looking at him the way he might a business partner. "Since the collapse of the Soviet Union, there has been a lot of argument over who controls the Caspian Sea. In addition to Russia and Iran, three other countries share the shoreline – Azerbaijan, Kazakhstan [CAUSE-uk-stan], and Turkmenistan [turk-MEN-eh-stan]. The argument centers on whether the Caspian is a sea or a lake. Some countries claim it is a sea because it's big and salty. Others say it is a lake because it's surrounded by land."

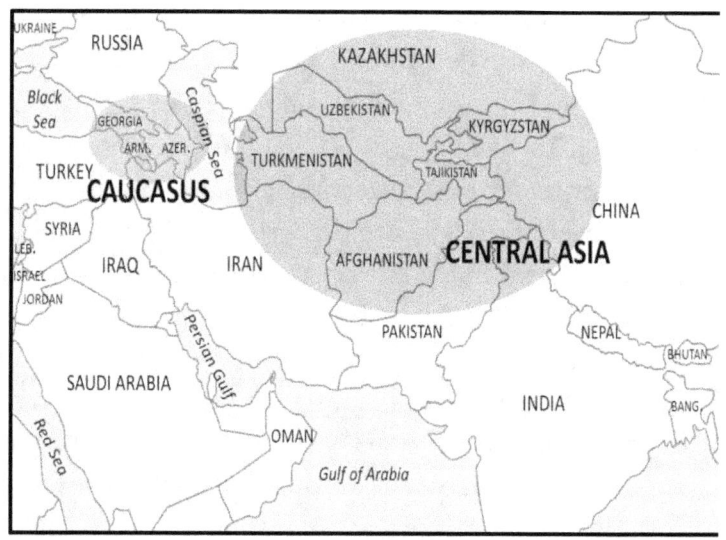

"Why does it matter?" Patrick asked.

Skip grinned at his dad, and then turned back to Patrick.

"The Caspian Sea sits on top of one of the world's largest reserves of oil and gas. It is also full of sturgeon – fish whose eggs are harvested to make caviar. Whether the Caspian is a sea or lake determines who owns these resources."

"Who gets to decide?" Patrick pressed.

Skip shot another look at Patrick's dad, and then answered, "That's the trillion-dollar question. Currently, there are many treaties – some nearly a century old – that divide the Caspian

74

among its neighbors. But the problem is that none of these treaties agrees with each other. Some were written when Russia and Persia controlled this region. Others were signed between the Soviet Union and Iran. More recent treaties have been created by the newly independent countries like Azerbaijan."

Seeing Patrick's puzzled look, Dad added, "It can be exasperating for us geologists, Patrick. We study science, but politics rule the day." Looking down at his dessert, he added, "Everyone wants a slice of the Caspian pie... if not the whole thing."

As they enjoyed Azeri pastries, Roger blustered in, looking troubled. He apologized for his tardy arrival and jumped immediately into the latest news. A couple of research ships owned by a British oil company had just had a close encounter with Iran's military. As the scientists aboard the vessels were mapping the seafloor, an Iranian warship passed close by. Soon after, an Iranian fighter jet buzzed overhead. Nobody had been hurt, but the encounter served as a grave reminder that the quarrel over the Caspian Sea could erupt into violence at any moment.

"These things happen from time to time," Roger continued. "The Iranians want the southern half of the Caspian. They argue that it has belonged to them for centuries – back when they were the Persian Empire. Of course, Azerbaijan has a different perspective of history." He laughed nervously and then added, "Probably nothing will come of this but finger-pointing and more arguing. But it has caused me quite a headache – I've been on the phone all day trying to get this sorted out. Anyway, that's why I'm late."

He took a deep breath, laced his fingers together on the table in front of him, and looked from Skip to Dad. "Not to worry. You guys should be fine to go ahead with your trip to Turkmenistan next week."

Patrick nearly choked on his drink. Turkmenistan? He looked at his dad, who was smiling at him.

"See? I told you things would pick up."

The next few days were relatively uneventful. The surprise news that they were headed to another country at least helped Patrick contain his restlessness. After their dinner with Roger and Skip, he had examined a map to find Turkmenistan. It lay to the east, on the other side of the Caspian Sea. Twenty four hours ago, Patrick had never even heard of the place. But according to Skip, Turkmenistan was a bonanza for oil and gas. In addition to drilling there, his company wanted to build a pipeline that would transport the Caspian Sea's oil and gas to the ocean, where it could then be shipped to other parts of the world. Roger planned to meet them in Turkmenistan, where he would give another briefing on the country's history, politics, and security.

In the meantime, Patrick had five days to kill before they left Baku. He had hoped to visit more sights around the city, but since Dad would be at the office, this idea was out of the question. His dad did not like the idea of his fourteen-year-old son roaming a foreign city. Although Ahmed volunteered to accompany him, Dad ruled against this option, as well. So, a week of hotel life it was…

Fortunately, Patrick was not starved for entertainment. Sitting by the hotel's lavish pool, sipping sweet pomegranate juice, he continued his great-grandfather's journal.

Reaching Mt. Ararat on May 1, 1928, Thomas devoted several journal pages to his brief stay there. Mostly, they focused on geology and geography.

The Mt. Ararat area contains two mountains, which in fact are really volcanoes. The larger one, Greater Ararat, reaches almost 17,000 feet above sea level and is the highest point in Turkey. To its east

76

lies a smaller volcano, Lesser Ararat, which is nearly 13,000 feet tall· Several eruptions have occurred throughout human history and, on occasion, have buried towns with their explosive force and pyroclastic flows· One of the earliest recorded eruptions was approximately 2500 B·C· - nearly five thousand years ago· It is thought to have buried an ancient settlement and killed many people· More recently, in 1840 A·D·, another major eruption occurred - this time with an earthquake - killing as many as ten thousand people and covering several cities·

Thomas went on to describe his efforts to locate some of the buried towns at the base of the volcano. Unfortunately, since these were deeply entombed in ash or pyroclastic rock, he found very little of archaeological interest. Perhaps frustrated – or just tired – Thomas decided to spend his last couple of days relaxing in local hot springs, which Marco Polo had named the finest in the world.

Patrick laid the journal on his lap and gazed at the mirrored surface of the pool. He felt a little confused about his great-grandfather's intentions. Given how little Thomas actually accomplished at Mt. Ararat – and how out of the way it was from the rest of his journey – it seemed strange that he had made this side trip. Aside from the fact that Polo had once visited this Biblical landmark, the two-week journey to Mt. Ararat seemed to be a waste of time – and completely unrelated to Thomas's goal of retracing the Silk Road. It just didn't seem like the behavior of a man who Grandpa had described as clear-minded and goal-focused, and certainly not a drifter or prone to dilly-dallying.

On the next page, Thomas answered his great-grandson's suspicions, as if he had anticipated the inquisitive mind of a future young Eaton when he wrote the words long ago.

May 8, 1928. After great deliberation, I have decided to amend my travel plans. Whereas my original intention was to proceed south from Mt. Ararat to Persia, I have decided instead to go east to Armenia. Misha's description of that land and its people has captivated me – and convinced me to see them with my own eyes. From there, I will continue to Baku in Azerbaijan – another ancient city with its own fascinating history and archaeological treasures.

But Thomas acknowledged that this new route brought considerably more risk. In 1928, the Soviets were solidifying their control over the Caspian Sea region. Unlike Persia, Armenia and Azerbaijan had already been absorbed into the Soviet Union. Their citizens were under total surveillance by the Soviet secret police. Freedom of speech was strictly prohibited, as was celebration of traditional culture. People who spoke out against the new communist government – or expressed any desire for their traditional way of life – could be arrested and sent to concentration camps in Siberia, or worse.

In addition to suppressing the local population, the Soviets were also on high alert for spies sent by other countries. It was rumored that secret agents from Europe were sneaking around behind Soviet lines, inciting rebellion against the communists. For this reason, any Westerner caught traveling here without paperwork risked being charged with espionage – a crime punishable by death. Thomas had no papers – after all, he had just made up his mind to go to Armenia and Azerbaijan. As an illegal

78

visitor, he could not afford to get caught. If arrested, it would be difficult to prove he was not a spy!

Once again, Thomas had to rely on his talents for making friends and blending in wherever he went. Just as importantly, he would depend upon the help and loyalty of his new friend, Misha.

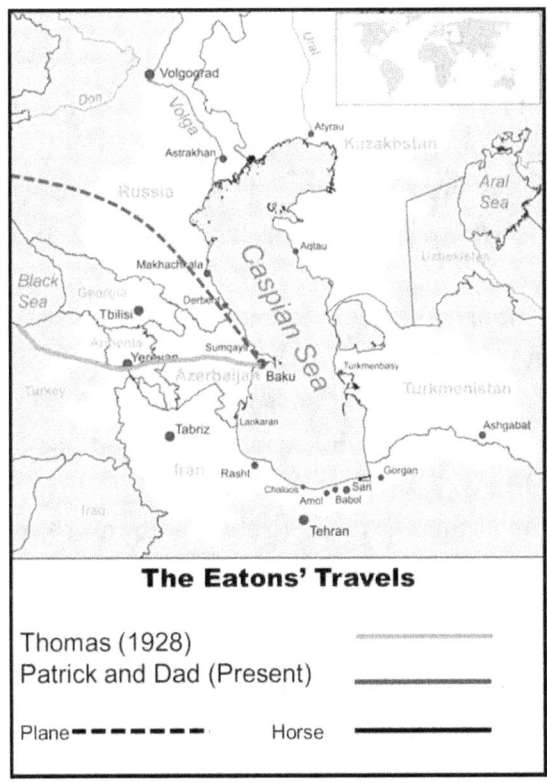

The Eatons' Travels

Thomas (1928)
Patrick and Dad (Present)

Plane -------   Horse ————

14 ENERGY MOVES THE WORLD

"The healthful balm, from Nature's secret spring,
The bloom of health, and life, to man will bring;
As from her depths the magic liquid flows,
To calm our sufferings, and assuage our woes."
– Seneca Oil Advertisement (circa 1850)

The company office occupied three floors of a high-rise building in modern downtown Baku – just a few miles from the caravanserais, fortress walls, and cobblestone roads of Old City. In true Azeri style, the office's interior décor blended east and west, old and new. A large hexagonal lobby of polished stone greeted visitors at the elevator. In the tradition of the Byzantines, tile mosaics and floor-to-ceiling pillars graced the area. Ornate fountains and lavish gold trim gave the receptionist area an Ottoman feel. A large Persian tapestry covered an entire wall, while local art and architecture lined various alcoves and bookshelves. Offsetting them were digital clocks, computers, flat-screen video monitors, and other features common to a modern office.

A young blonde woman in a smart black suit and phone headset greeted Patrick and his Dad when they entered. Sitting behind a large mahogany desk – its front emblazoned in gold with the company logo – she recognized Dad, smiled and waved them past. As they strolled down the hallway of offices and drawing rooms, Patrick tried to absorb as much imagery as he could. He wanted to remember where his dad spent his days when he was away on business.

Today was Saturday – a day of rest in many industries, but not for Dad's. As he so often pointed out, energy powers the world... and the world never stops. Oil and gas was an around-the-clock business. Besides, Dad and Skip needed to tie up loose ends in Baku before taking a boat across the Caspian Sea. This required getting paperwork in order, making phone calls, and fine-tuning goals and priorities. It also involved looking at maps – lots of maps.

"Howdy, boys!" Skip's voice boomed down the hallway when he saw them coming. Hanging out of a door and grinning widely, he waved one arm for them to join him, and then disappeared back inside. When they caught up, Patrick saw they were entering what looked like some sort of planning room. Compared to the rest of the office, it seemed rather modest. The area was clearly not for hosting guests – it was simply a place to get things done.

The tile floor, such as one might see in a grocery store, was crowded with ordinary brown office mats and plastic roller chairs. Rolled-up drawing papers leaned against every available corner of the room. An industrial-size coffee maker purred atop a stained kitchen counter. All types of maps covered the walls – physical, political, and geological. A few of Dad's coworkers sat at a long table discussing a large chart spread out before them. Between them, Patrick could make out red and blue lines showing the paths of oil and gas pipelines across Central Asia. Skip munched on a donut he had retrieved from one of several boxes on the counter, dribbling crumbs down his shirt as he spoke.

"Welcome to our 'war room,' Patrick! Nothing too fancy, but this is all we old geologists really need. Coffee, donuts, and maps."

"What about rocks?" Patrick asked. A couple heads at the table turned to look at him, plainly amused by the interrogation of their boss.

81

"Aha!" Skip replied, laying his donut on the counter. Wiping his mouth with a napkin, he crossed the room and pointed to a collage of maps on the wall. "All the rocks you need are right here! Carbonates, salts, sands, and lots of clay! Plus basalt, way below..." He hesitated while trying to figure out how to condense hundreds of millions of years of geologic history into a two-minute lecture. Seeing the look of interest on Patrick's face, he decided to give it his best shot.

"All right, partner, basically it's like this. The entire Caspian Sea sits in a topographical basin – that is, a gigantic depression in the earth's crust. This basin was forming as early as Paleozoic time – say, 400 million years ago. At one point, the Caspian Sea was part of the Black Sea. On its bottom, thousands of feet of mud and dead plants and animals settled on top of each other. At various times, the Caspian even had reefs growing in it – just like the ones you see today in the Caribbean Sea. Eventually, the mountains around the sea rose up again, cutting off the Caspian from the Black Sea. It was no longer part of the ocean. It became a lake, the way it is today."

"I thought it was a sea," Patrick interjected, one eyebrow raised. Skip laughed and slapped him on the back.

"Only the politicians care about the difference, buddy! I'm only concerned with the geology here. Lake, sea, whatever you want to call it... Essentially, the Caspian became land-locked." He pointed back to the map. "Then it started drying up. Sea water is very salty. As it began to evaporate, lots of salt was left behind. This salt settled on the bottom of the sea, on top of all the other mud, dead fish and plants, and so forth. Well, as the mountains continued to grow, more and more sand washed down into the sea, where it settled on the seafloor. Now think about the incredible weight of all those sediments (carbonates, salts, and sands) sitting on top of all the old mud and dead stuff. That's going to create a lot of pressure and heat. What's it all mean to a petroleum geologist?" He looked at Patrick, who shrugged.

Skip's smile widened and his eyes danced with excitement. "We've got a perfect oven for making oil and gas! All that pressure and heat essentially 'cooked' the mud and rotting plants and animals into oil and gas – over millions of years, of course. Now, we geologists are working to figure out where the sweet spots are – areas where the oil and gas have been trapped under the sediment. Once we find them, we drill down, tap into the reservoirs, and bring that precious cargo to the surface!" He stepped back and grinned at Patrick, looking proud of his explanation. But then he frowned and added, "Of course, that's assuming the politicians don't get in the way."

Patrick looked at the wall again. It included brightly colored maps, sheets with squiggly black lines, and various charts showing columns of rock types. He had seen stuff like this at his dad's office back home, or rolled up in the back of one of the closets in their house.

On another wall, framed black-and-white photos showed wooden oil derricks and shacks. There looked to be hundreds – or even thousands – of these towers packed together in a messy jumble of equipment, mud, and oily ponds. Some of the scenes were crisscrossed by railroad tracks, while others showed workers turning hand cranks, carrying pipes, or coaxing mules to pull carts through the thick sludge. Not a single tree could be seen in any of the photos.

"Is this Baku?" Patrick asked. Skip nodded, and they crossed the room to examine the pictures more closely. Meanwhile, Dad had joined his coworkers at the table.

"The land of eternal fire," Skip continued, cupping his coffee mug in both hands. "Baku has wept oil since long before humans walked the earth. These pictures show her back in the late 1800s. Quite a mess, huh? Back then, folks didn't understand the environmental impact of an oil operation. They would pump this stuff right into ponds, as you can see here." He pointed to one of the photos. "The effects of this damage lasted for a long time."

"But Baku doesn't look like this today," Patrick said.

"Nope. Technology and environmental awareness have come a long way. The oil and gas business is extremely clean and efficient now. Even if companies wanted to pollute – and I honestly don't know of any that feel this way – they would never be able to get away with it. People don't want to buy from a company that mistreats the environment."

"Earlier this week, Roger Neilson told me that, a hundred years ago, Baku provided half the world's oil," Patrick said. "But I always thought the Middle East was where oil comes from. I had no idea that the Caspian Sea was such an important place."

"You're exactly right. The Middle Eastern countries are big producers of oil – Saudi Arabia, in particular," Skip replied. "So are other countries around the world, like Russia and Venezuela. And, for that matter, so is the United States. However, in terms of natural gas, the Caspian Sea area is a monster. Look over here." He pointed to another map of the Caspian region.

"Russia owns a lot of territory in the Caspian region. And Russia has a third of the entire world's proven gas reserves. That's a lot of natural gas! The only country with more natural gas is Iran, which also happens to own part of the Caspian."

Patrick quietly studied the map. He had heard about oil and gas in the news and at school. But this was a lot of information, and he wasn't sure quite how to make sense of it all. Looking at him, Skip seemed to anticipate the boy's struggle to wrap his head around the issue.

"It's complex," Skip empathized. "Believe me, I have a hard time keeping track of it all, too. Here's what you need to know. Energy moves the world. For a country to prosper, it has to produce goods and services. And in order to produce these things, it has to have energy. There's no getting around this – that's just the way it is. Now, there are lots of other sources of energy: nuclear, wind, solar, hydroelectric, geothermal, biofuels, and others, too. But fossil fuels (oil, natural gas, and coal) provide

84

over ninety percent of the world's energy. Ninety percent! So, regardless what anybody *wants* for the environment – and no matter what you *hear* on television or in school – fossil fuels are not going away for a long time."

He took a sip of his coffee, and then looked at Patrick again before continuing.

"But oil and gas are only found in certain places in the world. Many countries don't have them. Even if they do, it's not easy to get them out of the ground. Developing an oil or gas reserve takes an incredible amount of time, money, and work. For example, Europe may be sitting on lots of energy resources, but it may be many years before they are able to access them. In the meantime, where are they getting their oil and gas?"

Looking uncertain, Patrick pointed to Russia.

"That's right!" Skip beamed. "Much of Europe is dependent on Russia for its energy."

"Okay," Patrick said, nodding. "But doesn't that give Russia a huge advantage? I mean, can't they basically call the shots?"

"You got it, buddy. Politics again! What happens if Russia decides to stop selling gas to Europe? Not good – maybe the lights go out in Budapest, or Prague, or Warsaw…"

Patrick nodded along.

Watching him, Skip decided to press on.

"But it's not just Europe that wants to buy the Caspian Sea's oil and gas," he said. "There's China and India, too – they need more and more energy to power their growing economies. Altogether, there is a lot of demand for oil and gas. And this means there's a lot of competition to control it. Whoever controls the oil and gas controls the world."

"So… this is why all these countries are arguing about who owns the Caspian?" Patrick asked.

"Yep. But like everything else in this part of the world, the issue is complex. Half the game is getting the oil and gas out of the ground, and the other half is getting it to market. It has to be transported by pipeline to the ocean, where it can be put on ships. But look at the geography of this region. There are as many as six or seven wars going on in the countries to the west of here. To the north and east of the Caspian are Russia and her friends, all of which are historical rivals of Europe and the United States. To the south is Iran and Afghanistan – another dicey part of the world. So when you look at the Caspian neighborhood, you can see that it's not exactly the safest or friendliest... That's where the politicians enter the game – they control the oil and gas."

A voice from the table called Skip's attention. He looked at Patrick for a moment longer. "That's a heck of a lot to think about, isn't it?" Patrick nodded slowly, still staring at the map. "When you get a chance, ask Roger to explain. That guy knows all about the politics and geography – and history, too. I'm just a geologist, after all. I try to leave the rest of this stuff to politicians and engineers!"

He smiled, slapped Patrick on the back, and joined the others at the table.

15 SHIFTING THOUGHTS

"Three things cannot be long hidden:
the sun, the moon, and the truth."
– Buddha

Leaving the geologists to their maps, Patrick decided to explore the office. Drifting through the hallways, he soon found a lounge area with vending machines and a television. Grabbing a candy bar and bottled water, he sprawled in an oversized chair to watch an American news channel. After a while, he got up and wandered over to the room's large window, where he stood peering out at the city. Far off, stretching across the horizon lay the dark, glimmering Caspian Sea, dotted with the black silhouettes of oil freighters and fishing trawlers. Nearer, he could make out the fortress walls and towers of Old City. Directly below him, cars and pedestrians marched along like thousands of worker ants. Baku was busy today, as it had always been.

He wondered what Grandpa would think of the city. Perhaps he had once visited with Grandma. After all, they seemed to have been to every corner of the earth. Patrick wished his old friend was here now. Together, they could explore the busy markets, poke around the alleys and back rooms of Old City, or stroll along the harbor to watch the hustle and bustle of exotic goods and people. Maybe they would simply spend a day at the beach, staring up at the clouds while sharing another of Thomas's grand adventures.

It would also be nice to have someone to explain everything he had heard and seen over the past week. Patrick's head was spinning with the details of Thomas's journal, Roger's lectures, Skip's talks about geology and pipelines, and Ahmed's account of Armenia and Azerbaijan. As best he could figure, Asia was not just old; it was really complex, too. There were so many perspectives to consider – culture, geography, history, politics, religion, and energy. He had studied Asia in his history classes, but the complexity of this place could hardly be packed into a library, let alone a few chapters of a textbook.

In any case, Patrick's time in Baku was at an end, at least for now. Tomorrow he would take a boat to Turkmenistan, where Dad assured him things would get more interesting. Patrick certainly hoped he was right. He wasn't sure he could bear another week of hotel life. What he craved was real adventure: wavy-dune deserts, camels and nomads, buried treasure, and danger lurking around every corner. That was the stuff of Eaton lore!

Recalling Thomas's journal, Patrick stepped away from the window and went to his backpack. Getting comfortable at a table, he opened the journal and continued reading.

May 9, 1928. After careful thought, I have decided to disband the caravan before entering Armenia. For one thing, the Soviets control the border with Turkey. Therefore, the likelihood of sneaking across with such a large a group is small. Secondly, while I trust Misha, I am not so confident about the dozen other members of our party. They have performed admirably thus far, but how will they react when confronted with the rifles and rough interrogation of Soviet border guards? Might a frightened Turk hand me over, perhaps naming me as a spy just to save his own skin?

Given the risks, I have decided to proceed with Misha only. My attendants and most of the baggage and horses have been dispatched back to Turkey. Keeping only the most important belongings – my digging tools, writing and mapping instruments, a handful of books, a few horses, and food and water – Misha and I can travel light and fast.

To minimize suspicion, it is imperative that I disguise my identity. We have agreed Misha will adopt the appearance of a local trader, while I will play the part of his humble servant. Maintaining this ruse will not be easy, as it requires me to perfectly mirror the dress, mannerisms, language, and customs of the local population. One slip-up (an out-of-place scarf, improper hand gesture, or misspoken phrase) and I could be discovered, arrested, and perhaps never seen or heard from again. As my accomplice, Misha would no doubt suffer a similar fate.

As luck would have it, there is probably no better place in Asia for a white-faced man to blend in than the Caucasus [CAW-keh-ses]. This geographic region comprises the three countries of Armenia, Azerbaijan, and Georgia. It is also thought to be the place of origin for the Caucasian race. Therefore, I will be surrounded by people who look very much like me (as opposed to when I was obviously *gweilo* in China). Also, Russian is commonly spoken here. If the worst occurs – I am stopped and questioned – my fluency in this language may be just enough to save my neck.

Misha has been extremely helpful with our preparations. His talent for clandestine operations is both impressive and surprising. For example, he has made several fine-tunings to my clothing – adjustments so slight that I would have overlooked them, but which he assures me a local would notice right away. He has fashioned a walking stick from a tree limb, atop which he fixed my compass so as to appear an inconspicuous decoration. How clever! After all, possession of a compass would be undeniable evidence that I am here on a covert map-making mission.

With each day, it becomes more obvious why Misha earned his military honors and the respect of the British. He is intelligent, perceptive, creative, thoughtful, steadfast, and honorable. I am very fortunate to have him along to keep me out of trouble these next few months.

Patrick laid the journal on the table in front of him and looked out the window. He tried to imagine the excitement and determination that must have coursed through Thomas's veins as he stole through Soviet territory disguised as a lowly servant. It was extraordinary the way his great-grandfather made decisions quickly and then turned his full energy and ambition toward accomplishing whatever new goals he had set. Self-doubt seemed to have been completely absent from the man's thoughts. Either he did not sense fear, or he simply chose to ignore it.

Grandpa once explained to Patrick that the key to success was to shift one's thoughts: to recognize a negative or fearful thought and to consciously choose its positive alternative. To focus on what you want, rather than what you don't. He must have learned this from his father. Indeed, Thomas had mastered the art of positive thought. Once he decided upon a goal, he refused to entertain any possibility of failure. He trained himself to view success as his inevitable destination.

Shaking his head with admiration, Patrick stretched his arm towards the water bottle on the table before him. Engrossed in his thoughts, Patrick misjudged his reach and knocked the drink over, gushing water onto the old yellowed pages of the journal. Leaping forward, he frantically wiped the pages with his shirt sleeve. Then he grabbed at the pile of napkins stacked nearby. His exasperation growing, Patrick switched from rubbing to dabbing, desperately trying to keep from ruining the gift that his Grandpa had entrusted to him.

Finally, Patrick collapsed in his chair and stared in horror at the smeared mess. A pain began to form in his stomach, followed by a lump in his throat, and then the burn of tears in his eyes. How careless and stupid. This was how things went for him at home and school, too. As soon as he thought he'd gotten on track and done something right, he would inevitably screw up or forget to turn in an assignment. But those failures paled in comparison to spilling water all over his great-grandfather's journal. How was he going to explain this to Grandpa? He cursed silently, laid his head in his arms on the desk and looked out the window.

In fact, he knew what Grandpa would say if he was here. *Shift your thoughts, Patrick. Stay positive.* His eyes returned to the journal. The writing had smeared into a large black stain in the middle of the page. Some of the letters were still readable, while others bled together. But in other places, letters appeared that were not there before! As the page dried, the letters faded away again.

Patrick lifted his head and wiped his eyes. There went another letter, and then another. What was going on?

Another sensation coursed through him – exhilaration. Picking up one of the wet napkins, he dabbed the top of the page where he had seen the writing. Nothing happened. He dipped the napkin and tried again. A couple of characters reappeared. Patrick heard his pulse pounding in his head. He knew exactly what this was – invisible writing!

Patrick dabbed more of the writing, and a line of characters became visible. He excitedly searched his backpack for a pencil and paper, and then began to write down the letters before they dried up again.

FOGK ZEBR NUUL MKAH LEMR SQXS

Patrick was looking at a cryptogram! Grandpa had taught him this four-group system of code writing. Putting letters in "fours" made the cipher easier to *en*code, and more difficult to *de*code – that is, except for someone who is familiar with the cipher. But how was Patrick going to crack this cryptogram? He did not know what code-writing method had been used, nor did he have the key for deciphering it. Or, did he?

Patrick leaned back in his chair, thinking. Thomas had instructed Grandpa in code-writing, and Grandpa had passed along this knowledge to Patrick. So, it was entirely possible that Patrick did possess the knowledge to crack this code.

But, he still needed the *key* – a word or phrase that would unlock the seemingly random arrangement of numbers or letters. Thomas could have chosen virtually anything as his key: the name of a friend or pet, his birthplace, favorite color, title of a book, acronym, or even a word spelled backwards. How was Patrick supposed to guess this? A trained code breaker might have a chance, but Patrick was merely an amateur. The task was impossible.

Shift your thoughts. Stay positive.

Patrick got up and paced the room. Why would Thomas have used a cipher in his journal? What kind of information would he have wanted to keep secret? And who was he afraid might discover it? The communists? Or perhaps bandits, which had been a threat during his travels in China?

In all likelihood, the key required some piece of knowledge that belonged only to Thomas. Perhaps he had committed it to memory. On the other hand, maybe he had hidden the key elsewhere in the journal. This way, if something terrible befell him, a trusted person would be able to retrieve the information he had encoded. It was a slim possibility. Putting a key into the same document as its cipher is risky. But Patrick decided to give it a shot. What did he have to lose?

He began flipping through page after page of writings, scribbles, and drawings. The journal was at least a couple hundred pages long. Thomas's cipher key could be hidden anywhere among all this information.

Then Patrick heard the faintest whisper somewhere deep in his mind. Ever so soft, he could not make out the words at first. Again, slightly louder this time, it toyed with him. Then, once more… That was it!

For my son (born 10/23/1927) – May the road rise up to meet you. May the wind always be at your back. May the sun shine warm upon your face, and rains fall soft upon your fields.

Something about this passage had grabbed Patrick's attention a week ago. For the second time, he found himself staring at the first page of Thomas's journal. *10/23/1927.* Was that his Grandpa's birthday? He'd had his doubts from the beginning, and now his suspicion was boiling.

He glanced back at the letters he had discovered. A shift cipher, he heard his Grandpa say, is a method of code writing often used by the Roman emperor, Julius Caesar, to write secret messages. The code writer begins by writing the alphabet across a page, and then below this message another alphabet is written – but shifted over a certain number of letters. The code letter is substituted for the real message letter. To decode the cipher, one must simply "shift" back over the correct number of letters. But how many letters to shift?

A date shift cipher is a clever variation of this method. The code-writer uses the numbers of a date as the key: each digit tells the decoder how many letters to "shift" each letter in the cipher.

Patrick began by writing out the alphabet as a guide. Below, he copied the four-group combination cipher. Then, beneath the cipher he wrote the date "key" (Grandpa's so-called birthday) back-to-back. 1-0-2-3-1-9-2-7, followed by 1-0-2-3-1-9-2-7, and then again. Slowly, he translated the cipher by shifting each letter to the right by however many spaces were indicated by the date key. For example, for the first letter, "F," Patrick shifted one letter to the right – "G" – because the first number of the date key was "1."

When he finished, his sheet looked like this:

A B C D E F G H I J K L M N O P Q R S T U V W X Y Z

F O G K   Z E B R   N U U L   M K A H   L E M R   S Q X S
1 0 2 3   1 9 2 7   1 0 2 3   1 9 2 7   1 0 2 3 1 9 2 7
G O I N   A N D Y   O U W O   N T C O   M E O U   T Z Z Z

Putting the letters together, the message spelled:

GOINANDYOUWONTCOMEOUTZZZ

Patrick stared at the characters. *Go in and you won't come out. ZZZ.* The last three letters might be "nulls" – space fillers that meant nothing.

"Patrick! There you are!" His dad stuck his head around the doorway. "We're ready to head back to the hotel. Ahmed's outside waiting for us."

"Okay, Dad," Patrick fumbled, cleaning up his mess of papers and napkins.

His dad moseyed in, looking down at the table. "What's this you're working on?"

Patrick slid the journal into his backpack and hastily stood. "Just messing around... Yeah, I'm ready to go."

"Good. I thought we'd head back in time for a swim and dinner. Then we need to pack. Tomorrow we're off to Turkmenistan."

Patrick grinned back at him and slung his backpack onto his shoulder. "Sounds good." Then, he halted to ask, "Hey Dad, when was Grandpa born?"

His dad gave him an amused look. "Grandpa? Um, 1932. Why?"

Patrick smiled. "No reason." As he brushed past his dad, it occurred to Patrick that there might be an adventure ahead of him, after all.

PART II: THE MIDDLEGAME

16 THE DAGESTAN

"Life is either a great adventure or nothing."
– Helen Keller

The view from the back of the ferry was breathtaking. A fantastically large sun blazed golden-orange above the horizon, its fiery radiance mirrored in the calm sea. The entire sky, in fact, was striped with shades of yellow, red, pink, purple, and finally dark gray from the sunset in the west to the arrival of night in the east. Silhouetted against the crimson skyline was a series of floating oil rigs. The black outlines of their platforms and towers looked like the hulls and masts of a massive fleet of ancient warships on its way to plunder some unsuspecting coastal town. Here and there, a twinkling star appeared above – soon joined by another – as darkness crept over the Caspian Sea.

Gathered shoulder-to-shoulder by the ship's railing, Patrick, his dad, Roger, Skip, and Ahmed gazed silently at the magnificent display. In the shadows behind them clanged and groaned the workings of the Dagestan ferry. Like an old plow horse, it seemed to know the task ahead of it and loudly protested every step. From its appearance, the ship had been making this crossing from Baku to Turkmenistan for a hundred years. Rusted and grimy, and crewed by a collection of apparent misfits, the ferry was one of only a few dilapidated vessels available to travelers wishing to cross the Caspian.

On previous trips, Dad had made the voyage by plane. But, he told Patrick, he had always hoped to take this ferry someday.

With his son along, now seemed the perfect occasion to experience the Caspian as it had been by countless previous generations of visitors. As seagulls squawked and wailed overhead and the engine rumbled within the ship's belly, Dad put his arm around Patrick's shoulders and drew him closer. Grateful for the flawlessness of the moment, no one in the group spoke for several minutes.

At last, they were snapped out of their trance by the blaring of the ship's horn – perhaps a greeting from the captain to an old comrade he had spotted in the distance. As if freed to speak, Ahmed said, "Look over there. Neft Desjlari [NEFT dosh-LAR-ee]." He pointed at what appeared to be a castle rising out of the middle of the sea.

Patrick strained his eyes trying to make sense of the startling sight. "What is that?" he asked.

"The Oil Rocks," said his dad. "It is also known as *Stalin's Atlantis*. Neft Desjlari is an entire city that was built for drilling oil. Joseph Stalin – the Soviet Union's most infamous leader – had the place constructed in the late-1940s, after World War Two. You're looking at what's left of the world's first offshore oil platform."

Patrick continued to stare, his brain trying to register what his eyes were telling him. "That's a city? But we're nowhere close to land. How is that possible?"

"It was built on the backs of ships," answered his dad. "They were deliberately sunk and dirt and rocks piled over them. On top of this artificial island, the Soviets built roads, homes, hotels – even cinemas and amusement parks. At one time, nearly five thousand people lived and worked there, drawing oil out of the ground that was then shipped to the Soviet Union."

"Does anybody still live there?" Patrick probed.

"Maybe a couple thousand workers. Oil Rocks is just a shadow of its former self. I don't think much oil is produced there anymore. Isn't that right, Skip?"

Skip nodded. Standing on the other side of Patrick's dad, his hands clasped over the railing, he added his take.

"Yeah, the place is falling apart. Most of it has been abandoned. There's so much collapsed steel in the surrounding waters that bringing ships anywhere close is just too dangerous now. The buildings are in shambles, roads have buckled, and oil is leaking into the sea... She won't be around much longer. Makes you wonder why the Russians don't just scrap her."

"It does, indeed, make you wonder," joined Roger from the far end of the railing. Everyone turned their heads to look at him. "For some reason, which isn't clear to me anyway, the Russians continue to guard her closely. They're funny that way... There are rumors that they might restore her, but those rumors have been floating around for a long time..."

"Maybe they have some kind of secret base there," Patrick piped in eagerly. "Like a James Bond movie!"

Roger laughed. "Well, I've heard stranger things. I would imagine that somebody in the intelligence community has considered the possibility, as well."

With that, the group was silent again. A couple of lights flickered faintly from Oil Rocks, and Patrick tried to imagine an entire city of people living, working, eating, and sleeping there. To him, it looked like an iron-caged island. Why would anyone want to stay there?

"Well, I don't know about you, but I'm hungry!" boomed Skip, jolting the group from their thoughts and rousing murmurs of agreement. "Let's see what the chef has for us tonight. In all likelihood, nothing!" He looked at Patrick, smiling. "That's how it goes on the Dagestan, partner. Everything about this operation is a big question mark! Fortunately, your old buddy Skip came prepared. Let's get below deck."

Carefully, they made their way across the dimly-lit deck towards a rusty hatch that led to the ship's cabin. Although it was too dark now to make out most of the ship's exterior features, when they boarded, Patrick had concluded it was held together by rust, duct tape, and plastic zip ties. What little metal had survived the ship's long life was now paper thin. Every clang from below deck reverberated throughout the vessel. Patrick grew increasingly apprehensive about what he would find in his cabin.

Everything about this operation is a huge question mark. Over the previous twenty-four hours, Patrick had found Skip's words to be spot on. In fact, the decision to travel by ferry had already delayed them by an entire day. They had intended to leave Sunday night, and were packed and ready to go then. But no ferry was available to carry them across. Patrick was perplexed by the news, while Dad seemed annoyed. But Skip just laughed it off.

"Welcome to Central Asia," he said to Patrick. "With luck, the ferry will be here tomorrow… if it didn't sink."

Fortunately, the ferry did arrive the next day, but not until late afternoon. The travelers had bought their tickets that morning, hoping to get underway before lunch. But when asked about the departure time, the clerk at the ticket office merely shrugged. In a thick Russian accent he grumbled, "Who knows? When it is ready, then you will go." Without further explanation, he lit a cigarette and turned back to his black-and-white television.

The delay, however, had a silver lining. Passing the time until the ferry left, the group strolled over to a nearby bakery. It was here that Roger turned up unexpectedly and surprised them further by announcing he would accompany them on the boat ride. Roger had already issued their visas on Sunday, so they had not planned to see him again until Turkmenbashi, after his plane landed. For a busy diplomat to find even a few extra hours in the day – let alone an entire night – to spend with travelers was rare and, for this group, very lucky. Aside from managing paperwork and diplomatic glitches, Roger was an expert on Central Asian history. His arrival guaranteed a night of interesting stories.

As the hatch clanged shut behind them, and the group began its shuffle down the narrow, dank, dimly lit passageway of the ship's interior, Patrick pinched himself to make sure it was all real. Two weeks ago he'd been sitting in Mr. Blackburn's class dreading another ordinary summer. One week ago he'd learned he would go to Asia and inherited his great-grandfather's personal diary. Five days ago he'd visited Old City and bathed in Baku's most lavish pool. And just three days ago he discovered a cipher written in invisible ink in Thomas's journal. Indeed, life appeared to be getting more interesting every day. But that wasn't all.

Last night, while Dad talked with Skip after dinner in the hotel restaurant, Patrick had gone upstairs early to take another shot at Thomas's cipher. Approaching his door, he was alarmed to see it open. A uniformed man with dark features and a pencil mustache stepped into the hallway. As he turned off the light and pulled the door shut, he noticed Patrick standing in the hallway. His eyes flashing, the man froze momentarily.

"Ah, yes sir," he stuttered. "I am with hotel maintenance. There was a problem with the air conditioning. It is fixed now."

He turned and walked quickly down the hall without looking back. Patrick glanced from him to the door, and then back to the man as he disappeared around a corner. Rather than entering, Patrick quickly returned to the elevators.

Downstairs, he found his dad paying the bill and excitedly explained what had happened. A brief chat with the hotel manager confirmed that no problems with the air conditioning had been reported, and that he had no employee who matched Patrick's description. Hotel security was summoned to search their room but, finding no evidence of tampering or theft, promised only to keep their eyes open. What else could be done? These things happen from time to time, they said.

They had been lucky tourists, fortunate to have had their passports and valuables with them. Had this happened a few days earlier, Patrick might have shrugged off the incident, which simply appeared to confirm the words of warning issued by Roger on their first night in Baku.

But Patrick wasn't convinced. Just yesterday, he had discovered a secret cipher written in invisible ink. Who knows what message it carried or who else might like to find out? However unlikely, Patrick couldn't help but wonder if the two events were somehow linked. In any case, the incident left him with a funny feeling, and he was thankful to bid goodbye to the hotel the next day.

As their ferry idled out of Baku's harbor, Patrick couldn't help but smile to himself. Watching Azerbaijan recede in the distance, it dawned on him that he was not the first Eaton to quietly slip away on a slow boat into Asia.

17 THE GREAT GAME

"All men can see these tactics whereby I conquer, but what none can see is the strategy out of which victory is evolved."
– Sun Tzu

It was a good thing Skip had brought food and drinks. His wisecrack about the unreliability of the Dagestan was prophetic. Not only was there no food on the ferry tonight, there was also no chef. According to a crewmember they passed on their way to the galley, the chef had a weakness for Turkmenbashi's nighttime festivities. Sometimes he would show up for the ferry the next morning and sometimes he would not. The crew member just shrugged and held up his hands in a gesture of helplessness.

Skip disappeared down a passageway while the others inspected the ship's galley. It was what one might expect the kitchen of a half-century-old Caspian Sea ferry to look like. The smell of diesel and the vibration of the engines permeated the compartment. Lining the room were steel bulkheads, which were barren save for a few rickety shelves and grimy portholes. Against one bulkhead leaned a sink, its surface cluttered with rusty pots and a stained coffee maker. In the galley's center, a couple of bare bulbs hung from the ceiling, casting a dim pallor over an ordinary metal table and folding chairs. Beyond this sphere of light, all was veiled in shadow. Perhaps that was a good thing, Patrick thought. Given what he could actually see of the galley, he wasn't sure he wanted to know what the darkness concealed.

Ahmed made a beeline for the kitchen cabinets to rummage for something to drink. Roger sauntered in, checking his satellite phone, seemingly indifferent to the gloom and grime. Dad entered leisurely, his hands in his pockets, glancing from the surroundings back to Patrick. With raised eyebrows, he quipped, "A bit different from our kitchen back home, eh?"

Patrick scanned the room with a combination of curiosity and trepidation. His dad's words were an understatement. The spectacle before him was like something out of a horror movie. For the second time in an hour, Patrick felt like pinching himself to make sure this was real.

Digging through the cupboards, Ahmed found some water bottles and tossed them to the others. A few minutes later Skip turned up with a huge grin and paper bag about to burst with food. Where had he gotten that? Patrick wondered.

They made themselves comfortable around one of the tables. From his bag of surprises Skip drew various cans and jars, a roll of bread, potato chips and bottles. He passed these around to the hurrahs of the group, none of whom had eaten since lunch. In short time, all forgot their misgivings about the Dagestan and were fully absorbed in the camaraderie of consumption and conversation.

"Turkmenistan is an odd place," Roger mused while crunching on a cracker. "It's a hodgepodge of nomadic tradition, Islam, totalitarianism... and amusement parks." He stopped chewing and wrinkled his brow. "It's kind of like Disney Land for dictators!"

Roger's comment drew a few laughs, but Patrick wasn't sure he meant it as a joke. The diplomat went on to explain that Turkmenistan was one of five "stans" – Central Asian countries that share the Persian suffix meaning "land of." The others included Uzbekistan, Kazakhstan, Tajikistan, and Kyrgyzstan. All had once been part of the Soviet Union.

"Turkmenistan is a difficult place to visit," Roger continued. "It's not easy for tourists to get permission to travel here. But since you guys already have visas, the authorities shouldn't hassle us too much. And having me along should grease the wheels, so to speak." He grinned.

"Maybe you can tell Patrick what makes Turkmenistan such an odd place," said Dad. Patrick got the feeling his dad already knew the answer.

Roger grunted and scratched his chin. "Well, let's see... For one thing, the country was ruled by one of the most repressive and crazy dictators the world has seen in modern times."

"And that's really saying something," Skip piped in, his voice laden with sarcasm. He passed around a bag of chips and then uncorked one of the bottles from his bag. Roger loaded his plate with bread and potato chips and then continued.

"This guy called himself 'Turkmenbashi,' which means 'Leader of the Turks.' Of course, that's also the name of the city where we're headed. Can you believe it – he actually named a city after himself! But then, he also gave his name to public buildings, airports, and stadiums – and even a meteorite."

"Must be tough to give directions in Turkmenistan," Skip joked again, trading a smile with Patrick. Roger and Dad chuckled, while Ahmed stared at his cup, apparently distracted by other thoughts.

"That's only the beginning. This Turkmenbashi fellow did lots of other bizarre stuff, too." Roger held up his hand and started ticking off fingers one by one. "He created a new alphabet, renamed the months of the year, and outlawed operas and ballet. He even banned news reporters from wearing makeup. Wherever he went, celebrations of dancing and music were required to greet him. That's just a handful of examples... I don't have enough fingers to count all the other wacky ones."

"It's hard to believe a nut job like that could hold onto power for so long," Skip replied, breaking off another piece of bread.

"It may seem that way at first," Roger agreed. "But when you consider Central Asia's history, it's not so surprising.

Totalitarianism is the norm here. For thousands of years, Central Asia has been ruled by dictators of one form or another. The Greeks, Romans, Persians, Mongols, and Russians all brought their own versions of oppression. Usually, their subjects were allowed to keep at least some of their traditions, so long as they paid tribute to whatever empire happened to rule them at the time. But the Soviets were different – they were determined to erase every bit of the native culture. They wanted to eliminate all practices or viewpoints that might challenge the communist system. This meant doing away with ancient kinships, historical boundaries, and religion. Essentially, the Soviets treated the people of Central Asia like cattle. They were herded, worked, milked, and slaughtered according to Moscow's orders."

Patrick recalled his great-grandfather's decision to travel through Soviet territory. The thought made him shiver.

"When the Soviet Union collapsed in the 1990s, the five 'stans' became independent countries. After almost seventy years of control by Moscow, they were suddenly on their own again. This situation created a 'power vacuum.' There was a lot of confusion about who was in charge and what types of government should be formed. Initially, many people hoped that moderate leaders would prevail to protect individual rights. But in the end, politicians from the old Soviet system won out. Most ditched their communist beliefs while rushing to seize control of their countries. It was a nasty fight that was won by the toughest, craziest, and meanest – like Turkmenbashi. Once in power, these guys treated their people just as ruthlessly as any previous emperor or dictator."

Skip leaned back in his chair and propped a cowboy boot against the stove. "A couple days ago, Patrick and I were chatting about Central Asia's geography and history. But I reminded Patrick that I'm only a crusty old geologist, and that we'd better leave the real story to you!"

The group laughed again, and Dad patted Patrick's back. "Well, Patrick's quite a history buff, too. He studied Genghis

Khan and the Silk Road in school this past year." All eyes turned to Patrick, who blushed. The galley grew quiet, and he felt he had to say something to fill the silence.

"Well, yeah," was all he managed at first. "In Mr. Blackburn's class we learned a little bit about Asia. I know that the Mongol Empire was the biggest in history. It stretched from China to Europe to the Middle East. I also read that Marco Polo traveled the Silk Road from Italy to China, where he served in the court of another Mongol king... Kublai Khan, I think. But Mr. Blackburn says Polo might have really been a spy, and not just a trader."

Roger bobbed his head and smiled. "Indeed, he may have been. In any case, he wasn't the first spy to travel the Silk Road or explore Central Asia." He took a sip before adding, "And he certainly wasn't the last, either. Due to its geography, this region has long been an epicenter of political intrigue. As its name implies, Central Asia is at the *center* of Asia. It sits between the four axes of power – Europe, China, Persia, and India. And it is where the world's four major religions overlap – Christianity, Islam, Buddhism, and Hinduism."

"Plus, it's full of natural resources," Skip added, winking at Patrick.

"That, too," Roger nodded. "If you can think of the world as a gigantic chessboard, Central Asia would be its middle. The players and rules may change over time, but the geography is the same as it ever was. Across history, great powers have sought control of Central Asia."

"The Great Game?" interjected Dad, and Patrick sensed a shift in the group's energy. It was as if his father's words placed a spell on the travelers, igniting their curiosity and transforming what had merely been a friendly chat into something far more tantalizing.

"Indeed," Roger nodded, cupping his drink on his lap as he reclined in the chair. His relaxed manner reminded Patrick of the way Grandpa would settle into his chair by the cabin's fireplace before launching into one of Thomas's grand adventures. Like Grandpa, Roger also appeared to relish the role of storyteller, teasing his eager audience by dragging out the tale's beginning with a bit of extra theater. He gazed up and sighed thoughtfully, as if searching the rust-stained ceiling for the words that came next.

"The Great Game was a contest among the world's empires for supremacy in Central Asia. Played throughout the 1700s and 1800s, it was essentially a political chess match between Great Britain and Tsarist Russia. It combined strategy and geography, spies and armies, and adventure and tragedy. And, Patrick, it all had its beginnings in the Mongol Empire."

Patrick stole a look at his dad, and then took Roger's bait. "What do you mean?"

Roger smiled and continued. "The Mongols are the reason why Russia has repeatedly tried to dominate Asia. You may recall that, among their many other victims, Genghis Khan's ferocious barbarian horde invaded and plundered Russia back in 1200 A.D. Back then, Russia was just a collection of tribes living in villages of wooden huts – nothing like the country of today. But even now, 800 years later, the memory of that horrific event still haunts the Russian people. Ever since the Mongol conquest, they have looked to their borders in dread of the next attack."

"Sounds like the Russians are paranoid about being invaded," Skip teased.

"Not really," Roger replied, his voice serious. "Their fears have been justified several times since – most notably by Napoleon, and then again by Nazi Germany during World War II. So, no, I wouldn't call them paranoid – just extremely guarded. In fact, their fear of invasion is one reason the Russian people tolerate such tyranny and abuse from their own leaders. They believe a strong government is necessary to keep them safe from outsiders."

Patrick nodded along. So far, Roger's explanation made sense. The diplomat continued his account.

"Geography and history have forced Russia to think carefully about how to protect itself from invaders. On the one hand, it can play defense – that is, build walls, sit behind them, and wait for the next attack. But Russia is the largest country on earth – and so it would be very difficult to fence off its entire border. So, what's the alternative?" He looked at Patrick, who shook his head, a look of puzzlement on his face.

"Sometimes the best defense is a good offense," Roger answered himself. "And this is the strategy that Russia has chosen. Over the last few centuries, its foreign policy has been to expand its borders. Rather than sitting around, waiting to be attacked again, Russia has repeatedly conquered the lands surrounding it. With each new expansion, it created a buffer zone, or ring of insulation, from which it could withdraw if needed. Going back to the chess analogy, you can think of this strategy as *controlling the middle of the board*."

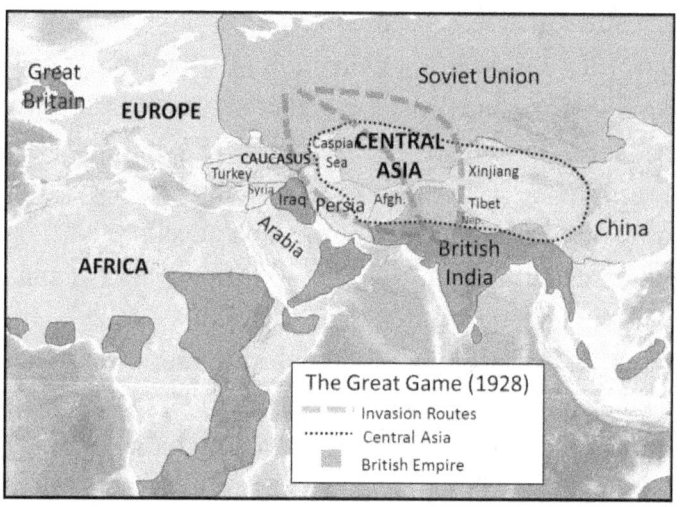

Dad interjected. "So this is why the Soviet Union invaded the countries of Eastern Europe and Central Asia – to create a buffer zone against future attacks?"

"Yes, partly," Roger confirmed. "But Russia adopted this strategy long before the Soviets came along. Way back in the 1700s, the Russian Empire was already expanding into the Caucasus – the region between the Black and Caspian Seas. As I pointed out at our dinner in Baku, the Caucasus is the most direct route from Russia to the Middle East. So it was vital to Russia that it controlled that territory – both to insulate itself from an attack through Turkey or the Middle East, as well as to create the option of invading those places itself."

"Russia wanted to conquer Turkey?" Patrick asked.

"Mmm," Roger nodded, wiping his mouth before continuing. "The idea has certainly crossed her mind. After all, Turkey's geographic location makes it an extremely valuable square on the world's chess board. Russia's empress during the 1700s, Catherine the Great, seized the Crimea in southern Ukraine and built a naval base there from which the Russian navy could sail to Istanbul. Her bigger goal was that Russia's navy gain access to the Mediterranean Sea."

Patrick crinkled his forehead. He'd recently heard Crimea mentioned in the news back home. It seemed like Russia had been involved there recently...

Outside, a passing ship's horn echoed somberly in the distance, momentarily reminding the travelers of where they were.

"Hey, Skip, give me a refill, will you?" Roger reached his cup out, which Skip promptly topped off. He took a sip before continuing.

"In the 1800s, Russia continued to spread its empire. But this time, Russia pushed south into Central Asia – the area between the Caspian Sea and China. Today, this region is occupied by the five 'stans.' But 200 years ago, it was a wild and dangerous territory that was divided between Muslim kingdoms, or 'khanates.' Patrick, these khanates had been around for a long time, and their leaders were a cruel and devious bunch. For centuries, they resisted the Russians, and often seized Russian soldiers as slaves. But by the 1800s, the Russian Empire had become too strong. No longer could the khanates hold off Russian artillery, and eventually they were toppled one by one."

"So, Russia invaded Central Asia for the same reason it conquered the Caucasus – to create a buffer zone?" Patrick asked.

"Yep. But, once again, these lands were a 'two-way street.' Britain began to suspect that Russia wanted to invade India. If you take a look at a map, you'll see that Central Asia lies between Russia and India." He reached into his bag to retrieve a glossy booklet, which he unfolded and spread on the table before them.

"Why would Russia want to invade India?" Patrick asked, examining the map.

"Well, if you recall from your history classes, India was a British colony in the 1800s. But not just any ordinary colony – India was the 'crown jewel' of the British Empire. It was known far and wide for its legendary riches, as well as for being a stepping stone to the markets of Asia. Christopher Columbus knew this when he set out to find it in 1492. Anyway, it's no surprise that Spain, Portugal, France and other European countries wanted India for themselves. At the time, it was a far more valuable prize than the American colonies ever were!"

Roger's voice had been building in intensity and he looked excitedly around the table at his audience. Suddenly realizing his zeal, he relaxed, took another drink, and then leaned back in his chair again.

"Eventually," he carried on, "Britain edged out its European rivals and had India all to itself. Therefore, the prospect of a new threat – this time a Russian invasion from the north – terrified the British. So Britain looked for a way to defend India. It ended up adopting Russia's strategy – a good offense. Britain invaded Afghanistan, a move that ended tragically for her soldiers. But that's another story…"

The lights flickered ominously, illuminating Roger's face with an eerie strobe-like effect. He paused and the group looked up at the ceiling, then around at each other, waiting to see what happened next. The flickering stopped, and Roger went on.

"In any case, neither Russia nor Britain knew much about the chessboard – that is, the deserts and mountains of Central Asia. Back then, most of it was still unexplored by Westerners, so the two empires sent spies to map these mysterious lands. Dressed as traders, monks, scientists or explorers, these brave men ventured into the dangerous wilderness on long missions to survey rivers and possible invasion routes, report movements of the other side, and hopefully win the loyalty of local khans and warlords. Many died there – some by cold or starvation, others by rifle or the sword."

"So who won the Great Game?" Patrick asked.

Roger scratched his chin again. "Well, eventually Russia conquered the 'stans' and the Great Game moved farther south into Afghanistan and then east into China. The competition fizzled out in 1907, when Britain and Russia signed a treaty establishing official borders between them." He paused for another sip. "But after World War I, the communists overthrew the Tsar, ripped up the treaties between Russia and Britain, and all bets were off again."

"So, the Great Game was a *stalemate*? Nobody won?" Patrick pressed.

"Tough to say," Roger said with a shrug. "As I said, the Soviet Union collapsed in the early 1990s. So, in the end the Russians lost Central Asia." He looked pleased.

"But, it's still not over, is it?" Skip interjected. Everyone turned to look at him. "The game continues today – this time over oil and gas."

"Right," Roger said, chuckling. He rocked forward and took another sip of his drink. "No doubt about it, the Great Game has begun again with a new player. And as the world's superpower, the United States has a number of strategic interests in Central Asia."

There it was again – the term *interests*. Roger had used this word on their first night in Baku. Patrick had been unsure what it meant, and now seemed like the perfect time to get some clarification.

"What do you mean by interests?" he asked.

For a moment, Roger said nothing. He broke off another piece of bread, slowly buttered it, and took a bite. At last, he looked at Patrick and said, "Well, for one thing, the United States needs to protect our allies in Europe. Russia already controls numerous oil and gas pipelines in Central Asia. Many of these deliver energy to Europe." Skip looked at Patrick and winked. "By controlling the flow of oil and gas, Russia could become as much of a threat as it was during the Cold War."

Roger cleared his throat and added, "And then there's Central Asia's other newest player in the game – or oldest, depending how far back you go – China. That country's navy is already threatening our allies in the Pacific Ocean. Here in Central Asia, the United States must balance China on land, too." Roger reached into the bag of chips, while his audience hung on his words.

"Lastly," he added, "The United States is committed to democracy in Central Asia. We don't want the newly liberated 'stans' to slide backwards into tyranny. And we want to prevent them from becoming breeding grounds for terrorists. It's important that Islamic militants do not disrupt progress there."

"So, it sounds like the United States has to be involved in the Great Game," Skip added.

Roger grinned, rubbed his hands together, and looked around the table. "Well, that's why we're here, isn't it? I mean, that's why we're headed to Turkmenistan. Sure, your company is negotiating a pipeline through Afghanistan. But this is about more than oil and gas. After all, America has plenty of energy. The United States' *real* interest in Central Asia is its geography."

"So, nothing's changed?" Patrick asked. "The Great Game goes on just as before?"

"Pretty much," Roger agreed. "But instead of pitting two adversaries against each other, today's game is like chess on steroids. The *New* Great Game, as some people call it, has more players and ever-changing rules. But the board – or *map* – is exactly the same as it was during the days of Alexander the Great or Genghis Khan. They knew then as well as the United States does now that to be the world's superpower, you must control the middle of the board!"

The group was silent for several minutes, and Patrick sensed an uneasiness in the air. As usual, it was Skip who brightened the mood again.

"And that calls for dessert!" He pulled a package of Azeri sweets from the bag, took two for himself, and passed the rest around. Gradually, laughter and conversation returned to the Dagestan's galley. Only Patrick and Ahmed remained silent, both deep in thought. They did not notice each other at the time, and it was only later that Patrick would recall this detail.

18 CROSSING BORDERS

"In chess, as in life, a man is his own most dangerous opponent."
– Vasily Smyslov

Their night on the Caspian was a restless one for Patrick. In Baku he had understood that he was far from home. But somehow the ferry trip had put an exclamation point on this reality. Just a few days ago he'd begun to think of himself as a confident voyager who could bear the ups and downs of globe trekking. But now he was starting to doubt whether this was true.

Now, if he felt tired, scared, or homesick he had no choice but to grin and bear it. He could not simply call his mom to come pick him up and whisk him back to the comforts of his own home. In fact, the Dagestan had no phone, so he couldn't even call her. Patrick had never gone this long without seeing or talking to his mom. What was worse, he had only been gone from home a week – he still had two months to go! His stomach grew queasy at the thought.

The galley festivities had carried on until midnight when Dad spied his son's eyelids drooping. He graciously reminded the others that they had another long day tomorrow and that he needed to get some sleep. The Eatons bade goodnight and made their way through the maze of ghostly passageways to their cabin. Standing outside the door, Patrick rubbed his eyes as Dad fished his pockets for the key.

As the hatch creaked open they peered in apprehensively. Dad groped around in the dark for a switch, and soon the room was immersed in the flickering glow of fluorescent ceiling light. On the other side of the threshold awaited a compartment the size of a large closet. It was sparsely adorned with wood-paneled walls and cabinets, stained carpet worn thin by decades of feet, and a slender bunk bed bolted to one wall. Across the cabin, a moth-eaten blanket hung from the ceiling as a makeshift curtain. Below, jammed between the bunk bed and cabinets, sprawled an oversized chair whose box-spring seat sagged nearly to the floor.

The spectacle reminded Patrick of a cabin where his family had almost stayed during a vacation to the mountains several years ago. Dad had tried to convince his mom that the place was "charming," but one glance was enough to persuade her otherwise. Without a word, she had simply walked back to the car, where she sat waiting for them to return the cabin keys. Laughing, the three of them had gone down the road to stay at a hotel.

At this moment, Patrick realized how his mom must have felt. He stared at the bunk bed, wondering what vermin crawled within and whether they liked the taste of human flesh. Dad's hand clasped his shoulder and Patrick looked up with nervous eyes.

"It'll be fine, buddy. A few guys from the office suggested I bring along extra sheets. That will get us through the night. Tomorrow, we'll take a shower at the hotel." Patrick hesitantly stepped across the threshold.

In spite of his dad's reassurance, they slept in their travel clothes. Minutes after turning out the light, Dad was already snoring on the lower bunk. But Patrick lay awake for hours with his eyes squeezed shut to drive away the thought of bed bugs scuttling up his legs. Eventually, his thoughts drifted to the galley discussion of the Great Game.

Patrick enjoyed the way Roger explained history. The diplomat glossed over the kinds of boring details he was required by his teachers to memorize. Instead, Roger focused on the big picture, which was what had always drawn Patrick to study history. Patrick was captivated by the interconnectedness of geography, culture, and strategy – and how they worked together to shape history. He liked thinking about how the world must have been long ago. During school field trips to historic places, he loved the sensation of standing in the same places others had stood centuries before. On these occasions, Patrick felt he could *see* and *feel* the past, the way others might experience art or music. But this special ability had yet to help him with school, where he struggled to remember the names of kings and dates of treaties.

Roger's analogy of the Great Game as a chess match between Russia and Britain made perfect sense to Patrick. Each empire schemed and plotted, as if protecting their kings. Russia's king was its "heartland" – the cities of St. Petersburg and Moscow, and the territory that surrounded them in the north. Far to the south lay Britain's own king – majestic India. Sandwiched between them was the vast chessboard of Central Asia. Just as controlling the center of the board is key to victory in chess, occupying Central Asia was crucial to mastering all of Asia. Clearly, the spies who charted the snow-capped mountains and harsh deserts were pawns in this game.

At dinner, Roger had initially said that the Great Game ended in the early 1900s – well before World War Two. But when pressed on this point, Roger confessed that the Great Game never really ended at all. In fact, it continued all through the Cold War when it introduced a new player, the United States. And the game went on even now, here in the twenty-first century. While it had since grown to embrace modern "kings" like oil and gas reserves, the age-old motivations of geography and political domination have never gone away. Players like the United States, Russia, and China were still trying to outwit and outmaneuver each other for control of the center of the chessboard.

Unable to sleep, Patrick crawled down from his bunk and crossed the room to his backpack. As his bare feet touched the floor, he remembered the filth hidden by the darkness and winced. From his bag he collected a small penlight and his great-grandfather's journal. Turning back to the bed, he paused. A circular glow pierced the curtain hanging over the ugly old chair. As much as he hated touching the soiled fabric, he could not resist the urge to take in one last glimpse of night on the Caspian. Drawing back the curtain, he peered through a grimy porthole. A half-moon hung over the calm water, its reflection illuminating a celestial path to Patrick's eyes. Far from the lights of civilization, the stars blazed brightly in the black sky.

Patrick let go of the curtain and leaped back to his bed in two long strides. Atop his bunk again, he opened the journal to the code he'd discovered in Baku. He still had no idea what it meant. But his only choice was to read on, looking for more invisible ciphers, and trying to discover the bigger pattern in the letters.

Although Thomas was entering lands far more dangerous than Turkey, he had no intention of giving up on his purpose for being in Asia: to follow the Silk Road and, wherever possible, explore the local archaeology. His expedition to Baku would require him to follow a lesser known caravan route to Asia. He intended to take up the main route again – the one taken by Marco Polo – once he reached the other side of the Caspian. But first, he wanted to explore the history, ruins, and artifacts of the Caucasus and, with luck, survive to tell his tale.

As it turned out, the two adventurers' arrival in the Caucasus passed without incident. In spite of the warnings they had been given in Turkey, Thomas and Misha slipped easily on horseback across the border into the Armenian Soviet Socialist Republic. Hoping to minimize attention, they spent their nights camped in the mountains or at the outskirts of towns, cooking and sleeping around small fires. In the hilly forests and away from Soviet-controlled roads and cities, they were warmly embraced by the local communities, and Thomas's proficiency with the Russian language helped them to make friends easily.

Despite their ferocious appearance and suspicious nature, the mountain people of Armenia are remarkably kind and generous. They bring food to Misha and me, for which we offer Persian rugs in return. While shy at first, the children are especially friendly. Once they have made up their minds to be sociable, they follow everywhere at our heels asking questions and inviting us to join in their games.

While negotiating prices of textiles or enjoying a bowl of *dzhash* – a brothy stew of meat and vegetables – Thomas also learned about Armenia's precarious situation in the Caucasus region. As a Christian nation, it lay between two Muslim states (Turkey and Azerbaijan) that were linked not only by faith and ethnicity, but also by their vicious territorial disputes with Armenia. Fortunately, Armenia was on relatively good terms with its Christian neighbor to the north (the Soviet Socialist Republic of Georgia), as well as with its Muslim neighbor to the south (Persia).

Its vulnerable location helped to explain why Armenia put up little resistance to the Soviet Red Army's arrival in 1920. Although not overjoyed about being ruled by Moscow again (which had made them part of the Russian Empire from the early-1800s until 1917), the Armenian population realized the Soviet military could protect them from their Muslim neighbors. With the Armenian Genocide still fresh in their minds, they did not want to stand against Turkey on their own. Listening to the old men quarrel around campfires, Thomas often heard the expression, "Better red than dead." In other words, Armenians would rather be occupied by Soviet communists than slaughtered by Muslim Turks.

The more Thomas heard, the more he realized how dangerous the situation was for Misha. If his hosts discovered that

Misha was a Turkish citizen, things would not end well for either of them. Like so many times before, Thomas's well-tuned antenna for danger told him it was time to move on.

Thomas and Misha were able to enter Azerbaijan undetected, as well, although this proved somewhat trickier than their previous border crossing. To avoid looking like Christian merchants, they needed to switch identities at the last moment before leaving one country and entering the other. This delicate operation required them to cross unobserved, so that Thomas could swap one forged passport for another and replace the cross around his neck with Islamic prayer beads. He had to quickly assume his new identity with no witnesses to raise the alarm.

In the black of night, standing in a forested valley with the howling of the wind and wolves all around us, Misha and I hurriedly changed clothes and stashed our Armenian documents under leaves and bushes. Our efforts were frequently interrupted by the sounds of trucks in the distance, the imagined beat of hooves on the road below, or the illusion of torches approaching us through the trees. I must confess that, of all our days and nights since departing Istanbul, this evening caused me the greatest distress. Fortunately, we were able to sneak across unseen. We walked all night to put as much distance as we could between ourselves and the border. The rugged terrain of the Azerbaijan Soviet Socialist Republic gave us ideal camouflage to once again blend in with our surroundings.

Patrick paused his reading. Somewhere over the Caspian, a distant horn blew solemnly. The muffled groan of the ferry's diesel engine mingled with the sloshing of waves against the hull. His eyelids grew heavy and the journal sagged closer to his body. Growing foggy, his mind recalled the cipher from the journal: *Go in and you won't come out.*

What could it mean? Go in where – Soviet territory? Over and over Patrick mouthed the words until at last he fell asleep with the journal atop his chest.

That night his dreams were filled with fantastic visions. The scuffling boots of Soviet secret police outside his cabin door. Ghostly caravans trudging through blinding sandstorms. The haunting songs of Muslim religious men calling their followers to prayer in the pale light of early morning. Ghoulish spirits visited him again and again during the night, uttering strange tongues from the past – whether warnings or provocations, Patrick could not tell. Long bony fingers tugged at his great-grandfather's journal in their frustrated attempts to pry it from Patrick's slumbering clutch. He hugged it tighter, murmuring his protests.

Finally, the spirits melted away, their voices fading into distant echoes. Left cold and sweaty, Patrick settled at last into a deep restful sleep as the Dagestan crossed quietly into the dark waters of Turkmenistan.

19 THE PRICE OF GOLD

"More gold has been mined from the thoughts
of men than has been taken from the Earth."
– Napoleon Hill (author, philosopher, entrepreneur)

The next morning, Patrick woke to screeching seagulls and the ship's blaring horn. He roused himself from the bunk and tried to gather his bearings. Scanning the cabin, he couldn't help noticing how much less intimidating it looked in the light of day. But even the warm sunshine streaming through the porthole did little to hide the filth and clutter. The Dagestan was an old horse, and it was doubtful she would plow the Caspian much longer.

He swung his feet over the bunk and hopped down, narrowly missing his dad who sat on the lower bunk working on his computer.

"Whoa!" his dad hooted, ducking the inbound tangle of legs and arms. "Look who's awake! How'd you sleep?"

"Not too well," Patrick replied, rubbing his eyes. "And I had some of the weirdest dreams."

His dad nodded understandingly. "Yep, travel does that to me, too. I think it must be the brain's way of making sense of new surroundings. I can't tell you how many times I've woken in strange places and couldn't remember where I was. Just be glad the bed bugs didn't gnaw your feet off... You *did* check to make sure you still have all your toes, didn't you?"

Patrick rolled his eyes as he walked over to look out the porthole. The Caspian waters shimmered under the morning sun. In the distance, he could make out a thin brown strip of land.

"How long until we can go ashore?" he asked, turning to his dad.

"An hour, maybe. But then again, Turkmenistan's port authorities have been known to keep ships waiting for hours, and sometimes even days, before allowing passengers to disembark."

"Days?" Patrick asked wide-eyed, panic beginning to rise in his throat.

"Yeah… days. What, you don't want to spend another week in this deluxe cabin?" Dad looked genuinely surprised, causing Patrick to stare back with a mix of bewilderment and horror. Unable to continue his performance any longer, Dad's face melted into a grin and he shook his head.

"Nah, don't worry. We'll be off in an hour or so. Otherwise, some poor official will have to endure the wrath of Roger!" Then he reached into his bag and pulled out a couple of granola bars. "Breakfast?"

It wasn't long before they heard Skip's laughter echoing down the passageway. He must have been teasing Roger or one of the ferry's crewmembers, because he seemed to laugh louder and longer with each outburst. Dad smiled and shook his head as he packed away his computer, then nodded towards the cabin door. He and Patrick slung their bags over their shoulders and headed out.

The bedraggled group of voyagers convened on the ship's deck. Noticing the others' wrinkled clothes and puffy eyes, it was obvious Patrick wasn't the only one who didn't sleep well. Based on the glances and ribbing between Roger and Skip, the storytelling and festivities must have stretched into the wee hours of the morning.

Spying a ring of plastic chairs in the shadow of the ship's bridge, the party of travelers decided to get comfortable while the ship idled towards port. Dad, Skip, and Roger chatted about business while Patrick reclined against a jumble of coiled ropes

122

and netting. He opened the journal to continue reading about his great-grandfather's progress through Azerbaijan.

Reaching Baku in the summer of 1928, Thomas described the city to be exactly like the pictures Patrick had seen on the walls of the "war room" at Dad's office.

I smelled the oil long before seeing the first derrick or grime-covered worker. From miles away, its acrid odor penetrated my nose, hair, clothes, and thoughts, and a thick black cloud hung over the horizon. Everything here smells like oil. As Misha and I got closer to the "Black City," we noticed oil glistening on the surface of our skin and all our belongings.

From time immemorial, the people of this place have cherished this naturally occurring, liquid treasure. I have read accounts of Baku's "black gold" in the writings of travelers and historians who visited this region as early as the fifth century. Almost a thousand years later, Marco Polo described how oil was used for healing purposes; he pointed out that oil-filled water-skins were carried by camels to markets as far away as Persia and India. By the sixteenth century oil wells were being dug in Baku, but it was not until the 1870s that the city's oil industry really grew. In 1916, more than one hundred international oil companies were operating in and around Baku.

When the Soviets conquered Azerbaijan in 1920, they nationalized its oil sector, which meant that the entire industry was placed under the control of Moscow. Business owners were ousted and their wells and equipment confiscated, prompting many to flee to places like Iran, Turkey, and Europe.

But strolling through the smoky oil yards of the "Black City," I can't help but doubt whether the Soviets can match the success of the original business owners. Just one year after Moscow took control of it, Baku's oil output declined to its lowest level in decades. The communists are finding that getting oil out of the ground is not so easy. The process requires skill, creativity, innovation, technology, planning, time, and money — in other words, capitalism — but this is the very economic system which the communists are determined to exterminate.

Despite Moscow's loathing of capitalism, the Soviet Union needs the money generated by Azerbaijan's oil industry to pay for its expanding military, as well as to fulfill the communist promise of a utopian society. This inconvenient paradox has forced Moscow to treat Baku differently from other parts of its empire. Essentially, the communist authorities "look the other way" while Baku's geologists and engineers apply science, innovation, and technology to mine oil. In exchange for their efforts, workers here are allowed to enjoy a better life than most citizens of the Soviet Union. One could even say (very quietly, of course) that the workers here are allowed to profit from their work.

124

But the "black gold" of Baku is not the only buried treasure to be found in these lands. Long before oil derricks dotted the landscape, Azerbaijan and Armenia – as well as the mountains of Central Asia – were famous for many other geologic riches. Minerals such as asbestos, copper, iron, jade, lead, manganese, mercury, rock crystal, salt, and zinc have been mined here for thousands of years. So have gemstones like topaz, rubies, emeralds, aquamarine, and lapis lazuli. These natural resources have lured one empire after the next to this region...the Soviets are only the latest in a long line of treasure-hungry occupiers.

But of all the riches buried in these lands, few have been so prized as gold, and the mountains of Central Asia are full of it. For thousands of years, this yellow metal has captivated locals and outsiders, rich and poor, vanquisher and vanquished. It has been fashioned into rings and necklaces, hammered into royal crowns and burial shrouds, poured into bars and ingots, and imprinted upon the domes of cathedrals, mosques, and temples.

Most significantly, gold has long been used as money, too. In fact, over the ages gold has consistently proven to be the world's most reliable and popular form of money. Since 650 B.C., when gold coins were first minted in Lydia (Anatolia), they have been used to pay soldiers and mercenaries, accompany royal processions, and grease the wheels of commerce.

While grains, animals, slaves, and paper have all served as money, none have retained their value across the millennia like gold. Empires, fashions, booms and busts have come and gone, but the demand for gold lives on.

Many gold coins have already been found by archaeologists and now sit behind museum glass for visitors to appreciate. Nonetheless, many more still lie buried along the Silk Road next to long-lost caravan routes, stashed in caves or mountain crevasses, and concealed under the floors of Buddhist temples. With a bit of luck, my expedition will yield additional discoveries that shed light upon the lives and deaths of the world's great empires, as well as the innumerable lesser-known people who traveled and traded along this famous route.

Patrick was roused from the journal by his dad's voice and looked up to see Roger, Skip, and Ahmed standing at the ferry's railing. His dad stood silhouetted against the sun, one hand clutching his bag over his shoulder. With his other, he waved for Patrick to come along.

Stuffing the journal into his bag, Patrick crossed the deck to join the others. Approaching the railing, he was surprised to see a vast harbor of cargo ships, a shore crowded with cranes, and tan desert mountains rising steeply in the background. There was no question that he was about to enter a world very different from – and much older than – anything he had experienced.

As if reading his mind, Skip turned to greet him. Recognizing the awe in Patrick's face, he grinned and said, "Welcome to Central Asia, partner."

20 QUIET MOVES

"Everything we hear is an opinion, not a fact.
Everything we see is a perspective, not the truth."
– Marcus Aurelius (Emperor of Rome, 161-180 A.D.)

At first, Turkmenbashi seemed to be a quaint, pleasant town – very different from the repressive dictatorship Patrick had anticipated. Taking in the scenery from the bow of the Dagestan, Patrick saw no evidence of iron-fisted tyrants or their strong-armed police that Roger had described the night before.   Squeezed between the calm gray waters of the Caspian Sea and desolate brown mountains to the east, the city seemed like a charming little seaside resort.

Once ashore, his initial impression of the country was barely tarnished by the three hours they spent waiting inside a crumbling harbor building for their visas to be checked. Even after paying hefty fees and having their bags searched by customs officials – all under the watchful eyes of brown-shirted guards – Patrick was eager to explore the resort town.

Finally, the travelers were cleared to enter the country. Crammed into a small taxi bus next to his dad, Patrick took in the melting pot of Turkmenistan that was on display outside his window.   As the bus made its way from the harbor, Patrick glimpsed a group of elderly women slowly making their way along the roadside carrying baskets and bread under their arms. They looked European and wore the traditional Russian garments Patrick had seen in his school textbooks – long black, blue, or gray dresses and headscarves. Farther along, Patrick saw another group of women – this time with somewhat darker skin, almost Asiatic in appearance, and outfitted in colorful patterned dresses. They were smiling and laughing and, even from this distance, Patrick recognized the glint of silver ornamenting their necks and wrists.

Here and there they passed men wearing black suits and ties, and sporting spotlessly shined shoes. They must be on their way to work, Patrick thought. Outside an abandoned warehouse, he spotted a group of children kicking a soccer ball. They were dressed in an assortment of western sports jerseys, jeans, and running shoes. With each new scene, the memory of the strict harbor guards faded, and Patrick began to wonder if Roger's opinions about the country were too harsh.

But as their taxi swept through the city, Patrick began to understand what the diplomat meant when he called Turkmenistan "bizarre." Sprawled across the horizon were austere cinder-block buildings and stark Soviet-era high-rise apartments cluttered with laundry and satellite dishes. From the back seat, Roger pointed out that these were homes for the majority of Turkmenbashi's inhabitants. People who could not afford these meager comforts spent their lives on street corners or in alleys, where they begged or peddled wares in the hopes of a coin or piece of bread. The smiling people of Turkmenbashi seemed to be barely hanging on.

On the other hand, everywhere Patrick looked, advertisements and artwork conveyed an impression of prosperity and leisure. Golden statues – some the size of garages – adorned intersections, and gigantic murals covered the sides of buildings. All depicted the country's former ruler. The smiling Leader of the Turks towered above the roads and sidewalks, at times wearing a cape, but always pointing or reaching out his hand in friendship – the way a father might beckon to his beloved children. High above abandoned buildings, huge billboards promoted marvelous monuments and theme parks. These must have been the expensive attractions which the great leader ordered to be built – and which he dedicated to himself.

One billboard exhibited an enormous alabaster palace that looked as if it were built a thousand years ago by a great Muslim empire. In its center bulged a colossal golden dome, reinforced by a white-pillared complex, and adorned with smaller gold-capped pyramids. Around this structure soared four slim cylindrical towers, also golden-domed. Surrounding the palace was a vast open square, its great floor slabs intricately laid in a mosaic pattern. The tiles were interspersed with dozens of fountains gushing water high into the thirsty desert air. A crowd of visitors held hands as they entered this regal monstrosity.

"Turkmenbashi mosque," Roger offered, seeing the look of curiosity on Patrick's face. "It's not as old as it looks. The Great Leader had it built a few years ago, just before he died. Some say it cost over one hundred million dollars! The place can hold a quarter-million people... but it is almost always empty."

Soon after, they passed another huge display advertising a theme park. Ferris wheels, roller coasters, and carousels were depicted below a row of colorful flags that fluttered against the blue sky. Again, throngs of visitors crowded the image – most of them smiling and laughing children.

"The 'Land of Fairy Tales,'" Roger added indifferently. "Another of the Great Leader's costly projects. But most of the rides don't work. And nobody can afford to go there, anyway."

At last they arrived at the Altin Hotel – an immaculately polished, almost sterile structure of silvery-white and gold, whose brightly lit interior still retained the look and smell of brand new construction.

"It's a gathering place for oil companies now," Roger explained. "But it was built to host pilgrims who were expected to come and worship the holy book that the Great Leader wrote – the *Ruhnama.*"

Unlike the hotel in Baku, however, the Altin was nearly empty. The travelers' footsteps and voices echoed down the vacant corridors as they made their way from the reception desk to the elevators. Upstairs they explored the large and lavishly decorated accommodations. They contained richly engraved furniture, luxurious beds, and silk curtains – a welcome change, indeed, from the cramped, flea-bitten quarters of the Dagestan, thought Patrick.

Most of their day was spent eating, napping, and planning the next week's itinerary. Dad invited Skip to their room, where the two lounged on velvet-covered chairs in front of a floor-to-ceiling window. As they traced their fingers over large maps spread on the ornamental coffee table between them, Patrick relaxed in the bedroom.

After a brief call to Mom, he opened Thomas's journal, but he was too tired to read. Instead, Patrick reached for a glass of water on the bedside table. Gingerly, he brushed a few pages with light strokes of water. No hidden words appeared. He tried a few more pages, but the result was the same. Too tired to continue, Patrick rolled over on the silky sheets and immediately fell asleep.

That evening Patrick attended his first diplomatic dinner. The event was held at the Turkmenbashi Hotel – the city's most elegant spot for hosting foreign envoys and businessmen. The resort boasted fifty stories with a revolving restaurant at its summit. Rotating slowly, diners could enjoy alternating views of the city's lights, the sun setting over the Caspian, and the pink glow of the mountains at dusk. As he peered up at the spectacle through the window of their taxi, Patrick couldn't help wondering why the world's most exquisite hotels seemed to be located in Asia.

Once inside, he kept close to his dad as they made their way along a line of state officials standing shoulder to shoulder, ceremonially greeting guests that entered the spinning restaurant. "Salaams" and "welcomes" were exchanged amid smiles and nods of people who spoke different languages. Not accustomed to

130

formal events, Patrick felt painfully out of place in his cargo pants, button-up striped shirt, and back pack. The hosts and other guests sported immaculately pressed suits.

Patrick noticed that the locals looked considerably different from their neighbors across the Caspian. They displayed darker skin, higher cheekbones, and flatter faces than the Azerbaijanis. But it was their eyes that grabbed Patrick's attention. They conveyed a striking perceptiveness, as if with a quick glance they could measure the full character of every guest who passed through the door.

Patrick breathed a sigh of relief as he moved beyond this eagle-eyed reception committee. He took a seat next to his dad at a massively long, white-clothed table festooned with origami-shaped gold napkins and purple flowers. Although he had hoped Skip would sit next to him, the big Texan was settling in farther down the table. Roger was a couple chairs to Patrick's left, speaking fluent Turkmen, smiling widely, and freely exchanging handshakes. Upon entering the hotel downstairs, Ahmed had melted from sight, probably to return to his taxi or drink tea in the lobby, as he was accustomed to do when waiting for them.

Just when the formality and calculating stares had raised Patrick's anxiety to the boiling point, he felt his dad's touch and looked up to meet his smiling eyes. Dad squeezed his hand, held his gaze a moment longer, and then turned to answer a question from an official across the table.

Somewhat reassured, Patrick took stock of his situation. At least twenty men sat at the long table. Most seemed to be local officials. A few Europeans were seated here and there, and a handful of Chinese occupied one end of the table.

Patrick glanced back at Roger again, envious of the diplomat's easy ability to make friends. He wondered how his great-grandfather would have handled such a dinner. No doubt Thomas would have charmed the crowd, winning their agreement and respect and even bringing smiles to the stony faces of the waiters. Grandpa had inherited this remarkable quality, as had Dad, who was now engaged in easy conversation with his table neighbors. But Patrick feared that the long line of Eaton charisma ended there. He sat uneasily, wondering if he should have just stayed at the hotel.

Stay positive, he heard his grandpa's words again. Patrick lifted his head and looked around the room. He could either withdraw into his shell and stay quiet, as he usually did, or take a risk or two... Feeling hot and sweaty all of a sudden, he reached for the crystal glass of ice water in front of him. As he did, he sensed the eyes of the man sitting across the table. Instinctively, Patrick looked up, but the observer's glance had already darted elsewhere.

Taking a sip of water, Patrick studied the stranger over the top of his glass. The man was stocky – not overweight, but bull-necked and broad-shouldered – with a build that tested the limitations of his dark blue suit. His hands were peculiarly small and moved continually as he spoke, occasionally flashing a large gold watch or bracelet under his shirt cuffs. Unlike the Turkmen at his sides, the man's face seemed to be of European origin. His silvery hair contrasted sharply with the dark manes surrounding the table. He had a big red nose that reminded Patrick of some of the old folks that lived near Grandpa. Maybe this was why he looked familiar...

Without so much as a pause in conversation, the man's eyes dashed back to Patrick. Between two narrow slits blazed eyes of different colors – one blue and the other green – both focused coolly upon him. Momentarily paralyzed, Patrick felt like an escaping inmate who, upon nearing the outer wall of the prison yard, was at the last moment caught in the blinding glare of spotlights. This was a clever man, Patrick recognized immediately, and perhaps dangerous.

Every fiber in him urged Patrick to retract farther into his shell, shift his chair closer to Dad, and pretend not so see this man.

132

Yet, another voice tugged him in the opposite direction. He could not hear the words, really – only gentle encouragement. As if by some supernatural force, he felt all of a sudden as if he had left his body and was now watching himself from high above. Looking down, he gasped as he saw himself put down his water, look directly at the man across the table and say, "Hello, I'm Patrick Eaton."

The man's eyes flashed momentary surprise. He had started to take a sip from his glass, but now put it down and reached across the table to shake hands.

"Uri Petrovsky," he replied with a deep, heavy accent. "I am with the Russian embassy. It is a pleasure to meet you, Patrick Eaton."

The Russian returned the glass to his lips but did not remove his eyes from Patrick, who waited, unsure what to say next.

"Are you enjoying your visit?" asked Uri, casually leaning forward and crossing his arms on the table. Patrick crashed back down into his own body again, returning from his mystical seat in the audience above. Once more, he was on center stage as the lead actor in what might turn out to be a comedy or tragedy.

"Yes," he answered. For a moment, Patrick could think of nothing else to say. Then, words began to flow, as if on their own. "It's my first time here. We just came from Baku. My dad's a geologist. He's here to study oil and gas." He pressed his lips shut, cutting off the torrent of anxiety-fueled blathering. What was the matter with him? Get a grip, he told himself, and reached for his water again.

"Turkmenistan has an interesting history," Uri replied matter-of-factly, paying no attention to Patrick's rambling. "Did you know it used to be part of the Soviet Union?"

Patrick nodded and tried to appear relaxed.

"In fact, Russians built this city. Of course, it was known as Krasnovodsk [KRAZ-nuh-vodsk] then. But it does not matter now. Things are different these days..." He shrugged, as if indifferent. But Patrick sensed the man cared more deeply than he let on.

"Where are you going from here?" Uri prodded.

"Um," Patrick looked to his dad, who was turned away from him in conversation. Patrick was all alone with the Russian. "I'm not really sure," he replied softly.

Uri grunted, as if to say, "I see." He continued to scrutinize Patrick, who was feeling more uncomfortable by the minute. Patrick glanced to his right again, but his dad was still preoccupied. Turning back to Uri, it occurred to Patrick that the man was trying to intimidate him.

Patrick tried a different tactic. "Why are *you* here, Mr. Petrovsky?"

Uri cast several long glances up and down the table, and then returned his eyes to Patrick. He was still leaning forward with his arms crossed on the table, as if his next words were meant only for the two of them.

"I am here to meet with Turkmenistan's energy secretary." He nodded at the official seated at the head of the table, surrounded by Chinese guests. "That man makes decisions about the country's oil and gas – where to drill, where to build pipelines, and when to sell. He also decides which companies are allowed to do business in Turkmenistan." Uri seemed to wince at these last words.

"Are there Russian oil companies in Turkmenistan?" Patrick asked, welcoming the fact that the conversation had turned away from him.

"Of course!" Uri seemed flabbergasted by the question. "This may not be Russia's territory anymore, but we are still interested in what our former republics do with their oil and gas... and particularly who they sell it to!"

Patrick must have looked puzzled, because Uri added, "How would your federal government react if Texas or Alaska decided to break away from the United States and sell its oil to China?" Patrick just stared back. Apparently his question had struck a deep nerve in the Russian.

Uri realized this, too, and his tone softened.

"Russia is committed to supporting its young neighbors in Central Asia. We want them to be happy and prosperous. Since Russia has been drilling oil here for many years, we have a great deal of knowledge and experience to share. It is good for everyone that we are involved here." He took another sip and squinted down the table at the Turkmen energy official.

Patrick was tempted to bring up the Great Game, but he thought better of it. Instead, he let Uri fill the silence.

"Besides, Central Asia has a complicated history," the Russian continued. "It may not seem this way to people in the West, but not everything can be fixed with oil and dollars. There are other forces at work here, too, which must be carefully managed. Many wrinkles must be ironed out before the people can live as you Americans do." He held Patrick's eyes, as if trying to gauge whether the fourteen-year-old appreciated his words.

Patrick stared back a few seconds, and then nodded slowly. "Yes, I realize that it must be hard to watch a people you ruled for so long create their own destiny." He gulped, instantly regretting his impulsiveness.

But Uri remained expressionless. He merely nodded, leaned back in his chair, and replied politely, "That is one perspective, Mr. Eaton... Mr. Neilson's, no doubt. In any case, I hope you enjoy the rest of your visit. Perhaps you will have an opportunity to venture beyond this city. If you do, I hope you will look with your own eyes and think with your own mind." With that, he turned to acknowledge the waiter who slid a crowded plate before him.

Patrick said little during the rest of the meal. From time to time, he and his dad exchanged approving nods and smiles over their food. But after his rash words to the Russian diplomat,

Patrick thought it more prudent to observe quietly. Uri, Roger, the Turkmen, and the Chinese... They were all fascinating characters in a complex drama or – perhaps more fittingly – chess match. Patrick sensed that quiet moves were being made at the table, but he could not see them or tell who was winning.

Given what Roger and Skip had said – that Turkmenistan sat on top of massive quantities of energy resources and that its strategic location made it part of a buffer zone for containing Russia – it was no wonder Uri was attending this dinner. He represented one of the Great Game's oldest players – once an adversary of the British Empire and, more recently, of the United States. Like his predecessors, he was undoubtedly here to win control of the center of the board. But was Uri merely a pawn in this game, or a more dangerous piece?

Patrick wiped his mouth with the origami napkin. Until he had an answer, he decided to take Uri's advice and to keep his eyes and mind open.

21 A LIGHT IN THE DARKNESS

"Only those who will risk going too far can
possibly find out how far one can go."
– T.S. Elliot (poet, playwright, social critic)

That night, something happened that not only changed the course of Patrick's summer, but his life as well. After several courses of dinner and speeches, the banquet atop the Altin Hotel concluded. After descending in glass elevators to the lobby on the ground floor, the Turkmen and their guests lingered – talking, laughing, shaking hands, and trading pledges of friendship and accommodation. When Ahmed appeared out of nowhere, Dad gave him and Patrick a look, as if to say, "It's going to be a while."

The two stepped from the hotel doors onto a brightly lit boulevard, its curb lined with cedar trees and shiny new European cars. A couple of storefront windows poured light onto the empty sidewalk in the hope of luring a chance pedestrian. Towering over the street, a handful of government buildings pierced the black sky.

Patrick breathed deeply, savoring the fresh sea breeze. It was a relief from the tense air of the diplomatic dinner. Ahmed drifted down the sidewalk to the opening of an alley and lit a cigarette. Patrick followed, hands in his pockets and his mind on the evening's conversation. He kicked a rock down a sidewalk grate, looked back through the hotel windows at the crowd in the lobby, and then let out a low whistle.

"Ahmed, all that schmoozing makes me tired." He shook his head, and then added, "Where have you been?"

"Ah, well, a diplomatic dinner is no place for a lowly interpreter such as me," Ahmed replied. His cigarette glowed, momentarily revealing his face in the dark alley.

Patrick laughed uneasily, unsure how to respond. "Well, it was nothing special. We just ate and talked, that's all. I felt pretty out of place, myself."

The two were quiet for some time. A car sped past, blaring music and laughter through its windows. Ahmed shuffled from one foot to the next, as if he were cold... or nervous.

"Why do you carry that backpack everywhere?" he asked, his face once more obscured by the shadows.

"This?" Patrick hooked his thumbs behind the straps and shrugged. "I don't know. I guess because I don't want to lose it."

"But we're not in Baku anymore," Ahmed countered. "The hotel here seems perfectly safe. You could leave it there, but you don't. What do you have in there that is so valuable?"

Patrick laughed nervously. The conversation was becoming awkward. "Nothing. Just books and stuff."

"No, no," Ahmed said, talking more excitedly. "I don't think so. You take it everywhere – what is in there?" He reached for it playfully with one hand and then again, more forcefully. Patrick pulled away, uncertain how to react. Was this some sort of joke?

"Let me see!" Ahmed suddenly cried, tearing at the zipper. Stunned, Patrick didn't know whether to laugh, play along, or fight back. His choice became obvious when Ahmed grabbed him from behind and yanked violently at the backpack.

"Get off!" Patrick screamed, terror clutching his chest and throat. Just fifty feet away, Dad stood chatting behind glass, completely unaware of his son's danger. If Patrick could just break free...

"Give me the book!" Ahmed grunted, straining to pull Patrick into the alley. The light from the street faded as Patrick was dragged farther into the lair of dumpsters and trash. Patrick's arms and legs burned with exertion, and his eyes with tears, as he wrestled desperately to break free.

Just when hope of escape was fading, he caught sight of a blurry silhouette in the mouth of the alley. As he was whipped about in his struggle with Ahmed, Patrick glimpsed the dark figure coming closer, rising in size as it approached. A split second later, the commotion exploded to a new level of ferocity, and Patrick was dropped to the ground amid shouting and violent pushing. From his hands and knees, he braced himself against the shuffling and kicking feet as the two characters grappled above. He curled into a ball, covering his face and pleading for rescue. And then, just like that, all was quiet.

Patrick withdrew to the wall of the alley, prepared to kick at whatever followed. He perceived no movement, but sensed the newcomer was still there, watching him in the darkness. Ahmed had run out of the alley, slipping and sliding on papers and trash, finally disappearing.

The figure seemed to come closer and Patrick frantically warned him away.

"It is okay, my friend," said a deep voice. "I am not going to hurt you. It is okay." The flick of a lighter exploded the alley in an orange glow, and the man kneeled before Patrick. "You are safe, my friend. I swear it on my life."

Breathing heavily, Patrick pulled his feet in, hugged his knees and glared. The man extended his hand to help him. "You will not need to worry about Ahmed anymore. I assure you he will not be back." The open hand lingered in front of Patrick.

Looking first at the alley entrance, and then back to the stranger, Patrick took a deep breath and cautiously reached for the hand. He was pulled up and closer to the stranger, whose Turkish features became clear in the dancing light.

"I am most pleased to be of service. My name is Ali. Let's get you back to your dad."

The hotel lobby was still abuzz, but now the casual laughter and stylish suits were replaced with tense questions and the stiff uniforms of Turkmenistan's police force. Patrick sat wide-eyed on a couch between his dad and Roger, nodding to a series of queries asked by a scribbling detective. He did his best to describe what had occurred just an hour ago outside the windows, while Dad's expression revealed the anguish and guilt he felt for having exposed his son to danger.

A break from the interrogation gave them an opportunity to call Mom. Awakened from her slumber on the far side of the world, she was verging on hysterical. Patrick could hear her shouting through the phone, which Dad instinctively pulled back from his ear.

His parents took turns arguing with raised voices over whose hair-brained scheme it had been to take Patrick to such a dangerous place. What had they been thinking? Their decision had endangered the life of their only child. For her part, Mom was adamant that their son be put on a plane for home that very night. Dad gingerly attempted to interject balance into the conversation, but for the most part he simply nodded his agreement. The two went on debating for a good twenty minutes while Patrick slouched on a nearby bench, listening to his dad's half of the conversation.

At first, the incident had left Patrick wanting to go home, too. He had spent the last week sleeping in strange places, deprived of his comfortable routine, and continually unsure what to expect. And now this! World travel was certainly not as glamorous – or as easy – as it seemed while reading his great-grandfather's journal or listening to Grandpa's stories.

From his place by the phone, Patrick could see Ali sitting in a chair, surrounded by police interrogators. It was obvious the man was being grilled about his identity and conveniently-timed arrival in the alley. In fact, he seemed a mystery to everyone. But

Patrick detected an element of goodness in Ali and – though he couldn't explain why – an odd familiarity.

He knew what Grandpa would say if he were here: *stay positive*. And what about Patrick's great-grandfather? Thomas believed every person faces a simple choice when faced with difficulties: to quit or go on. Over the course of his travels, he had endured much worse than a scuffle with a stranger in a dark alley. He had dodged bandits and secret police, cold and starvation. Thomas may have been scared, but he put one foot in front of the next – always determined to reach his goals. He never quit, and he never looked back. What would Thomas have done in this situation?

Finally, it was Patrick's turn to talk to his mom. She pleaded that he return home where she could keep him safe. Roaming around Central Asia was no place for an American boy who just graduated middle school. She would quit her lawyer job tomorrow and stay home as a good mother should. In fact, she had suspected all along that this trip was a terrible idea.

Patrick stood listening for a long time, slipping in an occasional "I know, Mom," and "I love you, too." He allowed the lawyer to make her case for his return, then waited as she circled back through her argument to add the emotion-filled proof of which only a mother is capable. At last, she paused, giving him a chance to speak. Recognizing that he was addressing not only the opposing lawyer, but the judge as well, Patrick delivered his testimony very carefully.

He began by acknowledging her concern. He agreed that the incident was serious, and admitted that if he were a parent he would be concerned, too. He thanked her for raising him to be strong and emphasized that all her warnings and instructions over the years – to fight back and yell for help if ever grabbed by a stranger – had saved him.

Then he made his case for staying the course, pointing out that he was not a little kid any more. He described the interesting perspectives he was learning, and explained that he was surrounded by people who were looking out for him. Then, before his mother could argue, he added, "We can be tough and scared at the same time, Mom."

Recognizing the advice she had given him the day of Grandpa's heart attack, she laughed through her tears. "You little stinker," she said. "If you decide not to be an explorer, you'll make a darn good lawyer!"

After several more assurances – he would stay within Dad's sight at all times, he would take no silly risks, he would not talk to strangers, and so forth – Mom finally capitulated. The court had ruled in favor of Central Asia.

The incident's impact upon Patrick's summer became immediately apparent. Deciding that he would stay with his dad rather than fly home, the two of them needed to decide where to go next.

Roger had already been absent from the Baku office for too long – he needed to get back right away. Skip intended to continue to the eastern part of Turkmenistan, where he would negotiate in favor of the company's pipeline. From there, he was considering a jaunt into northern Afghanistan, the next segment of the proposed pipeline. Of course, this prospect depended entirely on security – if Roger deemed it unsafe, based on military reports, then Skip would have no choice but to turn back.

Initially, Dad had planned for Patrick and him to return to Baku, but the incident with Ahmed forced them to reconsider. His actions came as a shock to everyone. The man had been employed as an interpreter by Roger and others at the U.S. embassy several times in past years. He had passed all his background investigations, which revealed no indications of his involvement with criminals or other nefarious characters. He had been friendly and cooperative up until now, which made the turn of events all the more curious. Why had he suddenly attacked Patrick?

Furthermore, that night's incident cast new suspicion on the mysterious "maintenance man" Patrick had discovered leaving their hotel room in Baku. Was he connected in some way to Ahmed? Patrick had his own ideas about this but decided to keep them to himself for the time being.

In any case, a return to Baku was out of the question until Ahmed was apprehended. There was no telling what he might try next. It was possible he might double back to Baku at some point. In fact, he might already be aboard a fishing trawler headed across the Caspian. Once back in Azerbaijan, he could draw upon his resources there and possibly mount another attack against Patrick.

Bit by bit, another option took shape for the Eatons. It was possible for Dad and Patrick to continue east across Turkmenistan with Skip. The Texan's destination was the city of Mary, another 600 miles across the Karakum (CARE-eh-KOOM) Desert. Mary's location was promising for several reasons. First, it was in the opposite direction of Baku, making it farther from Ahmed's base of operations. Second, it was an important node along the route of Skip's proposed pipeline, and close to a massive natural gas deposit that his company was interested in drilling. Finally, it was adjacent to several significant archeological sites along the Silk Road, which Patrick and his dad might have time to visit.

The group talked over the possibility. Skip rooted loudly for them to join him. In addition to wanting Dad along, whom Skip valued for friendship as much as geological prowess, the Texan was exasperated at the thought of having no one to kid around with for the next several days. Considering their options – and not entirely immune to Skip's cheerleading – Dad and Patrick selected Mary.

Unfortunately, by losing Ahmed, they'd lost their interpreter and guide. Aside from the fact that none of them spoke Turkmen, the government required visitors to hire an official guide if they plan to stay more than three days. Roger could not recommend anyone on such short notice. Without Ahmed, they were going nowhere.

Once again, Ali came to the rescue. As it turned out, the mysterious stranger was actually a retired middle school history teacher from Turkey. During summers, he moonlighted as an interpreter and tourist guide. It just so happened he was on his way through Turkmenistan, and he enthusiastically offered his services to the Americans. As one of the few foreigners on the government's list of approved tour guides, he seemed the perfect solution to their dilemma.

At first, Roger balked at the idea. He did not have time to properly investigate this newcomer whose arrival on scene, he reminded them, still seemed a bit fishy. On the other hand, he had no better suggestions. The Turkmenistan police vouched for Ali's identity, but this did little to soothe Roger. So he immediately placed a few phone calls to his embassy and, receiving no concerning "red flags" about Ali's background, reluctantly offered his approval.

In the end, the decision was left to Patrick. Did he want to return to the United States on the next flight, or was he up for continuing the expedition? He recalled the choice Thomas had made to trust Misha, even after having been double-crossed by a previous guide. Patrick went with his gut feeling about Ali and gave Dad a "thumbs up." The matter was settled.

The next afternoon, they would climb aboard the famous Trans-Caspian Railway and continue their journey eastward across the great desert of Turkmenistan.

22 PIPELINEISTAN

"We've made a substantial political investment in the
Caspian, and it's very important to us that both the
pipeline map and the politics come out right."
– Bill Clinton (42nd President of the United States)

The train station stood nearly empty, as seemed to be a rule
for Turkmenistan's most expensive public buildings and
attractions. On both sides of the wide marble floor, stretching
from floor to ceiling, were ornately decorated columns. Overhead,
gray light filtered through arched windows beneath the domed
roof. The footsteps of occasional passersby echoed like ghosts
from the railway's past.

Roger, Skip, Dad, and Patrick sat around a wrought-iron
table under a large train schedule board, drinking black tea, with
their luggage on the floor next to them. They had an hour until
boarding and were expecting Ali to join them any moment. The
travelers congratulated themselves on a trip well done thus far – in
spite of the difficulties they had faced along the way.

Roger planned to leave Turkmenbashi later that afternoon
on a plane to Baku, though he admitted being envious of their train
voyage.

"I know the train makes for a slower trip than simply flying
to Mary, but the experience is worth the extra time. The railroad
skirts the southern edge of the desert along the Silk Road. Out
your windows you'll see a landscape virtually unchanged since the
days of the old camel caravans. I wish I could go with you."

As he took a sip of tea, he glanced sideways at Patrick and added, "I also agree that it's safer than flying. I doubt Ahmed would expect a couple of oil men to take the slow train across Turkmenistan."

"When was this railroad built?" Patrick asked, brushing off the comment. He was in no mood to discuss their former interpreter.

"In the late-1800s, long after the Silk Road's heyday. The Trans-Caspian Railway was constructed to transport Russian soldiers into Central Asia to conquer the Muslim khanates. As I pointed out last week, these kingdoms had held out for centuries against Russian domination. But they were no match for modern artillery. At long last, they were swept into the growing Russian empire – all part of Moscow's efforts to expand and secure its borders."

"The Great Game again," Skip interjected, flashing Patrick a grin.

"Indeed," Roger said, peering up at the big clock on the wall and winding his watch. "And, of course, the game goes on... which brings us to the matter of your trip to Mary. How goes the pipeline project?"

Skip leaned back in his chair and crossed his arms in a rare moment of seriousness. "So far, so good, but we'll have to wait and see... Four countries have agreed to start building the pipeline in the next year or two. When finished, it will carry natural gas from the Caspian Sea east across the desert of Turkmenistan, south through the mountains of Afghanistan and Pakistan, and then finally to India. From India it will be loaded onto tanker ships and transported to markets around the world."

"So what's the hang up?" Roger teased him.

"Ha. Ha." Skip enunciated slowly, matching his friend's sarcasm with each syllable. Then he shook his head playfully and winked at Patrick. "Politics, Roger. You of all people know that! The big question is whether the pipeline can be kept safe in

146

Afghanistan. Nobody really knows for sure. That's why most oil and gas companies have been reluctant to invest there so far. But I still think it's worth checking out."

"It is certainly a door worth opening," Roger echoed. "In Pipelineistan [Pipe-LINE-is-stan] it's always good to have options."

Patrick listened quietly. Last night he'd vowed to be less impulsive with his questions. But after Skip's encouraging wink he couldn't resist the temptation.

"Pipelineistan?" he asked, looking around the table. His dad merely smiled, evidently content to sit this discussion out. Whenever Dad was quiet back home, Patrick assumed he had his mind on other things. But now, it seemed like Dad simply enjoyed watching Patrick figure things out on his own.

"Pipelineistan is a nickname for Central Asia," explained Roger. "The whole region is crisscrossed by a spider's web of pipelines and, as you know, many of the country names end with 'stan.' So, put the two together and, presto, you have... *Pipelineistan*!" He held up his hands like a magician who'd just made a rabbit appear.

Above their heads, the train schedule fluttered noisily – clickety-clickety-clickety – as it rolled out the latest departure and arrival times.

"Remember our conversation about the challenges of getting fossil fuels out of the Caspian Sea region?" Skip asked. Patrick nodded, recalling their meal together at the hotel in Baku. "Since the sea is land-locked, the only way to move oil and gas is by pipeline."

"That's right," Roger jumped in again. "Everybody builds pipelines. Russia's pipelines carry oil and gas north to Moscow – or west to the cities of Europe. China's go east to provide power for its growing population. Iran transports it south... Of course, none of these countries are what you might call 'pals' of the United States."

"How come?"

Roger looked caught off guard. "Well, that's a long story. For the time being, let's just say our *interests* don't always line up."

"So, you want to build a pipeline that doesn't depend upon these countries being friendly towards us?" Patrick pressed.

"You got it." Roger nodded agreement while tapping his fingers on the top of his tea cup. "Of course, the United States doesn't actually have its own pipelines here, but we do help our friends to build theirs. Our role here is to promote regional cooperation. For instance, a few years ago we helped Azerbaijan, Armenia, and Turkey construct an oil pipeline from Baku to the Mediterranean Sea." He smiled proudly.

Again – the term *regional cooperation* that Patrick had heard their first night in Baku. He'd meant to ask Roger what it meant.

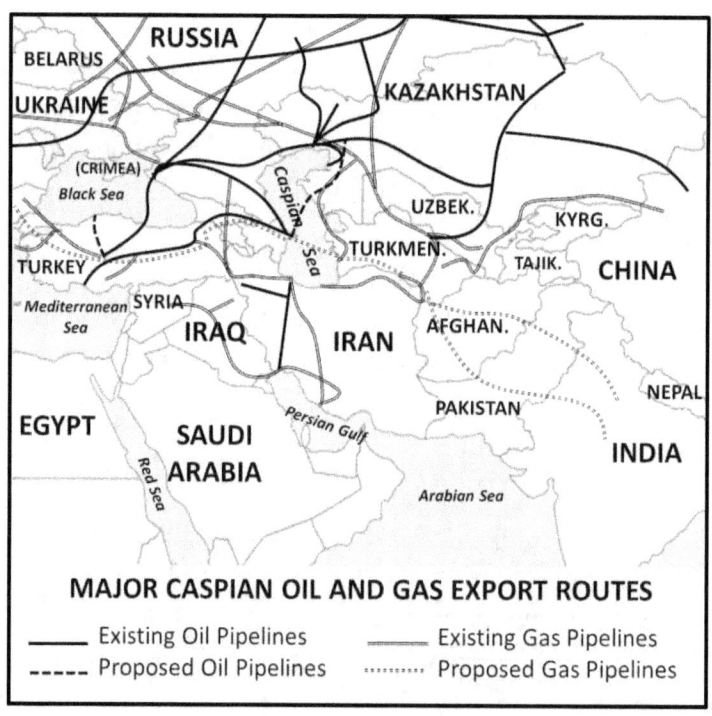

MAJOR CASPIAN OIL AND GAS EXPORT ROUTES

———— Existing Oil Pipelines   ———— Existing Gas Pipelines
- - - - Proposed Oil Pipelines   ·········· Proposed Gas Pipelines

"How did we help them?" Patrick prodded.

"Uh... well, with various incentives. Mostly money and technology. For other countries, we provided assistance with security or negotiations... Sometimes we merely tweaked the political climate."

"So what's wrong with the current pipeline?"

"The one through Azerbaijan and Turkey? For the moment, nothing. But, as I said, it's good to have options. You never know when the next war is going to break out here... and if it will put a pipeline out of action. Plus, you can't count on the allegiance of these countries. Sure, Azerbaijan is friendly to the United States today. But what if, tomorrow, its government decides to be pals with Russia instead?"

"No more oil." Patrick acknowledged. "So the pipeline through Afghanistan will be like a 'back-up plan?'"

"Pretty much," Skip interjected again. "But for natural gas instead of oil."

Patrick shook his head, trying to fit together the puzzle pieces. "But there's a war in Afghanistan. Isn't that kind of a dangerous place to build a pipeline?"

Skip laughed and pointed to Roger, passing the question like a hot potato. Even Dad chuckled. Patrick winced at the ensuing hilarity, hoping it was not at his expense.

"I guess I'll answer that..." Roger sighed, clearly amused. Then, more seriously, he responded, "It's a good question, Patrick. Yes, Afghanistan is a dangerous place today. But hopefully that will soon change. The United States must act *strategically* – for the future, that is. And Central Asia's energy security is a big strategic interest of ours." There was another term Roger had used weeks ago – "energy security." Bit by bit, Patrick thought he was beginning to understand.

Roger continued: "A stable and democratic Afghanistan – one that is friendly to the United States – will be able to resist the political pressures of Russia, China, and Iran. It will not be swayed by their threats and demands, their meddling and scheming. A pipeline through Afghanistan will deliver affordable energy to the world, as well as serve as a back-up to the existing pipelines. Of course, to succeed, this plan needs the violence in Afghanistan to decrease. For the time being, the United States will have to help provide security there – but it's important that we do whatever it takes to see Afghanistan succeed."

"But the other night you said the United States has plenty of oil and gas. Don't we already have 'energy security'?" With this, Patrick wondered if he was pushing too far again.

Skip laughed uneasily, while Roger shifted in his chair. Dad looked relaxed with one ankle crossed over his knee. He simply smiled at Patrick's question.

"Well, we do have a lot of energy resources," Roger replied. "But, as I said, our reason for being in Afghanistan is not just oil. We also have an interest in balancing power in the region. And, of course, we are committed to supporting democracy and rooting out terrorists and ..."

"But at dinner last night I was talking with Uri..." Patrick interrupted, caught up in his thoughts. He knew he should probably stay quiet, but he wanted to make sense of it all.

"I'd take anything Uri Petrovsky says with a grain of salt," Roger countered sharply. "If it were left up to him, Turkmenistan would be a puppet of Moscow again. He's just here to gum up the works."

"What do you mean?"

"I mean he'll try to torpedo any progress we make here." Roger laced his hands together on the table and took a deep breath. "Here's the thing... Uri has been at this game a long time. What I mean is, he worked in Soviet intelligence back in the old days."

"Intelligence... He was a spy?" Patrick asked, wide-eyed. This was getting really interesting.

150

Roger pressed his lips together, apparently not wanting to share more detail. "The Soviet Union may be gone, but in Uri's mind nothing has changed – it's still Mother Russia against everyone else. He's an old-school chess player, and he's in this game to win. There's no doubt he's up to his old antics in Pipelineistan."

Roger reached for his tea and, seeing it was empty, busily patted his pockets for his wallet. Evidently, the discussion was over. Skip yawned and stretched, while Dad checked their tickets again. It was almost time to go.

Patrick sat quietly, recalling the blue and green eyes that scrutinized him from across the table last night. The image sent a shiver down his spine. Perhaps Roger was right. Maybe Uri really was the devious, calculating plan-wrecker than Roger described. Then again, it was Uri who had advised Patrick to keep his eyes and mind open.

Each player in the Great Game seemed to have his own reasons for "torpedoing" the plans of the other. Patrick had heard the American viewpoint. Now he couldn't help but wonder what Uri would say about Roger, if asked. Patrick regretted not finding out when he had the chance.

23 THE BLACK SAND

"If light is in your heart you will find your way home."
– Rumi (Persian poet, 13th century)

Once again, Ali arrived in the nick of time. The travelers had assembled on the platform outside, preparing to bid farewell to Roger alongside the idling diesel engines, when Patrick spotted him in the distance. He strode towards them casually, a massive duffel bag slung over his shoulder and one hand loosely tucked in the front pocket of his slacks. Seeing Patrick, he raised it in a carefree wave.

Last night, while he was being grilled by police under the spotlights of the hotel lobby, Patrick had had little opportunity to study his mysterious rescuer. Now, in the light of day, he was startled by how tall the man was. Well over six feet, with broad shoulders and an athletic gait, Ali stood out from the local Turkmen. His short salt-and-pepper hair framed dark eyebrows, an angular bronze face, and square jaw. Dressed in khakis and a white silk shirt, Ali looked like as if he'd just stepped off the pages of a yachting magazine.

Nearing them, he grinned, held out his hand, and said in perfect English, "Salaam, Patrick. It is good to see you again."

"Wa alaykum," Patrick answered, tilting his bead back to look at him. Up close, Ali was also older than Patrick recalled – at least twenty years his dad's elder.

Skip nodded hello. "We were starting to wonder whether you'd show."

152

Ali laughed and swung the duffle bag to the ground. "I thought you might want some time to yourselves this morning." He looked at Dad and bowed his head. Dad returned the gesture by taking the man's hand in a warm handshake, pumping it with gratitude.

The hissing brakes and whine of the engines alerted them it was time to go. Final salaams and backslaps sent Roger on his way, while the remaining four climbed aboard. Reaching up to grab a handrail, Patrick shifted his bag to avoid dropping it under the rails. As he did, he glanced once more down the line of passenger cars. Here and there a traveler hurried across the platform to join the departing train. Several cars down, partly veiled in the shadows, a stocky-framed man with silver hair was boarding. Patrick squinted and blinked, working to focus his vision, but in seconds the man was gone. Sensing Dad's gentle nudge from behind, Patrick shook his head and stepped inside.

The voyagers easily found their cabin, which was one of only six on the old passenger car. It had two modest bunk beds on each side and a vinyl table and chairs centered beneath a large window. On the whole, their quarters seemed a relatively comfortable way to cross one of the more forsaken regions of Central Asia. Dad said the trip would take over twenty hours, leaving Patrick to ponder how difficult it must have been by camel.

"Dad, can I look around?" he asked. The others drew short straws for bottom bunks, traded jokes and grumbles, and stuffed their luggage wherever they could find room.

"Yeah, that's fine... I think." Dad looked at Skip hesitantly and then poked his head out the cabin door, glancing up and down the passageway. "Just stay close by... and don't be gone more than a few minutes."

Patrick stepped out, bracing himself as the car jerked, its couplers tightly grasping the car in front of it as the train lurched forward. He moved slowly, examining the passageway as he went. One side framed a solid bank of large windows, and the other side was lined with cabin doors. Drab Soviet-era beige and red colors, threadbare carpet, and thin wood-paneled walls reminded him of the Dagestan. As his thoughts crept back to bed bugs and diesel fumes, he quickly tried to refocus them on something less disturbing.

Reaching the far end of the passageway, he leaned against the window and peered outside. Block after block of monotonous tan and gray buildings, lifeless construction cranes, and empty boulevards passed by at a quickening pace. He was not sorry to leave Turkmenbashi. They had just stepped off the Dagestan yesterday morning, but already he felt much older.

Although he had sidestepped Roger's reference to Ahmed at the train station, the incident was still very much at the front of Patrick's mind. However true it was that he didn't want to return home, the incident with Ahmed still rattled him.

Last night, Patrick had felt scared, but now, in the light of day, he was bothered by something else. Even though he had only known Ahmed for a couple of weeks, he'd begun to view him as a friend and someone he could trust. Patrick had been stirred by Ahmed's torn allegiance between Azerbaijan and his childhood home in Armenia. He had laughed at the man's jokes and hung on every word of his history teachings.

Less than twenty four hours later, Patrick had no idea who Ahmed really was. He couldn't be sure if the tales Ahmed had told at the caravanserai – or, for that matter, anything he had said – were true. Had Patrick simply been a "mark" all along – someone Ahmed had lied to and used from the beginning? While everyone around Patrick was concerned for his safety, it was the plain-old betrayal that sank his heart.

As the train picked up speed, the large government offices and boulevards gradually gave way to brick shops and homes, then narrow alleys, and finally a jumble of rickety shacks strewn along the city's fringe. At then, just like that, all signs of civilization vanished. In their place, only flat and empty desert unfolded as far

154

as he could see – nothing but sun-scorched sand, occasional scrub brush, and more sand. From his vantage point inside the air-conditioned sleeper, the desert appeared tranquil – almost innocent. *Almost.*

"The Black Sand," Ali said, as if on cue.

Startled, Patrick turned to stare. The rhythmic clickety-clack of the car's wheels over the track had muffled the man's approach. He now stood gazing out the window alongside Patrick – relaxed, as if he had been there the entire time. When Patrick said nothing, Ali lifted his finger at the glass and spoke again.

"Karakum is Turkic for 'Black Sand.'"

Patrick turned back to the window. He was silent for a moment, and then asked, "Why is it called that?"

Another pause.

"I have no idea," Ali answered, chuckling. "Doesn't look very black, does it?"

Patrick shook his head. "Maybe it's so hot that it turns everything black?"

Ali nodded, considering the prospect. "Possibly. After all, it *is* the hottest desert in Central Asia. Hard to believe there are people who make it their home."

Patrick squinted at the desolate landscape. "How do they survive?"

"These days, irrigation canals bring water that supports farming. But even centuries ago, people had adapted to this environment. As desolate as it looks out there, there's enough vegetation for goats to live on. Nomadic pastoralism [raising livestock by moving the herds to richer grazing areas] was the main lifestyle throughout Turkestan's history."

Patrick hesitated. "Turkmenistan?"

"No – *Turkestan.* Turkmenistan is a country. Turkestan is a region far bigger than any one country. Its name means 'land of the Turks.' Turkestan stretches from modern-day Turkey all the

155

way to China – and from Kazakhstan in the north to Afghanistan in the south."

Patrick was quiet. "Basically," Ali continued, "*Turkestan is Central Asia.* They are one and the same."

"But if it includes all of Central Asia, why is it called the 'home of the Turks'?"

"Because the people of this region all descended from the same ethnicity and culture. They're all Turkmen. Today, they are spread through Azerbaijan, Turkey, Kazakhstan, Tajikistan, Kyrgyzstan, Uzbekistan, and Afghanistan...even Iran."

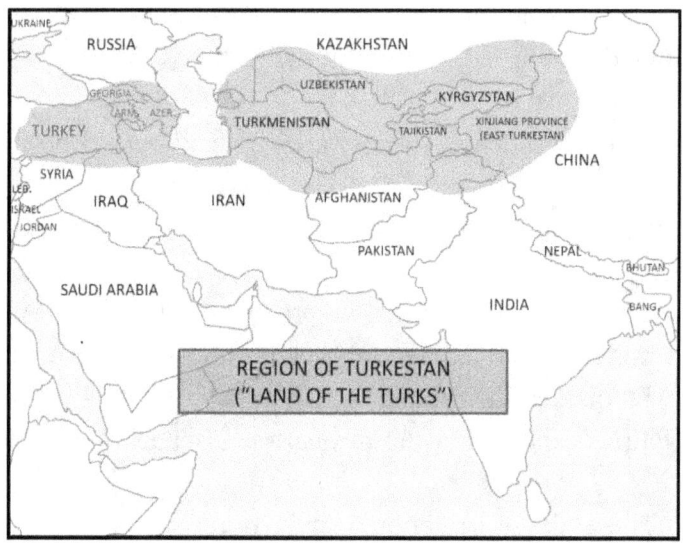

Patrick recognized a few countries Ali listed. "So, you're a Turkmen?"

Ali nodded and grinned. "Guilty as charged. I'm a *citizen* of Turkey. But *ethnically*, I'm a Turkmen. If I traced my family tree back far enough, I'd probably find that I am related to the people here, perhaps also the Uzbeks in the north... maybe even people in western China!"

"Wow," Patrick said. "How come there are so many different countries? If you're all Turkmen, why not just live together?"

"Ah, good question. Over centuries, geography and politics have separated us. Mountains and rivers divided us naturally, of course, as we migrated farther apart. Various groups adopted lifestyles that best suited their different environments."

Ali gestured out the window. "And empires divided us further. For example, the borders we see on the map today were drawn by the Soviet dictator, Joseph Stalin, almost a century ago. He intentionally split Turkestan into many smaller countries."

"Why?"

"Well, he felt threated by a united Turkestan. Stalin wanted Turkmen to be good communists – all equal to each other, and all obedient to him. To accomplish this, he had to abolish any other allegiances. So he separated family, friends, and neighbors, and split ethnic and religious groups. While some people were physically relocated to other parts of the Soviet Union, others simply had borders drawn between them."

The two stood quietly looking out at the barren wasteland. Between wide flat sheets of sand, great dunes rose up – some of them as tall as buildings. Ripple marks stretched across their surfaces, far into the distance. Sometimes wavy patterns were marred by the tracks of some desert creature that had struggled by. Every so often, a scraggly bush could be seen clinging to a rock – the only sign of life outside the railway car.

"Do you miss home?" Patrick asked finally.

"Do you?" Ali countered.

Patrick thought for a moment. "Some. Especially after last night."

Ali nodded. He slipped his hands into his pockets and stood up straight. After a long pause he said, "When life deals us a card like Ahmed… it is natural to want to sit out a hand or two."

"So, do you miss home?" Patrick asked again.

"What is home but a state of mind?" He looked down at the boy. "I have what I need in my duffel bag. I live the life I choose. I am traveling Central Asia, studying its history and enjoying its people. I am here in this moment with a new friend who, I think, might feel a little bit as I do. I *am* home."

Ali took a deep breath, gazing beyond the dunes. Then, clicking his lips, he added, "Poor Ahmed... Where will that wretched soul go? Back to Azerbaijan, where his treachery will continue to weigh on him like an anchor? He deceives himself if he thinks he can find solace there. Ahmed is a ship without a lighthouse – lost on a stormy sea."

As the train rounded a bend, Patrick could see the diesel engines chugging along out front. The rhythmic clickety-clack and gentle sway of the car relaxed him, slowly dissolving the burden of worry from his mind.

Ali looked down at the boy. "You, on the other hand, are really quite fortunate. Though somewhat bruised, you have chosen to go on. A clear conscience lights your path... Perhaps you are closer to home than you think?"

He patted Patrick's shoulder, then turned and walked away.

24 INTO TURKESTAN

"A single death is a tragedy; a million deaths is a statistic."
– Joseph Stalin
(Leader of the Soviet Union, 1924-1953)

The travelers spent their day lazily swaying to the gentle rhythm of the train. Their cramped quarters impelled them to take occasional strolls in the passageway. Every so often, someone slid open the cabin door, walked to the end of the car to stare out at the endless desert, and then returned. The waltz reminded Patrick of the way his classmates back home took turns raising their hands, asked permission from the teacher to get a drink of water, and then strolled the hallways for as long as possible before returning.

Lively discussion monopolized the first couple of hours, but eventually gave way to card games, crossword puzzles, reading, and a nap or two as the trip wore on. By late afternoon Patrick was engrossed once more in his great-grandfather's journal. Stretched out on the top bunk, he thumbed through the pages, studying their details, inspecting sketches, and keeping his eyes peeled for another cipher.

As it turned out, Thomas's voyage was becoming more exciting with every mile he covered on his way east. His last days in Baku were filled with exploring the ruins on the Apsheron (AP-share-on) Peninsula, the large finger of land that juts eastward into the Caspian Sea.

The peninsula has a fascinating history. Inhabited for millennia, it became one of the major centers of fire-worshipping by the fifth century A.D. Misha and I poked around one of its famous fire temples for an hour or two. But we were unable to get our picks and shovels dirty. Recognizing that we were drawing attention – after all, what about this place could possibly interest a couple of carpet traders? – we reluctantly moved along.

From the temple we drifted over to an especially mysterious feature of the peninsula. Carved into the earth of open fields are ancient "stone roads." They resemble ruts made by the wheels of carts, but they extend directly into the Caspian Sea. Similar roads have been found along the coasts of Greece, Italy, and France. Amazingly, those date back over 7000 years. What is most astounding is that archaeologists have found similar stone roads on the seafloors of the Caspian and Mediterranean. Were they all built by a great civilization that existed long before the Egyptians built the pyramids? Do they lead to the ruins of an ancient "Atlantis" buried far beneath the waters?

Next to his writing, Thomas included a sketch of the roads. He showed how their parallel ruts topped a hill dotted with grass and scrub. In the background, they descended to the sea, threading through a Soviet oil complex and troop garrison along the way. Thomas included various other notes and dimensions, as well, including a chart of coordinates that he must have gathered clandestinely using the compass fixed atop his staff.

The mysterious stone roads of the Apsheron Peninsula.

Despite their fascination with Baku's history, Thomas and Misha realized their time in the "land of fire" was running out. Soviet troops were everywhere, walking through the streets or rushing along in the backs of huge transport trucks. Thomas was increasingly concerned by what they could not see but knew were all around – the Soviet secret police. Dressed as locals, these sinister agents were relentlessly on the hunt for trouble makers, rebels, spies, or anyone who did not show enough "enthusiasm" for the new communist system. Most worryingly, the secret police had the unlimited power to arrest whomever they wanted. Already, hundreds of thousands of Azerbaijanis – and millions of others around the Soviet empire – had "disappeared" at the hands of this dreaded unit.

It was of little surprise to Thomas and Misha when they were roused in the middle of the night by a soft knock at the door of the inn where they stayed. Outside stood one of the locals Thomas had befriended since arriving – an Azerbaijani woman whose husband had "disappeared" the previous year. People in the neighborhood were talking, she told them, and it was likely the secret police had caught wind of the whispers. In fact, on her way to warn them she had spotted a pair of well-dressed characters lingering in an alley outside the inn. Rather *too* elegant for this part of town, she emphasized. Another shadowy figure lurked outside a tavern farther down the street. Thomas needed no more convincing. It was time to go.

During our travels in the Caucasus, Misha and I have gone to sleep every night with our bags packed. By doing this, we are always ready to flee at a moment's notice. This night, our cautious habit paid off. In less than a minute, we were hurrying down the inn's rickety wooden steps. We climbed out a back window and hid behind a pile of rubbish. There we lay quietly, waiting to see if the alarm had been raised. Reassured that our getaway had not been detected, we hurried off. Our friend led us this way and that through a maze of alleys and backstreets, until at last we felt safe from any possible pursuit.

We offered our brave rescuer a handsome financial reward, but she politely refused (with the explanation that bamboozling the communists was gratification enough.) So we bid adieu and made our way down to

162

the waterfront· At four o'clock in the morning, we had little need of stealth· The streets were empty, except for an occasional band of soldiers singing loudly and stumbling back to their barracks·

Within an hour of fleeing the inn, we had snuck aboard an oil tanker and hidden amidst a jumble of barrels, crates, and netting piled atop its deck· The waves lapping against the ship's hull thumped a charming lullaby that quickly carried me off to sleep· The next day, we stayed put as the crew went about their business, oblivious to our presence· We were quite relieved to feel the ship push off in late afternoon·

Ships departing Baku were typically destined for either Kazakhstan or Turkmenistan. As it turned out – fortunately for the two stowaways bent on following the Silk Road – this tanker was headed for the second destination. Arriving in Krasnovodsk (known today as Turkmenbashi), the bedraggled figures slipped ashore in the soft light of early morning – perhaps no more than a stone's throw from where Patrick departed the Dagestan eighty years later. They quickly hid themselves in the back alleys, where they planned their next move.

In order to reach the legendary Silk Road towns in the East, the travelers had to find their way across the Karakum Desert. But in 1928, this was not just wild and dangerous territory, it was also off-limits to outsiders, and rebellion by the local Muslims was an ever-present threat. Having only recently conquered these lands, the Soviets were determined to prevent any more trouble-making there. Spies sent by other countries might try to stir up a *jihad* – or holy war – to weaken this southern border of the Soviet Union.

Despite the dangers of traveling in disguise, Thomas realized it was their best option for continuing along the Silk Road. Even "official" guests – those who had gotten permission from Moscow – were rarely allowed to visit Soviet Turkestan. If Thomas applied for a visa and was denied, his entire expedition would be at an end. So, he proceeded as an "unofficial" visitor, knowing that if he was caught he would be probably be arrested as a spy… and punished accordingly.

Since official visas were required to buy tickets for the Trans-Caspian Railway, taking a train across the Karakum Desert was out of the question. Thomas's disguise and forged travel documents had been sufficient to pass him off as a local in the Caucasus. But in the frontier lands of Soviet Turkestan – where even the locals' paperwork was routinely checked – a man with western features and a shaky backstory would be easily discovered. Thomas and Misha needed another plan.

Avoiding the railway station, the two travelers headed for the bazaar in Krasnovodsk. Here they combed the crowded stalls and kiosks, banking on their natural assets – Thomas's charisma, Misha's knowledge of the language and customs, and their combined resourcefulness – to make friends and gather information. As it turned out, a caravan was leaving for the cotton-rich province of Mary the following morning. Thomas and Misha decided to join it.

Who were they? asked the caravan's leader. *Just brothers on their way to visit family*, they replied. Why didn't they just take the train? *It was too expensive.* Did they carry anything valuable? *Of course not!* Though skeptical, the man invited them along. The caravan would set out just after midnight to avoid the scorching heat of day.

At last, Thomas would be back in the heart of Central Asia – the land that captured his imagination in Kashgar four years earlier. From the city of Mary it was only a few hours' camel ride to Merv, one of the world's oldest cities and a legend among archaeologists. Even by 1928, few Westerners had ever laid eyes upon this ancient Silk Road oasis. Thomas might be the first American to visit. But first he would have to elude secret police, outfox devious camel traders, and survive the 600-mile trek across the scorched Black Sand. With his usual resolve, Thomas fixed his gaze to the east – and stepped confidently into his next adventure.

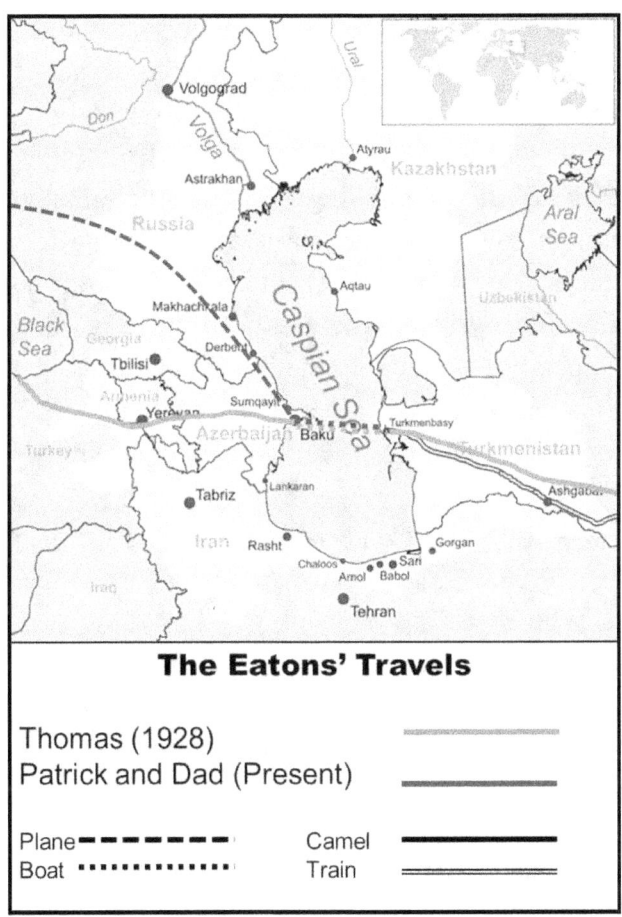

The Eatons' Travels

Thomas (1928)
Patrick and Dad (Present)

Plane ▪ ▪ ▪ ▪ ▪ ▪ ▪   Camel
Boat • • • • • • • • • • •   Train

25 SHADOWS OF THE GREAT GAME

"It is the secret of the world that all things subsist, and do not die,
but only retire a little from sight, and return again..."
– Ralph Waldo Emerson

Patrick felt himself falling. Not a mile-a-minute plunge
from some great height, but the slow, steady sinking feeling as if
mired in quicksand. With each effort to free himself, he became
more stuck, gradually losing the ability to move at all. First his
legs became paralyzed, and after that he could not move his arms.
Then, only his lungs worked. Finally, descending farther, he could
not breathe. Desperate for air, Patrick awoke gasping in the dark
train cabin.

All was still. The clickety-clack that had vibrated through
his body for the preceding fifteen hours was gone. The train sat
motionless. Where were they?

"Dad?" he whispered into the darkness. "Dad?"

"Hey, buddy," came the soft reply from below, followed by
a rustle of linens and creaking springs. "We must be in Ashgabat
[ASH-guh-bot]."

"Huh?"

"Ashgabat!" Dad whispered again. "The train stops here
on its way to Mary. Probably only for a half-hour or so." More
rustling. "It's only five o'clock. You can go back to sleep... or do
you want to stretch your legs?"

Patrick propped himself up on an elbow as his eyes
searched for a hint of light to make out his surroundings. "Stretch
my legs?"

"Yeah," his dad whispered back. "Get your shoes on and we'll go check out the platform outside."

"Okay!" The two fumbled in the darkness, trying to stifle their laughter as they bumped heads and tripped over luggage, all while trying to keep from waking Skip or Ali. Finally, they pieced together what they hoped was a satisfactory ensemble of shirts, pants, and shoes. Tiptoeing out of the cabin, they quietly shut the door and headed down the corridor.

Stepping off the train, it occurred to Patrick that he might actually be dreaming. With sunrise still hours away, the dark platform lay eerily swathed in fog, illuminated only by the occasional blurry orb of an overhead lamp. Muffled voices permeated the gloom every so often, though it was impossible to tell from where they came. A sudden hiss echoed down the line of cars, causing Patrick to jump. As pressure slowly bled from their brakes, the platform grew quiet once more. Except for his heartbeat, Patrick perceived only the muffled growl of the engines somewhere out in the blackness.

The two looked at each other with raised eyebrows, and then crossed the concrete platform, their hands stuffed in their pockets. Braced against the cold air, Patrick was struck by how vastly different the days and nights were here. From his geography studies he knew that the extreme temperatures of the desert were due to an absence of clouds, which served as insulators. But until now he would hardly have believed such contrast was possible within just a few hours. Yesterday's afternoon heat had been suffocating.

"This way," his dad said, nodding in the direction of a hazy red light. "Stay close."

As they moved parallel to the train, ethereal voices whispered in Patrick's ears through the swirling vapor – evidence they were not alone. When they reached the station it looked vacant. They peered in the windows, rattled a couple doors, and walked its perimeter, examining the murals on its walls. Every one of the gigantic paintings was dedicated to Turkmenistan's Great Leader, who was depicted in various self-important poses. Some were of his head only, flashing large white teeth and a vain smile. In others he stood, his hand gently outstretched in fatherly reassurance to his people. One showed him relaxing in a chair, chin resting in hand as if reflecting deeply upon the divine importance of his life.

"Here," Dad said, holding out his hand. Patrick reached for a granola bar. "Breakfast of champions, eh?"

Patrick tore open the wrapper and took a bite. The cold air felt good on his face, which was still a little puffy from sleep. Actually, he hadn't slept well since leaving Baku. The nonstop pace and nighttime travel had jumbled his body's internal clock. When he was awake he felt exhausted, and when he was supposed to sleep he was wide awake.

"Is Ashgabat a big city?" he asked.

"Yeah, pretty big…" Dad replied, thinking. "Half a million, I'd say – maybe more. It's the capital of Turkmenistan."

"Then why aren't we visiting it?" Patrick pressed.

"Mmm," Dad replied, his mouth full of granola. "We might stop here on the way back – depends how the negotiations go. Maybe we'll go to the 'Land of Fairy Tales'!" His eyebrows bounced up and down.

A muffled clang, followed by a shout, resounded from out of the mist. Then came what sounded like laughter. Someone must have dropped heavy luggage on his toe, thought Patrick, smiling a little as he reflected on their own attempt to navigate the shadows.

Noticing the sign on a nearby door, Dad handed his granola bar to Patrick. "Here – I gotta use the bathroom … I'll be right back."

He ducked inside, leaving Patrick standing alone on the dark, empty platform. He took a bite of his dad's granola bar, smiling at the thought of his dad's reaction upon finding it whittled in half. After the last few days' diet of granola, crackers, and dried fruit, Patrick was looking forward to local food again. He wondered if Turkmenistan served the *pahklava* and pomegranate juice he'd come to enjoy in Baku. That had been Ahmed's favorite dish, as well... He was shaking the thought from his head when what appeared to be his dad's silhouette rose out of the vapor again.

"Hey," Patrick said, stifling a giggle. "Sorry, but I had to even up our granola bars."

He smiled up at him – and then froze. Returning his gaze were the green and blue spotlights that had scrutinized him two nights ago. A shock of silvery hair glistened under the platform lamps. Staring down at him was the figure he knew he had spotted yesterday – if only for an instant – climbing aboard the train. When the man spoke, his accent left no doubt about his identity.

"Hello again, Mr. Eaton," growled Uri Petrovsky. "Fancy meeting you here, all alone in the wilds of Central Asia." Patrick stood paralyzed, the sensation of quicksand once again forcing him to gasp for air.

"On your way to Mary, I presume?" Uri continued, his small hands hanging motionless by his sides, yet somehow appearing coiled to strike. Patrick took a step back and stole a glance towards the restroom door. Where was his dad? Uri followed his eyes. "It is unwise to get off a train in Turkmenistan in the middle of the night. You never know what mischief is lurking about."

Abruptly, he took a step forward and reached out. Patrick dropped the granola bar and clenched his fists instinctively. Uri paused, his hand frozen in the air between them. For a moment, Patrick thought he spotted astonishment in the man's face, followed by a slight softening around his eyes. Uri's hand slowly dropped back to his side, and he stood for a moment longer, considering the boy in front of him.

169

At last, he grunted – whether irritated or gratified, Patrick couldn't tell – and then nodded. "I see… Enjoy the rest of your trip, Mr. Eaton. Perhaps we'll meet again down the road." Then he was gone, consumed by the swirling fog.

Patrick looked after him for a second, and then hurried to the restroom door. As he pushed it open he ran smack into another body and fell backwards onto the ground. He rose to his knees, fists out once more, and then looked up at his dad.

"Patrick!" His dad's eyes widened with alarm. "Are you okay? What happened?" He reached a helping hand toward his son.

Patrick's eyes filled with tears, quickly followed by violent sobs and gasps. His dad held him there on the dark platform, squeezing him tightly and rubbing his back as his shoulder grew wet. Patrick had been stoic in Turkmenbashi, but this was too much.

Dad pulled him close, wrapping his arms around Patrick's body. He said nothing about being strong or staying positive. Nothing about quitting or going on, either. Dad only stood there holding him as Patrick cried. They stayed like that for a while, swathed in the solitude of fog and darkness, a father and son alone yet together on the far side of the world.

After a while, Patrick pulled back and wiped his cheeks. He looked at his dad and smiled half-heartedly, then lowered his eyes. They picked up the spilt granola bars together. As his shock slowly subsided, Patrick did his best to explain what had happened. He told his dad how Uri had appeared out of nowhere – describing how the Russian had sized him up through those venomous eyes. He recalled Uri's veiled threat – the dangers of being alone at night – and reached out to grab him.

But as he put the incident into words, Patrick couldn't help wondering if he was mistaken. Had Uri really threatened him? He recalled the odd look in Uri's face when Patrick drew up his fists in quickness to battle. It had seemed like a surprise at the time, as

170

if the Russian was caught off guard – foiled in his attack. Then Uri's expression had softened, as if with sadness... or understanding. The bulky Russian spy could have grabbed Patrick if he had wanted to. Instead, he politely bade goodbye.

Why was Uri here at all? Could it be that the man was stalking them? On second thought, was it really so surprising that a Russian diplomat would travel to Turkmenistan's capital? In fact, that was probably where the Russian embassy was located. Wasn't it more likely that Uri was simply on his way home?

As Patrick talked through the incident with his dad, his impression of Uri softened. The Russian didn't come off quite as villainous as he had seemed earlier. While Dad was clearly concerned for his son, they were both hesitant to go to the police with what might well have been a misunderstanding with a high-ranking Russian official. So that's where they left it – a chance encounter in the hinterlands of Central Asia.

As they made their way back to the train, it occurred to Patrick that the incident may not have been so different from countless other meetings between adversaries of the Great Game. According to Roger, those shadowy encounters had also taken place along far-flung train stations, barren deserts, or snow-capped mountains – swirled in fog, sand, snow, and the blurred line between diplomacy and danger. The prize then had been the middle of the board...

Climbing aboard the passenger car, Patrick imagined a new chapter in the game beginning to play out – one that pitted him against Uri for new stakes. Although, exactly what those stakes were, he hadn't the faintest notion...

26 SAND AND STARS

"The Stars are setting and the Caravan
Starts for the Dawn of Nothing – Oh, make haste!"
– Omar Khayyam
(Persian mathematician, astronomer, philosopher, and poet)

June 12, 1928· Endless sand· Blowing, stinging, blinding red sand· Not a single piece of equipment, seam of clothing, or body part escapes its steady assault· Carried over us in gray and pink clouds, it dances lightly across the dunes and swirls into the hot dry air we breathe· It penetrates my head scarf, chafes my lips, coats my beard, and collects in my nose and ears· Each morning when we stop to rest, and at night when we prepare to ride again, I cough crimson dust, painfully wipe it from my eyes, and grind it between my teeth· Even as I sleep, it continues to burrow into my clothes, setting up like concrete wherever it meets the moisture of my body· For a Montanan, the Karakum Desert is a strange and most inhospitable place·

Fortunately, the incredible romance of traveling by caravan more than compensates for its hazards· Our first week in the Black Sand brought us to Geok-

172

Tepe [YOKE tuppa] *and the remains of a fortress destroyed by the Russians decades ago. Time and wind have reduced its once-great walls and towers to dirt mounds. The crumbling ruins strain the mind's ability to imagine that a great population once lived and died here.*

The battle of Geok-Tepe (1879) was one of the final clashes in the long struggle between the Russian Empire and Turkmen tribes for control of Central Asia. After a siege lasting several days, the Russians detonated explosives under one of the fortress's main walls, poured in, and slaughtered the defenders. Those who survived the initial blast died in the ensuing massacre, which dragged out for miles east of the fortress as its previous occupants fled into the desert. Their bleached bones can still be found there to this day.

As we passed the ruins, I couldn't help but wonder if the Turkmen people have really changed all that much since Geok-Tepe. Certainly, they are not as strong or free as they once were. Yet, my hosts appear to have retained much of their independent nature. Even under the oppressive fist of the Soviet Union – which is determined to abolish all traces of local tradition and self-rule – these people have clung to their nomadic ways.

Our caravan is commanded by Rahim, a large, quiet Muslim whose authority over the caravan is without dispute. In his tow are seventy-five camels, forty men and women, and an assortment of children, goats, and dogs. He rides out front, away from the rest of the group. He rarely speaks, but when he does it is only to a handful of his subordinates. Rahim's black beard hangs down his chest and a large, furry, black sheepskin hat – known as a "telpek" – covers his head. Falling to his knees is a long flowing robe, under which he wears trousers and riding boots.

All men of the clan are dressed like this, although some have mustaches rather than beards. The women dress much more flamboyantly. They are decorated in vibrantly dyed robes and beaded vests. Intricately woven silver and gold jewelry adorns their bodies from head to waist. And their long black hair is tied in braids bound by colorful fabric. In contrast, the children are outfitted in a haphazard mixture of whatever seems to be available. Some wear smaller versions of the grown-ups' clothing, while others are clad in little more than blankets tied with leather cord.

Misha has swiftly endeared himself to the group, as he seems to do wherever we go. His laughter and theirs mix easily, such that I sometimes have difficulty picking him out from them. I, on the other hand, have found their acceptance surprisingly difficult to earn – and remain alone with my thoughts. It may be these people doubt my true identity. They are likely suspicious of all foreigners – but especially those with

174

European features. After half a century of brutal treatment by their northern neighbors, I can't say that I blame them. Evidently, the cruelty they once endured with the Tsar continues today under their Soviet rulers.

During one evening's conversation with a caravan member, I inquired about an aspect of Central Asia – the camel – that has baffled me since my earlier travels through China. Did he really think them pleasant creatures? I asked. Were they not bad-tempered, stubborn, and foul-smelling beasts – as I had found them to be while crossing the deserts of China?

Camels were like women, he replied flatly. They can be gentle and beautiful, yet dangerous and contemptuous. In this respect, he said, their feelings must be tenderly but firmly managed. This is why Rahim had assigned camel duties to Abdu, a man who seemed to speak their language. He pointed at an eccentric old character that walked barefoot alongside the caravan. The man was quarrelling with a biting and spitting camel. His high cackling voice and the camel's grunts and groans reminded me of an argument between a long-married husband and wife.

Later I was astonished by another tale. My new caravan friend told me of the real pride of his people – horses. In fact, his family had once bred the finest horses in the world. The Golden Horses, he said, were prized afar for their speed, intelligence, and beauty.

But this tradition ended under the communist system. Stalin – their new king in the north – wants the Turkmen to be cotton farmers instead of nomads. So they are being forced to give up their horses and work on plantations, growing food for the Soviet Union.

To speed up this transition, Stalin has ordered all the Golden Horses to be slaughtered. Already, thousands have been butchered across Turkestan. As a final insult, the meat of this cherished herd is then returned as food to the Turkmen. All part of the new communist paradise, snarled the Turkmen, who spat on the ground to make his view on the matter perfectly clear. At this point, I realized he had either decided I was not Soviet secret police, or he simply did not care. Or worse... he does not intend to let me escape to report his treason. This final possibility prevented me from sleeping much during the journey.

Despite Stalin's efforts, the Turkmen remain a high-spirited and unpredictable people. Just a few decades ago they were bandits – raiding Russian caravans and enslaving their unfortunate passengers. How much they have changed since then, I do not know. There's no telling what might happen to me if they suspect I am Russian...

As I looked around at the impressive array of revolvers, knives and swords dangling from their belts, it occurred to me just how defenseless I was. Should their present attitude toward me change – for whatever reason – my bleached bones might quickly join those of Geok-Tepe and countless others who never escaped the Black Sand.

Misha spotted my anxious look. Before setting out that night, he slipped me a bejeweled dagger to carry beneath my robes. While it would be futile against the caravan's entire arsenal, it might help me fend off a lone attacker and buy a few moments to escape. Of course, I wasn't sure where I could possibly go from there. My situation would be little different from the survivors of Geok-Tepe who, ousted from their fortress, ran blindly out into the endless sand to try to escape death. As I scanned the barren horizon, my prospect of survival seemed equally bleak. Misha simply grinned at me. "Iyi sanslar [EE-shon-slar]," he whispered, patting my arm, and walked away. "Good luck."

In the Karakum, the viciousness of the desert sun is balanced by the tranquility of its nights. Sweltering heat and blistering winds give way to clear crisp air and an almost unsettling calm. Although it gets unbelievably cold, the absence of clouds reveals the night sky in all its cosmic glory. Traveling at night, wrapped in blankets on the back of my camel, I sometimes lean back and stare up at the heavens above. Back on our ranch in Montana, I spent many nights lying out in the field or atop the barn, staring at these very same planets and constellations and fantasizing

177

about traveling the world. Now here I am - living my dream under this very same canvas. Ambling along, I recognize many of my old friends.

Out in front of our caravan, to the northwest and hanging by its handle, is the Big Dipper. Above a half moon twinkles the red planet, Mars. Just after dusk, Vega becomes the brightest star in the east. It sits atop the big Summer Triangle, accompanied by Deneb to its lower left, and Altair to its right. Over the course of the next couple months, this triangle will slowly climb higher into the sky, until by fall it will perch directly overhead at dusk. When it finally does, I hope to be in the Fergana [Fur-GONE-eh] Valley - far to the northeast of here - making preparations to cross the mighty Tien Shan [Tee-EN SHAWN] Mountains into China.

Three weeks after setting out from Krasnovodsk, we finally arrived in Mary - a small, flat, unremarkable oasis town on the Murghab River. As we circled around the town to its caravanserai, I reflected on my journey. Although it seemed that I carried a bucket's worth of sand in my hair and clothes, I have survived the desiccating heat and winds of the notorious Karakum. I managed to avoid contact with the Soviets, or any hostile strangers, for that matter. And I escaped the wrath of the Turkmen traders.

In truth, I have enjoyed these people - and grown to deeply respect them, as well. Once assured that I do not report to Moscow, their initial suspicion and coldness gave way to friendly conversation, followed by an almost brotherly acceptance. As a Montanan, I couldn't help but empathize with their free and easy ways. In truth, they were little different from the cowboys I grew up with back home.

But, like the American cowboys, how long can these friendly, intelligent, and independent nomads continue to roam the sands of Turkestan? Having seen with my own eyes communism's brutal consequences in the Caucasus, my guess is that the days of the caravan are numbered. As a steam locomotive chugged into Mary's station in the early morning, blowing its whistle loudly, it occurred to me once more that I am a witness to the collision of two worlds. Old and new, East and West. Whatever the future brings, I am at least glad to have known these people when they were here – once proud and free.

27 THE PRICE OF PETROLEUM

"A century ago, petroleum – what we call oil –
was just an obscure commodity; today it is
almost as vital to human existence as water."
– James Buchan
(Scottish novelist and historian)

As the train approached the Mary station, sounding its whistle as it slowed, Patrick scanned the landscape that was gradually coming into focus outside his window. It took little effort to imagine his great-grandfather amid the dunes and tangles of scrub littering the outskirts of the town. From out of the Karakum Desert, Mary would have been a most welcome sight to Thomas – a green, tropical island in the middle of an ocean of sand.

After spending twenty hours on a train to get here, Patrick could only wonder at the relief Thomas must have felt after three weeks in the desert. Ambling along on the back of his camel, he may have even glanced at a passing train on this very spot of track. In that instant, Patrick felt the decades separating them melt away, leaving nothing but a window between him and the man he was getting to know so well but would never meet.

The train puffed to a stop and, luggage in hand, the foursome stepped off, made their way outside the station, and hailed a taxi. As it whisked them through the streets to their hotel, Patrick noted that his great-grandfather's description of Mary as an "unremarkable" place still seemed to be true. In the town's center stretched mile after mile of dull, monotonous, Soviet-era government buildings, fountains, and apartments. To Patrick, it looked as if they had been designed by architects too afraid to create something original.

At last they reached their destination, the Margiana (Mar-gī-AN-uh) Hotel, located on a bank of the concrete-lined Murghab (mer-GOB) River. Its elegant alabaster walls, circular façade, and tall mirrored windows must have been built after the Soviets left Turkmenistan. Inside, Patrick was relieved to find it clean, modern, and staffed with smiling attendants. Surprisingly, it was also quite busy – the first sign of bustle he'd seen since arriving in the country.

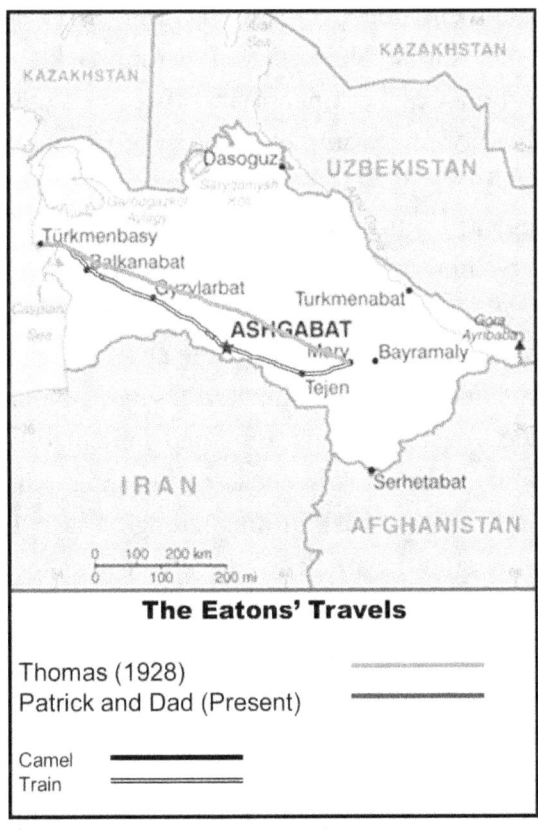

The Eatons' Travels

Thomas (1928)
Patrick and Dad (Present)

Camel
Train

The next couple of days were devoted to business. Dad was pulled once more into a whirlwind of meetings and phones calls. Unlike in Azerbaijan, however, here there was no luxurious pool for Patrick to while away his days sipping pomegranate juice and cooling his feet. And no strolling about the town, either – Dad kept him close at all times, determined to avoid any more surprise encounters.

Fortunately, Patrick did not have to wait around long. On the afternoon of their second day, Skip, Dad, and Patrick were offered a tour of the Galkynysh (GAUL-ken-ISH) gas field that lay southwest of the city. In addition to the Turkmen officials, visiting businessmen, and engineers aboard the tour bus, Patrick noted another group of visitors. He'd spotted them in Baku, and again at the diplomatic dinner in Turkmenbashi. It seemed the farther east he ventured, the more he would encounter the Great Game's other key player – China.

The field trip introduced Patrick to the intense desert heat once suffered by his great-grandfather. Stepping out of the air-conditioned hotel, Patrick felt the moisture pulled from his lungs and skin. True to character, Skip proclaimed to the entire bus how pleasant the weather was here compared to his native south Texas. For added effect, he rubbed his arms and lamented not bringing along a jacket. Patrick shook his head and grinned while the other passengers stared incredulously at this strange man. Though they remained politely silent, Patrick felt he could hear their thoughts. *"Gweilo..."*

Over the course of several hours, the bus made its way south of Mary, halting at various locations along the dusty desert roads. At each stop, its passengers streamed out to consult their maps and notebooks in huddled groups. The Turkmen driver would amble out, too, deliver a quick and impassive talk, and then hurry back to the comfort of the cool van. During one of these stops, Skip and Patrick found themselves standing off to the side of the crowd.

Taking in the expanse of sand and scraggly vegetation, Skip reflected to Patrick: "Talk about beauty in the eye of the beholder, eh?"

"What do you mean?" Patrick asked, straining to see what about the empty land could possibly be mistaken for beautiful.

"The Galkynysh gas field is the second largest in the world. Right out there under all that ugly sand..." He pointed out at the horizon. "To a geologist, that's beautiful."

Patrick looked over his shoulder at a brown-shirted agent of Turkmenistan's government, who stood ominously by the van, his arms crossed. At least two of these automatons had been within sight since they arrived in Mary.

"Do you really think the people of Turkmenistan will benefit from the oil and gas?" he asked.

Skip looked at him blankly. "The people?" Following Patrick's eyes to the van, his expression softened. "No, probably not. The government will enjoy handsome profits, of course. But you're right – the lives of ordinary Turkmen will not change much."

"Don't you feel bad about that?" Patrick asked again, feeling a bit pushy in the heat.

Skip was quiet for a moment. When he spoke, his voice was oddly serious.

"Patrick, my job here is to find fossil fuels – a resource that benefits everyone whose lives it touches. But I don't decide who gets to use it. And I can't control where the oil and gas is buried, either – geology determines that. Unfortunately, petroleum is all too often found in oppressive countries like this." He jerked his thumb at the brown-shirt.

"Here's how I see it," he continued. "Every drop of oil or gas I bring to the surface has the potential for improving someone's life. More energy means more jobs. It means a family somewhere that can turn on their lights at home, or drive their car to school or work. It means someone can benefit from plastic products – medicine bottles, shoes, phones, water bottles, or whatever – which might not be available otherwise. Are there downsides to the oil and gas business? Yeah. No situation is perfect."

Skip took off his sunglasses and wiped sweat from his brow. As he put them on again, he raised a finger to emphasize one final point.

"But make no mistake, Patrick, the people of Turkmenistan are poor because their government keeps them that way. My company spends a lot of money here to extract a very beneficial resource, but by themselves, neither oil nor gas – nor the taxes that my company pays to the politicians – can do anything to help the average Turkmen. Only freedom can do that. Until the government gets off their backs, the people here will continue to suffer."

On the ride back to the hotel, Skip sat in the rear of the bus, his voice booming nonstop about the topics most important to a geologist from Texas: oil and gas, barbequing, and football. At one point, Patrick turned to peek at the scene behind him. Skip was sprawled in his seat, one leg stretched into the aisle, and an arm draped around the shoulders of a little Chinese engineer who sat awkwardly beside him. Skip's other hand flew wildly in the air to emphasize a joke he told. This was followed by hearty laughter, slapping his knee, and jabbing one elbow into the side of his other unsuspecting neighbor.

Surrounded by Turkmen and Asians, Skip looked and sounded like a giant. His audience simply stared back open-mouthed – though Patrick couldn't say whether they were fascinated, flabbergasted, or frightened by the audacious Texan. Patrick grinned and turned back around.

Next to him, Dad scribbled vigorously in his field book. From time to time, he punched away on his calculator or peered at the map lying in his lap, nodding or shaking his head. Under a sweat-lined baseball cap, his eyes crinkled and his mouth worked furiously as he sketched a diagram here, or jotted a figure there. Patrick noticed that his dad's face and forearms were tanning a golden brown from their week in the desert sun, and the rough shadow of a beard appeared where his face was normally smooth. His fingernails were lined with dirt, having sifted through the sandy red matrix next to the bus. Rather than his usual office attire, he wore faded jeans and the well-worn hiking boots that Patrick hadn't seen in years.

Patrick wanted to say something, but hesitated. His dad looked so content.

"What do you think?" Dad asked, rotating his field book into view. On the page was something that looked like a graph – a series of lines, cross-stitching, and shading, dotted by an assortment of strange symbols.

"What is it?" Patrick asked, wrinkling his nose.

"It's a geologic cross section – my best guess about what lies beneath all this sand."

"Oh... Well, in that case, it looks really good!" They traded smiles and examined the drawing a moment longer. Then, Patrick asked, "Is this what you do, Dad? I mean, when you go on business trips?"

His dad looked around, as if seeing his surroundings for the first time.

"Not so much anymore," he replied, shaking his head. "Most of my trips are bogged down with office meetings or time spent working in my hotel room. Which is not so bad, really... it's all part of the job." Then he grinned and patted Patrick's knee. "But I have to admit, I'd rather be outside like today!"

"How come?"

His dad looked surprised, then thoughtful. "Well... I guess I just like playing in the dirt. That's what drew me to geology in the first place. Back when I was a kid – about your age, really – I spent most of my time outdoors. My dad – your Grandpa, that is – was gone a lot on business." He paused and looked at Patrick, as if a thought had just occurred to him. Then he continued.

"So, every day after school I headed off to hike the woods or wade through streams collecting rocks and fossils. Later, when I went to college, geology just seemed like the obvious thing to study."

"Were you outside more when you first started working?"

"Yeah, there was definitely more field work back then. Most of my days or weeks were spent out in the wilderness – mapping the geology for my company. It was a blast! I traveled all over, met some incredible people, and experienced the most amazing natural wonders."

His dad gazed out the window, as if looking beyond the barren land that raced past. The late afternoon sun cast a warm orange glow onto his face. He pushed up his cap to reveal an uncharacteristic mess of sweaty hair. Watching him, it occurred to Patrick how much his dad resembled the young man from the photo on Mom's dresser back home.

"But," he went on, "As I gained experience, I found myself working more and more in an office. I can't complain too much. I was making a lot more money and got to spend more time with your mom. Then, you came along – and I knew I didn't want to be gone all the time." He playfully bumped his shoulder against Patrick's.

"Do you miss the traveling and adventure?" Patrick asked, his hands clasped in his lap, looking expectantly up at his dad. "Do you regret giving up your time outside?"

His dad wrapped his arm around Patrick's shoulders. They swayed gently as the bus cruised along the highway back to Mary. After a few seconds, he said, "When I'm gone on trips, I miss you guys. The only thing I regret is that you don't already know that."

As the sun began its descent in the fire-red sky, Patrick leaned against his dad. They sat like that for the rest of the trip.

28 STUCK IN THE MIDDLE

"It is not in the stars to hold our destiny but in ourselves."
– William Shakespeare

It's easy to understand how Merv [Mer] got its name – Marv-i-shah-jihan – or Queen of the World. Simply look at its geography. The ancient oasis-city lies at the intersection of Silk Road caravan routes that once stretched from Persia to Samarkand [SAM-mar-KAND], and from Afghanistan to the Caspian. It is strategically located on the Murghab River, which flows out of the Hindu Kush Mountains before vanishing in the hot, thirsty desert to the north. With its continuous supply of water, Merv has long been prized both as a watering hole for animals and a cradle of agriculture in an otherwise barren region. Situated near the border of Afghanistan, the town serves as a gateway to Hindustan [northwestern India]. It's no wonder that, when the Russians captured Merv in 1884, Britain was convinced that an invasion of India would soon follow.

Founded by Cyrus the Great in the sixth century B.C., Merv saw a change in rulers many times. For a brief period it even adopted the name "Alexandria" in honor of the great conqueror from Macedonia. By the twelfth century A.D., Merv was one of the largest cities in the world – rivaling Damascus, Cairo, and Baghdad in size – and served as a lighthouse for the study of religion, history, and literature. But, in a fate shared by so many other societies of Central Asia, Merv was sacked by the Mongols in 1221. The extent of its devastation was impressive even by ancient standards. The Mongols are said to have slaughtered as many as one million people in a single day.

Today, I find Merv a much quieter place – and rather ideal, I think, for studying Silk Road coins. Several Roman and Byzantine types have already been discovered here by Russian archaeologists. But Merv has contributed its own chapter to the history of money, too. Around 200 A.D., the city was assigned the important task of minting coins for the Persian Empire. Several types were produced locally – golden denarii, silver drachmas, and various bronze types. Many were cast with characteristically Persian designs – and with great uniformity – such that, wherever they are discovered, these coins help estimate the ages of other archaeological sites.

With luck, our little excavation of Merv will proceed without much ado. The site's abandoned condition virtually ensures that we will have no onlookers. Nowadays, almost nothing remains of the once great city. It lies uninhabited – its towering walls

189

and tree-lined boulevards mostly buried or eroded· Its emptiness, combined with its distance some twenty miles east of Mary, should help our party avoid any unwanted attention·

We are making final preparations and hope to be off to Merv in a day or so· As I write, Misha is discreetly recruiting a handful of Mary's citizens to assist with digging· We've replenished our supplies at the local bazaars, purchased fresh camels, and made several important new contacts· This last point is especially vital· Aside from the enjoyment of making new friends, the value of information in this strange and perilous land is immeasurable – something we learned once already in Baku· Should the Soviet authorities catch wind of our doings and decide to pay us a visit, news will with luck reach us before they do·

Patrick closed the journal and stared at its cover. He swept his hand over the cracked leather as he reflected on the thousands of miles it had traveled – and was traveling still. Relaxing in the air conditioned hotel room, Patrick wondered how Thomas would feel about his great-grandson retracing his footsteps. Clearly, the journey had been riskier and far more grueling back then. But from what Patrick had seen over the past three weeks, Central Asia had not really changed so much. The desert heat and government seemed just as oppressive as in Thomas's time. According to Roger, the region's resources and geography still enticed great powers as they had during the Great Game. With so many parallels between their experiences, what words of advice or warning might Thomas have offered his great-grandson?

Stretched out on the cool cotton sheets, his dad asleep in the other bed, Patrick smiled knowingly. Although Thomas could not speak to him in person, his guidance transcended time in the pages of his journal. The universe seemed to be conspiring once again to bring them together through circumstance. As it turned out, what had begun as a day of disappointment and doubt had ended in excitement and possibility – and the likelihood that Patrick would learn even more about his great-grandfather.

Patrick reached over and turned off the bedside lamp. Clutching the journal on his chest in the dark room, he reflected on the day's twists and turns.

Their third day in Mary began with a trip to the office of a natural gas company owned by Turkmenistan's government. Skip, Ali, Dad, and Patrick piled into a taxi early that morning for the half-hour drive across town.

Arriving at the surprisingly modern complex, the party was escorted upstairs to a large and bustling conference room. Under a high ceiling of bright fluorescent lights, Turkmen officials and various international businessmen lingered around large tables scattered with maps, pastries, tea and coffee. Smiling to himself, Patrick concluded that donuts must be the official food of geologists across the world. Near the doors lurked a handful of brown-shirted sentries.

As Skip and Dad injected themselves into the noisy throng, Patrick and Ali retired to a quiet corner on the other side of the room. Sipping tea, the retired teacher and student spent the next couple hours trading perspectives about middle school. The discussion wandered from class schedules and homework to the challenges and frustrations of being a middle schooler and opinions of lunch food. Inevitably, they turned to history – a favorite subject of both.

"The topics that Americans and Turks study in eighth grade are similar," Ali acknowledged. "We both read about Ancient Rome and China, the Byzantine Empire, and Genghis Khan. We take a look at the American Revolution and the world wars, too. But I'm not so sure we *interpret* them quite the same as Americans do."

"What do you mean?" Patrick asked.

"Well, we study these topics from the perspective of Turks, rather than Americans."

"Okay… but I still don't understand."

"History affects us differently," Ali explained, resting an ankle on his other knee. "For example, your colonists first settled America some five hundred years ago. My ancestors lived in Turkey as many as five *thousand* years ago. America is protected by vast oceans and has never been conquered. We Turks are sandwiched between great powers and have been invaded more times than we can count. To Americans, these ancient empires existed long ago and far away. We, on the other hand, are direct descendants of them."

Patrick nodded, thinking. "I have heard that people in other countries don't like Americans because we are free – and because our country is so rich. Is that true?"

Ali smiled and shrugged. "I think that is a simplistic view. Perhaps some people feel that way. Many others don't. There are over seven *billion* people in the world today – so my guess is there are just as many opinions. In any case, I suspect that everybody – regardless of where they live – wants freedom and prosperity. These things are desired, not resented."

"What about Turks?" Patrick pressed. "How do you feel about Americans?"

"Again, there are millions of Turks, so I can't possibly claim to know what they all think. But as a whole, I would say we like Americans. Certainly, we have a history together. Our governments were allies against the Soviet Union, and today we still look to you as friends." Ali swirled his tea, and then went on.

"But like I explained, Turkish history is *thousands* of years old. We have watched countless empires come and go. In contrast, the United States has been a world power for what – less than a hundred years? That's a very short amount of time in the context of world history. All empires fall. Her time will also come. Since Turkey lies at the crossroads of the world, we Turks must always keep our eyes and minds open."

Keep our eyes and minds open… a message that Patrick had heard more than once during the past few weeks. He had many more questions for Ali, but the clamor of lunch interrupted their discussion.

Dad and Skip rejoined them and the foursome merged with a line of hungry guests threading its way through the buffet of exotic foods. Patrick was delighted to see that his favorite new dish, pahklava, was back on the menu. But, loading his plate, he noticed that his dad's mood had changed considerably. Dad and Skip both appeared somber, as if discouraged or even troubled by the morning's proceedings. When Patrick overheard Skip grumbling about "stonewalling politicians," followed by "back to the drawing board," it confirmed his suspicions. Things were not going quite as planned.

Convening around a table, Skip shared the news with Patrick and Ali.

"Negotiations here are at a stand-still. It seems our friends, the Turkmen, are having second thoughts about building a pipeline through Afghanistan. They want to hold off making any plans until they have time to reconsider their options."

Patrick looked at his dad, who offered his view on the matter. "They may have had some encouragement whispered into their ears." He glanced over at a table of Chinese officials. "If built, this pipeline would rival another that was constructed a few years ago – and which runs east to China."

This time Ali spoke. "I am surprised. It was my understanding that Turkmenistan wants to reduce its dependence on China. That's why it was looking to build a pipeline through Afghanistan to India."

Skip glumly pushed food around his plate with a fork. "Yeah, Ali, that was our impression, too." Then, looking at Patrick, he smiled weakly. "Politics again... where's Roger when we need him?"

Then the conversation took another turn for the worse. Patrick listened wide-eyed while his dad explained that, in light of this morning's developments, their purpose for being in Turkmenistan was temporarily at an end. And with Ahmed still on the loose, a return to Baku was out of the question, as well. They were stuck in the middle – unable to make further progress in Central Asia. This only meant one thing. Patrick braced himself for what he knew would follow.

"The trip has stalled out," his dad said. "There's really nothing left to do but go home."

The next hour at the table was a blur. Sitting dumbfounded, Patrick heard little and said less. His pahklava grew cold on the plate in front of him. As Dad and Skip grumbled about the turn of events, Patrick despaired over the end of their trip. Despite the difficulties he had faced, he was enjoying Central Asia. After only three weeks, it was just too soon for his once-in-a-lifetime adventure to end.

Following lunch, the foursome returned to the hotel. The afternoon was subdued, with Skip and Dad making phone calls and trying to figure out what to do next. They decided that Skip would return to Baku to consult with the rest of his team there. His company clearly needed to summon additional political muscle for negotiating with the Turkmen – and for undoing the Chinese efforts to axe the Afghanistan pipeline.

Sitting on the bed in their room, Patrick watched his dad, who stood facing the window. In one hand he clutched his field notes, while the other held a phone to his ear. After several minutes of silence – listening to whoever was on the other end of the line – he flung the papers onto the table in frustration.

"Okay," he said softly. "That's it, then. We'll just have to hold off." He hung up but continued to stare out the window sullenly.

Patrick said nothing for a few seconds. Finally, unable to control himself, he blurted, "Are we going home?"

His dad slowly turned, looked at him, then sighed and nodded. "I don't see any way around it. There isn't much else we can do here." Seeing the expression on Patrick's face, he added, "I'm sorry, son."

Patrick glanced down at the floor, feeling the sting of disappointment in his eyes. He reached over and picked up Thomas's journal, turning it over in his hands regretfully. His dad stood facing him, hands in his pockets. Neither spoke for a while.

"What do you have there?" Dad finally inquired, wrinkling his brow. "I've been meaning to ask you about that."

Patrick held the journal aloft, as if inspecting it for the first time. "Something Grandpa gave me," he answered casually. "It's *his* dad's journal from when he traveled here."

Dad appeared to tense. He stared for several seconds, as if making sense of what Patrick had said. Then he slowly replied, "Grandpa gave you that? When?"

Patrick recalled their last night in the States when they had visited Grandpa at his cabin. He told his dad of the old man's instructions to read the journal after reaching Baku. Then he briefly summarized Thomas's expedition from Istanbul to Mary.

At first, his Dad looked stunned. But the longer he listened, the more he relaxed. At last, a faint smile crept across his lips.

"I remember something about that…" he said musingly, his voice drifting off. "When I was a boy, your Grandpa told me about Thomas – *my* grandfather.... He was quite a character!" He chuckled to himself. "Can I take a look?"

Patrick handed him the journal and watched as his dad flipped through the pages, clearly amused. "I'll be darned," he kept saying to himself, shaking his head. Then he froze, his attention focused on one of the pages. Slowly, he turned it around to show Patrick, who recognized his own penciled translation of the cipher. Dad raised his eyebrows.

Patrick rubbed his hands together and took a deep breath. Then, he explained the spilled water, the jumble of mysterious numbers, and how he came to doubt Grandpa's unseemly birth date. His dad's eyes shined with interest, so Patrick went on. He showed him the string of mysterious letters he had decoded, and the message – *Go in and you won't come out.* He explained why he thought it odd that Thomas would have used code writing in the first place. Then, as Patrick watched his dad's excitement grow, he went one step further. He shared his suspicion that the incident in the Baku hotel room and Ahmed's inexplicable behavior might somehow be related to the journal.

By the time he had finished, Dad was sitting in the chair with his elbows on his knees, leaning forward, with enchantment in his face.

"I'll be darned," he kept saying, shaking his head and turning the journal over in his hands. "And you've been working on this the whole time... Why didn't you tell me?"

"I don't know," Patrick said softly. "You were busy, and I... I don't know."

"Unbelievable... Have you read it all? Where does it end?"

Patrick shook his head. "No I haven't read it all... but I couldn't help taking a peek at the back. There's no more writing after the city of Kokand. I'm not sure why."

"Huh," his dad said thoughtfully. The room was silent for several minutes. At last, his dad leaned back and smacked his hands on his knees, the way he did when he'd suddenly made a decision.

"The oil business is on hold for a while – there's nothing we can do about that. But here we are in Turkmenistan – father and son – with a mysterious journal. Seems to me like a perfect reason for us to stay in Central Asia."

Patrick looked up, dumbfounded. His dad was grinning at him. Patrick smiled slowly, unsure what to say.

"Let's follow that journal," Dad continued. "If it only takes us to Kokand, that's fine. But it beats going home with our tails between our legs. By golly, we're going to get something accomplished on this trip!"

With that, they stayed committed to Central Asia. Ali was happy to extend his services to them for another couple weeks. Skip agreed to give Dad the next month off work. He only regretted he could not go along, and wished them the best of luck.

Tomorrow, Dad would wrap up a few loose ends in Mary. Then they would be off to see the ruins of Merv – once the greatest city in the world – and for a father and son, the first step of their new great adventure.

PART III: THE ENDGAME

29 QUEEN OF THE WORLD

I met a traveller from an antique land
Who said: "Two vast and trunkless legs of stone
Stand in the desert. Near them, on the sand,
Half sunk, a shattered visage lies, whose frown,
And wrinkled lip, and sneer of cold command,
Tell that its sculptor well those passions read
Which yet survive, stamped on these lifeless things,
The hand that mocked them and the heart that fed:
And on the pedestal these words appear:
'My name is Ozymandias, king of kings:
Look on my works, ye Mighty, and despair!'
Nothing beside remains. Round the decay
Of that colossal wreck, boundless and bare
The lone and level sands stretch far away."

– Percy Bysshe Shelley (Ozymandias, 1818)

The glossy travel brochure explained that the historical site of Merv included the remains of at least five different cities, constructed one after the next due to one calamity or another, over some 2500 years. However, each city was built a little farther west of its predecessor. Sometimes the winding Murghab River forced the townspeople to abandon their homes, and other times it was the destruction wrought by invaders such as the Mongols. Standing atop a dirt hill, Patrick looked west across the empty expanse of grass and sand. He tried to imagine what the largest city of its time had once looked like.

Over his shoulder, Patrick heard shouting from the direction where they had parked. Ali was waving his arms and yelling at a pack of dogs sniffing around the car. Picking up a stick, he went running at them. Weighing their chances against the big Turk, the dogs retreated, barking and whining, over a hill and out of sight. Reaching Patrick and his dad a minute later, Ali grinned, slightly out of breath. He held up a brown paper bag.

"They were after your lunch, Patrick. Now you know how far a Turk will go to help his American friends!"

Before exploring the ruins, Dad, Ali, and Patrick ate their lunch atop the hill. Behind them, the sun still crouched low in the pink morning sky, yet Patrick's skin was already sticky with sweat. Along the horizon, dancing heat waves began to form the infamous "mirages" known for giving false hope to thirsty desert wanderers. Aside from the howls of unseen dogs and an occasional vulture flying overhead, the trio appeared to have the ancient city to themselves.

"In addition to its importance to Silk Road trade," Ali explained as they ate, "Merv was a center for science, philosophy, and literature. The city was home to several great libraries, mosques, and madrassas (religious schools). Islamic scholars here made important contributions to our knowledge of geography, astronomy, and mathematics. It's even rumored that Merv was the inspiration for the famous tales in *Arabian Nights*."

Ali pointed to one of the few standing structures, at least half a mile away. "That's the Mausoleum of Sultan Sanjar [SAN-jar]. The Sultan had it built just a few decades before the Mongols arrived. Legend has it that the mausoleum could be seen by caravans a day away from Merv." He took a bite of his sandwich as his eyes scanned the horizon.

The **tomb of Sultan Sanjar**, located in the ancient Silk Road oasis-city of Merv (Turkmenistan). Legend has it that the mausoleum could be seen by caravans a day out from Merv. The Sultan's body was moved shortly before the Mongols arrived; the tomb now stands empty.

"There's the Great Kyz Kala [KIZ kah-LA]," he said, pointing at the ruins of a massive, four-sided structure shimmering in the distance. "It's a fortress of some kind. Or at least, that's what they think. Nobody knows for sure. It's generally thought to have been built in the seventh century..."

Ali continued the history lesson for another half hour while Patrick and his dad munched on rice, mutton, and flat bread. Finally, the conversation returned to present day and what approach they should adopt for exploring the site.

The group began by walking around Sultan Kala [KUH-la] – an area of Merv that flourished in the eleventh century during the Silk Road's climax. To get there, they walked along a mud berm that had once been part of a great fortress wall. Inside the wall's perimeter, a vast system of canals, roads, caravanserais, palaces, administrative buildings, and defenses had once stretched for miles. Now, only a field of grass and barren mounds remained. According to Ali, Sultan Kala had also been known for manufacturing elaborate clay bowls and vases that were popular among traders from around the world. Here and there, Patrick spotted a pottery shard or brick that hinted at the city's former greatness.

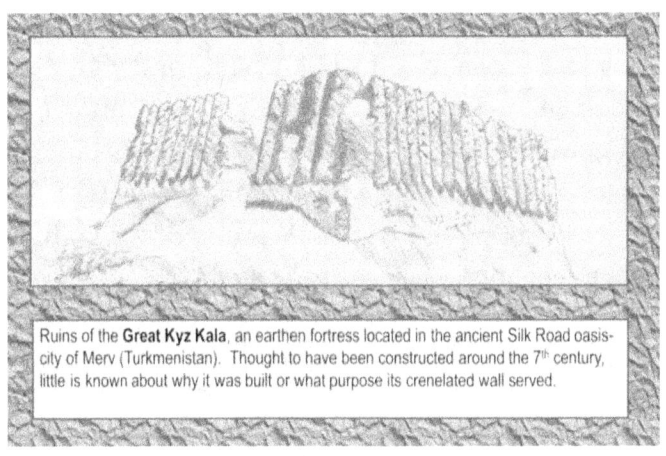

Ruins of the **Great Kyz Kala**, an earthen fortress located in the ancient Silk Road oasis-city of Merv (Turkmenistan). Thought to have been constructed around the 7th century, little is known about why it was built or what purpose its crenelated wall served.

Approaching the Mausoleum of Sultan Sanjar, Patrick was surprised by its well-preserved condition. Seeing his look of astonishment, Ali remarked, "This landmark has been restored over the years. It is still a very popular place to visit – a sort of pilgrimage for many."

Patrick tilted his head back to take in the tomb's full grandeur. The colossal building stood at least one hundred feet tall, constructed of tan mud bricks expertly fitted together. Where the walls met, they formed the sharp corners of a perfect square. High above were richly adorned arches that served as the underpinning of a large brick dome.

"Is the Sultan buried here?" Patrick asked, awed by the sight.

Ali shook his head while drinking from his canteen. "When news arrived that the Mongols were coming, the Sultan's body was moved. Nobody knows where his bones lie today. The tomb is empty."

Patrick pointed at an inscription etched in the brick wall. The characters were written in the elegant beauty of a strange language. He raised his eyebrows questioningly.

"Ah, yes," the Turk said, wiping his mouth with his sleeve and stepping closer. "Let's see... It says:

> "This place is ennobled by the remains of the one who was called Sultan Sanjar, from the descendants of Turks-Seljuks... He was Alexander the Great of his time; he was the patron of scientists and poets, and was accepted by the Islamic world in the state of prosperity and happiness owing to his love of sciences and arts."

The trio stood in silent contemplation. A sudden gust of wind swirled about and whistled through the arches high above their heads, giving the impression that the mosque was breathing. When it exhaled a blast of cold air through the large door before them, Patrick felt himself shiver in the desert heat. Sensing their enchantment, Ali decided to tell a local legend.

"It is said that the Sultan fell in love with a magical woman and wanted to wed her. Before she would marry him, he had to agree to three conditions: never to hug her waist, to look at her feet while she ran, or to watch her brush her hair. The Sultan agreed, but his wife was so beautiful that he could not help himself. He soon broke all three of his promises. However, when he hugged her waist, he found no bones there. When he looked at her feet, he saw they did not touch the ground. Watching her brush her hair, he discovered that she first had to remove her head. Learning of his deceit, the woman turned into a white bird and flew into the sky. The Sultan begged her not to go, saying he would die without her. She told him to construct the tallest and most beautiful building in the city – and to leave the roof open.

And so he did." Ali looked up at the windowed dome. "And every week she flew over so that he could be with her."

They stepped through the arched gateway into the cool, musty interior. As Patrick's eyes adjusted to the light, he made out a large empty room with a tile floor. In its center, a rectangular slab marked the spot where the Sultan's body had once lain. The walls of the chamber were lined with simple, yet beautiful, patterned engravings. Birds fluttered in the rafters overhead. Otherwise, the tomb was quiet and still.

Patrick pondered the contrast between the grand mausoleum and what little remained of Merv. A great city had once flourished here – home to powerful rulers and magnificent architecture, attracting great thinkers and merchants from all corners of the world. According to Thomas, Merv had been one of the largest cities of its time. Now it was gone – relegated to history and packs of wild dogs. Empires came and went. Ali had said as much the other day, and here was the proof.

It was strange to think that his great-grandfather had been here long ago. Thomas must have camped nearby with Misha and his crew of diggers. He had probably stood where Patrick now stood and stared up at the same great dome, pondering Merv's rise and fall. I'll bet it all looks exactly the same, Patrick thought, as he drifted over to a bench along the wall.

As his dad roamed the tomb's smaller chambers and Ali poked around outside, Patrick pulled the journal out of his backpack. Flipping through the well-worn pages, he paused at a familiar sketch. Indeed, there was the mausoleum exactly as it looked today. Beneath the drawing, Thomas had penned a translation of the inscription that was engraved in the wall outside – the same that Ali had interpreted for them.

The next several pages included a description of Merv's archaeology and the artifacts Thomas's party had found, as well as an analysis of the great city's importance along the Silk Road. Evidently, Thomas had also found several coins, some of which were sketched and described in detail. Greek and Roman coins made of silver and gold in the older sections of town. Bronze pieces from the Byzantine era. And mixed coins of the Sassanid and Seljuk empires.

Patrick dabbed water on the pages, but no hidden cipher appeared. He sighed, wondering what to do next. During the past week, he had tried several of the other pages throughout the journal, as well, but there was no evidence of any further coding.

Sensing someone nearby, he looked up to see his dad leaning against the wall, wiping sweat from his forehead. He kneeled next to Patrick and inquired, "Well?"

Patrick shook his head. "I don't know." His eyes returned to the journal. "I'm not sure what to look for."

"You used the water?" Dad asked, glancing at the plastic bottle. Patrick nodded.

"Hmm." He lifted his cap to scratch his head. "What's another way to uncover hidden writing?"

Patrick thought for a while. He knew of inks that could be made to reappear by adding a certain chemical. But he didn't have any of those ingredients with him. Grandpa had shown him how to use a black lamp, too, but that was also out of the question.

"I think I remember something from when I was a boy..." his dad mused. "Your Grandpa showed me how heat can be applied to reveal invisible citrus ink. In the old days, spies sometimes wrote in lemon or grapefruit juice, which disappeared when it dried. A hot lightbulb or stove can be used to make the code visible again." Patrick nodded, remembering the idea, as well.

"Let me see..." His Dad took the journal and reached into his own bag. He pulled out a plastic lighter and held it below one of the pages. "I'll try not to light your great-grandfather's journal on fire. Now, let's see if I remember how to do this..."

He flicked the lighter and slowly waved it back and forth, at first several inches under the paper. Bringing it closer, he moved the flame in circles, sending a curl of smoke wafting up towards the mausoleum's dome. No words appeared. He turned the page and tried more writing. Still nothing. He paused and the two stared at the journal, puzzled.

Then, Patrick brightened. "What about the pictures?" he asked. Dad nodded. He repeated the heating process, this time under Thomas's sketch of Merv. At first, the same frustrating result – nothing. Then, very faintly at first, letters began to form among the roads and buildings. As Patrick's dad moved the lighter beneath the page, more letters appeared. At last, another cipher: XORHZEXS.

The two looked at each other, wide-eyed and giddy. A quick translation using the false birth-date cipher revealed "YOTKANZZ." As with the last cipher, the Z's were probably just space holders, or "dummy" letters. Patrick and his dad had no idea what YOTKAN could mean. But at least it was something…

Thomas ended his journal entry with a mention of his travel plans. He would next venture to Bukhara (boo-CAR-uh), another legendary Silk Road oasis-city. It lay farther to the north, deep inside Soviet Turkestan. Recognizing this as their next destination, Patrick and his dad packed the journal away.

As if on cue, they heard gravel crunching, and Ali's shadow appeared at the door. It was now late afternoon and time to get back to Mary. With wild dogs and spirits roaming about, nobody wanted to be caught in the ruins after sundown.

Taking one last look up at the dome, Patrick imagined a white bird flying overhead – the Queen of the World. Her beauty had been lovely but fleeting – much like Merv, or any other great civilization, had once been. Here for one glorious moment, and then gone forever. Patrick slung his backpack over his shoulder and stepped into the sunshine.

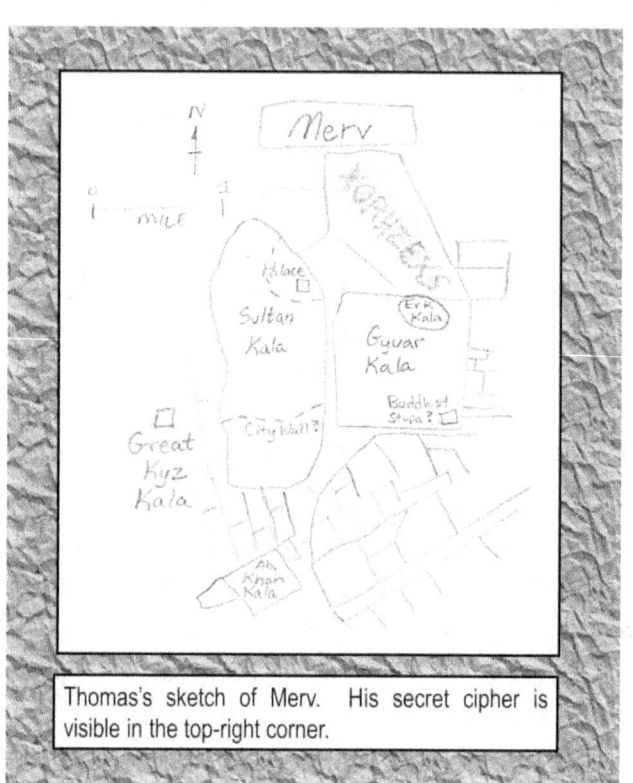

Thomas's sketch of Merv. His secret cipher is visible in the top-right corner.

30 NO MAN'S LAND

"Never look back unless you are planning to go that way."
– Henry David Thoreau

The trio cooled their heels in Mary while waiting for their paperwork. Though they were eager to visit Bukhara, they hadn't received visas to enter Uzbekistan. This process often delayed tourists a week or longer, but a quick call to Roger cut their wait to two days. They spent the extra time touring Mary, inspecting the local architecture and learning more of its history. Patrick and his dad also made long overdue phone calls to Mom and Grandpa. After initial hellos and small talk, Patrick excitedly described their exploits during the previous weeks.

"Well, well…" Grandpa had chuckled from his porch half a world away. "It seems you are making an adventure of it, after all."

Patrick went on to explain the strange ciphers he'd discovered in the journal while in Baku, then talked of the one they'd just found in Merv, which they had translated to spell "Yotkan", using Grandpa's false birthdate.

"Sounds Chinese," Grandpa replied, his voice sounding soft and distant over the line. His next words were garbled, but Patrick could hear him say, "Keep your eyes and mind open." The phone connection was failing, so the two quickly said goodbye and hung up. *Chinese…* Patrick repeated to himself, intrigued.

It was now mid-June. The Black Sand was at its hottest and deadliest when Patrick, Dad, and Ali finally set out for Uzbekistan. Once again, they boarded the Trans-Caspian Railway

– this time for a short, four-hour trip to the city of Turkmenabat (turk-MEN-uh-bot) in the northern part of the country. From his seat in the nearly empty passenger car, Patrick peered out at the limitless stretch of sand – a scene to which he had grown accustomed during their prior train ride. An occasional shrub, mound of dirt, or group of camel herders passed by his window, offering temporary relief from the endless brown and gray landscape.

The train's rhythmic sway prompted Patrick to lean his head against the window and reflect on his great-grandfather's journal. Thomas had left Merv with a sense of accomplishment, having spent nearly two weeks mapping the site at Sultan Kala. He had collected several coins, pottery shards, and other artifacts left over from some of the world's great empires.

Upon returning to Mary, however, Thomas was startled to learn that its bazaar buzzed with news of his expedition. Worse, his contacts reported that gossip had also reached the ears of the Soviet secret police, who it was rumored were prowling about for a mysterious Westerner believed to be disguised as a local. There was little doubt Thomas was their prey. He and Misha packed immediately.

Thomas also included an odd reference to an acquaintance he made while in Merv. His writing – usually clear and detailed – was oddly vague on this matter. He simply wrote:

My departure from Merv was eased by a fellow outsider whose sympathy for my situation resulted in a significant measure of support.

As the car swayed back and forth lazily, Patrick couldn't help wondering if this unnamed associate was somehow related to the secret ciphers in the journal. He contemplated other possibilities, too, which had nibbled at his subconscious since leaving Baku. As he turned them over in his mind, they bled

208

together in a haze of truth and dreamy imagination. When he woke a couple of hours later, the train had stopped.

Like most cities in Central Asia, Turkmenabat has a very long history. According to Ali, it had been founded two thousand years ago and served as an important junction along the Silk Road. Like so many of its neighbors, Turkmenabat was obliterated by the Mongols, ruled for centuries by local emirs, and finally subjugated by the Soviets in the 1920s. As part of one of Moscow's Five-Year Plans in that era, the town's artisans and traders were forcefully converted to farmers and assigned the collective duty of filling the Soviet Union's demand for cotton.

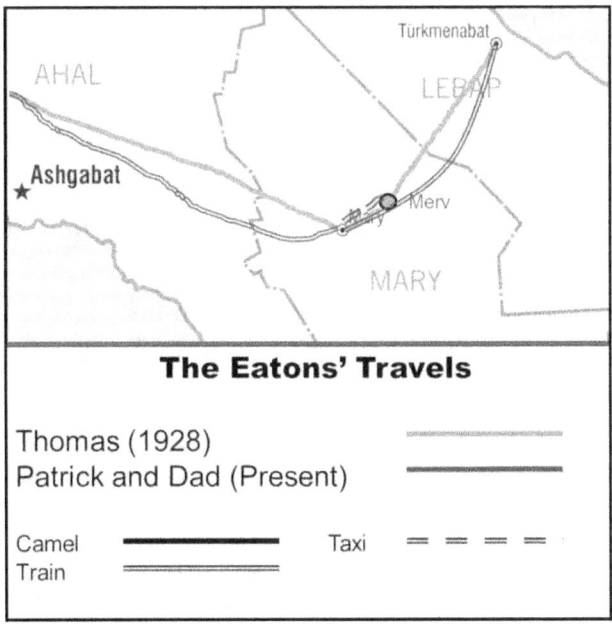

"There's the famous Amu Darya [AH-moo DAR-ya] River," Ali said, pointing at the wide expanse of slow-moving brown water in the distance. "Known to the ancient Greeks as the Oxus, countless armies have crossed it throughout history. Originally, the river drained into both the Aral and Caspian seas.

But a thousand years ago, the locals built a dam to divert water to the Aral Sea only, irrigating their fields along the way. The Mongols destroyed the dam, but today the river still follows this course. Sadly, very little water reaches these fields today. The Soviets destroyed the region by over-farming it. Now, even the Aral Sea is nearly gone."

To Patrick, Turkmenabat looked much the same as Turkmenbashi and Mary. It was filled with large, white-washed government buildings, golden statues of the Great Leader, and mile after mile of rundown, concrete apartments that were mass-produced by the Soviets. According to Dad, the city was also the starting point of a newly built gas pipeline to China. This was the strategic energy route to which Skip had alluded the other day. Spotting the drilling rigs that dotted the skyline, Patrick recalled the large number of Chinese workers he had seen over the past week.

Despite its growing prominence on the world stage, Turkmenabat was merely a layover for this trio of Silk Road wanderers. At the train station they hailed a taxi for a forty-mile drive to the dusty border town of Farab. From here, Patrick was startled to learn, travelers wishing to enter Uzbekistan had to undertake a one-mile hike through the sweltering desert. Due to an apparent diplomatic mix-up years ago, the borders of the two countries did not touch. Instead, they were separated by a desolate "neutral zone." Since transportation through this zone was unpredictable, most border crossers simply hoofed it.

"You are welcome to take a taxi shuttle across," smirked the Turkmen guard as he looked over their passports. "They sometimes arrive once or twice a day." Patrick gazed at the trail of dust swirling behind their disappearing taxi. As soon as his passengers had gotten out, the driver spun a U-turn and floored it back to Turkmenabat.

"This ought to be fun," his dad said, grinning. "I think we should buy a few more waters before heading out... What do you think?"

Patrick looked at him incredulously. He squinted down the bleak stretch of road leading to the border and watched it disappear over the horizon in a shimmering haze of heat. He turned back to his dad again.

"It'll be okay." Dad reassured him, rubbing sunblock on his face and neck. He handed the bottle to Patrick. "Just think... you'll never forget this day."

Patrick reached for the bottle while Ali headed to the bazaar across the street for water. As he tightened his shoelaces and then adjusted the straps on his back, Patrick took stock of his situation. All those years he'd spent listening to stories about the Eatons – climbing this mountain, splashing across that ocean, or slogging along another far-flung desert... And now, here he was, getting what he'd always asked for. As unlikely as it would have seemed a month ago, Patrick was about to cross a deserted no-man's land between two former Soviet republics – along the very same route taken by his great-grandfather, and Marco Polo eight hundred years before that.

Stay positive, he heard his Grandpa say. Then, in the words of Thomas: *Don't give up, and don't ever look back.*

Ten minutes into their trek, Patrick looked back. With sweat dripping off his brow, he shielded his eyes and peered south towards Turkmenistan. Only a dark line on the horizon – along with the occasional glint of the metal border fence – hinted at the presence of distant Farab. Turning back to the north, his eyes met an identical view. They were halfway across.

It was boiling hot. Though he sweated profusely, his clothes were dry. The thirsty desert air lapped up the moisture as quickly as it left his body.

Ahead of them, Ali strolled in long, easy strides, his thumbs leisurely tucked under the straps of his pack. Tolerance to this heat must be in the man's blood, Patrick thought, or perhaps he had simply adapted over countless trips here. The Turk wore a checkered scarf around his head and neck, which seemed to Patrick like a silly thing to wear in the middle of the desert. As if sensing eyes on him, Ali stopped and turned to looked back. Seeing the boy's red face and heaving chest, Ali dropped his pack and reached into one of the pockets. He pulled out a second scarf and waited for Patrick to catch up.

"Here. Let me show you how to wear the *keffiyeh* [kūffiyah]." He skillfully wrapped the colorful cotton cloth around Patrick's head and neck. Stepping back to inspect his work, his eyes danced with satisfaction. "Now, my friend, you look like a Turk!"

The three carried on in silence. Occasional gusts of wind pelted them with sand, while offering a brief reprieve from the static heat. Larger squalls howled farther out in the desert, every so often spinning up massive sand devils that reached high into the blue sky. At one point, it sounded as if one of these desert twisters was approaching them from behind. Patrick ignored the roar at first. But as it became louder, he turned to look.

A car was quickly approaching them, swirling dust in its wake. Dad and Ali stopped at the sound, too. The trio moved to the side of the road, prepared to shield their eyes and let the vehicle rumble pass. But instead, it slowed. As a dust-coated Mercedes Benz limousine rolled to a stop next to them, its tinted rear window opened. Stepping closer, the trio peered into its dark interior.

"Going to Bukhara?" came a familiar voice from the shadows. An arm stretched into the sunlight, and the small bejeweled hand of Uri Petrovsky beckoned them to enter. "I would be most honored to offer the Eatons and their Turkish friend a ride."

212

Stunned, Patrick took a step back and glanced at his father, whose expression mirrored his surprise. Gathering himself, Dad allowed a sly grin to creep across his face. He glanced at Ali with raised eyebrows, then slowly turned back to the window.

"We'd be most grateful, Mr. Petrovsky. It's a tad warm out here."

Instantly, the driver's door flew open. Its occupant stepped briskly to the back of the vehicle, where he opened the trunk and stowed their bags. As Patrick handed him his pack, he glanced up at the man. Something about him looked familiar. The thin face, tight skin, and dark mustache... How did Patrick know him?

"Your bag, Mr. Eaton?" the driver asked, seemingly amused by the boy's puzzlement. Patrick nodded dumbly, handing over the pack.

As he stepped from the hot sun into the dimly lit, air-conditioned limousine, his head spun. Five minutes ago, he would not have believed that his circumstances could grow more fantastic. One moment, he was hiking through the Central Asian desert dressed as a camel trader. Now he was hitching a ride with a Russian spy. What would Grandpa say if he could see them now?

31 OUT OF THE SHADOWS

"Be extremely subtle, even to the point of formlessness.
Be extremely mysterious, even to the point of soundlessness.
Thereby you can be the director of the opponent's fate."
— Sun Tzu

Although a quarter-century had passed since the collapse of the Soviet Union, Russia clearly retained a powerful influence in Central Asia. At the Uzbekistan border, the group was delayed no more than ten minutes as their paperwork was hastily checked and stamped. The passengers weren't even asked to get out of the limousine. After returning their passports and visas through the car window, the uniformed guard nodded courteously and waved them through.

Ali leaned over to Patrick and whispered, "This is unheard of. I've never been through this checkpoint in fewer than two hours!" Patrick nodded, recalling the two hours of red tape they had endured in Farab.

Relishing the admiration displayed by his guests, Uri sat across from them with his fingers laced over his belly. Relaxed in a pin-striped suit, he looked like a mob boss awaiting the townspeople to come and kiss his ringed fingers. All he needed was a crooked-nosed, ex-boxer sitting beside him, Patrick thought. Instead, a tall, academic-looking man sat next to Uri, clutching a briefcase atop bony knees. Below his dark, close-cropped hair, a pair of wire-rimmed glasses perched delicately on his pointed nose.

"This is Comrade Bukov," Uri introduced the man, who nodded coolly. "He is also with the Russian embassy." With that,

Uri paid the man no more attention. "I am glad to have found you."

"Thanks again for the ride," Dad replied, spooning caviar onto a cracker from the plate between them.

"My pleasure." The Russian's blue and green eyes twinkled. "When I heard that a couple of Americans and a Turk were crossing into Uzbekistan, I knew it had to be you."

The guests smiled back. Patrick wondered how Uri knew about Ali. Nothing in Central Asia seemed to escape this man's attention.

"I apologize for startling you at the train station in Ashgabat," Uri said unexpectedly. "I would have stuck around, but I was in a hurry to get to a meeting at the Ministry of Oil and Gas."

"That's okay," Patrick replied, playing with his hands. "You just surprised me. With the fog and all…"

"These trips to Central Asia are like that now," Uri went on. "From one place to the next, then back again. So little time to spare. Those of us who work in energy are busy bees. You understand, of course…" He glanced at Patrick's dad, who nodded.

"But in the Soviet days, the ministers of these republics came to see us," Uri continued, his voice tinged with melancholy. "Not the other way around. When I was a young delegate, I worked in Tashkent (the capital of Uzbekistan) for a while. Our meetings were held in extravagant parlors and halls, and all of the country's important people came to visit us." He looked out the window. "But things have changed… at least for now. We no longer sit at the head of the table."

"So what exactly do you do?" Dad asked the question which had been on Patrick's mind since Turkmenbashi. For some time, Uri gazed out the window in silence.

At last, he replied, "I am what you might call a *facilitator*." A hint of a smile appeared on his red cheeks. "I make

215

arrangements, look for opportunities, share perspectives…and help friends when I can."

The highway to Bukhara started to smooth and, after twenty minutes of bumping along the potholed roads, the car's interior suddenly became quiet.

"Are you a communist?" Patrick asked abruptly, causing his dad to nearly choke on his caviar. Ali let out a snort. Cool as ever, Uri merely smiled. Then he gently shook his head.

"No, I am not a communist, Mr. Eaton. Very few Russians are… or ever were, for that matter. The old communist hardliners began to lose their power decades ago, well before the Soviet Union collapsed. Since then, we Russians have become much more *practical*."

"What does that mean?" Patrick queried, eyeing the caviar but lacking courage to try it.

Noticing his conundrum, Uri chuckled. "It is the best caviar in the world – from the eggs of Caspian Sea sturgeon. One of the few luxuries we Russian diplomats can still count on…"

Patrick sucked in his cheeks and shook his head. "No, thank you."

Uri laughed deeply. "Okay, Mr. Eaton! No caviar for now, but you may still come around yet…" He sipped from a fancy-looking glass next to his seat and went on.

"As I was saying, we Russians admit that communism does not work. Today, we are much more realistic. In the coming decades, the world will need natural resources, not silly ideas." He grinned and added, "Fortunately, Russia has a lot of natural resources."

Patrick recalled his conversations with Skip and Roger, but decided not to interrupt Uri again.

"Russia has oil, gas, and coal," Uri continued. "Lots of uranium, too. Did you know that the United States imports almost all of the uranium that it uses to produce nuclear energy?" Patrick shook his head. "As a matter of fact, natural resources account for

216

nearly all the goods we export to your country. One must never forget that ideas come and go, Mr. Eaton. Raw materials, however, are a very different matter."

Patrick's dad joined in: "I had the pleasure of visiting Russia years ago. I studied the geology of the Ural Mountains, and even visited Moscow."

Uri did not look surprised, but he smiled politely. "I hope you enjoyed your stay. Russians are the most hospitable hosts you will find anywhere. At least to our *invited* guests…"

Patrick gave him a questioning look.

"We Russians have had to defend our country several times from outsiders. But you already know this, I think."

Patrick couldn't resist the bait. "That's why Russia has expanded its borders throughout history – to create a buffer zone against future invasions." He controlled his urge to smile, proud of his recently acquired knowledge. He glanced at his dad instead, who grinned back.

"Indeed," Uri agreed. "And we have good reason. But invasion is not the only threat to Russia. Outsiders have long tried to seal us off from the rest of the world in order to keep Asia's markets for themselves. The colonial powers of Europe wanted to keep Russia penned-up in the steppes of the north."

"How did they do that?" Patrick asked, peering out at the desert.

"By encircling us with their armies and navies. By sending their spies into Central Asia to map our lands and resources, stir up the local Muslim population, and cause trouble in our hinterlands. For centuries, foreign agents infiltrated our borders, disguised as geographers, traders, scientists… even archaeologists."

Patrick turned sharply from the window to lock eyes with Uri.

Trying to mask his surprise, Patrick blurted, "But I thought Russia wanted to invade India."

217

Uri flicked his hand, dismissing the notion. "Some Russians may have desired this. Few believed it possible. This was mostly a myth created by British propaganda – an excuse for Her Majesty's government to spread its own empire across Asia. *The Russians are coming!* they cried! *The Russians are coming!* Pure nonsense."

"But what about the Soviet Union?" Dad asked. "Doesn't that prove that the British were correct?"

Uri shook his head. "As I said, Russia had no choice but to occupy the lands around it – otherwise we would have been suffocated. It is the same situation today."

Hearing Uri's words, Bukov lightly patted his briefcase. Uri continued, as if reinforced by this cue.

"After World War II, the United States stepped into the shoes of the British Empire – and surrounded Russia with its own army and navy under the banner of NATO. In the name of 'containing communism,' your government positioned its military in Europe, the Middle East, Korea, Vietnam, and Japan. *The Russians are coming!* you cried, repeating the old British myth. But look around now. The Cold War is over, and communism is no longer a threat... Yet your armies have not gone home. Now it is 'terrorism' you claim to be fighting, rather than communism. So you occupy Afghanistan and Iraq, too. Just a few years ago, the United States even had a base here in Uzbekistan – right in our backyard! Can you imagine how Americans would react if Russia placed its bombers in Mexico?"

The air was tense for several seconds. Patrick thought he detected a faint smile on the lips of Bukov – although whether it amounted to amusement or approval, Patrick couldn't say.

Uri took a sip from his glass and then added, more calmly this time, "Once again, Russia finds itself surrounded. So we do what we have always done – we play The Game. The past couple of decades have been difficult for us, but we will rise from the shadows. We always do. Russia has long been a great power, and it will be again."

Small talk then replaced geopolitics for the remainder of the drive to Bukhara, but the earlier conversation stayed with Patrick. Mostly, he felt sorry for confronting Uri again. The man had been kind enough to offer them a ride and Patrick felt he had challenged the man's motive for being there.

Besides, Uri had made some good points. It was hard to deny that foreign militaries had repeatedly surrounded Russia. Patrick had never seen this perspective in his school textbooks. Still, he was undecided about the whole matter. Everyone with whom he spoke seemed to have a different perspective about the Great Game.

As their ride together drew to an end, Uri seemed to make an attempt to ease Patrick's guilt.

"You are a thinker, Mr. Eaton. Like your father... and his before. Don't ever apologize for thinking for yourself."

With these words, Patrick breathed a sigh of relief, leaned back in his seat, and immersed himself in the sights of legendary Bukhara.

32 BUKHARA THE NOBLE

"In all other parts of the world, light descends
upon the earth from above; but in Bukhara
it comes from below, and rises."
– Ancient Proverb

Ever since my first visit to Asia, I have dreamed
of going to Bukhara [boo-CAR-uh]. Though few
Westerners have seen it, this remote oasis is the most
legendary of Silk Road towns. During its golden years
in the ninth and tenth centuries, Bukhara was called
the "Pillar of Islam" because it was the center of
Islamic religious and intellectual thought in Central Asia.
It became known far and wide for its more than one
hundred mosques, three hundred madrassas, and the
region's finest bazaar.

But like most of its neighbors, Bukhara also has a
long history of suppression and violence. It has been
conquered and ruled by countless foreigners – one of its
earliest being Alexander the Great, who found his bride
in this region. The Persians, Bactrians, Sogdians, and
Arabs all had their turns reigning over the city. It was
pillaged by the Mongols and then conquered by
Tamerlane. Since the 1700s it has been governed by

220

tight-fisted Muslim emirs who sealed it off from Westerners. And just a few years ago, Bukhara was conquered once again – this time by the Soviet Red Army.

On a late afternoon in July 1928, I became one of only a handful of Americans to lay eyes on this fabled place. As Misha and I led our camels up the stone road to one of the city's eleven gates, the sun glistened off the white fortifications and eighty-one watchtowers, making the city appear as if it were glowing. The effect was breathtaking. This was exactly how I had imagined Bukhara would look.

But as we passed through the gates, my exhilaration began to fade. Inside the great walls lay the dilapidated remnants of what once must have been extravagant gardens and brick homes. As we strolled farther along the main road, we observed the crumbling ruins of other once-majestic structures, many of which had been destroyed by Soviet artillery just a few years ago.

What survived the Soviet siege now deteriorates from pure neglect. The communists not only seem aware of this process, but even welcome it. Perhaps recognizing the impossibility of converting this "Pillar of Islam" to godless communism, they have decided to let it slowly die on its own. With Bukhara's emir gone, its water diverted to Soviet cotton farms, and trade routes cut off, the city is like a heart that has been cut out from the rest of its body.

Fortunately, enough of Bukhara remains to satisfy our imagination and sense of adventure. Finding a local caravanserai to care for our camels, we set off through the maze of narrow alleys where the city came to life for us. Men in gray khalats (robes) and black skullcaps relax in chai-khanas (teahouses), where they play chess, sit on rugs, and smoke. Children in colorful khalats halt their street games to eye us warily. Occasionally, we pass anonymous burka-clad women. Everywhere, the exotic aromas of incense and cooked lamb float into the streets. Ancient Bukhara survives, after all, even though she is retreating bit by bit into the back alleys or behind the heavy wooden doors of madrassas.

All visitors are required to register with the local Soviet office. However, this is an encounter we must avoid at all costs. Despite our camouflage as Muslim traders and our proficiency with the local language, we would almost certainly be unmasked. Disguised, we may be able to stretch our stay to at least a week. When the noose begins to tighten as it did in Merv, we'll beat a hasty escape to Samarkand.

Over several pages, Thomas went on to document his stay in Bukhara. He described and sketched the city's most remarkable sights, including its distinctive blue-domed mosques. He noted the infamous Tower of Death – a 150-foot-tall minaret from which criminals were thrown to their deaths in previous centuries. For

222

thousands of years, it was the highest building in all of Central Asia, and legend has it the minaret was the only structure Genghis Khan left standing when his Mongols demolished the city.

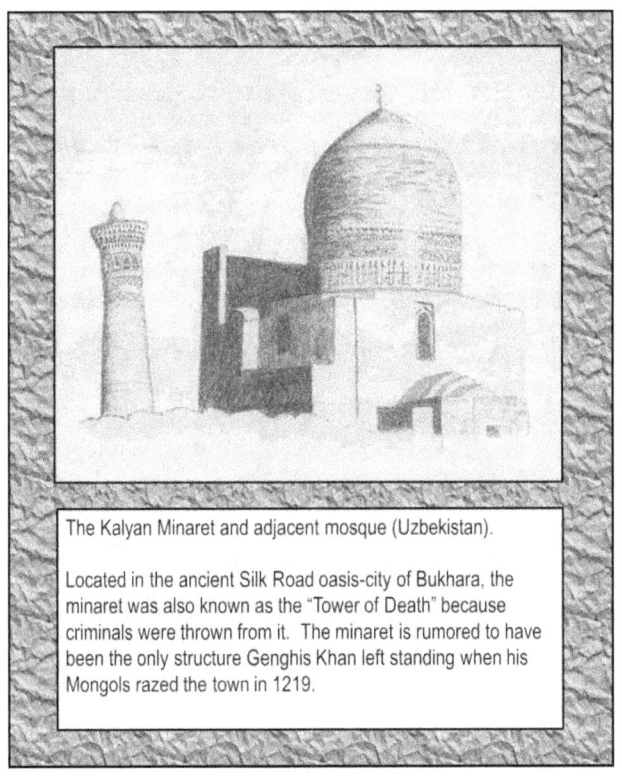

The Kalyan Minaret and adjacent mosque (Uzbekistan).

Located in the ancient Silk Road oasis-city of Bukhara, the minaret was also known as the "Tower of Death" because criminals were thrown from it. The minaret is rumored to have been the only structure Genghis Khan left standing when his Mongols razed the town in 1219.

Thomas also included his impressions of the Ark – a massive fortress in the center of the city. Just a century earlier, a particularly notorious emir ordered two British officers beheaded outside its gates. Their executions came after having spent several years in the fortress's infamous "bug pit." Ironically, one of the prisoners, Captain Arthur Connolly, had been the first person to use the term "The Great Game" just a few years earlier. Ultimately, however, the Ark proved no match for the artillery of the Soviet Red Army, and its walls now crumbled like the rest of Bukhara.

In addition to local culture and architecture, Thomas chronicled his archaeological efforts.

We got to work immediately. First, I scouted a part of the city under which Central Asia's oldest mosque is rumored to be buried. According to the locals, when their ancestors learned the Mongols were approaching, they covered the mosque with sand to keep it safe. Today, the top of the structure peeks above the surface, as if teasing us. Unfortunately, since it lies in plain view of the rest of the town, digging here would be impossible without attracting suspicion.

Reluctantly, I switched my focus to the town's ancient trash piles instead. Fortunately, these lie off beaten paths, meaning I can dig more freely. This advantage has paid off handsomely – I have discovered several old coins, each establishing the influence of former empires here. I've found Byzantine and Kushan coins, as well as silver imitations of the Persian drachmas that were minted in Merv. There are also copper varieties with square holes in their centers, such as were common in China. These may have been exchanged by eastern traders for local horses or pottery, or to hire Bukharans as mercenaries. Altogether, a very satisfying find!

But as it turns out, most coins left Bukhara long ago – they went east to China. After Genghis's death, the Mongol empire split apart. Genghis's grandson, Kublai Khan, established the Yuan Dynasty in Beijing in 1272 and became the first foreigner to rule China. The Yuan was the most powerful and ferocious Mongol khanate in all of Asia. At least half of China's population is thought to have perished under his rule. Interestingly, it was Kublai who had hosted Marco Polo for seventeen years at his court.

However, the Yuan dynasty ultimately went the way of all empires. Kublai's lust for war and glory proved very expensive. As his gigantic army, extensive bureaucracy, and lavish public works projects drained the treasury of its gold and silver, Kublai was forced to look elsewhere for revenue. He imposed heavy taxes on the people (rather than simply slaughtering them as he had done before). He ordered raids of the tombs of past Song Dynasty emperors for their gold and silver. His government nationalized the economy – that is, it took control of businesses and kept the profits (much as the Soviets have done in Baku).

Then, with his gold and silver reserves dwindling, Kublai issued paper money called Chao. Upon seeing this, Polo – a Venetian merchant who understood money and was all too familiar with Rome's demise – was taken aback. He wrote: "With these pieces of paper they can buy anything and pay for anything. And I can tell you that the papers that reckon as ten bezants do not weight one." Backed only by

225

government promises, the Chao inevitably lost value as more of it was printed.

War, taxes, and inflation are paths to a society's destruction. The fall of the Roman Empire demonstrated this lesson all too well. Ultimately, the same fate awaited the Yuan, but not before these Mongol warriors carted off tons of gold, silver, and other riches from Central Asia. Some of their treasure-laden caravans survived the Silk Road to reach Kublai's capital in Beijing. But many others did not...

The reverence Thomas had felt for Bukhara was shared by his great-grandson three-quarters of a century later. Looking down at the city from atop the Kalyan Minaret – the "Tower of Death" – Patrick reflected upon its thousands of years of history. He'd always felt this way when he visited historic places. There was something fascinating about standing where civilizations had existed long before. This tower was perhaps the very place where Genghis Khan or Tamerlane had once looked west in bloodthirsty anticipation of new victories, territory, and plunder.

"Bukhara looks different from what I expected," Patrick said. "It doesn't look like it's falling apart."

His dad and Ali stood nearby, shielding their eyes from the sun. From this height, the jumble of citizens and sightseers below looked like a horde of ants.

"Yes, indeed," Ali replied. "It has become quite a tourist destination. Bukhara still has a mythical reputation. And for Muslims it remains a holy place."

Patrick had seen the prayers during his stay in Central Asia. Five times a day, Muslims ritually face Mecca, kneel, and recite a statement of their faith. As a Muslim, Ali participated, too, but not every time. "I am a believer, but not a strict one," he had once explained to Patrick with a sheepish grin.

Earlier that morning, Patrick heard a man – called a *muezzin*, according to Ali – recite the call to prayer from atop one of the city's minarets. "Allahu akhbar!" or "God is great!" The man's melodious and hauntingly beautiful voice echoed across the rooftops and through the alleys. As he listened from his hotel window, Patrick watched the sun rise – silhouetting the minarets and domed mosques against the pink morning sky. Below lay the golden mud-walled homes and tan brick streets of ancient Bukhara. Still foggy from sleep, the experience had felt like a dream to Patrick. It was as if he had stepped back in time a thousand years. The fragrance of incense and cooked lamb floated up to his window, carrying Patrick's thoughts back to his great-grandfather's journal.

As Thomas's first week in Bukhara drew to a close, so too had the noose of the Soviet secret police. Once again, contacts he had made warned him that newcomers to the city were inquiring about a Western traveler. In the minds of communist agents, an American traveling in Central Asia could mean only that he was a spy sent to orchestrate an uprising against Moscow's rule. After three hundred years of tug-of-war with the Muslims of Turkestan, the Soviets had finally managed to extinguish the region's fiery resistance to Russian domination. Now, the last thing they wanted on their hands was a new *jihad* – or holy war – against their occupation. This American – whoever he was – could not be allowed to make trouble. He needed to be quickly found and dealt with.

Regret tinged Thomas's writing as he bid goodbye to the city he had dreamed for years of visiting. After midnight, he and Misha set out again, this time to the east towards Samarkand, another fabled Silk Road town. Glancing back at the moonlit city, he wrote:

Bukhara the Noble has survived thousands of years. Perhaps at no other time since the Mongols has it been closer to death than now. But, despite the Soviets, something tells me that Bukhara will endure a thousand years more.

33 THE GOLDEN ROAD

> We travel not for trafficking alone.
> By hotter winds our fiery hearts are fanned.
> For lust of knowing what should not be known.
> We take the Golden Road to Samarkand.
> – James Elroy Flecker
> "The Golden Road to Samarkand"

The merchant sniffed indignantly at the offer by the well-dressed man, who was most likely a tourist from Europe or America. The customer turned helplessly to his blonde wife, who nodded and patted him encouragingly. Reassured, he upped his bid.

On the other side of the booth, the merchant draped a brightly colored, finely embroidered rug across his arms, the way a mother holds her newborn for a friend to admire. The merchant cast forlorn eyes at his merchandise – as if reluctant to let it go at any price – and then shook his head again. His skinny finger wagged from under the tapestry as he expounded on its magnificent, hand-crafted quality.

These rugs are the pride of our women, he seemed to say over the ruckus of the bazaar. They represent Samarkand's long history of culture and commerce, and harken back to the great Silk Road days. For such a treasure he could not accept less than, say, two hundred American dollars.

Watching from the restaurant terrace across the street, Ali provided a running commentary of the negotiation the way a sportscaster might describe a soccer match. He explained to

Patrick and his dad that prices of *suzani* embroideries had soared after the Soviet Union collapsed. Finally allowed to visit a land that had been off-limits to them for centuries, Western tourists had poured into Samarkand. They came for its fabled sights, to taste the exotic flavors of Central Asia, and to scour bazaars for collectibles. Sometimes they got a good price, as perhaps these tourists might.

At last, the buyer made an acceptable offer, and the rug and money exchanged hands. Delighted and looking quite proud, the couple strolled off hand-in-hand through the crowded market with their new purchase tucked under his arm. When Patrick's eyes returned to the dealer, another embroidery – seemingly identical to the one he had just sold – lay atop the table for the next tourist. Patrick smiled and took another bite of his pastry. At least he had gotten *his* money's worth, he thought.

The past two days in Samarkand had been fascinating but exhausting. The trio had worked up tremendous appetites walking around the congested streets in the stuffy heat. After taking the high-speed train from Bukhara, they had embarked on a whirlwind tour of the city, determined to see each of its three sections.

The first day they visited the western side of Samarkand. This was the newest part of the city, having been built by the Russians in the 1800s. It appeared clean, modern, and energetic. But, as Ali explained, the circumstances had been quite different just a few decades ago.

"Life under Soviet rule was very hard for the Uzbeks. They were forced to give up their traditional lifestyles and become cotton farmers. Soon after the Soviets arrived, most Uzbek artists and intellectuals were put to death during the infamous Great Purge. This was Stalin's effort to wipe out all political opposition. It was a terrifying time to live through… and many did not. No one knew who would be next to disappear, or why. At any time, the secret police might show up and drag someone off, never to be seen again."

230

On their second day in Samarkand, they poked around an area called "Afrosiab" – just north of the modern city. Built three thousand years ago, it had once been the capital of the Sogdian Empire. Like so many other cities in Central Asia, it was ruled by one power after the next before being annihilated by Genghis Khan. Now an archaeological preserve, Afrosiab sat quiet and empty.

Today – their third and final day in Samarkand – the trio enjoyed the cuisine, customs, and attractions of the city's south side. It was here during the 1300s – after being destroyed by the Mongols – that Samarkand was reborn as a great place of learning and sophistication. Ironically, its resurrection occurred under Tamerlane, a notoriously cruel Muslim ruler whose army massacred millions across Asia in an attempt to recreate the Mongol empire. Despite his viciousness, however, Tamerlane was a supporter of the arts and sciences. He commissioned extraordinary architectural works to be crafted by artisans who were brought to Samarkand from all over his empire and whose lives he had spared for this very purpose.

"Believe it or not," Ali said, dabbing his mouth with a napkin, "Tamerlane is a national hero in Uzbekistan these days. In the capital, his statue has replaced that of Karl Marx, the icon of Soviet socialism."

Patrick shook his head, wondering how anyone could celebrate a man known for leaving behind pyramids of decapitated heads in the cities he conquered. What did this choice of hero say about the Uzbeks, a people who seemed peaceful enough selling carpets to Western tourists?

Seeing his expression, Ali continued. "Uzbeks are good people. But like many inhabitants of Central Asia, their perspective is three-thousand years old. They have been both the vanquishers and the vanquished... just like us Turks!" He looked sad for a moment, and then thoughtful. "Actually, many Uzbeks

231

are descended from Turks – either that, or Persians. Uzbekistan did not even exist until Stalin created its borders."

"So why would modern Uzbeks worship a mass murderer – especially after seeing their families and friends murdered by Stalin?" Patrick pressed.

Ali shrugged and then replied coolly, "Tamerlane may have been a mass murderer, but he was *their* mass murderer. Under his rule, Samarkand was the center of a great empire. While this memory may be a distant one, it is far more appealing than the Uzbeks' most recent status... as serfs of Moscow. Pride is a powerful thing. When it is lost, a nation will go to any length to get it back."

"Hmm... A lot of wars have started that way," Dad interjected. Ali raised his glass in a silent toast. Patrick sat quietly, contemplating what he had heard.

Earlier that morning, the travelers visited the Shah-i-Zinda (SHAW-ē-Zinda) mausoleum – or "Tomb of the Living King." This was a place of holy pilgrimage for Muslims, for it was believed to contain the body of the prophet Mohammed's cousin. From there they'd walked to the Bibi-Khanym (BEE-bee CON-ĕm) mosque, an enormous and stunningly beautiful blue-domed structure. It was rumored to have been built by Tamerlane's Chinese wife as a surprise while he was away. Legend has it the builder fell in love with her and gave her a kiss. Upon returning, Tamerlane learned of this and had the man killed. From then on, all women in his empire were required to wear veils.

Now, as the sun burned high in the July sky, the trio finished their lunch and set out for the Registan (REJ-ē-stŏn). This was to be their last stop in Samarkand and one of the most impressive sights in all of Central Asia. The large plaza was surrounded by three imposing Islamic madrassas whose minarets rise above the medieval city. It had probably been a wall-to-wall bazaar in the days of Tamerlane. Now, it was equally busy, but with tourists clicking away on their cameras, reading maps and

232

brochures, pointing and gawking, or resting in the shade as they sipped bottled water.

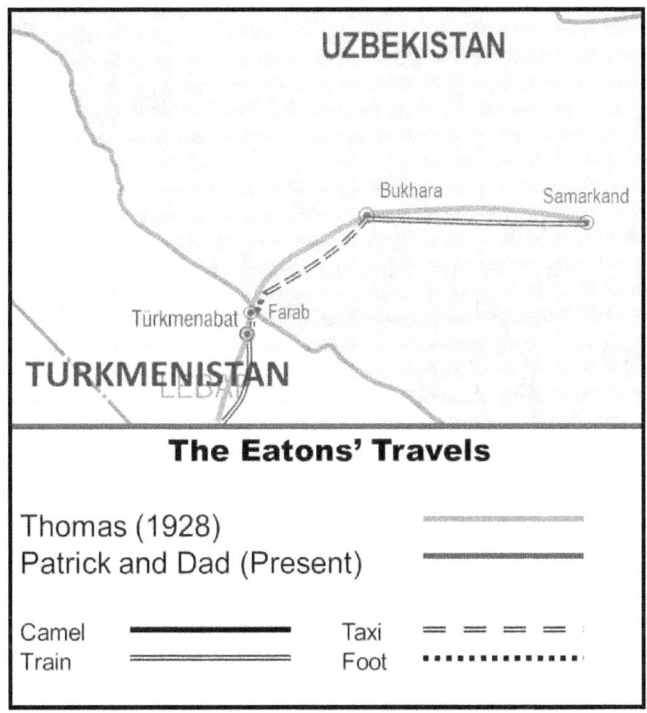

"What do Uzbeks think of all this?" Patrick asked, thinking of the mixture of ancient history and modern commercialism.

Ali looked puzzled. "Think of what? The tourists?" Patrick nodded. "They are welcome here. As I mentioned earlier, Uzbekistan was a very difficult place to live under the Soviets. Now it is beginning to thrive again…" He spread his arms out wide. "Once more, people from around the world take the Golden Road to Samarkand!"

They crossed the plaza, admiring the elaborate tile mosaics that adorned the tan walls of the madrassas. As Patrick strolled along the well-worn, beige stones of the square, he tried to imagine them filled with traders from the distant corners of the continent.

No wonder his great-grandfather had been determined to get here. Everywhere he looked, history seemed to gaze back.

Last night, while he lay in bed in the small room they had rented above a bustling street – the windows open to let in the warm night air – Patrick had thumbed through the final pages of Thomas's journal. He read slowly, savoring each word and sketch, not wanting the adventure to end. But he knew it did end in Kokand, though he could only speculate why. Thomas had written nothing beyond that final destination. The remainder of the journal had only yellowed sheets of blank paper.

In one of his final entries, Thomas described Samarkand's history and archaeology. As in Bukhara, Thomas found an abundance of ancient coins in Samarkand – of all types and from all places. Some bore images of Roman or Greek mythology, others of Persian kings. Still others had the familiar square holes of Chinese origin.

Along with the collection of coins, Thomas went into detail about a particularly fascinating find:

From a small pit that we dug near the ruins of a celestial observatory, I discovered the remains of an ancient board game. Out of the hole, I retrieved seven figurines, all made of ivory – a king, chariot, vizier, horse, elephant, and two soldiers – as well as a coin that dates these artifacts to the eighth century. Here in Samarkand, the game would have been known as Chatrang by the Persians, and later as Shatranj by the Arabs.

But the origin of this game of strategy is actually much older. It was developed in the Gupta Empire of India during the fifth century, where it was

234

known as *Chaturanga* – a Sanskrit word meaning "four divisions." From India, *Chaturanga* spread outward along the Silk Road, where it became popular among all classes – merchants, soldiers, and rulers. Over time and across thousands of miles, the game evolved. Today, the rules of *Chaturanga* are a bit of a mystery. Some versions involve two players, others four or more. Some require players to take turns, whereas others allow them to move simultaneously.

Equally mysterious is the ornately decorated board on which the game was played. Some think it also served as a type of hieroglyphic rulebook, or perhaps a scorecard. Alternatively, the board designs may have had nothing to do with the game. Instead, they may have been maps, business transactions or family histories.

In any case, descendants of this ancient game eventually spread beyond Asia to Europe, where it is known as chess. Many versions of *Chaturanga* endure today, though the rules and strategies still depend on where and by whom they are played.

Thomas's unearthing of the *Chaturanga* pieces seemed a fitting analogy for his situation in Samarkand. He had played a dangerous game against the Soviets – upon a vast and mysterious board, and with rules that were unwritten and constantly changing. As Patrick read, he realized his perception of the man whom he had grown to admire from stories at Grandpa's cabin was slowly changing through reading the words of his journal.

Was Thomas really an archaeologist, or something else? Aliases, disguises, invisible ciphers, camouflaged map-making equipment, a sudden and unexplained trip through the Caucasus, and then the Soviet secret police hot on his trail... To Patrick, this all sounded like part of the Great Game.

In any case, Central Asia was a wild and dangerous place for all outsiders, regardless of their motivations. The region pitted ancient cultures and traditions against a backdrop of unforgiving terrain and weather. Furthermore, as Roger had explained during their night aboard the Dagestan, Central Asia had long been a battleground of empires. It was a difficult place to conquer and even more difficult to rule. In 1928, when Thomas traveled through Central Asia, it was caught between two world wars and surrounded by the violent clashes of great powers, revolutionary ideas, tribal feuds, and religious extremism.

Equally alarming, Thomas's quest along the Silk Road was leading him back to China – a country from which he had barely escaped four years earlier and which in those days was torn by civil war. Thomas could have chosen to follow the Silk Road's southern route – from Mary to either Persia or Afghanistan – where he might have been safer. Instead, his eyes were fixed on the east, upon the Fergana Valley and the distant Tien Shan Mountains on China's border. His path was not leading him away from danger, but seemed to be taking him directly into it. *Go in and you won't come out*, his invisible cipher warned.

On the other hand, Patrick knew Thomas had not been one to shy away from peril. Certainly, he had left San Francisco and Shanghai when his friends' lives were in danger. But when it came to his own safety, the man did not deviate from his mission. Even when things got really dicey, he pushed on, determined to make his mark. Never quit, and never look back, he had said.

With his own time in Central Asia winding down, it occurred to Patrick that the advice of his great-grandfather had never been more relevant, nor had it weighed heavier on his mind.

He couldn't help but wonder if the words were meant for him, as well. Tomorrow, they would go to Kokand, and perhaps Patrick would find out.

34 CHECKMATE

"Fergana is a small country, abounding in grain and fruits.
It is girt round by mountains except on the west,
i.e. towards Khujand and Samarkand, and in winter an
enemy can enter only on that side."
— Babur (first Mughal ruler)
from *Baburnama* (Memoirs of Babur)

As they threaded their way east through the Kamchik Pass
– surveying the twisting descent into the Fergana Valley – Patrick
inhaled the cool mountain air gusting through the taxi window.
The old diesel engine growled and sputtered every mile of its two-
hour climb from the city of Tashkent, and Patrick felt his shoulders
relax as the taxi leveled out atop the notch in the Tien Shan range,
7500 feet above sea level. Outside, a leaden sky hung over the
barren, boulder-strewn peaks, tinting the countryside a cool
grayish-blue. It was a striking relief from the sweltering khaki-
colored desert they had left behind.

Dad sat next to him in the back seat eating the last bites of
his breakfast – *plov* wrapped in greasy paper bought from a
roadside stand a few miles back. Ali sat in front, chatting with the
driver – a plump, lively fellow who seemed intent on chain-
smoking throughout the entire trip. Drums and flutes kept a
snappy beat on the radio, punctuated only by the driver's howling
at Ali's jokes or bellowing one of his own.

Patrick tried again to rub the sleep from his eyes. The cold
air helped, but the sway of the taxi and the prayer beads swinging
from the rear view mirror stubbornly tempted him back to sleep.

He drank from his water bottle and held it out to his dad, who smiled and traded him a map in return. Patrick examined their route through Uzbekistan, highlighted in red ink. From Samarkand they had taken the bullet-train to Tashkent, the country's capital, where they had done a bit of sight-seeing and checked into flights to the United States. Early this morning they had set out to the east towards Kokand, where they planned to spend their final couple of days before returning to Tashkent and home.

"We'll cross the Syr Daria River again down in the valley." Ali's voice from the front beckoned Patrick to lean forward, straining to hear over the noisy taxi. "You remember crossing it on the train to Tashkent?" Patrick nodded. "The river feeds this entire valley. Makes for very good farmland, but also a lot of conflict."

"Why?" Patrick asked, almost shouting, and placed his hands on the headrest of Ali's seat.

"This valley is bordered by three countries – Uzbekistan, Tajikistan, and Kyrgyzstan. Each wants the farmland and water, but nobody is quite sure who owns it."

Dad leaned forward to join the huddle between the front seats.

"The Fergana Valley is one of the most heavily populated regions in all of Central Asia," Ali continued, turning slightly so they could hear better. "The Greeks were here once, and the Persians too. Even the Chinese. This area has long been valued for its cropland, but made world famous by its race horses!"

Patrick gazed through the windshield at the broad basin ringed by mountains. The black Syr Darya snaked back and forth along the valley floor below, sparkling here and there where it reflected the occasional ray of sunlight. The driver shouted something in Uzbek and motioned with one of his hands. Ali listened and then translated.

"He says he grew up here, back in the Soviet days. It was more peaceful then." The man barked something else and laughed.

Ali nodded his head and smiled, then added, "But that was because the Soviets did not allow any quarreling. They made all decisions about who got land and water!"

"Whose land was this before the Soviets?" Dad asked.

"Various peoples," Ali replied. "For many centuries, the valley was divided according to the customs and lifestyles of its different tribal groups. Some were settlers and farmers who needed land by the river. Others were nomads who came from higher up in the mountains. But when the Soviets took over, Stalin carved up the valley according to his own ideas. He drew new borders that cut across traditional lines – splitting families, tribes, and territories. Now that the Soviets are gone, the boundaries are being sorted out again."

The taxi driver shouted another stream of Uzbek, while Ali sat patiently listening. Then, he translated once more over the wind and radio.

"The Fergana valley is a holy place for Muslims. It's also a stronghold of resistance to outsiders. Muslim *Bashmachi* warriors fought the Soviets here in 1918. Today, the valley and surrounding hills are again home to Muslim militants. Some have suspected ties to international terrorists and jihadists. Others are simply local rebels fighting over farmland or water."

With this, Patrick looked wide-eyed at the valley ahead of them and then over at his dad. Seeing his expression, Dad smiled and reassured him. "No worries, Patrick. We have this Turk to keep us out of trouble!" He slapped Ali on his shoulder. "Besides, we'll just be here a couple of days, and then it's back to Tashkent. Best enjoy the ride before it's over."

Patrick nodded and settled back in his seat, his hair blowing in the cool air. Dad was right. Their trip, at least as they knew it, was indeed coming to an end.

They began the evening with a stroll through downtown Kokand. Walking along a tree-lined boulevard, Patrick was captivated by the sights and sounds of the old city. He marveled at the architecture, which reflected the contrasting influences of East and West. There were the colorful, tiled pillars, arches, carved doors, and domes built by the Muslim khans, offset by the rectangular, drab, flat-roofed brick structures erected under Moscow's rule.

The street was busy with cars that honked and weaved past the road-side carts of merchants selling the valley's fruits and grains. Both young and old were enjoying the cool evening air, browsing the market on their way home, playing chess under a lamp post, kicking a soccer ball, or chatting with friends and neighbors. Their golden skin, high cheekbones, and dark hair revealed their Mongol and Turkic heritage. Men wore traditional vests and slacks, while women and girls were clad in long veiled dresses of brilliant hues. Patrick was surprised to see the boys wearing Western-style clothes – jeans, t-shirts, and athletic shoes or sandals. But almost all of them donned the distinctive white *khalats* (skull-caps) signifying their Muslim faith.

"Kokand has a modern feel about it," Ali explained, as they walked along side-by-side. "But it is more traditional than other parts of the country. You see how the women cover their hair here?"

They stopped at a cart vendor selling bread, where Patrick bought a loaf with *som* – the local currency Ali had exchanged earlier for dollars on the black market. Apparently, this was an acceptable (even if technically illegal) way of doing business here in Uzbekistan. Patrick couldn't resist a quick glance around for the blue uniforms of the police.

Not long after, the trio settled into the street-side patio of a busy restaurant, where they enjoyed a front-row view of Uzbek nightlife unfolding in the street before them. Soft music from overhead speakers blended traditional Uzbek instruments with modern rock melodies. The overall effect was exotic – perfectly suited to their final hours in Central Asia.

"What do you think?" Dad asked Patrick, elbowing him playfully. "Not a bad way to end our trip, huh?"

Patrick nodded his head, while he wrapped the keffiyah more tightly around his neck to ward off the cool air.

"I'm glad we decided to stick around a while," Patrick replied. "And that we didn't go home after the whole gas deal thing in Mary."

"Me too," Ali echoed, smiling across the table. "I've been through Central Asia many times before, but this is without a doubt my most enjoyable trip. If only there was a way to prolong the fun..." He winked at Patrick.

"What was your favorite part of the trip?" Dad asked. Patrick thought for a moment. He wasn't sure. The journal was a nice surprise. The codes had been exciting, even if he'd never figured out what they meant. But his favorite part? He looked up at his Dad and smiled. He couldn't remember when they had ever spent this much time together.

"I don't know," Patrick said finally. "The pool in Baku was pretty awesome." He blushed at their laughter, and Dad rustled his hair playfully.

Patrick looked away for a moment, surprised by a dampness in his eyes. It was true – he really didn't want the trip to end. Once home, he'd be back to getting ready for school at Central High and Dad would be off to work again. Now was one of those moments he knew he would never get back – when he truly appreciated life in the moment. He wouldn't trade this for anything or anywhere in the world.

Patrick would have dwelled on the sentimentalism of the moment had a dark shape not caught the corner of his eye. Turning his head, he saw a long, black, familiar limousine pull along the curb and halt under the street lamp. Straightening, he elbowed Dad and pointed. Recognizing their carriage to Bukhara, the three travelers sat motionless, staring over the patio railing.

Springing from the front, nimble as ever, the driver with the pencil mustache circled around to the rear door, opened it, and waited at attention while his passenger climbed out. Patrick squinted at him and then tensed. What was it about the driver? Sure, he'd seemed familiar when Patrick handed him his luggage two weeks ago. But did Patrick know him from somewhere else? The thin face, tight skin, and shifty eyes...

Suddenly, Patrick remembered, and a cold sweat spread over his body. No doubt about it, the driver was the stranger Patrick had caught slipping out of their hotel room in Baku.

Dazed, Patrick barely stiffened when Uri Petrovsky emerged a second later – his silvery hair glinting under street lamps. He snapped his black pea coat around his neck, adjusting it as he said something to his chauffeur. When he turned to look at them his hands paused briefly at his collar, and for several seconds the world seemed to stop. Then Uri flashed his viper grin and headed directly for them.

However, that wasn't what Patrick recalled most from Kokand, or even from that summer. Rather, the memory that stuck with him for the rest of his life was the words Uri uttered upon reaching them. Placing both hands on the patio railing and leaning forward, he growled, "I am afraid you cannot go home tomorrow. There is a certain matter that must be addressed first." As his blue and green eyes fixed on Patrick, he added, "It seems you are in possession of a certain journal..."

PART IV: THE OPENING

35 A STEP FARTHER

"Wherever there is danger, there lurks opportunity;
wherever there is opportunity, there lurks danger.
The two are inseparable."
– Earl Nightingale
(American radio personality, writer, speaker)

The limousine sailed east along the highway past gently rolling hills, lush green fields, and the clear cold streams of the Fergana Valley. Higher up on the surrounding slopes, the dark silhouettes of grazing horses could be seen among groves of pine trees or below rocky bluffs. The morning sun evaporated the last remnants of heavy fog that had blanketed the valley at sunrise. Only the glistening dew on the grassy meadows remained. It was a fitting scene for Patrick to reflect on the dreamlike twist his life had taken during the past twelve hours.

Uri's appearance at dinner the previous evening had been surprising. But the story he told the travelers was downright incredible. Patrick was alarmed by the big man's menacing reference to the journal, and even Dad tensed at the implication that they would be unable to leave Central Asia. What could the Russian diplomat have in store for them? The travelers had exchanged uneasy glances as Uri circled the patio railing to join their table.

"What's all this about?" Dad had asked.

"Unfinished business," Uri replied coolly, settling into a chair across from them, next to Ali, and lacing his hands together

244

on his belly. "I understand you've wrapped up your travels and plan to leave for home."

"We've made it to Kokand, yes. It's been a great trip, but this is the end of the line. Now it's back to the good old USA for us."

Uri made a funny sound deep in his throat. He sprawled out, one leg cocked beneath his chair, and his small hands in his lap. Patrick marveled again at the man's uncanny ability to appear at once relaxed and coiled to strike. He caught Uri eyeing him and sat up warily.

"I'd like you to consider another option," Uri said. "If you are willing to hear me out, I want to tell you a story... one that I hope will convince you to go a step farther in your journey."

"Well, we're all here," replied Dad, smiling uneasily and holding out his hands. "Your captive audience, once more!"

Uri flashed a devious grin. "Indeed." He looked from one Eaton to the other, measuring his next move.

"Three-quarters of a century ago, your great-grandfather..." His eyes shifted to Patrick. "...came to Central Asia to retrace the Silk Road. Setting out from Turkey, he was accompanied by a Turk guide – a gallant soldier and loyal friend."

Uri subtly bowed his head in Ali's direction.

"Together, they traveled to Armenia and Azerbaijan, then stole across the Caspian Sea. Of course, in those days Soviet Turkestan was off-limits to Westerners. But Thomas Eaton was never one to be told what he could not do. He decided to go forward anyway... in disguise. Together, the two travelers mapped ancient cities, uncovered artifacts, and searched for coins of long-dead civilizations. From Krasnovodsk to Merv, and Bukhara to Samarkand, Thomas and his guide, Misha, explored the past, all the while rushing to stay ahead of the Soviet authorities on their trail. You already know this from the journal, yes?"

Patrick gave his dad a questioning look, and then nodded.

245

"But of course, the journal ends here in Kokand... Thomas never had the chance to finish writing it."

Uri paused again, blowing on his tea. Patrick sat perfectly still, spellbound at hearing his great-grandfather's story retold by a Russian secret agent. Dad looked tense, sitting forward with his fingers intertwined, his knuckles white.

"In Samarkand, Stalin's hounds were closing in on them," Uri continued. "Realizing this, Thomas and Misha attempted a bold deception. Their backs against the wall, Thomas decided to impersonate a Soviet secret police agent, and Misha posed as his prisoner. Together they set off for the China border, with Thomas pretending to escort his 'captive' to a prison camp in Siberia. The two almost pulled it off... but not quite."

Uri lifted his arm to point over Patrick's shoulder. "Your great-grandfather and his Turkish friend were arrested just down the street from where we now sit. They were thrown in jail for three days, and Thomas's journal and equipment were confiscated. After being harshly interrogated, the two were declared spies – secret agents who had been sent to gather information and agitate the local Muslims against Soviet rule. They were to be shot the next morning."

The table fell quiet for what seemed like a full minute. Now Patrick understood why nothing more was written in the journal after Kokand. Yet, he was sure his great-grandfather had survived and returned to America. What had happened?

"He had help from a friend," Uri stated, seeing the puzzled look on Patrick's face. "A man he had met in the city of Mary a couple of months earlier... a rival archaeologist... a Russian. Mary was not so big then, and it is of little surprise that two archaeologists working there would have met. One encounter led to another, and their friendship grew. Somehow, their intellectual interests outweighed political allegiances. Of course, a good Soviet should have reported someone like your great-grandfather to the authorities. But Thomas and this Russian shared something

246

much stronger than 'civic duty.' Their friendship was born of mutual respect, a love of things past and the freedom to inquire about them – bonds that transcend time and political borders. So it was that, when faced with the impending execution of his friends and colleagues, the Russian arranged a daring jailbreak in the dead of night. On camels, the three men – an American, a Turk, and a Russian – made off for China."

Patrick was stunned. He recalled Thomas's mention of a "fellow outsider" in his journal entry at Mary. This must have been the Russian.

"But how can you know this?" Patrick blurted out.

Uri sighed and, once more, Patrick perceived a faint softening in the Russian's face. His menacing grin was gone, and a gentle smile crinkled his ruddy cheeks. The fierce glow had subsided from his blue and green eyes. In its place, Patrick sensed compassion and perhaps even kindness. Uri cleared his throat solemnly.

"The Russian's name was Dmitri Petrovsky. He was my father."

Patrick was unsure what to say. He sat dazed, trying to fit the pieces together in his mind. Uri carried on, filling the void.

"The three friends made their way east across the Torugart Pass and into Chinese Turkestan, now known as Xinjiang [pronounced *Shin Jung*]. But they were not only running from a Soviet firing squad... There was another reason they went to China. As it turns out, the three of them had pieced together a most interesting story about the Silk Road. In Merv, they discovered evidence of a treasure-laden Mongol caravan that had set out for Kublai Khan's capital in Beijing. However, this caravan never completed its mission and it vanished without a trace in the Taklamakan."

"Go in and you won't come out," Ali added in quiet awe.

Patrick stared at him. He wasn't sure he had heard him correctly.

247

"What did you say?"

Ali gazed back. "Taklamakan is an old Turkic word. It means, 'Go in and you won't come out.' The desert is one of the deadliest in the world."

Patrick took a deep breath and slumped back in his chair. *Go in and you won't come out.* The code from his great-grandfather's journal.

"Yotkan..." Patrick whispered to himself, remembering the other code.

Uri looked up, his eyes narrowing. "Yotkan? Is that what you said? Yes, indeed. Yotkan was a Silk Road oasis located on the southern route around the Taklamakan. It was a stopover for traders headed to China. It is in the vicinity of where this Mongol caravan disappeared. What do you know of it?"

Patrick shook his head, uncertain how to reply. Uri already knew about the journal, but could he really be aware of the codes, too? Was he merely toying with Patrick – playing dumb to draw out whatever additional information he could? Patrick needed time to think. He glanced over at the limousine from which the chauffeur was undoubtedly watching them through its tinted windows.

"Did you think I wouldn't recognize your driver?" he asked. "He was in our hotel room in Baku."

Patrick hoped his words would shake Uri, but the Russian only smiled. "Believe it or not, Patrick, he was there for your protection. Mr. Neilson hired a scoundrel for a translator, as you now know. Perhaps he should have consulted us Russians first..." He snorted his amusement. "We keep long records on folks like Ahmed. When I found out he was your interpreter, I put my man on him." He nodded towards the limousine to indicate his driver.

"You suspected Ahmed?" Dad asked, shifting his weight. "How come? And why didn't you say anything?"

Uri held his palms out innocently. "I knew he was rotten, but what could I do? Mr. Neilson and I are not exactly friends, as you may have guessed already, so I doubt he would have heeded my warning. Besides, I didn't want to alert Ahmed of my suspicions…I thought it safer to keep my eye on him. Though he made a show of being an unfortunate refugee, he is really just a mercenary – a thief for hire. In Baku he was probably working for some treasure-hunting outfit, or perhaps the Chinese."

"The Chinese?" Patrick asked, startled.

"Possibly," Uri replied, his eyes cold again. "It's conceivable they know the journal has returned to Asia. If so, I guarantee you they have not forgotten Thomas Eaton… *gweilo* that he was. The Chinese do not have fond memories of the *foreign devils* that plundered their cultural treasures. If the Chinese know about the journal, they will want it."

Patrick shook his head, trying to make sense of it all.

"So Ahmed simply wanted to steal the journal? He never meant to hurt Patrick?" Dad asked.

Uri shrugged. "In all likelihood, Ahmed would have preferred lifting the journal from your hotel room. That would have been much easier and less risky than ambushing an American outside a diplomatic dinner. But you never let the journal out of your sight, Patrick… By the time you reached Turkmenbashi, Ahmed evidently felt he had no other choice but to take it by force. Perhaps his employers were pushing him for results…"

"So where is he now?" Dad asked gravely.

Uri took a deep breath and looked out at the busy street. "I wish I could say. We lost him in Turkmenbashi. Perhaps he returned to the sanctuary of the Caucasus Mountains… or maybe he is here in the Tien Shan. One thing about rats like Ahmed – they are very good at keeping to the shadows and they only reveal themselves when they have the advantage."

The table was quiet as they contemplated Uri's words.

In the days following his violent encounter with Ahmed, Patrick had begun to suspect a connection between his former interpreter and the journal. Its invisible codes appeared to be evidence that the journal hid important information, which Thomas obviously had feared falling into the wrong hands. However, in the weeks since Roger's lecture aboard the Dagestan, Patrick's imagination had entertained other possibilities, as well. For instance, what if the codes were somehow related to the Great Game? Perhaps Thomas really had been one of the secret agents described by Roger – the brave men disguised as geographers or archaeologists who mapped the mysterious center of the board. Maybe his invisible messages referred to Soviet troop movements, invasion routes, or the names of contacts...

But now, Uri's revelation suggested another exciting possibility – that the codes were clues to buried treasure! Patrick racked his mind for some detail from one of Grandpa's stories at the cabin – anything that might help answer the question that grew with each step he took along the Silk Road. Who was his great-grandfather, really? An archaeologist or spy – or both?

Patrick tapped his finger on the table, debating whether to put the question straight to Uri. If anyone knew the answer, Uri would. According to Roger, the Russian had worked in Soviet intelligence in the "old days." If a file existed on Thomas – perhaps tucked away in the dusty archives of some basement in Moscow – Uri might know of it and possibly have access to it. What is more, the Russian's own father had saved Thomas's life. So if Dmitri had told his son of the treasure, perhaps he had also told him of Thomas's real purpose for being in Central Asia.

Patrick decided he had little to lose from asking. He rolled the dice.

"Was my great-grandfather a spy?"

An exotic melody sifted down from the overhead speakers, dancing lightly over the table, and creating a perfectly mysterious ambiance. All eyes turned to Uri. The Russian looked at Patrick for some time. The compassion was back in his eyes again.

"Thomas... a spy? No." He shook his head slowly. "A reporter, an adventurer, and a stubborn archaeologist... definitely.

But not a spy." Then, almost as an afterthought, he added casually, "Your grandfather, on the other hand…"

For several seconds, Patrick didn't register what he had just heard. But as he turned the words over in his head, their significance gradually came into focus. Then, he began to feel light-headed. The music was suddenly gone from the restaurant speakers, and the pedestrians and cars passed silently in the street. Later on, he would recall Dad sitting openmouthed, slowly shaking his head, equally stunned by the Russian's insinuation. All the while, Ali had sat motionless across from them, chin in one hand, his dark eyes moving back and forth between Patrick and his Dad. The Turk looked amused by the impact of this unexpected news.

"Yes." Uri drew the word out slowly. "Your grandfather was a spy …" He glanced from Patrick to Dad. "After World War Two, the United States formed its famous intelligence agency – the CIA. Your grandfather became one of its first Cold War agents. He spent most of his career playing a secret chess match against the Soviet Union. That's when I met him."

"You knew Grandpa?" Patrick asked. How many more surprises did this Russian have in store for them?

"I did… and, in fact, I still do." He grinned at their astonishment. "Your grandfather and I had heard of each other from our fathers. Eventually we met and became friends, too. Of course, this was all done in secrecy. During the Cold War, friendship between a Soviet and American spy was a dangerous gamble. Back then, there were only two teams – the United States and the Soviet Union – and you either played for one side or the other. Right and wrong all depended on which flag you waved. Either way, the penalty for losing was severe."

He reached for his tea again, measuring his audience over the rim of his cup.

"As our friendship grew, your grandfather and I learned a lot from each other. We began to see beyond simplistic political allegiances and borders, just as our fathers had. Your grandfather discovered that I didn't embody the immoral, ruthless, brainwashed communist that your government made all Russians out to be. And he wasn't exactly the greedy, slave-driving, imperialist that Moscow claimed all Americans were. Rather, we came to realize that both of us were simply pawns caught up in a much larger game – a game in which truth and morality was often forgotten or pushed aside in an all-encompassing scramble for world supremacy."

Uri put his hands flat on the table in front of him, as if he were laying his cards down for the other players to see.

"Your grandfather and I stayed in touch throughout the Cold War. When the Soviet Union collapsed in the early 1990s, everything changed... After digging around, I located Thomas's journal in Moscow – along with a couple of other items – and mailed them to back your grandfather. That's how he ended up with the journal and then could pass it on to you. We still talk today... the American, the Russian... and the Turk.

Uri looked over at Ali, smiled, and put his hand on the Turk's shoulder. "Ali, too, seeks the treasure found by his father, Misha."

"You? What?" Patrick stammered, his eyes wide again. At last, he managed only, "The Mongol caravan?"

Ali nodded and grinned. "Our fathers discovered it buried under sand. It had been preserved for centuries by the hot, dry air of the desert and contains an immense cache of gold and silver. But circumstances forced them to leave it there and, after all their efforts, they departed Central Asia empty-handed. For years, your grandfather, Uri, and I made plans to find it... all of them foiled by political conditions or bad luck. We planned to reunite one day... to finish the work of our fathers. But when your grandfather called to tell us of his heart attack, we thought we had waited too long. Then he told us his son and grandson were on their way to Asia... he said you might take his place."

"But why the secrecy?" Dad pleaded. "Why not just tell us from the start?"

"Your father made us promise to keep quiet," Uri replied to Dad. "He wanted you to have your own adventure, to choose your own path. Ali and I only intervened when Ahmed made his attempt on Patrick. The safety of the Eaton boy trumped all other considerations." His eyes radiated a warmth that Patrick knew well. He had seen it many times in Grandpa's face.

"But what about everything you said in the limo? About Russia and the United States, and the Great Game?" Patrick asked.

"All correct," Uri replied matter-of-factly. "At least from the perspective of Moscow... You Americans have your own views, I know. But no matter. Politics is irrelevant where my friendship with the Eatons is concerned.

"And Bukov?"

Uri rubbed his hands together. "Bukov is a patriot who lives for Mother Russia. With men like Bukov, it's best they hear what they want to hear."

"I'll be darned," Dad whispered, shaking his head. "So, what are you proposing we do now? You said something about continuing our journey?"

"Ah!" Uri smiled, leaning forward and folding his hands on the table. The blue and green eyes glowed once more. "You have come this far in the footsteps of your ancestor. Now we are asking you to go a little farther... with Ali and me... to the Taklamakan Desert. Let us find this buried Mongol caravan and finish the work of our forefathers."

Over the next half-hour, Uri set about persuading Patrick and his dad. To each of their "yeah buts" and "what ifs," Uri had a convincing reply. It seemed he had the expedition planned to perfection, and at last the table fell quiet while they contemplated his words. Uri used this opening to deliver his coup de grace.

"You grew up listening to your grandfather's stories of Thomas," the Russian said quietly, looking at Patrick. "Perhaps you wondered if you could fill his shoes, or whether you would ever have the opportunity. Fortune placed you here in Central Asia – in his footsteps, as it were. But I don't think you are here to fill his shoes. You are not your great-grandfather... nor are you your grandfather... or your father. Yes, you are an Eaton, but your life is your own game, Patrick, to play however you choose. The next move belongs to you."

The next morning, Patrick watched the Fergana valley come to life outside the limousine window. Across from him, Uri and Ali debated various points about the history of Turkestan, continuing a friendly argument they'd begun just after leaving Kokand – or perhaps many years earlier. Dad stared at a map in his lap, taking notes in his field book, his hat pushed up on his head to reveal his suntanned face.

Patrick smiled to himself. *My life is my own game*, he thought contentedly. And the next move is . . . to China.

36 PUSH PULL

"The natural liberty of man is to be free from any superior power
on Earth, and not to be under the will or legislative authority of
man, but only to have the law of nature for his rule."
– Samuel Adams
(One of America's Founding Fathers)

In the bright sunshine of mid-morning, the limousine swept
through Andijon at the very eastern edge of Uzbekistan. Andijon
was one of the oldest cities in the Fergana Valley and had been yet
another important stop along the Silk Road. According to Ali, it
also happened to be the birthplace of Babur – the first ruler of
India's Mughal Empire. (Mughal is the Muslim word for Mongol.)

But as they rolled through its busy streets, Ali described a
more recent and tragic chapter in the city's history. In 2005, local
authorities had arrested several residents for being Islamic
extremists. They were said to be separatists who were trying to
split Andijon away from the rest of Uzbekistan. A trial was held
and thousands of civilians gathered in protest. One thing led to
another, and police opened fire on the protestors. Hundreds were
killed in the shooting.

"Very sad," said Ali, shaking his head. "Unfortunately, it
is an episode far too common in Central Asia's history. Political
dissent is dealt with harshly here."

"But they were religious fundamentalists, no?" Uri
countered from the seat next to him, one eyebrow raised.

"I'm not so sure, Uri..." Ali replied. "*Perhaps* a few. But
it is also possible the government was simply getting rid of

255

political competition. The citizens on trial were greatly respected leaders in their community. In fact, their popularity may have been viewed as a threat to other politicians. There are rumors that these people were simply businessman who refused to pay the exorbitant taxes and bribes demanded by the local authorities, and so they were made an example of what happens when you oppose the government."

Uri lifted a finger sternly as he looked at Patrick, "To rule in Central Asia, you must be strong and unwavering. Everywhere, forces of resistance simmer below the surface. Religious fundamentalism, tribalism, nationalism… they are always at work here. If a ruler shows weakness or indecision – even for a moment – these forces will rise and overwhelm him. Genghis Khan and Tamerlane knew this, and so did the Soviets. Uzbekistan's current government surely knows this, too."

Patrick shook his head. "But why shouldn't the people of Andijon have the right to live as they choose? Who cares if they decide to split away and form their own country? Didn't you say that the borders of Central Asia are artificial anyway – that Stalin drew them intentionally to divide ethnic and religious groups?"

Uri's face relaxed as he elbowed Ali. "This one's an Eaton, all right." He laughed softly. "Well, you may be right … But I assure you that Uzbekistan's government will not give up control of this region without a fight. Think about it… If Andijon secedes, what next? The entire Fergana Valley? Will the seeds of separatism spread through the region and break apart other countries, too?" He shook his head with a rueful smile. "It won't be allowed to happen."

To this, Ali added, "Rest assured, Patrick, nothing – absolutely *nothing* – terrifies government like talk of secession."

Patrick looked out the window and, half to himself, replied, "That doesn't make it right. A people should be free to live how they choose…"

256

"Your heart is good, Patrick," replied Ali. "But Uri's point is valid. In Central Asia, it is strength that matters and it has always been that way. Self-rule is rare. And liberty? Virtually unheard of. Five thousand years of history do not suggest these people will get a Samuel Adams anytime soon." He then shrugged, as if the point he made were self-evident.

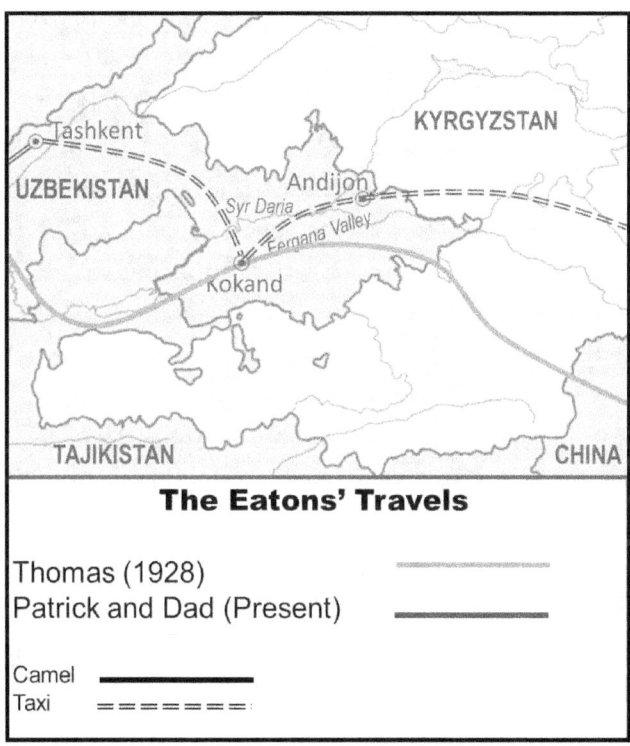

From the lush green meadows surrounding Andijon, the limousine crossed into the country of Kyrgyzstan and began its long climb to the dark peaks of the Tien Shan – or "Mountains of Heaven." Ali took advantage of the change of scenery to talk about something else.

"As you probably know from your studies, Patrick, China has long been isolated from the West by natural barriers." He pointed out the window at the barren landscape of rock and snow which stretched as far as the eye could see. "But as daunting as it was to cross these mountains a thousand years ago, the journey into China can be almost as difficult today."

"What do you mean?" Patrick asked.

"China's border police," Uri grunted in reply. "The Torugart Pass is often closed for weather. But even when it's open, you never know for sure whether you will get across. Security up there is strict... and the mood of the guards unpredictable. Fortunately, yours truly has a VIP pass." He tapped the breast pocket of his suit jacket and flashed Patrick a grin. Then, he added solemnly, "When we enter China, we may be accompanied by an official escort. If so, let me do the talking..."

With each mile the road became rougher and the ride more slow and arduous. Every so often the limousine struck a pothole, jarring its passengers and tossing their gear about. But as they neared the border checkpoint, traffic slowed to a crawl, giving Uri's driver more time to dodge the craters in the asphalt. In front of them, semi-trucks groaned up the steep incline, loaded with various goods headed to China. Finally, the line of traffic ground to a halt.

Spotting the approaching limousine, a Kyrgyz guard smiled and motioned them to go around. After passing a quarter-mile of stopped trucks, they pulled alongside a crumbling, single-story concrete building near the top of the pass. Several Kyrgyz guards in heavy coats loitered outside, chatting or shouting jokes to truck drivers they recognized as they passed by. The limousine passengers got out and entered the building to have their paperwork inspected.

Patrick marveled at Uri's diplomatic talent for moving things along. His friendliness with the guards was subtly balanced with the aura of authority. While they laughed and kidded with him, it was obvious the guards were anxious to get this mysterious Russian out of their hair and across the border. Much better for him to be China's problem...

Thirty minutes later they piled back into the limo, wheeled through the opening in the fence, and entered a three-mile stretch of no-man's land between the two countries. As they arrived at the top of the pass and entered the check-point at the border of the People's Republic of China, Patrick detected a sharp change in attitude. Gone were the pleasant smiles of the Kyrgyz guards. Staring at them were stone-faced sentries, one of whom waved them into a sort of holding pen where vehicles were being checked. Obeying the order, Uri's driver shut off the engine, and the passengers sat quietly for several seconds. Then came a knock at the window.

The Chinese guard was far younger than Patrick would have expected. When he jammed his pimpled face through the limo window, giving the interior a callous going-over, it was obvious he couldn't be more than twenty years old. But from the way he spoke, it was clear he had grown accustomed to his authority.

Uri greeted him in Russian, and the guard raised his eyebrows warily. To each question barked by the guard, Uri gave an equally terse answer. Gone was the friendliness Uri had shown on the Kyrgyz side. Here, negotiations were clearly a pushing match won by the more brazen. At last the guard nodded and retreated across the gravel lot to his outpost building.

"I think that went well," Uri said, rolling the window up. "He wanted seven hundred dollars to let us through. I talked him down to three. Typically, tourists cannot drive their own cars across, but an exception has been made. As for our political escort..." He nodded out the window at a fat little man waddling towards them through the mud. "It seems he will be accompanying us to the immigration office."

The Chinese official bade them a polite nod as he settled his hefty frame into the seat next to Uri. He looked to be in his fifties or so, but it was hard to say for sure. The crinkled corners of his eyes hinted at middle age, but his neatly combed jet-black

259

hair had none of the silver that peppered Dad's or that dominated the regal manes of Uri or Ali. A pair of gold wire-rimmed glasses framed inscrutable brown eyes. Soft hands and a rotund figure – which was squeezed into a modest gray suit – suggested he was used to a life far more comfortable than guard duty atop the Torugart Pass. Glancing over at Uri, Patrick saw this appraisal mirrored in the Russian's blue and green eyes. *Be careful*, they seemed to signal him.

As the limousine pulled back onto the highway, Uri and the official conversed for several minutes in Russian. Patrick admired the calm and polished way that Uri managed diplomatic issues. But the Chinese official seemed to be a worthy adversary. Finally, Uri spoke in English.

"This is Chen Li. He'll be escorting us for the next hour. Mr. Chen, this is Ali Kaptan, Dan Eaton, and his son, Patrick."

Li bowed his head slightly. "Your first time to China?"

Patrick nodded, while Dad and Ali explained that they'd visited years ago. Li folded his hands in his lap and began a monotone lecture. Patrick was astonished at how well he spoke English.

"Western China – or Xinjiang [pronounced *Shin Jung*] – has changed a great deal in recent years. It used to be something of a backwater, as you may recall from your previous visits. But the government has a great plan for developing this region, and Xinjiang is growing quickly as a result. New highways, railways, and energy pipelines are being built to integrate this region with our cities in the east. It is a very exciting time for China."

The visitors nodded politely, but no one spoke. Uri's words of caution were still fresh in their minds. Li took their silence as encouragement to continue.

"And the government's plan is helping the people of this region, too. Take Kashgar, for example. This city is the not only Xinjiang's economic center, but its cultural heart, as well. It is home to thousands of artisans who practice the trades and crafts of their forefathers. But they are poor. In fact, many of them live in the same buildings as their ancestors did. These structures are hundreds of years old and in danger of collapsing. Therefore, the government is replacing them with brand new apartments, where they will be safe and happy."

"Tell us how that is going," Uri interjected. "Are the people taking it well?"

"Yes, of course," Li replied. "The people are very grateful to the government and they are enjoying the benefits of a modern city."

"What about the violence here?" Uri pressed. "We have heard reports of terror attacks…"

"Ah, well, yes," Li answered quietly. "Like all great powers, China has its challenges, too." He gazed out the limousine window. "Just like Russia, America, and Turkey – China faces the rising threat of terrorism. The region of Xinjiang is mostly Muslim and some of its inhabitants have ties to Islamic extremist groups in the neighboring countries of Kyrgyzstan, Afghanistan, and Pakistan. Several terror attacks have been carried out here in China, but our government is getting better at security. We will not let the terrorists win."

"What do they want?" asked Uri, and then winked at Patrick as if to say, *This one's for you.*

"The terrorists? To create fear."

"But why? What is their goal?"

Li studied him with a look of amusement. Patrick glanced back and forth between them. He sensed something beneath the surface of words – a subtle tension that exists between old adversaries. He'd had a similar feeling when listening to Uri and Roger Neilson chat in Turkmenbashi.

"They are separatists, Mr. Petrovsky. They want to form their own state."

There was that word again – *separatism*. Uri had explained that it meant *secession* – breaking away from one country and government to form another. First, separatists in Andijon. Now, in Xinjiang, too? It seemed all of Central Asia was torn between empire and independence. Maybe it had always been this way – despotic rulers pushing people together, while religion, ethnicity, and tradition pulled them apart again.

"They don't want to be part of China?"

"No. They want to establish their own state – East Turkestan." Li studied Uri for another few seconds. Then he added, "They have tried this in the past, when they had help from other countries... as you surely know. Countries that would prefer to see China bottled up in the east."

Li paused again, allowing his words to linger. Uri merely shrugged, his lips drawn in a thin smile. The silence continued until it became awkward, and Patrick shifted uneasily in his seat. Li finally smiled back, and then continued speaking to his other guests.

"You see, the natives of Xinjiang are not really Chinese—" He quickly corrected himself. "That is, they are not *Han* Chinese. They are a Turkic people – more closely related to the people of Uzbekistan or Kyrgyzstan. They are known as the Uyghur [WEE-gur]. Ten million of them live here in western China." He rubbed his hands together methodically, weighing his next words carefully.

"The region of Xinjiang has a complex history. Thousands of years ago it belonged to the Han Chinese. Since then, it has been invaded many times, including by Turkic peoples. In 1949, the region officially became part of the People's Republic of China. Of course, not everyone has come to terms with this... But make no mistake, Xinjiang is part of China."

He glanced at Uri before retrieving a file from his briefcase. He opened it and silently inspected the contents. Without looking up, he abruptly began reading a long list of questions. What was their reason for visiting China? How did they know each other? How long would they be there? Where did they plan to travel?

Uri answered most of the questions – rather curtly, Patrick thought – while Dad and Ali nodded along in agreement. They would stay for a couple of weeks to visit the Silk Road, to take in the scenery and culture, and maybe to visit the markets for souvenirs. They planned to travel to Kashgar, Yarkand, and Khotan.

To each of their answers, Li smiled or clicked his tongue agreeably, almost apologetically, as if the entire proceeding were merely a formality. At last, apparently satisfied, he closed the file and looked out the window. Patrick gently let out his breath, relieved the interrogation was over. Then, Li started to speak again.

"China is an ancient place," he said softly, his head still turned to the window. "Our people have known much tragedy, yet we are proud of our history. We try to protect it when we can, but sometimes we must give up a little history for the sake of progress... Such is the case in the region of Xinjiang. These decisions are never easy, of course. But they are *Chinese* decisions, no?" He turned to his audience. "China should decide what stays and what goes in China. Not other people – not foreigners."

His face revealed no emotion as he continued.

"Yet, not so long ago, spies and treasure-hunters from Europe and Russia – even America – came to western China. They filled our people's heads with false ideas about ethnicity and independence. Some stole our cultural treasures, taking them home to sell or display in their museums. Of course, we do not tolerate this sort of crime now. We are a patient people and someday we will get back what was taken from us."

Patrick sat perfectly still. He felt a trickle of sweat down his back. The Chinese eyes settled on Ali for a moment, then moved to his dad, and finally to Patrick, where they rested.

263

"Eaton," Li pondered. "That is a common American name, yes?" He peered at Patrick over the top of his glasses. "There was a treasure-hunter by that name who visited China many years ago. Thomas Eaton. Any relation to him?"

"He was my great-grandfather," Patrick blurted, his chin up and a touch of pride in his voice.

"Hmm. I see." Li continued to stare at him. "Well, that was many years ago. *You* are not here to steal artifacts, I presume?" Li let out a strange giggle. Patrick shook his head no, but Li had already moved on. "I have approved your visit to Kashgar. But first, a bit more paperwork, I'm afraid."

He inclined his head towards the window. Patrick turned to see they were approaching an immigration station. As the limousine slowed, he reached for his backpack. Hauling it onto his lap, he felt Li's eyes on him again, and Uri's words echoed in his head. *The Chinese have not forgotten Thomas Eaton...* Instinctively, Patrick pressed the bag close to him. He would be glad to be rid of Li and his piercing questions.

37 CROSSROADS

"Kashgar is a region lying between north-east and east,
and constituted a kingdom in former days, but now it is
subject to the Great Khan. The people worship Mohammed.
There are a good number of towns and villages,
but the greatest and finest is Kashgar itself."
– Marco Polo, *The Travels of Marco Polo*

The pale orange sun continued its slow slide across the hazy sky. Within the hour it would be gone behind the jagged black peaks in the west, and the weary travelers would be safe and sound in Kashgar.

Their day had begun two countries away on the far side of the Tien Shan. After a brief stop at the Chinese immigration station, the limousine descended eight thousand feet in just four hours, popping Patrick's ears and turning his face the color of jade. After winding through dark canyons and desert arroyos, the highway flattened out along the sun-baked Tarim Basin. They were on the final stretch of road to Kashgar. Any moment now they would be able to make out the city's lights on the horizon.

Not quite the grueling journeys his great-grandfather had undertaken to reach Kashgar, Patrick had to admit. It was incredible to think that Thomas had made this trip on camelback – not once, but twice. Still, today's trip hadn't been easy. Ever since the sun rose in Andijon, the group of travelers had spent hours waiting to have passports stamped and bags searched, fended off interrogations by unfriendly border guards, and careened along slender passes while dodging overloaded semi-trucks. Even with air-conditioning and bottled water, the trip was not exactly a run-of-the-mill Saturday drive to Grandpa's cabin on the lake.

Fortunately, Patrick could ask for no better entertainment along the way. A former Russian spy and Turkish history teacher will guarantee some pretty interesting stories, especially when the tales involve espionage and buried treasure.

"I was in Western China several times during the Cold War," Uri explained as the limousine twisted through the mountain passes. "At first officially, and later... uh, *unofficially*. Early in my career, Moscow and Beijing were friends, and I served here as an aide to the Russian envoy. However, in the late-1960s the situation changed, along with my mission. I suppose this bit of history is not lost on Chen Li – who, by the way, didn't strike me as any ordinary border guard."

"It did seem like you two knew each other," Patrick replied.

Uri chuckled softly. "I'm sure he knows *of* me... The Chinese government undoubtedly has a file on me. It may be he's seen it. In all likelihood, Li is a member of China's security services. But it doesn't really matter – I'm just a gray-haired old Russian diplomat now... nearly retired... I'm only here in China to do a little sight-seeing." At this, his blue and green eyes seemed to twinkle with mischief.

"It seemed as if he was expecting us..." Dad added tensely. "He knew about Thomas, anyway."

Uri blew through his lips slowly. "Yes, the Chinese have their ways of finding out about these things. It's impossible to say how much they really know – or how long they've known it. Perhaps they hired Ahmed... or perhaps not." He rubbed his hands together. "It's possible that Thomas's name simply popped up during a routine computer search."

"Possible... but not *likely*?" Dad pressed. Uri answered with a weak smile.

"So... do we need to be worried?" Patrick asked. "Are we going to see him again?"

Uri shrugged. "Hopefully not. I am a Russian diplomat and you are American citizens. That should be enough to protect us." He peered at Ali through narrow lids. "As for this Turk... I'm afraid your goose is cooked, my friend." Everyone laughed at this.

"So why was my father here?" Dad continued.

Uri rubbed his hands together. "It was the 1960s – during the Cold War. As a CIA officer, your dad's orders were to try to play the Soviets and Chinese against each other, recruit local agents, and keep tabs on everyone in between. Of course, he and I already knew of each other from the stories of our fathers, so it wasn't long before we met and became friends – *off the record*, of course. We talked a lot about the Mongol treasure but couldn't find a proper excuse to go looking for it." Uri looked over at Ali. "Then, things changed."

Uri went on to explain how the relationship between the Soviet Union and China worsened during the 1960s. The two governments argued over which should be the international leader of communism. Then, in 1967, Moscow officially announced its support for the East Turkestan separatists. From then on, Uri's mission was to support the local struggle against Chinese rule. He did this by providing the Uyghur people with money and supplies, a role that required him to operate covertly – as a spy.

"So there we were..." Uri continued, looking at Dad. "Your father and I, together in Western China... officially as enemies... unofficially as spies... but, most importantly, as friends." He laughed and gazed out his window. "Our unique circumstances allowed us to operate with a great deal of autonomy. We mostly traveled when and where we liked... Nobody suspected we were also looking for treasure. We quickly got in touch with Misha's son, Ali, who agreed to join us. As an ethnic Turk, he had no problem blending in."

Ali grinned. "The three of us met in Kashgar and started to make plans. But wouldn't you know it? Things fell apart before they even got started. The political situation – which was at first a helpful smokescreen – soon grew to be a wildfire."

Uri interrupted. "The Chinese started testing their nuclear bombs in the Taklamakan. This led to more tension with Russia. Soon, the two countries were shooting at each other along the border. Xinjiang became a battleground."

Ali again: "Meanwhile, the Vietnam War was heating up, and the CIA reassigned your grandfather there. And that's when our plans fell apart... we never got another chance to go after the caravan." He shrugged at this, while Uri merely nodded.

Patrick shook his head in amazement. So this was what Grandpa had really been doing while he was "traveling the world."

As the limousine glided out of the canyon shadows and into the flat desert, Ali filled them in on the history and geography of Xinjiang – or East Turkestan, as it had been known for much longer. He explained that the region was ruthlessly fought over by empire after empire across thousands of years. Glancing at the bone-dry arroyos and gnarled trees through his window, Patrick wondered aloud why anyone would bother fighting over such as desolate place.

Ali smiled and said, "Geography. Throughout history, the region's location has made it strategically valuable for both military and economic reasons." He spread a map on his knees and ran his fingers over the area surrounding Kashgar.

"Situated in the middle of Central Asia, Xinjiang is a natural buffer zone. Its mountains and deserts separate Russia, China, India, and Iran (Persia)."

"In fact," Uri pointed out, "There are really only three ways Russia can be invaded from the south: through Iran, over the peaks of Afghanistan... or across the deserts of Xinjiang."

Patrick nodded slowly, turning the information over in his mind. He recalled seeing Iran and Afghanistan mentioned often in the news back home. At last he countered, "Isn't that also true for a Russian army trying to invade India?"

Uri grinned at this. "Roger Neilson taught you well. Indeed, both the Russians and British used Kashgar as a sort of... observation post... to keep tabs on each other." He spread his hands on his knees – his "tell" that he was about to reveal important information. "In the 1800s, the two governments tried to win the favor of local khans and warlords. Britain and Russia each promised the rulers of Kashgar riches and prestige in exchange for keeping out the other."

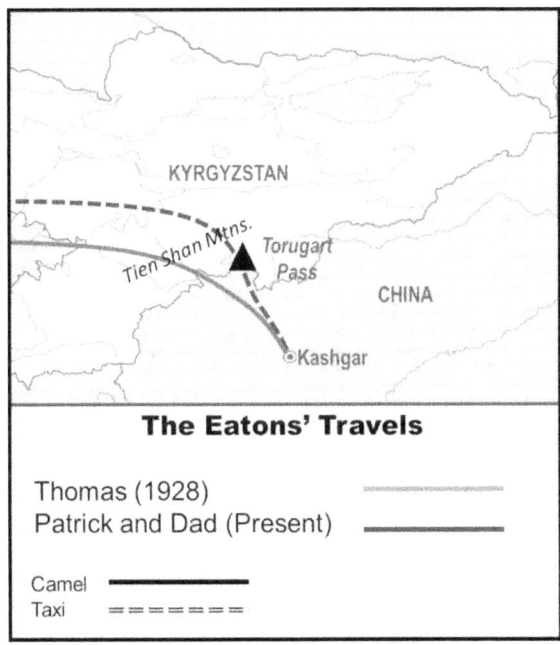

The Eatons' Travels

Thomas (1928)
Patrick and Dad (Present)

Camel
Taxi

Ali then explained why Kashgar was also an important economic crossroads. Its location within Xinjiang made it the hub of a gigantic wheel, whose "spokes" were roads that extend outwards in all directions. From Kashgar, merchants could travel to Kokand, Afghanistan, India, or China. As early as the thirteenth century, Marco Polo described the oasis-city as the largest and most important in the province. Seeing the large Turkic Muslim population that made its living through trade and handcraft, Polo named the area the "Land of the Uyghur." For two thousand years, the city's caravanserais provided refuge for Silk Road merchants crossing the vast and dangerous wilderness.

And the region was just as important today.

"There is a lot of oil and gas here," Dad said. "And mining, too."

Ali nodded. "And agriculture. The spring snowmelt from the surrounding mountains feeds fruit orchards and cotton fields.

Uri snorted. "Xinjiang has three-quarters of China's natural resources and it seems the entire world wants them."

After this, the passengers fell quiet as the limousine approached Kashgar. Patrick reflected on what he had heard. Buffer zones and trade routes, empires and rebellions, spies and war, gold and silver, cotton... and now oil and pipelines. Like the rest of Turkestan, Xinjiang seemed to have it all.

Aboard the Dagestan, Roger had confessed that the Great Game never really ended. Now, listening to Ali's history lesson, Patrick couldn't help but agree. Although today's contest had grown to include fossil fuels, little else had changed in a hundred years... or even a thousand. Just as in Polo's time, Central Asia lay in the middle of a grand chessboard – surrounded by players vying for control of it.

Bicycles, animals, frolicking children, and the buzz of commerce crammed the maze of narrow cobblestone alleys. Every manner of good seemed to be for sale here – prominently displayed in booths, draped over carts pulled by donkeys, or hanging in the open windows of workshops and bakeries. Brightly colored rugs, clothes, melons, seeds and nuts, lamb meat, jewelry, books, handcrafted musical instruments, animals... the choices seemed endless. Everywhere, the mouthwatering aroma of *nan* (clay-fired bread) permeated the air.

To Patrick, the people of Kashgar were as diverse as the wares they sold. Women clad in black *paranjas* – some entirely veiled, and others with only their eyes showing – quietly perused the merchandise, carrying shopping bags or loaves of bread tucked under their arms. Other women wore brightly colored head scarves and dresses, proudly displaying their faces and arms, and vigorously engaging each other in conversation. Countless men wore the khalats and circular hats (known by the Uyghur as *doppas*) similar to the skull-caps Patrick had seen throughout Western Turkestan, and many of them had beards down to their chests. Others doffed soft black or gray workers' caps, which Dad said were common to the people of China.

Here and there Patrick recognized the dark-skinned people of the mountains – perhaps hailing from Tibet or Pakistan. Every so often, he spotted a child with red or blond hair and skin as pale as his – they could just have easily lived down the street from him back home. Wherever he looked, eyes of all colors – hazel, olive, indigo, and ash gray – stared back. Kashgar truly was a crossroads of culture, Patrick marveled.

As Ali steered them through the cool, shadow-filled backstreets, Patrick reflected on how quickly an outsider could become lost here. Kashgar's historic downtown was a labyrinth of narrow lanes and passages – many only a few feet across. They were jammed with traffic, confined by mud brick walls interspersed with ornately carved wooden doors, all nearly identical. Alleys split off at every angle – some of them seemingly dead ends, until at the last moment they miraculously opened into another busy lane. Even Uri, who had once lived here, seemed momentarily disoriented. Thank goodness for Ali, thought Patrick. He halted every so often, waiting for them to catch up. "Stay close," Ali would say, grinning. "We don't want to be late to our meeting!"

They'd been in Kashgar two days already and were staying at the old Seman Hotel in downtown. The building's exterior had the tired, gaudy look of a cheap gambling establishment, Patrick thought. Entering the lobby, he glanced around anxiously at the antique, baroque-style foyer, which looked like the combination of a cathedral and funeral parlor. The sight gave him the willies – it reminded Patrick of a photo one would expect to see in a book of "haunted places." Eyeing the chipped columns, faded frescoes, and dusty alcoves, he groaned when Uri asked the hotel attendant for rooms in the oldest part of the building.

When Patrick started to protest, Uri put his hand on the boy's shoulder, leaned his head back, and sniffed the air. "This place is over a hundred years old. Before it was the Seman Hotel..." he whispered, "It was the Russian consulate...headed by one Nicholas Petrovsky, I may add. Once a dinner host to Thomas Eaton, I believe. And great-uncle of yours truly!" He looked down at Patrick and grinned. "I know this place like the back of my hand." A reassuring nod from Ali hushed Patrick.

Despite its tired appearance and modest comforts, the hotel had its upsides. For one, it truly was full of history, as Patrick soon found out. While Uri and Ali made some phone calls, Patrick and his dad wandered the corridors, taking in the architecture and décor. The old wing was adorned in traditional Uyghur mosaics, high ceilings, and military-style oil paintings. Patrick almost felt like he was on a movie set, apart from the inescapable smell of boiled cabbage and cigarette smoke that clung to the walls, carpets, and linens.

Another advantage of the Seman was its location. Situated in the middle of the old city, the hotel was a convenient base from which to explore the nearby warren of open-air bazaars, mosques, and historic city buildings and fountains. While sightseeing on their first day, Uri stopped them outside a somewhat newer but modest-looking hotel called the Chini Bagh (CHIN-ee bog). He stood for a while with his hands in his pockets, staring at the building, waiting for his companions' impatience to boil over.

"What's so special about this place?" Patrick finally asked. Uri smiled and waved them to follow him around back, where an older, low-lying building was concealed under a canopy of trees.

"This is the old British consulate," he explained. "One of Her Majesty's most important listening posts during the Great Game. Many well-known explorers and archaeologists stayed here over the years, including your great-grandfather. I'm told he frequently took tea on these very steps, hailing friends as they passed. It's just an out-of-the-way little building now, forgotten or unrecognized by most."

They sat on the steps for a while, removed from the commotion of the streets, savoring the cool shade. Patrick was overcome by the same sensation he had felt atop the minaret in Samarkand. Sitting where countless others had sat centuries earlier, it seemed almost as if he could reach out and touch the ghosts of the past. He half expected to turn and see Thomas sitting next to him, raising his teacup in a silent salute.

Continuing their tour, Patrick was shocked by the amount of construction he saw. Block after block of the old city was being demolished by cranes and heavy equipment. Towering piles of rubble stood between centuries-old brick structures and modern malls and apartments. This must have been the development plan Chen Li had told them about. Patrick couldn't help but notice there were few smiling faces among the onlookers. Along the way, he spotted an old man gazing sadly at a bulldozer pushing down what looked to have been a house. A block away, they passed a parade of residents pushing luggage-loaded carts through the street as uniformed Chinese police stood by talking on radios. Everywhere, security seemed tight, and Patrick didn't get the impression that *everyone* was quite as happy and "grateful" to the government as Li had indicated.

At the end of their second day, after a dizzying trek through the city's alleys, Ali finally brought them to their destination. Awaiting them was a quaint restaurant tucked into the side of a mud brick building. It teemed with locals, resonated with the poetic melody of stringed instruments, and was filled with the inviting aroma of cooked lamb and freshly baked nan.

Checking his watch, Ali said, "We're here. Inside are some people who will help us on the final leg of our journey." He straightened Patrick's keffiyah, solemnly nodded to Dad, and glanced warily up and down the street. A few feet away, Uri did the same, as if scanning for something… or someone. Then, with a nod, Ali simply said, "Time to eat." And in they went.

38 SHIFTING SANDS

"Lives of great men all remind us we can make our lives sublime.
And, departing, leave behind us footprints on the sands of time."
– Henry Wadsworth Longfellow

Entering the restaurant from the sunlit street, Patrick waited for his eyes to adjust to the dim light. Slowly, a large, crowded room came into focus – its patrons squeezed together around tables, shrouded in a smoky haze. Scattered among them were various stone fountains, statues, and intricately carved wooden screens. The customers looked local – and all were men. They wore khalats and doppas, smoked and sipped tea, and chatted with friends. In the faint light, Patrick couldn't be sure how many recognized them as foreigners. But a few nods and smiles conveyed a friendly atmosphere.

Ali led them past the tables to the back of the restaurant. Brushing aside a curtain of hanging beads, they entered a low-ceilinged, windowless room with a stone floor. Except for a handful of old-fashioned brass lamps, the only light came from dozens of candles flickering atop tables or inside wall nooks. The place had the ethereal feel of a Buddhist temple.

Sitting around wooden tables was a motley-looking crew of men, young and old, traditionally dressed or clad in suits. All bore the Turkic features of the Uyghur – there was not a Han Chinese among them. Spotting the newcomers, a few turned and stared. One got up and approached them.

"Salaam, Ali," the old man spoke softly. His drooping gray mustache turned up in a smile and his eyes radiated warmth.

"Wa alaykum salaam," Ali replied, embracing him. "It is good to see you, Yusuf."

"And you. I was most pleased to hear your voice after all these years." He turned to Uri. "Ah, and life has been good to our neighbor from the north, I see." He pointed at Uri's belly and laughed, then shook his hand warmly.

"These are the friends I told you about," Ali continued, turning to wave them forward. "Dan and Patrick Eaton."

"*Qarshi alimiz*. Welcome," said Yusuf. He raised an eyebrow at Dad. "Yes, I see the resemblance... my prayers to your father." Shifting his gaze to Patrick, he added, "...and to your grandfather. He is a good man. He will be around for many more years, *inshallah* (God willing)."

Yusuf beckoned them to the table, where he introduced the old men sitting round it. In turn, they nodded their heads politely, whereupon Yusuf invited his guests to join them. Patrick was instantly distracted by the sumptuous array of dishes spread around the table. A sizzling stir-fry with peppers, tomatoes, onions, garlic, and green beans tantalized his nose. A platter of mutton dumplings got his mouth watering. Large round flat breads fresh from their clay-fired ovens made his stomach growl. And then... Patrick spotted the dark purple juice which filled several of his hosts' glasses. Could it be?

"Pomegranate juice?" Ali asked, seeing him gaping. He signaled a server. "A round for all of us, please." He smiled at Patrick. "I thought you might like this place, my friend."

A couple of dumplings and a kebab of mutton and vegetables later, Patrick studied his table mates while sipping the cold sweet drink he'd come to love in Baku. Four other men sat around the table. Like Yusuf, each of them wore an embroidered doppa perched atop his shaved head, and an old-style suit that conveyed both modesty and dignity. Deep wrinkles etched their bronzed faces, and the beards hanging over their chests had lost their color long ago. They spoke quietly and deliberately, their fingers curled around their teacups or artfully dancing in the air to emphasize a point. Only their eyes were youthful, darting from one speaker to the next, to their guests, to the door... Wise men, Patrick thought, perhaps city elders.

They spoke a strange tongue, which Ali said was Uyghur. "They want to know how you like Kashgar," he translated to Patrick, who smiled bashfully. "They say they are honored by your visit. And they hope you will carry home the memory of this place, which may soon be gone."

One of the elders spoke at length. An index finger wagged in the air as he lectured with his eyes fixed on Patrick. The others fiddled with their teacups and nodded from time to time.

"He says he is from the desert. For generations, his family has worked as merchants, carrying jade and silk back and forth across the sands." The old man's speech strengthened as he went, captivating Patrick with its poetic lilt. "He says the desert is tranquil and beautiful, as well as violent and deadly. It can capture your heart in one moment, and take your life in the next."

He carried on for a minute or more with Ali translating and the others grunting or bobbing their heads in agreement. At last, he said, "Great sand dunes travel far and wide, grow old, and die upon the slopes of distant mountains. One generation after the next, they keep coming, though no two dunes are ever quite the same. Forever moving, shifting, like waves on the ocean – they mark time upon the eternal clock of the world."

The man stopped talking and looked at Patrick.

"Do you see?" Ali asked, a playful grin on his face. Patrick nodded, but he was not so sure. "He wishes you luck on an ancient journey."

A shout from the next table startled them, followed by roaring laughter. A crowd of younger men – locals in their late-twenties or so, it seemed to Patrick – were giving each other a hard time, obviously enjoying themselves. The old men at Patrick's table did not look up from their tea.

One of the young fellows got up as if to leave. He passed a haphazard glance in their direction and hesitated with an expression of uncertainty on his face.

"Hasan!" Yusuf cried out. He lifted a bony arm to wave him over and said, "Come here a moment. I have guests for you to meet."

The young man bowed his head respectfully as he approached, greeted Yusuf warmly – with a "salaam" and kiss on the cheek – and took a seat.

"Hasan is my great-nephew," Yusuf said cheerfully. "He is training to be a blacksmith, like his father." Hasan shrugged, apparently not as excited about his future. Under his white doppa, wisps of black hair fell over his eyes and ears, framing a dark angular face. His body pulsed with an energy that Patrick could feel across the table.

"Perhaps, Yusuf," Hasan replied. "But there are other opportunities these days. I will have to wait and see…"

Yusuf clearly didn't like the sound of this, but it seemed to Patrick they'd had this conversation before. "Blacksmithing is a family tradition. It is a good living. And your father has worked hard to give you this chance. That is what you should do."

Hasan shrugged again, rubbing his hands together on the table in front of him. "We don't even know if his shop will still be standing in a month, let alone a year from now." He looked up at Ali. "Our neighborhood is scheduled to be demolished as part of China's Dangerous House Reform Project."

"I'm sorry to hear that," Ali replied. "I have noticed many changes since last I was here."

"Changes? Oh, yes!" Hasan bit back, his face clouding. Ali said nothing, sensing he had touched upon a sore spot. But Hasan was not to be put off. "The Chinese tear down our houses… for our 'safety,' they say – to protect us from earthquakes. But our ancestors lived with earthquakes, too… And they constructed homes to survive them – far better than the ugly high-rise buildings

278

the Chinese build. Did you know that eighty-five per cent of the old city is scheduled to be demolished?" He was almost shouting now, and Yusuf patted his arm to calm him, but he jerked it away and continued.

"Have you seen the mounds of rubble that were once our homes, our businesses, our history, our lives? And for what? To make room for Han Chinese who are moving here by the thousands, pushing us out. You want to know the real reason they are destroying the old city? They think it is a breeding ground for insurgency... for the courageous citizens of Kashgar who oppose them. And you know what? They are right! Here in our narrow alleys, hidden courtyards, and secret back rooms we meet and make plans to kick them out!"

"Hasan!" Yusuf bellowed. "That is enough!" The table fell uneasily silent. Even the shouts and laughter from the table next to them died down, and a few heads turned to see what the fuss was about.

"Hasan is young and hotheaded," Yusuf continued in a hoarse whisper. "He sees the changes to his city and he feels sadness. He hears the surveillance helicopters flying overhead and he feels trapped. He is searched at roadblocks and insulted by Chinese police... and he feels fear."

"I am not scared!" Hasan let fly again. "I am angry! They stomp on our religion and culture, destroy our lives, and then call us terrorists because we don't roll over and submit to their rule!" Yusuf's hand tightened on Hasan's arm, and Patrick could see the purple veins bulging from the effort. A shout of encouragement went up from the table next to them.

"I know, Hasan, but you must be careful. The Chinese have eyes and ears everywhere, and violence solves nothing."

"Oh? Was that what you said when you fought against China in your youth?" Hasan replied with a smirk, and nodded in Uri's direction. "With this Russian?"

Yusuf was aghast, his jaw working furiously as he strained to come up with a worthy tongue lashing. Always the diplomat, Uri stepped in with a few words of his own.

"You are both right – there is more than one way to protect your land and people. History has not been easy for the Uyghur. But you have been here a long time and, I think, you will not be going anywhere soon." He smiled and the tension seemed to ease.

"Yes, you are right," Hasan said quietly, his head bowed. "I am sorry... to you both. I meant no disrespect. I just get so frustrated..."

"No offense taken," Uri replied before Yusuf could speak. The old man's temple was still throbbing over the matter.

"Is this the man you said will help us?" Ali added, looking from Hasan to Yusuf.

Still flustered, Yusuf managed a nod. "Yes, despite his youthful impudence, Hasan is an expert guide. He knows the city and will outfit your expedition with whatever you need. It is the least we can do for our guests." He scowled at the man next to him, but Hasan's face brightened nevertheless.

"Yusuf has told me about your trip to the Taklamakan Desert. Very exciting! I have arranged for an SUV, food, water, and gear for your expedition. They are hidden just two blocks from here."

"Hidden... why?" Dad asked.

"We should avoid unnecessary attention," Uri interjected, the old glint in his eye. At the dinner in Turkmenbashi, Patrick had perceived the cool and easy manner of the Russian. Uri seemed equally comfortable at the Chinese checkpoint, too. Now, conspiring in the back room of a dusty oasis-town, Uri was once more like a fish in water. No wonder he had made such a good spy, Patrick smiled to himself. Like Ali, the man seemed to be at home wherever he was.

"Tomorrow morning we'll leave for Yarkand," Uri continued. He looked at Dad. "Southeast of here. Chen Li will have reported our travel plans by now... so it's best we stick to them."

Yusuf's irritation had subsided, and he seemed at ease again. "Who would have thought we'd all be back together as old men. It seems like another life that we—"

His next words were drowned by a clamor in the front of the building. An eruption of angry shouting and scuffling feet turned heads. At the next table a man jumped out of his chair, knocking it backwards onto the floor. Another man came running in, alarm upon his face.

"*Sahci!*" he cried, waving his arms in the air.

"Police!" Ali translated, summoning them out of their chairs. Yusuf spoke rapidly to Hasan as commotion overtook the small room.

"Hasan will take you from here," Yusuf explained as he stood. "Go with him. And go with God, my friends." He shook their hands quickly before Hasan whisked them to the back of the room, past another curtain, and out into the back alley. Threading their way past empty cartons and boxes, the five of them returned to the dizzying labyrinth of the old city, darting up one narrow alley and down another. At last they emerged onto a busy street several blocks away.

"What was that about?" Dad cried, breathing hard and glancing back from where they'd come.

"Police raid. Happens all the time." Hasan let out a whoop of excitement.

"What did they want?" Patrick asked.

"Better not to find out." Hasan grinned. "Let's get you back to your hotel."

———————————————————

It was dusk outside when they returned to the Seman Hotel. Standing in the hallway outside their rooms, Uri shared some final thoughts before they retired for the night.

"Pack tonight," he said. "And be ready to leave early. We want to be gone before the sun is up."

"Anything else we need to bring?" Dad asked, lifting his cap to scratch at his sweat-drenched hair.

"Everything else has been prepared," Uri said. Then he paused, considering something more. "Actually, have Ali loan you another keffiyah, and lose the ball cap, Dan. Up close, anyone can see you are Westerners, but from a distance, you might pass as Uyghur. No need to advertise our presence here."

Back in their room, although Patrick and Dad tried to relax, it was difficult to contain their excitement. Patrick flipped through television channels, while Dad repacked his bag and took a shower. Exhausted from the day, they found themselves lying in their beds at dusk, staring up at the ceiling and talking about the trip.

"Do you think we'll find the treasure?" Patrick pondered aloud, watching the ceiling fan spin slowly overhead.

"I don't know," Dad said. "Uri and Ali seem to know where it is located – a place by the Karakash River, Ali said, north of Yotkan in the desert. The area is world-famous for the jade deposited there by the rivers that flow out of the mountains. If nothing else, it'll be an adventure, won't it?"

"Yeah," Patrick said, letting out his breath. "I still can't believe I'm here." His thoughts wandered back through the previous months – from Kashgar to the oasis-cities of Samarkand and Bukhara, back to Turkmenistan, across the Caspian Sea, Baku, and the flight from Germany that seemed like an eternity ago.

"Your grandpa…" Dad chuckled softly. "I should have known he was up to something when he proposed bringing you on this trip."

"You mean it never even crossed your mind that he was a spy?"

"No," Dad answered. "I mean, as a boy I might have wished for a story like that. He had different careers. Sometimes he was a photojournalist... other times a travel writer. I saw many photos and heard even more stories. But since I didn't go with him on his trips, I never got to see what he actually did when he was gone from home." He was silent for several seconds. "He and I never took a trip together like this."

The sounds of the old city wafted through their open hotel window, and the last remnants of daylight cast a gray afterglow over the room. They lay on their backs, atop the sheets in their travel clothes, deep in their own thoughts. How long he lay there before falling asleep, Patrick did not know, but the room was pitch black when he awoke to knocking on the door.

He heard his dad fumbling from his bed to the door, muttering in his half-sleep. He cracked the door to reveal the light from the hall and silhouette of a familiar bull-necked figure.

"We need to go," Uri growled. "Hurry – grab your gear!"

Stepping into their shoes and snatching their bags, they followed Uri down the hallway. Ali was waiting for them at its end, perfectly still, his eyes and ears trained on an intersecting corridor that led to the lobby. He raised one finger to his mouth and then motioned them forward.

"Let's move. Quickly but quietly!" Patrick and Dad looked pleadingly at him, but Ali shook off their questions. Now was not the time, his eyes seemed to say.

Uri led them away from the lobby, down ghostly corridors lit by century-old chandeliers. At the end of one passageway, he stopped to pry open the door of what appeared to be a janitor's closet. In they piled and Patrick half-expected them to be jammed together next to mops and buckets. Indeed they were, but only for a moment. With a sleight of hand, Uri adjusted something – a piece of furniture or a light switch, Patrick couldn't tell – and one wall of the closet opened to reveal another dark corridor. In they went, one-by-one, each holding onto the belt of the person in front of him, while Uri had only the spark of a small penlight as his guide.

For several minutes they shuffled through a stone tunnel, their footsteps echoing into the gloom ahead. A twist here or turn there set them on a new bearing, so much so that Patrick quickly became disoriented. He sensed they were somewhere beneath the city, probably heading away from the hotel. But Uri seemed to know exactly where he was going, and a few minutes later they approached a narrow stairwell, which they climbed as a single, stumbling, line. Emerging through a hatch into another dark room, Patrick thought he felt straw beneath his shoes. They shuffled through the dark until Uri stopped them and cracked open a door, letting in a yellow sliver of light.

They remained there for only a few minutes, but the suspense made it seem like hours – completely still, trying to control their heavy breathing, listening... At last, they slipped out into another alley. Ali took the lead, guiding them past empty kiosks and numerous wooden doors, and over or around an occasional pallet or empty cart lingering from the previous day. Patrick marveled at the early-morning tranquility of the streets that been bustling just hours before. He recalled Hasan's comment about the shelter that Kashgar provided insurgents... Indeed, it would be nearly impossible to find a person who did not want to be found.

At last they reached a wooden-beamed adobe building that had the look of a barn. Ali halted and knocked gently. For several seconds there was no answer, and Uri cast an anxious glance back up the alley. Somewhere in the distance a dog barked, echoed by an angry shout. Then a heavy wooden door rolled open, and Hasan's smiling face appeared from the shadows.

"Everything's ready," he whispered excitedly. "Let's go."

"What about your driver?" Dad asked Uri.

"He'll pretend to be confused under interrogation. Then he'll wait around for my instructions." They followed Hasan into the barn. "Don't worry, Dan. He's an old hand – he knows what to do."

Two hours later, Patrick gazed out the SUV's window as the morning sun crept above the Taklamakan. Outside, no sign of life – or pursuit – was evident among the endless dunes and desolate highway. Uri's foresight to bribe the hotel staff on their first day had paid off tremendously. When Chinese police had entered the lobby just hours ago, the front desk attendant discreetly buzzed Uri's phone three times – the agreed-upon warning. Having selected rooms near the old consulate's underground passage, Uri had put their escape plan into place within the first hour of their arrival in Kashgar. Patrick shook his head in admiration. Had Grandpa been this good?

Uri wasn't certain why the police were looking for them, but as Hasan had pointed out, sometimes it is better not to hang around to find out. Discarding their plans for Yarkand, the travelers pushed eastward into the world's most foreboding place – towards the Karakash, away from their pursuers, in search of treasure in the Taklamakan Desert.

39 PLACE OF RUINS

"The desert, to those who do listen, is more likely to
provoke awe than to invite conquest."
– Joseph Wood Krutch

The thermometer in the vehicle registered 101 degrees, but
Patrick swore it had to be hotter than that.   The sun blazed high
overhead, reflecting its heat off the sand in shimmering waves.
Staring out at the endless expanse of barren dunes, Patrick
wondered if he had not reached the end of the world.

It was mid-day as the travelers headed south along a
desolate stretch of one of the few highways that cross the
Taklamakan. Rolling along at sixty miles an hour, the SUV looked
like a safari wagon from one of Patrick's adventure magazines. It
was outfitted with all manner of gear suitable for an expedition
into the wilderness. Two spare tires and several large plastic water
containers were secured to the roof with netting. Strapped to the
sides of the vehicle was an assortment of shovels, tent poles, camp
equipment, tools, and various other items. Inside, the rear cargo
hold was piled full of crates, duffel bags, tarps, and boxes of tinned
and dried food.

The air conditioner whirred at full blast, blowing the
passengers' hair and making conversation difficult. Sitting in front
with *doppas* atop their heads, Hasan drove while Ali acted as
navigator, his finger tracing a large map spread across his lap. In
the back seat, Uri, Dad and Patrick were squeezed shoulder-to-
shoulder, wrapped in keffiyahs, and sporting the light-weight shirts
and trousers Hasan had purchased for them.   As Dad pointed out

286

various facts about the geology of the Taklamakan, Uri punched the buttons of a global positioning system (GPS) unit, halting every so often to wipe sweat from his brow. A photograph of the expedition would have been right at home in National Geographic, Patrick thought.

"The Taklamakan is the largest, driest, and hottest desert in all of China," Dad explained, his voice raised over the background noise. "It's also the world's second largest sand-shifting desert." Seeing the quizzical look on Patrick's face, he added, "Believe it or not, sand dunes grow and move all the time. Only the Sahara Desert has more active dunes."

"Why are they here?" Patrick asked.

"I'm glad you asked!" Dad smiled back. "Millions of years ago, the surrounding mountains began to rise up, and in the middle of them, a gigantic bowl formed. This bowl is known today as the Tarim Basin, and the Taklamakan Desert lies in its center. Since the basin lies in the 'rain shadow' of the adjacent mountains, almost no precipitation reaches it. The only water here comes from rivers that are fed by mountain snow and glaciers. For thousands of years, the glaciers have been shrinking. As the basin continues to dry out, its sand is blown into great dunes that travel hundreds of miles. Because of that movement of the sand, the desert is growing."

"The Taklamakan was here long before my people," Hasan echoed from the front. "It has devoured many of our cities. Some were covered slowly, over many years, while others were buried in a single day by sandstorms."

"Sandstorms?" Patrick looked alarmed. "Are there still sandstorms today?"

"Oh, yes!" Hasan replied excitedly. "All the time. In fact, now is the height of sandstorm season." Patrick felt his stomach tighten, and Dad bumped his shoulder reassuringly.

"If the Taklamakan is such a terrible place..." Patrick continued, "How did the Silk Road caravans survive here?"

287

"They went *around* it," Ali answered. "From Kashgar, travelers who wished to reach China could choose from a northern or southern route along the desert's perimeter. Both avenues were dotted with oasis-cities, which were themselves watered by mountain streams, nourished by agriculture, and enriched by the passing caravans."

The group was silent for several minutes as they stared out at the wasteland. Some of the dunes looked to be two hundred feet high – maybe more – with no trace of life. It was little surprise that Silk Road traders avoided this place, Patrick reflected. Without a modern vehicle, air conditioning, and huge amounts of water, attempting to cross the sands seemed like sheer madness.

"In the centuries after the Mongol Empire, the trade routes dried up with the rivers," Ali continued. "It wasn't until the 1800s, during the Great Game, that the region started to regain the world's attention. Spies and geographers came to explore and chart its lands, which at the time were merely 'blank spots' on European maps. Not long after, Western archaeologists arrived. Men like your great-grandfather uncovered remarkable finds that shed light on the region's important resources. Gradually, the world began to rediscover the Tarim Basin."

"And then the Qing Dynasty made the Tarim Basin an official province of China," Hasan grumbled. "At first, the Uyghur were promised we could keep our homeland. We were powerful then, and we had friends like Britain and Russia. Even when the Communist Party took control of China, they mostly left us alone. But the situation is very different now. China has become strong – and its hunger for our land and resources grows. Today, the Uyghur need friends more than ever. Who will help us, I wonder?" He eyed Uri in the rearview mirror.

Catching his glance, Uri calmly replied, "We are still friends, Hasan, but as you say, the situation here is quite different from what it was during the 1960s. China is stronger now and its claim to Xinjiang carries more weight. Keep in mind that Russia is in a similar position. Like China, we have our own 'frontiers' to consider – namely, our former republics. We must tread carefully with China…a great power with which we share a long border, as well as responsibility for Central Asia."

"But Xinjiang belongs to the Uyghur! Are you saying Russia will sell out my people to get back Kyrgyzstan?" Hasan snapped.

"I mean it is complicated…" Uri repeated. "China watched the collapse of our Soviet Union. Beijing does not want to lose Xinjiang the same way Moscow lost its republics." He placed his hands flat on his knees, a habit Patrick had detected weeks earlier. "Believe me, Hasan, I sympathize with your people…"

"We need to stay focused," Ali interrupted. "Only an hour to our destination, and I see we are not alone."

At first, Patrick thought Ali was merely defusing the tension, but when he turned to peer over the piles of baggage and through the back window, he realized Ali's warning was more than a peacekeeping gesture. On the highway, miles behind them, he could make out something twinkling through the shimmering heat. In this vast emptiness, only the glint of sun on metal could create such a spectacle.

"I wonder who they are," said Dad, trying to turn in his seat to have a look.

"Probably nothing to worry about," Ali replied, his eyes fixed on the side mirror. "But just the same, let's remember we are all on the same team… Today, we are not Russian, Turk, American, or Uyghur. We are friends and comrades."

"*Inshallah*," Hasan said, nodding agreement. "I will drink to that. Pomegranate juice, anyone?" He waved a bottle in the air, dissolving the tension amid shouts of thirsty delight.

On the southern edge of the Tarim Basin, two rivers spill out of the Kunlun Mountains: the Yurungkash (White Jade River) and Karakash (Black Jade River). On a satellite image, they appear as two long, skinny green fingers that stretch far into the immense golden sands before finally merging to form the Khotan River. Hundreds of miles to the north, the Khotan joins the Tarim River, which eventually drains into a small desert lake in the northeast. It is where the twin jade rivers first leave the mountains that the famed oasis-cities of Khotan and Yotkan once prospered, offering sanctuary to ancient Silk Road travelers from as far away as Beijing or Rome.

The SUV turned off the main highway and was now rumbling south on a dirt road that paralleled the westernmost river, the Karakash. Outside Uri's window lay more sand and silt, which was now peppered with scraggly bushes and small trees. To their right, on Patrick's side of the vehicle, the vegetation thickened where it approached the boulder-strewn waters of the river. Green tamarisks and poplar trees grew amid a tangle of tall grasses and reeds. Ahead of them, far to the south and partly veiled in the desert haze, loomed the snow-covered peaks of the Kunlun Mountains.

The hum of rubber on asphalt gave way to the crunching of gravel beneath the tires. Hasan slowed to weave around the frequent holes and ruts, while Uri fiddled with the GPS, tilting it this way and that to try to get a better reception.

"Our fathers logged the coordinates of the buried caravan," Ali said, turning in his seat. "But even so, our search won't be easy. This landscape has changed a great deal since Thomas, Dmitri and my father were here. Plus, their mapping equipment was not as precise as our modern technology." He winced as Uri repeatedly smacked his hand on the GPS while muttering in Russian. "Easy there, old friend. She is the only one we have!"

Uri glared back as he gave the unit another whack. "We're getting close, but the reception is weak here." He glanced up at the sky, as if he expected to spot a satellite overhead. Ali followed his glance.

"We should find a place to spend the night," Ali said. "Let's head closer to the river. That'll get us out of sight of the main road and allow us to fine-tune our GPS. Also, we need to set up camp before it gets dark." Glancing at Patrick, he explained, "It's hot now, but when the sun goes down it'll be freezing."

The engine groaned as the SUV climbed over river rocks the size of bowling balls, bouncing equipment and its passengers inside. Carefully, Hasan edged them closer to the water, and then turned for higher ground. He brought the vehicle to a halt upon a sandy stretch, and switched off the engine.

"Shouldn't we camp closer to the river?" Patrick asked his dad, eyeing the clear and likely cold water flowing more than 150 feet away.

"Not a good idea in the desert," Dad replied quietly. "Rains here are rare, but if they do come, a small river can turn into a surging flood in seconds."

An hour later, four tents ringed the sandy clearing. A large canopy had been erected in its center, under which the band of explorers relaxed in folding chairs. A circle of rocks enclosed a fire over which tins of beans and rice gurgled and sputtered. Patrick drank often from his water bottle and tried to move as little as possible in the suffocating heat. Aside from the buzz of an occasional flying insect and the babbling of the Karakash beyond a thicket of tall grass, the desert was silent and still.

"We should survey the area this evening," Ali mused aloud, stroking his chin. "When the temperature cools, we can walk along the river." The others nodded, quietly sipping their water. "If the GPS is correct, we are close to the caravan. My father said it was on the east side of the Karakash, buried in an old river bed. However, like the sand dunes, the rivers of the Taklamakan can migrate considerable distances. No telling what this area looked like in the late 1920s."

"Have you been to the Taklamakan before?" Patrick asked.

"No," Ali replied, smiling. "Khotan and Yotkan, yes, but never into the sands where we are now."

"How far are we from Yotkan?" Dad inquired as he slapped at a biting fly.

"Thirty miles or so. But these days, Yotkan is little more than an empty hill among overgrown fields. Khotan is the nearest modern city, but it lies farther east."

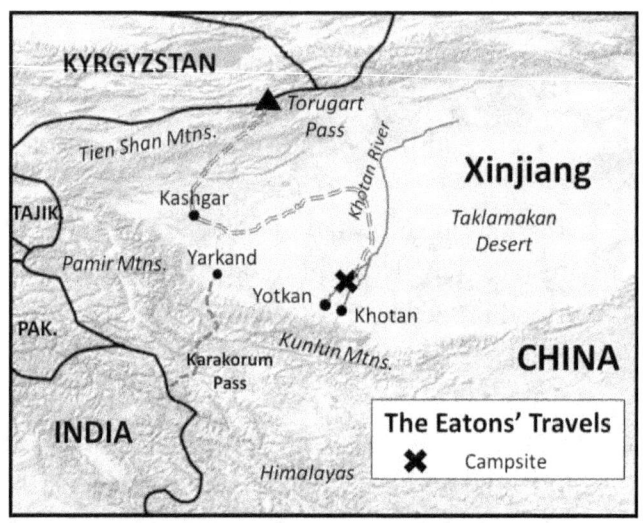

"What happened to Yotkan?" Patrick pressed.

"It was buried by sand. At one time, thousands of years ago, Yotkan was the capital of a great kingdom." He wiped water from his mouth with his sleeve. "But it wasn't the only ancient oasis-city along the Taklamakan's southern road. This area was originally settled by Tibetans as well as Indians, and the Tarim Basin became the center of Buddhism. Silk and agriculture allowed its people to prosper."

"And jade," Dad added. "We are in one of the most famous jade-producing regions in the world."

Ali nodded. "Of all varieties, and carved into every manner of jewelry, statues, pipes, tools... even burial suits. Jade was

292

valued as much as gold or diamonds. Actually, it still is... White 'mutton-fat' jade sometimes sells for two or three times the price of gold!"

Dad slapped his knee enthusiastically. "Well, that does it, Ali! You've gotten me all worked up to go treasure-hunting! Gold, silver, jade... I'm all for it. What do you say we have a look?"

The sun burned orange in the western sky. It was still hot, but no longer the furnace it was when they first set up camp.

"Yes, my friends," Ali smiled back. "Let's go for a walk."

Years later, Patrick would still remember that evening vividly. Of his entire summer in Central Asia, the imagery and sentiment of that hike stood above even the minarets of Samarkand. The surrounding dunes glowed like embers under a warm pink sky, while grasses and scrub cast long shadows that danced in a gentle wind. The empty, inhospitable desert came to life as birds chirped from the shrubs and lizards scampered under rocks in advance of the explorers. The cold, clear water of the Karakash tumbled gently over cobblestones which had begun their lives millions of years ago as jagged granite boulders. The dreamlike sensation of that evening dissolved any concerns about Chinese police or mysterious pursuers.

Patrick tightened the keffiyah around his neck and swatted at the cloud of gnats orbiting his head. Uri and Ali conferred around the GPS, arguing as old friends sometimes do. Hasan sat on a rock, looking deep in thought as he smoked his pipe. Dad had already discarded his shoes, rolled up his pants, and waded into the shallow river. He splashed along, scrutinizing the riverbed and occasionally stopping to pluck a rock from its bottom.

"Hey, Patrick," he called out, flipping a pebble through the air. "Check it out!"

Catching the specimen and turning it over in his fingers, Patrick beheld the waxy, translucent glow of green jade. He'd seen its final, polished form in books, but he was surprised by how

293

dull the mineral was in its natural form. Patrick looked up with a grin but his dad had already moved on – slipping on a rock here and there, splashing and laughing cheerfully as he explored the riverbed. As Patrick watched him, he again recognized the enthusiastic, young sun-tanned man from the photo on his mother's dresser. His dad was a boy once more – at play in the mountains of his home, captivated by his natural surroundings, relaxed and carefree in his thoughts.

Patrick decided to join the fun. Kicking off his shoes, he waded into the icy water, probing the sandy bottom with his toes. A couple of glistening stones caught his attention, but upon closer inspection proved to be nothing out of the ordinary. Minnows darted through the current, their metallic scales flashing in the sun, momentarily giving the impression of silver or gold. Turning his focus to a tranquil pool encircled by driftwood and cobblestones, Patrick scooped up a handful of gravel. He let it slowly sift through his fingers, then listened as it kerplunked back into the water. A dark-colored pebble stood out and he quickly closed his hands around it. Amid the black grains of sand on his fingers, a familiar-looking nugget the size and color of an olive shone back at him.

Pocketing the jade, Patrick tilted his face to the sky, which was fading to violet as the sun sank in the west. He glanced to the Kunlun Mountains in the south, and then turned his attention once more to his dad splashing merrily in the Black Jade River. It all felt so perfect and natural – as if this place and moment in time had been waiting for him.

"When you boys are done with your fun, come have a look at our map!" Ali shouted from the bank. Hasan had finished his pipe and joined their huddle, where he was now pointing down-river.

Once ashore, Patrick and his dad listened as Ali summarized their efforts at locating the treasure. "According to our fathers, the caravan had been trying to save time by crossing

294

the desert in winter. It was following an old riverbed when it became stranded, or perhaps was attacked and robbed. We think their final site now lies in that hillside," he said, indicating a grass-covered knoll nearby. "The GPS won't get us any closer than this... Dan, what do you think?" He handed Patrick's father a yellowed piece of crinkled paper.

Dad looked at it thoughtfully. "This map is from your father?" Ali nodded. "Hmm. Sand and gravel everywhere... It'll be tough to tell one old river bed from the next." His eyes scanned the length of the river. Pointing at a hill in the distance, he said, "There's a sandstone outcrop. We can assume that it's been here for a while. And I think it's on the map here." He jabbed his finger at the paper.

"So, we're close?" Hasan asked excitedly.

"I think so," Dad replied. "We'll have to probe with shovels and the metal-detector tomorrow. It'll be long, hot work." He tousled Patrick's hair. "Good old-fashioned field work!"

Pulsing with excitement, the party returned to their campsite and toasted the expedition with another bottle of pomegranate juice. As the sun slipped behind the mountains, Ali excused himself from the group and climbed to higher ground, where he stood sipping his drink in solitude. Patrick watched him for several minutes, thinking Ali might kneel to pray as he had done occasionally over the past few weeks. Instead, Ali stared at the horizon, at one point bringing binoculars to his eyes. When he returned to the tents, his expression was sour.

"We never heard any cars pass on the highway today," he said matter-of-factly. "And there are lights in the distance. There's no movement, which means they have probably stopped for the night."

"Who are those guys?" Dad asked.

Ali shook his head. "Perhaps we will find out tomorrow." As he walked to his tent, he added over his shoulder, "But hopefully not!"

40 History Rhymes

"Only the wisest and stupidest of men never change."
– Confucius

The wind howled like banshees through the night – rattling gear and pelting the tents with sand – as if wailing the names of those who perished here long ago. Patrick lay next to his dad, bundled under a heavy blanket to protect him from the chilly night air. He awoke several times in the darkness, listening to the blustering squalls and imagining the ghosts of ancient caravans passing silently by. Once, when the spirits seemed just outside the tent, he tried to rouse his dad. Unsuccessful, he buried his head under the covers, squeezed his eyes shut, and tried to force his thoughts elsewhere.

When he awoke, all was quiet and still. Sweeping open the tent flap, Patrick peered out. The campsite was bathed in the pale lavender light of early morning. Sand drifts anchored one corner of their tent and half-buried the folding chairs that ringed the fire. Their footsteps from the day before were gone, as if they had never been here, and only pristine sheets of rippled sand covered the area between their tents.

Ali was on his hill already, silhouetted by the purple morning sky, peering through binoculars. Hasan stood below him, smoking his pipe and chatting away excitedly. Patrick couldn't make out their words, but Hasan's wild gesturing and Ali's icy stillness told him their mysterious shadows had not moved from last night. A couple of tents away, Uri dusted off a food cooler, grumbling as he dug in it for breakfast. Retrieving a package wrapped in plastic, he held it aloft with a Russian exclamation of triumph.

A half-hour later, as the sun stole over the grassy dunes, the adventurers convened around a crackling fire. Lamb, potatoes, nan, and Uri's beloved coffee sizzled over an iron grate. Hasan poked the tinder as he described the campfire smoke that he and Ali had spotted on the horizon.

"Besides us, who would possibly be out here?" Dad asked, looking from Hasan to Uri.

Uri shrugged as he turned one of the kebabs over the fire. "Perhaps other tourists like us..."

"No, no," Hasan interjected excitedly, his cheeks full of bread. "Nobody but shepherds would ever camp in this wretched place."

"Probably shepherds then," Ali repeated quietly, fingering the ringlet of his tin mug, but the crinkled lines around his eyes seemed to betray doubt.

"Pack enough water for the day," Dad instructed, focusing the group on the task at hand. "At least a gallon per person." He squelched his walkie-talkie, echoing static in the other radios around the fire. "We'll use channel 2, and channel 5 as back-up. Be sure to keep the volume up." The uncertainty in his son's eyes led him to add, "Just in case we get separated."

"I'll carry the metal detector," Ali volunteered. "We'll take turns when we get there. Hasan, you bring the probing rod. Shovels for everyone. It'll be hot, so take breaks as needed."

Uri dabbed sunblock across his nose and cheeks, appearing comical for once. Spotting a smile on Patrick's lips, Uri growled, "We Russians have pale skin!" His defensiveness only drew laughter from the group, causing him to scowl as he rewrapped the checkered scarf around his neck.

Minutes later, the crew stood next to the river by the grassy knoll they'd surveyed the previous evening. Dropping their packs, they wiped away sweat, which already flowed freely under the hot sun. Ali adjusted Patrick's keffiyah, effortlessly knotting it behind his ear with experienced hands.

"Your show, Dan," Ali said, handing Dad the yellowed paper. While the others adjusted their gear, choosing only what they needed for excavating, Patrick's dad turned his compass expertly, glancing from it to the knoll and then back to the map. His brow furrowed with concentration, but the twist in his lips gave away his delight in the challenge.

Pointing at the same spot in the sand, he said, "That's gotta be it. Nothing to do now but dig."

As he threw his first shovel-load of sand over his shoulder, Patrick was bursting with optimism. Despite the lack of sleep, his mind and body felt fresh and buoyant. Glancing at the others slogging away to his left and right, he knew it could not be long before he heard the ring of metal on metal, followed by the triumphant shout of "Eureka!"

By noon, however, Patrick's cheerfulness was evaporating as fast as the sweat from his brow. It was extremely hot, and his muscles and hands were becoming knotted from the strain of digging. Sand gnats continued to find their way under his keffiyah to gnaw red welts along his neck, forcing him to stop, smack them away, and rewrap the scarf. A liter of water had already passed his lips and the thought of a river bath seemed like ecstasy. When he saw Hasan peering ravenously at the water, his red face puffing from his efforts, Patrick knew he was not alone.

One after the other, without speaking a word, the digging party headed for the river. After a refreshing swim, they gathered under the shade of a tamarisk bush for lunch and revisited their plan. The sandy bank looked like Swiss cheese from their efforts, and the tools lay where they'd dropped them in their trek to the water.

"Why don't you help Uri with the metal detector?" Dad suggested, seeing the discouraged look on his son's face. Patrick nodded weakly as he finished the last of his nan.

The group lingered in the shade for another few minutes before resuming the search. Uri and Patrick roamed along the top of the knoll, the Russian slowly sweeping the detector's disk left and right over the ground. Every so often he would stop to let Patrick poke the sand with the iron rod, trade a discouraging head shake, and then move on. Despite his hefty build and pasty skin, Uri somehow managed to look at ease in his work. The man never ceased to amaze, thought Patrick.

Spotting his wonder, Uri remarked softly, "It's all a mindset, Patrick. Pain, heat, fatigue… the power of mind over body is remarkable. You must go somewhere in your head that feels cool and refreshing, then convince your body that's really where you are. *Stay positive*."

"How do you do it?" Patrick asked.

"I take my thoughts to the lake where I swam as a boy," he answered. "It is cold and clear, under the shade of tall birch trees. That memory has carried me through many hardships."

Patrick recalled the lake by Grandpa's cabin. He imagined the revitalizing cold, the sensation of floating, and the gentle splash of waves lapping against the dock.

"Was it hard to be Grandpa's friend, and yet his enemy, too?" Patrick asked, already feeling cooler.

"Not as difficult as you might think." Uri considered him out of the corner of his eye. "Our work never pitted us directly against each other, so we were only enemies in theory."

"What if it had?"

"Friendship always trumps politics."

"But Mr. Neilson said that you want Russia to be an empire again… that you are in Central Asia to torpedo America's pipeline plans. It seems like politics is pretty important to you."

Uri laughed softly but remained silent for a while. At last, he replied, "The world is not really as black-and-white as it looks in the news. Peoples and governments are not the same thing, Patrick – and rarely does one stand for the other. There are people

299

in the Russian government who want to reestablish their lost empire, but many others do not. As for pipelines, I will not deny that Russia protects its energy interests, just as the United States does."

He rested the metal detector on the sand while he wiped away sweat with his scarf.

Putting his hand on Patrick's shoulder, he added, "As for America, I admire her people very much… so do many Russians. But the United States is not the same as America. America is a land, a people, an *idea*… On the other hand, the United States is a government – like any other if you ask me. And if you choose to look more closely, I suspect you will question how closely it represents you. Of course, the same can be said of Russia. I love my people and my country, but that does not mean I always agree with my government."

"Is this how my Grandpa feels?"

"You'll have to ask him," Uri replied, smiling. "He is his own man, just as you are yours."

After a fruitless hour of searching, it was time for Hasan to take a turn with the metal detector. Uri went back to digging but insisted Patrick keep his job with the metal rod.

"The desert is not an easy place, eh?" Hasan asked, grinning as they began. For a few minutes he followed Uri's careful method, but before long he was waving the detector about haphazardly, his thoughts consumed by friendly banter. Despite his quick temper, this man's energy and enthusiasm seemed to be unlimited.

"Many have never returned from these sands," he said cheerily. "Our people even say the Taklamakan is cursed. Legend has it there are immense treasures buried in the middle of the desert – gold, silver, diamonds and jade. It is said that anyone who finds them and fills his pockets with riches will become bewitched. When he attempts to leave, he will be unable to find his way, walking only in circles until he falls. Wild animals will then descend upon him, nipping and tearing away his flesh.   Only by tossing away the treasure can a man break the spell, free himself of the beasts, and find his way out of the desert."

"Do you believe that story?" Patrick asked.   "It seems a little far-fetched."

Hasan looked amused.   "Who knows?   A man is most optimistic when he starts his journey... A week in the desert may change his mind."

As they walked among the brush and sand, their conversation was relaxed and easy.   Hasan was indeed impetuous, as Yusuf had claimed, but his boundless energy was also alluring and contagious.   It was clear that he would not take life lying down, a conviction that was particularly evident in his loyalty to the Uyghur.

"Uri is a good man," Hasan admitted.   "My uncle has told me this.   But we live in a very different world today, as even Uri admits.   My people can no longer depend on Russia.   We must look elsewhere for help against the Chinese."

"Where will you get it?" Patrick pressed.

"We have friends," Hasan replied matter-of-factly.   "There are other Muslims who feel as we do.   They also fight to be free, to protect their religion, land, and way of life."   Patrick wasn't sure he liked where this was going.   "We are in touch with our brothers in Pakistan and Afghanistan.   They have much more money and experience than we do."

"Terrorists?" Patrick asked, wide-eyed.

Hasan's face reddened.   "That is an over-statement.   Those people wage *jihad* to free themselves of the invaders who occupy their lands.   They do not have tanks and fighter planes as Russia, China, or your country does, so they do what they can.   They fight as *guerillas*, just as your American colonists did against the British.   Would you call Samuel Adams or Patrick Henry terrorists?"

Patrick said nothing. It was uncomfortable when Hasan got worked up. Sensing this, the Uyghur relaxed his expression.

"I do not mean to frighten you, Patrick. You think I want violence? I don't... and neither do most Uyghur. We only want to defend what we feel belongs to us. If there were another way, we would try it... But when our backs are against the wall – when no one helps us and we are displaced, arrested, tortured, and worse in our own land – we do what we must. This includes making friends with whoever will help us. As an American, you can't possibly fault us for wanting to be free, can you?"

Patrick had never considered this point of view, so he stayed quiet. He liked Hasan and did not doubt the man meant well. However, as an American who had been born after the attacks of September 11, 2001, and who had grown up in a safe and quiet neighborhood, it was difficult to relate to the plight of the Uyghur. If his own family were threatened like Hasan's, then perhaps Patrick would fight back, too. He just didn't know...

After an hour or so, Hasan reluctantly handed over the metal detector to Ali. Once more, they both insisted Patrick continue with the metal rod. Unlike Hasan, Ali adopted a more methodical approach. He seemed deeply attuned to his surroundings, as if he were channeling a frequency beyond the one which triggered beeps in the detector's headphones. On television, Patrick had once seen a documentary where diviners used wooden sticks as "tuning forks" to find water. It had seemed a bit like voodoo, but watching Ali, Patrick felt he was witnessing a similar kind of magic.

The Turk's eyes narrowed from time to time, when he would stop and signal for Patrick to drive the metal rod into the sand. With a shake of his head Ali continued, meticulously working up and down the knoll in the straight rows marked by their earlier footprints.

"Do you think we'll find the treasure, Ali?" Patrick asked after twenty minutes of silent work.

302

"Haven't we already?" Ali replied without looking up. For a moment, Patrick wasn't sure what he meant. Then, he recalled their conversation from weeks earlier on the train across the Karakum Desert.

"What is home but a state of mind?" he repeated Ali's words aloud and smiled.

Ali nodded. "You have already traveled a long way and discovered much. Perhaps we will find the caravan, as well."

They walked a while longer before Patrick mused, "You are a Muslim, Ali..." The Turk nodded slowly. "And yet you are not angry like Hasan. Is that how most Muslims feel?"

"About what?"

"I don't know. About religion, independence, *jihad*, whatever..."

Ali did not say anything for several seconds. Then, he answered, "Do you remember when I said there are billions of people in this world?" Patrick nodded. "There are billions of Muslims, too – of all different countries, languages, and political beliefs. I do not know how they all feel, but my guess is they each have their own perspective of this world and their place in it. Certainly, not all Muslims – or even Uyghur, for that matter – feel as Hasan does."

Patrick wrinkled his nose, trying to sort out the words. Seeing this, Ali added, "History does not repeat, Patrick, it only rhymes. No one likes to be ruled, regardless of his religion. The reasons for conflict in Central Asia may be old, but with each generation the possibility of peace and friendship is also renewed."

He paused while they drank from their water bottles. A faint wind stirred the sand about their feet, and a distant thumping reverberated over the emptiness. Ali gazed in the direction of the sound, and for a moment Patrick thought he saw apprehension in the Turk's face. But when he continued speaking, his expression was untroubled.

"The banner of Islam unites many oppressed peoples around the world. Like any idea or religion, it is a hammer that can be used to build... or to destroy. Ultimately, every Muslim – indeed, every person – must think for himself. Our thoughts create our reality, my friend... not the other way around. If we choose to focus on bending others to our will, we will only get more war and conflict. On the other hand, if we choose to focus our thoughts upon happiness, abundance, and freedom, then we will get more of that."

They worked quietly for some time. At last, Patrick announced, "I like the second choice."

"I know you do," Ali said, pausing in their search. "Your thoughts have brought you here to Central Asia and they will take you wherever you want to go in life. Keep love and joy in your heart, trust yourself, and the universe will show you the way. It always does."

They worked for another hour as the sun began its slow slide toward the mountains in the west. When Uri's thick-accented growl echoed over the radio, telling them to bring it in for the day, Patrick felt a mix of emotions. He was hot, tired, and hungry. They'd toiled all day under the blistering sun without as much as a hint of discovery of the caravan. Yet he was also grateful for the time he had shared with his friends, and for simply being here in this time and place. If he were to be perfectly honest, he also had to admit they had made decent progress, even if they had found no gold or silver today. At least they knew where *not* to dig tomorrow, Patrick thought with a smile.

The search continued the next day, the one after that, and again on the fourth day. Long hours, hard work, and tempers that sometimes flared as hot as the sun... yet the band settled into a routine that felt like a dance, their camaraderie growing with the shared labors, hopes, and frustrations. Each day began by eating breakfast by the fire, followed by carrying water and tools to the river, formulating a plan, and then digging. At mid-day they enjoyed a river bath and lunch, returned to digging, and finally trekked back to camp too exhausted to be disappointed. At first, they occasionally turned their eyes to the north – toward the white smoke that rose from the mysterious campsite in the early or late hours. As the days passed, however, their concern faded. They were too tired to jump at shadows.

The fourth morning began like the others before. But on this day, it occurred to the crew that the caravan's grave could be within sight of their tents, so they decided to dig closer to camp. Patrick and Ali canvassed the top of the knoll with the metal detector and rod, silent in their work after three days of talk. It was already blistering hot and, having drunk his customary liter by mid-morning, Patrick headed toward a tamarisk bush to relieve what he hadn't already sweated out.

He went to the edge of the knoll, away from the others, and inched down over the side for privacy. Standing alone with one eye peeled for scorpions, he recalled the mysterious campsite and squinted at the horizon. It seemed strange that there had been no contact between the two parties yet, given that they were practically camped on top of one another in the middle of nowhere.

Patrick was so engrossed in his thoughts, while trying not to fall down the knoll as he finished his business, that he initially overlooked the man crouched several yards to his right. Though perfectly still, something about the stranger's outline stood out from the soft, smooth curves of the sand, and Patrick's eyes quickly returned to him. His skin was dark, and he wore the colors of the flowered shrub under which he perched: a gray silken shirt, khaki-colored pants, and snowy white doppa. He might have been content to let Patrick proceed unaware, but when their eyes connected they both knew the game was up, and he rose with a sly grin.

Patrick cursed himself for not running when he had the chance. Seconds later, when the stranger's associates appeared from the tangle of scrub and reeds, Patrick realized there would have been no point in trying to escape. After all, there were five of them – wiry, shifty-eyed, sinister looking men who could no doubt scramble over sand faster than he could. They were dressed like bandits, some wearing turbans or desert scarves, others doppas, but all bedecked with waist daggers, rifles, and bandoliers across their chests. Despairingly, Patrick realized that he was finally looking at his mysterious camp neighbors. From their appearance, it was obvious they were not innocent tourists.

They had yet to speak when a sixth man approached, his features veiled in the shadow of the sun behind him. Shielding his eyes, Patrick beheld a small and pudgy figure whose steps were nevertheless sure and confident. Nimbly climbing the dune, the man lifted his head to meet them, revealing black eyes and a crooked smile that struck Patrick with the force of a dagger. Although he had grown a scraggly black beard and his skin was tan as leather, Ahmed Batuk wore the same sinister sneer that was burned in Patrick's memory from Turkmenbashi. Had it not been for one of his henchmen standing behind Patrick, with vise-like grips on his shoulders, the shock of seeing Ahmed might have tumbled him backwards down the dune.

"We meet again, Patrick," said the man whom Uri had fittingly called a scoundrel. "But no guardian angel will rescue you this time." Fingering the revolver in his belt, he added, "In fact, I'd like to have a word with that big Turk. Let's go find him, shall we?"

As his eyes narrowed with malice, Ahmed pointed up the sandy ridge, toward which his men shoved Patrick forward.

41 KARA-BURAN

When a man is riding by night through this desert, he hears
spirits talking. These voices make him stray from
the path so he never finds it again.
– Marco Polo
(Description of the Lop Nor Desert, just east of the Taklamakan.
Translated from *The Travels of Marco Polo*)

They sat in a circle in the sand, silently watching their
captors through narrow eyes. Patrick was seated cross-legged next
to his dad, who despite his best attempt at stoicism could not hide
the worry from his face.   Their adventure was no longer an
innocent game, as it had seemed back in Kokand, atop the Torugart
Pass, or even in the tunnels below Kashgar. Aside from Ahmed's
attempt in Turkmenbashi, Patrick and his dad had managed to stay
out of danger, as if by floating high above Central Asia...
seemingly untouchable. Across more than two thousand miles,
they had avoided as much as a scratch. Even Roger Neilson's
travel warnings had seemed meant for others – naïve or unlucky
tourists maybe – but not for them.   Surely, nothing unfortunate
could possibly befall them.

After all, they were no ordinary or inexperienced party of
travelers. Their crew included Uri, the veteran Russian spy, to
smooth their way with his credentials and diplomacy. Then there
was Ali, a native and expert guide, fluent in the languages and
ways of the locals. Finally there was Dad... In Patrick's mind, at
least, he was the epitome of sureness and safety. Nothing could
possibly go wrong on his watch.

But it had gone wrong after all – terribly wrong. Their crystal fantasy had been shattered in absolutely the worst possible place, hundreds of miles from safety – and in the hands of the worst possible people, a gang of treasure-hungry outlaws.

Surrounded by Ahmed's men, Patrick would have gladly welcomed the blue uniforms of China's police force, which had seemed so grim just days earlier. As heavy-handed and prejudiced as Hasan said they were towards the Uyghur, at least the Chinese would show some consideration for Americans and Russians. Ahmed and company, on the other hand, behaved as if they were beyond the reach of any law. They seemed beyond sanity, even, with bloodshot eyes and faces and hands that twitched relentlessly. Patrick guessed their trigger fingers were no steadier than their minds.

At least they hadn't harmed their hostages yet, Patrick reflected, and perhaps this was reason enough to stay hopeful. When Ahmed had first come face to face with Ali atop the knoll, Patrick had been certain the scoundrel would lash out with his rifle butt or worse. But Ahmed only smiled, quietly reveling in the twist of fate. When he finally spoke, his voice was chillingly calm.

"I owe you for that night in the alley," he said, twisting his beard with his fingers as he no doubt fantasized the various tortures he would inflict upon the Turk. "But we'll settle that score later. In the meantime, you can use that heroic strength of yours for digging."

Ali had revealed no hint of emotion. He was a full head taller than Ahmed, and despite having an advantage in numbers and weaponry, the bandit appeared hesitant to get too close. Instead, Ahmed leveled insults at Ali from several feet away, behind the protective guard of his henchmen. At last, perhaps frustrated that he could get no reaction from the Turk, Ahmed marched his captives back to their tents. While two of his men searched the campsite and vehicle, Ahmed assembled the prisoners in a circle, and then proceeded to boast of his cleverness.

"I thought you might end up in Kashgar," he taunted, twirling the keys of their SUV around his finger. "It was obvious that the Russian here would choose the Seman Hotel. What's that about old dogs and new tricks?" He chuckled. "From there, tracking you through the old city was child's play. I admit, we did not know about the hotel's secret tunnels… But by then we had already followed this youngster to his uncle's barn." He looked at Hasan. "So my men were waiting when you emerged early that morning." His eyes danced arrogantly. "And you were so confident you'd gotten away…"

"What do you want?" Uri grumbled, his hands taking on their peculiar habit of looking at once relaxed and coiled to strike.

"The treasure, of course," Ahmed smirked. "The same thing I wanted when I tried to take the boy's journal. Did you really think your fathers' secret would stay safe for eighty-five years?"

"Who told you?" Ali asked.

"It doesn't matter. In Xinjiang, talk of treasure is as common as sand. Truth is not contained in any one grain. One must know how to sift it from the legends and wishes of old men!" He laughed again. "In any case, we are here now, aren't we? It is time to finish the job."

Ahmed pointed at the shovels, his arm outstretched in silent command. Behind him, his henchmen snickered at the ironic fate of their captives. Ali was the first to stand, his face still expressionless. Dusting off his pants, he looked coldly at Ahmed and picked up his shovel.

Uri followed Ali's lead, then Hasan, and finally Dad and Patrick. Shuffling over to the sandbank, they looked like a prison chain gang laboring shoulder-to-shoulder under the cold, watchful eyes of its armed guards. All that was missing were ankle chains and striped suits. For several hours they toiled without rest or any hope of a refreshing swim in the river. Ahmed's crew permitted them occasional sips of water, but lunch was refused amid cackles

309

and snarls. By early afternoon, the sun had assumed its imperious throne high overhead, lashing the work party with its searing rays.

Patrick was scared, and if his muscles had had any remaining strength, they would undoubtedly have shaken with fear. As it was, trepidation hung over him like a heavy blanket, paralyzing his body under its weight. He looked to his dad for reassurance, but got only hopeless compassion in return.

"I love you, son," Dad repeated painfully. "Whatever happens, I want you to know that. I shouldn't have brought you here. I should have known better..."

Patrick didn't know what to say. Maybe he had expected something else – comfort or optimism, perhaps – but a plan, for sure. Dad had never been short of solutions – he had always known how to fix a situation, no matter how bad or tough it got. Flat tires, jammed fingers, bruised feelings... he had always been there to save the day. But not now... he looked broken, as Patrick had never seen him. Was the situation really that hopeless?

If his dad could see no reason for optimism, neither could he. So Patrick merely kept digging, mechanically tossing one shovel of sand after the next over his shoulder. Even supposing they found the treasure, it was doubtful Ahmed would let them go. Why would he take chances with loose ends? Better to wrap up the business of hostages here in the desert – where there were no meddlesome witnesses...

Patrick paused, resting one hand on the shovel's handle as he wiped the sweat from his eyes. He looked up at the clear blue desert sky – the same view that had filled him with such peace and appreciation and possibility only a day earlier. It was so hot. If only he could rest a while longer...

When the blow fell upon his back it forced the air from his lungs, knocking him violently to his knees and mashing his face into the dirt. Rolling over, half in shock, his lips encrusted with sand, he looked up at the menacing jeer on the guard's face. The man's rifle was already cocked over his shoulder for a second strike. Dad dropped his shovel – his fists bunched and face snarling in rage – but Ali grabbed his wrist, momentarily restraining him.

"That's enough!" Ahmed bellowed from the shade of a tamarisk tree. "Let them be, Malik. Unless you want to dig yourself…"

The bandit swore under his breath but relaxed the rifle and stepped back. "Keep digging, fools!" he barked. "No breaks until we find the gold. Then you can rest." A sickening, knowing grin curled the mustache under his crooked nose.

Patrick rubbed his back where the rifle butt had bruised his shoulder blade. But as his dad helped him up, the fear which had gripped Patrick a moment ago seemed to subside. It was as if the guard's attack had released the tortuous anticipation of what might happen. No longer did the veiled possibility of violence hang over Patrick, paralyzing his thoughts. In fact, the pain seemed to have shocked his conscience – clearing his mind so that he could focus his thoughts. Even the heat seemed to ease, as if a bucket of cool water had been poured over him. Gradually, he was overcome by the sensation of bobbing weightlessly upon the lake by Grandpa's cabin.

It was true their situation was grim. But Patrick still had control over his thoughts. And he had a choice to make. As he picked up the shovel, he felt strength coursing back into his forearms. Drawing the handle back to strike the earth, he paused, and his eyes momentarily locked with his dad's. Patrick smiled before driving his spade deep into the sand. He would not give up.

As he laid into the knoll with renewed vigor, fortified by his decision to go on, Patrick became aware of another sensation. At first, he thought it was merely his pulse in his ears. But when he saw Ali glance over his shoulder, Patrick realized it came from beyond, somewhere to the west. Initially, the boom was not so much a sound as it was a vibration, which Patrick felt rumbling his

311

bones.   But growing louder, it became like a thumping or knocking noise. As it echoed off the sand bank, one of the guards turned to stare.   Far across the Karakash, away on the distant horizon, the sky threatened black and ominous. Rain might be rare in the Taklamakan, Patrick thought, but back home he had only seen clouds like this gather before a massive storm.

Another boom met his ears, and Patrick again searched the horizon for its source. As he did, he suddenly remembered the guard's warning and braced himself for the blow that was sure to follow.   When none came, he opened his eyes warily.   No menacing sneers or rifle barrels awaited him. Instead, he saw the wild, gleeful expressions of his captors focused on Uri. The noise reverberated again. This time it was more clearly a thump – the echo of a hammer on hollow wood.

"The treasure!" Ahmed whooped from his sitting place beneath the bush. He leaped up and careened through the sand towards them, tying his turban about his head as he ran. "We've found it!" He rushed to Uri, yanked the shovel from the Russian's hands, and began to attack the sand himself. "Quickly, uncover it!" he shrieked to his comrades.

Ahmed's eyes danced crazily, as if the man had become possessed by demons. Forgetting about their captives, the crew of bandits fell upon the sandbank with zeal, one of them on his knees, clawing at the earth with his bare fingers and squealing like a pig.

The prisoners backed away slowly, shocked by the bizarre sight, but careful not to interrupt their bewitched captors. Dad put his outstretched hand on Patrick's chest, inching him backwards, and glanced sharply at Ali beside him. Ali brought his finger to his lips, looking over his shoulder as he backtracked.

As the wind picked up, the knocking on the horizon gave way to howling, followed by a distant roar. Blowing sand stung their faces, prompting them to pull their scarves over their noses and mouths. Several yards from the sandbank, they reached their tents. Opening the flaps, they grabbed whatever was close and then ducked around the back of the campsite. At first, they fled slowly, still stunned by the strange behavior of their guards – and suspicious it might all be a trick. But by the time they reached the river they were at a full run, leaping over rocks and driftwood as they made their way upriver.

"What's the plan?" Dad shouted ahead to Ali.

Turning his head as he ran, the Turk yelled back, "We go south – towards Khotan!"

"But you said that's fifty miles from here!" Patrick shouted back.

"Yeah… but it's our only hope!"

"Is it rain?" Patrick shouted again. The Turk's response was carried away by the wind, which momentarily blinded Patrick with sand. Wiping his eyes, he yelled his question again.

Ali halted and turned, his eyelids narrow and coated with sand. "Kara-buran! The black sandstorm! Whatever you do, stay close! If we get separated, we will never find each other again!"

The wind had reached gale force now, whipping sand and leaves into the air, laying vegetation on its side and thrashing the group mercilessly. Patrick adjusted his scarf to leave only a slit through which to see, but even that could not keep the sand out. In no time, grit caked the corners of his eyes and crunched between his teeth. He trudged behind Ali, straining to keep his balance against the violent onslaught. His dad was close behind him, followed by Hasan and Uri.

They lumbered along for what seemed like an hour… But it could have been fifteen minutes or three hours for all Patrick knew. Wrapped in his scarf, enshrouded by the thick sand cloud and nearly deafened by the shrieking wind, Patrick lost all sense of time and space. At first, the storm only blocked out the sun, then it thickened to hide the dunes on their left. Soon, the Karakash faded from sight, though it couldn't have been more than ten or twenty feet from them.

Finally, Patrick could only make out Ali's heels in front of him. Desperate not to lose sight of them, he quickened his step every time the Turk's boots began to fade. But without warning, they would inevitably reappear, forcing Patrick almost to a halt to avoid getting tangled. This waltz required all his attention, but it was a merciful distraction from their perilous situation.

Sandstorms have buried cities and caravans in a day, Hasan had told him. Even Thomas had warned of this. *Go in and you won't come out*, he had written. The Taklamakan's reputation was indeed fierce, and many who entered were never seen again. But at least his party had the river as a guide, Patrick thought. If they followed it, eventually they would have to reach civilization. But the sandstorm had grown to apocalyptic proportions. It had turned day into night, drowning their voices, hammering their senses... as if spirits were calling to them, luring the voyagers from safety to join the desert's other victims in eternal sleep.

When Ali stopped and looked from left to right, Patrick knew his fears had already come true. Ali pointed to their right, but the words he screamed were carried away on the current. The Turk grabbed Patrick's hand and put it on his shirttail, and the others followed his example. Holding on to each other, the crew moved in the direction of the Karakash, but it was not there. They kept going, cantilevered into the wind, while Patrick choked down the panic that rose in his throat. Still, the river did not appear. They were lost.

The group stopped and huddled together, partly blocking the sandblasting with their backs, as Dad pulled out his compass. South! he seemed to shout as he pointed over Patrick's shoulder.

"Hold onto the man in front of you!" Dad managed to yell over what sounded like a jet engine. "Don't get separated!"

Again they set off, half blind, deaf, and numbed by the desert's brutality. Conscious thought melted into a subliminal hum, and existence was counted only in footsteps. Left, right, left... Keep going, Patrick repeated to himself. Just don't stop.

314

How long they continued like that – moving as one, ragged, pitiful beast – Patrick did not know. Time became a blur strewn with dreamlike visions of wild animals nipping at their heels, and of long ghoulish faces shrieking with wide black mouths, their clothes tattered and torn, and bony fingers reaching out to claw at him. Patrick squeezed his eyes closed and clutched Ali's shirt. When he opened them again, the ghouls were replaced by the apparitions of turbaned riders, wrapped in shawls and wearing goggles.

What peculiar horses, Patrick thought, and realized he was laughing out loud. I've gone mad, he thought, and laughed harder. One eye half open, he squinted through the blowing sand again, trying to make out the horses. Ali had stopped, and as Patrick stood dumbly, holding onto the Turk's shirt, he realized the horses were close enough to be touched. He reached out for one, and felt hair as thick and matted as a sheep's. Were these real, or was he delirious? His hand clung to the wool at first, and then his hand encountered an arm or some other body part protruding from the animal's side. Confused, he moved his hand up and sensed what felt like cloth. Moving down again, he realized the object was a boot – he was holding onto a man's leg!

The next he knew, he was being lifted up and into the saddle behind the rider. He felt his dad pat his leg and shout something, and then the animal began moving. Voices slipped by on the wind, but he could not make out the words. He reached his arms around the rider, burying his face in the stranger's back. Was it all a dream? Was this how it ended, he wondered, as the animal rocked back and forth, lumbering over the sand. As his mind clouded, the shrieking gradually retreated, his body grew heavy, fatigue overtook him and all went dark.

42 FOREIGN DEVILS

"The wise man in the storm prays to God,
not for safety from danger,
but deliverance from fear."
– Ralph Waldo Emerson

When he opened his eyes, Patrick found himself staring up at the thatched roof of a small hut. Slivers of sunlight pierced the woven reeds, cut through the dust that hung motionless in the air and speckled the dirt floor where he lay. He remained motionless for several minutes, collecting his thoughts, then working to fully open his sand-encrusted eyelids. Lifting a hand to his face, he realized he was covered in the fine-powdered sand of the desert. It matted his hair and ears, and crunched between his teeth. He tried to lick moisture back to his parched lips, but his tongue stuck to the dry insides of his cheeks.

Propping himself up on an elbow, Patrick squinted as he tried to make out his surroundings. The hut was no bigger than a small shed and furnished just as meagerly. A handful of crude wooden tools and dusty clay bowls lined the walls. In one corner, several cloth sacks lay atop a pile of hay. Next to it, a field mouse stood on hind legs, whiskers twitching as it considered Patrick through beady black eyes, then scampered into the shadows. Leaning against another wall, as if it had been transported from another world, his shiny, nylon backpack reflected the light that silhouetted the door. A gentle breeze wafted through the reed walls.

Rousing himself, Patrick groaned as he rubbed his back, which still throbbed where Ahmed's man had struck him. He was startled to see that his shirt had been replaced by a beige khalat, its long sleeves rolled up to his elbows. As he gathered his feet under him, Patrick realized his legs and rear end were equally tender. The lumbering gait of whatever beast he had ridden to get here had strained his joints and bruised his thighs. Pushing open the reed door, he tensed at the fiery sensation of his stiff cloth pants rubbing against chafed skin.

Patrick stumbled outside, where he stood on unsteady legs, his hands shielding his eyes from the glare of the midday sun that found his skin once more, immediately assaulting him with its blistering rays. A soft wind provided some relief, lightly blowing his hair and tickling his ears.

A tremendous roar shocked Patrick's senses, setting his heart pounding as his body released a reserve of adrenaline. Instinctively, he raised his hands for battle and squinted through the dazzling light in search of the noise. Seeing nothing close by, he relaxed his fists, rubbed his eyes, and looked around again.

No more than ten paces from him, tethered under a large tree, stood a large, furry two-humped camel. The shaggy animal gazed back at him through glassy black eyes, blinked its long eyelashes, and unleashed another vulgar bawl. Patrick's body relaxed at the spectacle, and he was surprised to find himself laughing. The camel's jaw worked back and forth, milling the hay which hung between its lips. Then it dunked its head into one of the buckets at its feet and sloshed thirstily with its long tongue.

"Her name is Melwah," came a familiar voice from behind. Patrick turned to see his dad and went to hug him. His dad chuckled quietly, deeply, the way he did when he was too joyful for words. "How do you feel?"

Patrick's fingers clasped his dad's shirt, while his arms hugged him as tightly as his weary muscles would allow. Dad put his lips to Patrick's hair.

"Tired," Patrick whispered back. "Thirsty…"

Smiling, his dad freed one arm to hand Patrick a water bottle, but the corners of his eyes were moist as he looked upon his son. The two stood quietly for several minutes watching Melwah. The wind stirred again, flapping Patrick's khalat in its breeze and briefly chasing away the sun's heat. The water felt cool and sweet on his tongue, and he sensed every inch of its journey down his throat to an empty belly. He could not remember anything tasting so delicious.

"She's thirsty too, eh?" Patrick looked up to see his Dad nod at the camel. "She carried you forty miles through a sandstorm." Melwah stopped chewing and stared at them for a moment, then bellowed again, its tongue flapping wildly about its lips.

"Where are we?" Patrick asked, as Melwah plunged her head into the bucket for another mouthful.

His dad scratched his head as he looked around. "A shepherds' camp. Evidently, these men had been out looking for us." He pointed at the crowd of figures on the far side of a clearing. "Hasan seems to know them. As soon as you're ready, they'll take us the rest of the way to Khotan. Another sandstorm could arrive at any moment."

Patrick nodded and went to retrieve his backpack from the hut. When he returned, the two of them crossed the clearing to where the others were already mounting camels for the final leg of the journey.

"Well, well… we don't have to leave him after all!" Uri shouted merrily from atop his camel. "Ali offered to leave you with the shepherds, but I insisted we bring you along with us!"

A strong hand grasped Patrick's shoulder. Turning, he saw the grinning, keffiyah-swathed face of Ali. "Good to see you, my friend. You would make a fine shepherd, I have no doubt." He glanced at Patrick's dad and subtly nodded his head. "But I think

318

your destiny lies beyond the Taklamakan, wouldn't you agree?" Patrick nodded. "Good. Then it is time we finish our adventure."

They rode for several hours through ragged scrub and dense thickets, sometimes approaching the Karakash River, which at other times was concealed among the narrow arroyos of low-lying hills.

Swaying atop Melwah, Patrick studied their rescuers. Wrapped in light-colored khalats and capped with the familiar doppas, the men were undoubtedly Uyghur. There were five of them – two adults about Dad's age, and the others younger, teenagers perhaps. They rode effortlessly, as if they had been born atop their animals, reminding Patrick of the cowboys he had seen back home. Although they had rifles slung over their backs, their faces were relaxed and friendly.

The sun descended as the caravan left the vacant desert for a wide, flat dirt road. Scrub gradually gave way to straight rows of poplar trees, at least a hundred feet tall and lining the thoroughfare as far as Patrick could see. Bit by bit, sandy mounds faded away, replaced by grassy clearings, then a sprinkling of roadside huts and stone walls, and finally the mud-brick buildings which marked the outskirts of a city. An occasional pedestrian quickly grew to groups of three or four, then carts pulled by donkeys and mules, and finally the sputtering of motorbikes and flat-bed trucks.

At last, the caravan was parading down a crowded asphalt road between rows of low-lying shops and restaurants, much like those which Patrick recalled from the other bazaars he had seen along the Silk Road. Everywhere, people displayed the common mixture of Turkic and Chinese features and traditional clothes of East Turkestan. Above the rooftops, a lonely minaret pierced the skyline.

The caravan continued for another mile through crowded streets before peeling off onto a quiet side road. Their escorts led them past stone walls dotted with elaborately carved wooden doors, similar to the ones Patrick had seen in Samarkand,

Khokand, and Kashgar. Finally, the lead rider halted and dismounted. As if on cue, a large gate wheeled open, and the party ducked their heads under the frame as they were lead into a large, walled compound. Children ran about the dirt yard, laughing and shouting, followed by barking dogs. Supervising them was a crowd of women adorned in colorful headscarves. A couple of older boys assisted with the camels, helping the riders dismount and taking the reins. Hasan greeted these boys merrily, kissing and "salaaming" them among laughter and boisterous talk. Smiling widely, he waved for the others to follow him inside.

"This is the home of Nur Azizi," Hasan proclaimed as he led them through a hallway and into an inner courtyard. In its open-roofed center, sitting cross-legged and alone on a wooden platform, waited an elderly man in a black khalat and white doppa. A long gray beard hung straight down his chest, and his hands lay folded gently in his lap. Looking up at them, his eyes crinkled as if with recognition, and he held out a palm for them to join him.

Hasan greeted him respectfully and then introduced his friends. The old man smiled and nodded, his eyes sharply appraising his disheveled guests. Dusting themselves off, the weary travelers stepped onto the platform, looking uncertainly at each other.

"Nur Azizi is a family friend," Hasan announced to the others. "He and Yusuf go back many years together."

Ali spoke in Uyghur, evidently bestowing compliments to the old man, who smiled and repeatedly bowed his head.

"You are safe here," Hasan reassured Patrick and his dad. "Nur Azizi is a friend. We can stay as long as we need to."

"Please tell him 'thank you,'" Dad requested, and Hasan obliged by translating. The old man nodded, watching them with a faint smile. Then he responded in Uyghur.

"You are most welcome," Hasan translated. "He is honored to have guests from so far."

A young woman brought a platter with drinks, and Patrick helped himself to a steaming cup of black tea. The party sat cross-legged in a circle on the wooden platform, surrounded by a covered walkway and the four inner walls of the home. The compound's arrangement reminded Patrick of a fortress. The courtyard was enclosed by a large wall, its perimeter devoid of as much as a peephole. All evidence of domestic life was confined to the interior of the home, where colorful tapestries hung from the walls and lush, potted plants gave the courtyard a garden-like feel.

"Yusuf sent word ahead of our journey," Hasan continued. "When the kara-buran approached, Nur Azizi became concerned and sent out his men to look for us. It is a miracle they succeeded."

The men spoke at length as Hasan translated back and forth. Nur Azizi wanted to learn more about Uri and Ali, and he smiled when they told him of their long-held fascination with the Tarim Basin. But the old man's eyes continually returned to Patrick, for whom they seemed to twinkle with amusement. Patrick shifted uncomfortably, pretending not to notice. Finally, he could not ignore the old man's behavior any longer.

"With respect, I am curious why he stares at me," Patrick whispered to Hasan, who in turn looked puzzled.

"I don't know," Hasan confessed. "Nur Azizi is very old. Perhaps you remind him of someone else."

Patrick returned his attention to the old man, who was now smiling. As Nur Azizi spoke to Hasan again, his eyes remained fixed on Patrick.

"He is most impressed by the fact we have crossed the Taklamakan and survived the kara-buran," Hasan translated. "He has known many who have not been so fortunate. He says that the desert is cursed – its promise of empire and riches has turned men into savage animals." With a wink, Hasan added, "See, I told you!"

The old man sipped his tea before continuing. His voice was high pitched but soft. He occasionally bobbed his head or lifted an index finger to make a point. As he listened, Hasan's eyes grew wide with wonder. At last, he translated.

"Nur Azizi says you are not the first from the far continent to stay as his guest. When he was a boy, a man from America—"

All of a sudden, shouts and screaming echoed down one of the inner corridors, spilling out into the courtyard. Two of Nur Azizi's men scrambled out of the doorway, looking at him with their palms bared and mouths wide in apology. Immediately after them poured a mob of blue uniforms – attire Patrick would have given his arm for a day earlier. Bringing up the rear of this entourage of Chinese police came the man who must have been their leader. He burst into the courtyard with his thumbs tucked into his jacket like a circus-master.

"It has come to my attention that you are stationing illegals here!" he shouted in broken English, pointing at Nur Azizi. "Fugitives from the Chinese government. Under the authority granted me as chief of police, I hereby announce you all under arrest!"

"For what?" Uri responded disbelievingly.

The man stared at the Russian and with an icy smile replied, "For stealing the cultural treasures of the People's Republic. You *gweilo* will all stand trial for theft!"

43 LOST OR FOUND

"Giving up doesn't always mean you are weak;
sometimes it means that you are strong enough to let go."
– Author Unknown

The police official stood motionless in the center of the courtyard, his hands clasped behind his back while his subordinates searched the house. The man's face was inscrutable, betraying neither anger nor arrogance. Only his eyes moved, shifting between his captives and the efforts of his squad. Now and again he barked what must have been a command, to which his men snapped salutes and dashed off to fulfill his instructions. Evidently, the man's name was Bin Lo and he was a regional chief in China's security services.

For the second time in twenty-four hours, the weary travelers sat in a circle with various expressions of helplessness, waiting to learn their fates from their captors. Twice, Uri's protests were cut short with flicks of Bin Lo's hand. Unaccustomed to this treatment, the Russian sat close-lipped on the edge of the platform, his arms dangling in their characteristically odd way. Patrick could not tell if he was dejected or angry – or merely reevaluating his strategy. After what seemed like a quarter-hour, one of the officers approached Bin Lo and the two conferred quietly. Bin Lo nodded curtly and dismissed him. At last, he spoke.

"Where is the treasure?" he demanded loudly, studying the ring of prisoners.

Ali traded glances with Dad, while Uri simply stared back at Bin Lo. Hasan shifted his weight nervously, and Nur Azizi sat expressionless. No one spoke.

"Where is the treasure?" Bin Lo repeated, this time with a touch of annoyance. "I know you seek a caravan of gold and silver. Tell me where it is."

Still, Uri said nothing. He looked down at his hands and then thoughtfully adjusted the cuffs on his sleeves. He looked remarkably at ease, as if he could have been relaxing in his limousine, perusing a dossier as he snacked on caviar.

Patrick sensed the official's anger rising. Despite his impassive face, the man's eyes looked as if a fire were raging behind them. He yapped another order. Two of his men stepped forward and yanked Nur Azizi to his feet, spilling the old man's tea cup to the floor, where it shattered against the wooden boards. Hasan let out a cry.

"I suspected you were up to something in Kashgar," Bin Lo said. "When you fled my officers at the Seman Hotel, you confirmed your guilt. Only criminals run from the police."

"Unless the police are the criminals!" Hasan shouted back.

"Hasan..." Ali said softly, placing his hand on the young man's shoulder.

Bin Lo considered Hasan coldly. "You will soon have an opportunity to elaborate on those sentiments. In fact, we have several questions we have been meaning to ask you..."

"What other lies did Ahmed tell you?" Uri interjected, turning heads and causing Bin Lo to tense. The question had clearly caught him off guard.

"Who?" he retorted instinctively, then removed his glasses and set about carefully polishing the lenses. Apparently, everyone has his "tell," Patrick thought wryly.

"The animal you hired in Azerbaijan," Uri replied calmly. "The one you paid to commit theft, kidnapping and... murder."

A long pause followed. Bin Lo continued buffing his glasses, but Patrick could see the man was shaken. Had he lifted his eyes to meet Uri's, the flames blazing behind them might have leapt forward out of their sockets. Nearby, Nur Azizi sagged between the two guards who clasped his shoulders. The thin old man looked as if he were suspended on a coat hanger, waiting to be neatly filed away in a police van. He looked up momentarily, and as their eyes met Patrick felt his own face flush with anger.

"You can have the treasure," Patrick heard himself announce. All heads turned to look at him. Once again, he felt as if he were floating above the room, removed from his body, an onlooker to the drama unfolding below him. "Let Nur Azizi go. He has done nothing but serve us tea."

Bin Lo's hands paused, but he continued to stare at his glasses. For what seemed like a full minute, no one moved. Then Bin Lo carefully placed his glasses back on his nose and looked up at Patrick.

"You are not in a position to make demands of me," Bin Lo snarled. "This is China, not America. Your government has no power here."

"But he *is* an American," Uri interrupted again. "And *I* am a Russian diplomat. You and I both know how this will end, Bin Lo... Your superiors will not back you on this one."

"Who says they need to know?" Bin Lo replied, a thin smile creeping across his lips. "Xinjiang is a large and dangerous place... rife with rebellion and corruption. People disappear here all the time. I am merely a district chief. Who will blame me for a few missing tourists?"

"Take the treasure," Patrick said again, surprised by the strength of his voice. He started to reach for the journal in his backpack but stopped when he heard Ali's voice.

"This is my father's map," the Turk offered Bin Lo. "It shows where the caravan lies... next to the Karakash. If you hurry, perhaps you will reach Ahmed before he takes it all for himself."

325

Bin Lo looked uncertain at first, but Patrick could sense the impact of Ali's words upon him. A seed of doubt had been planted, and it would not be long before it had grown into full-blown distrust of his accomplice. Bin Lo's eyes darted from Ali to Uri, to Patrick, and finally back to the Turk. Striding hastily to Ali, he snatched the paper from his fingers, briefly examined it, then folded and placed it in his pocket. He stayed a moment longer, his eyes searching his captives once more, and then he barked an order in Chinese. Instantly, his guards let go of Nur Azizi, who fell to the floor in a crumpled heap. Without another word, the uninvited visitors marched out of the building.

Suddenly freed from captivity, Hasan rushed forward to help Nur Azizi. They were quickly joined by several of the elder's family members who poured into the courtyard. Dad exhaled a loud sigh of relief and wrapped an arm around Patrick. Next to him, Ali sat motionless with his chin on his chest – though whether he was relieved or disappointed, Patrick could not tell. The man's decades-long quest was at an end, as was his father's legacy. Gone was any hope of recovering the treasure Misha and Thomas had discovered. As Patrick's mind searched for some words to ease his pain, Ali raised his head. Unexpectedly, he smiled and nodded.

Uri was halfway across the courtyard when Dad called after him. "What now?"

The Russian turned to peer at them through narrow slits. "Now I must place a phone call." Seeing the puzzled looks of his friends, he added, "To Chen Li – our chaperon from the Torugart Pass. I do not think he will be pleased to learn that his despised *gweilo* is actually one of his own men." Uri's green and blue eyes flashed, and then he spun on his heels and walked out.

Turning back to Patrick, Dad teased, "Something tells me we've seen the last of Bin Lo."

"And Ahmed, too," Ali added, rising to his feet. "His hunger for treasure will be his demise. If it hasn't already…"

"What do you mean?" Patrick asked.

Ali placed his hands in his pockets and looked up at the sky, where dark clouds swirled ominously. They heard a familiar howl in the distance, followed by a breeze that rustled their hair. Grinning, he looked at Patrick and said, "Go in and you won't come out."

The sandstorm subsided by early evening. Nur Azizi had invited his guests inside to wait out the blowing sand, and when the skies finally cleared they returned to the open-roofed courtyard. Reconvening on the wooden platform – now illuminated by the flickering light of torches and the stars overhead – the group sipped black tea. Patrick's journey was nearly over and, knowing he was now safe from Ahmed, he was infused with a strange calm. He felt like he had the night of their hike alongside the Karakash, when everything seemed exactly as it was meant to be. The others must have shared his sentiments, for they all sat quietly for what seemed like an hour – each member lost in his own thoughts.

At last, Nur Azizi interrupted the silence by speaking softly in Uyghur. As he did, the old man looked at Patrick and smiled again.

"He says you are like your great-grandfather," Hasan translated. Even the dim light could not hide the look of astonishment on Hasan's face. "Like Thomas, you are kind and courageous. You are a good man."

Patrick sat cross-legged with his teacup in his lap, uncertain how to respond. This revelation explained the man's earlier behavior. For some reason, Patrick was not surprised by his words.

"He says he was a young boy when he met Thomas," Hasan continued, directing his words to Patrick. "Your great-grandfather arrived in Khotan in the year of a severe drought, when the Karakash was no more than a dry, dusty river bed. He had been camped in the Taklamakan with two friends – a Russian and a

Turk. Having run out of water, Thomas crawled out of the desert to summon help for his friends. He was a man who never quit."

Patrick looked at Ali, who in turn bowed his head. Across the circle, Uri seemed to smile in the crimson light of the torches. Before Hasan could continue, the pattering of feet turned their attention to a young girl carrying a carved wooden chest. Setting it down at Nur Azizi's feet, the child kissed the top of his head and retreated back to the house.

Seeing the box, Hasan's face lit up and he rubbed his hands excitedly. "Ah, games!" he cried. "Just like when I came here as a boy."

Nur Azizi opened the box and withdrew what looked like a roll of parchment, which was faded and tattered at its edges. With shaking hands, the old man untied the golden cords that bound the material and unrolled it on the timber planks before him. Leaning forward, Patrick strained his eyes to make out the images in the flickering shadows. Printed upon the large, square cloth was the checkered pattern of a chess board. Stitched into the design were dozens of smaller images – human figures, animals, mountains, and rivers – as well as cryptic writing.

Reaching back into the wooden chest, Nur Azizi retrieved a smaller box and placed it at his feet. One by one, he took out various ornately carved statuettes – kings, horses, soldiers, and elephants – and passed them along the circle until every person had his own pieces. Nur Azizi carefully arranged his statuettes on the squares closest to him, with Hasan and Ali following his example.

Nur Azizi spoke again and Hasan translated. "Long ago, this game came to us from the mountains to the south."

"From India, centuries before Islam arrived in China," Ali quietly added. Patrick nodded, remembering Thomas's mention of the game in his journal.

"How do we play?" Patrick asked.

"Like chess," Hasan replied merrily. "You try to capture the others' kings."

"We all play at once?" Patrick pressed.

"Yes," Hasan answered. "And there is not always a clear winner."

"When is it over?"

Ali smiled and raised his eyebrows. "Ha! Good question." He chuckled and handed Patrick a jade elephant. "Here – the mysterious *gaja*. It's similar to the bishop in chess, but it is one of the most respected pieces in this game. The elephant has long been worshipped by the people here. It represents wisdom, power, and peace."

Patrick placed the elephant on the parchment, lining it up with the others as Hasan had done. Turning the conversation back to his great-grandfather, he asked, "What happened to them? I mean, how did it end for Thomas, Misha, and Dmitri?"

Patrick's words seemed to hang in the air between the players. When he got no answer, Hasan quietly interpreted Patrick's question to Nur Azizi, who chuckled softly. The old man bobbed his head as he responded, his expression hidden by the shadows.

"Your great-grandfather intended to return to the caravan," Hasan translated, "But the Russian was sick. So Thomas and Misha stayed, refusing to go back without him."

Nur Azizi advanced one of his pieces across the board, triggering a cry of frustration from Hasan. Regaining his composure, Hasan continued, "Thomas and Misha faced a choice. Recover the gold or save their friend…"

Uri grunted as he pondered Nur Azizi's move. At last, he pushed forward one of his own soldiers, no doubt preparing a counterstrike. Then he added, "Your great-grandfather and Misha gave up their hunt for the gold. Instead, they carried my father to India."

Ali sat with his chin on his hand, pondering Uri's previous move. Shaking his head with frustration, he hugged his knees, rocked back, and looked over at Patrick. Seeing the questioning look in Patrick's face, the Turk added: "They went over the Karakorum Pass." He pointed at the wall over Patrick's shoulder. "To the south – to India."

Instinctively, Patrick turned to look at the wall, envisioning the mighty mountain range he knew to lay just beyond it. He recalled the story Grandpa had told him in the hospital – about when Thomas had stood atop the pass with a promise in his heart to return to Asia. Thomas had indeed returned, but his mission to retrace the entire Silk Road was clearly a failure. His plans had been to reach Xi'an (SHE-an) – the eastern starting point of the Silk Road – and then continue to Beijing. Instead, crossing the Karakorum Pass for the second time, he returned with nothing – no treasure and no fame.

Patrick furrowed his brow. "Now we've lost the treasure, too. Your dreams... and your fathers' dreams!" He looked at his dad. "Grandpa's, too... We failed again."

Uri chuckled softly, but it was Ali who spoke next. "Thomas viewed life as a journey towards enlightenment. Now, here we sit – fathers, sons, and friends from far corners of the world – linked by history, but with our own paths to follow. We have discovered much on our journey, don't you think?"

As he considered these words, Patrick tilted his head back and gazed up at the star-filled night sky. Sparkling overhead was the Summer Triangle – the stars Vega, Deneb, and Altair – the same constellation Thomas had predicted would mark his arrival in China. Perhaps his great-grandfather had sat in this very spot when he made the decision to give up his expedition for the sake of a friend.

They played the game into the wee hours of the morning, until Patrick became sleepy and lost track of time. He vaguely remembered Hasan snapping a picture of the group before he fell asleep. When he awoke at dawn he was wrapped warmly in a soft sheepskin. The others had slumbered on the platform nearby, wrapped in their own blankets against the cold. The old man was gone, causing Patrick to briefly wonder if he had really been there at all.

44 TABIYA

"We are what we think. All that we are arises with our thoughts.
With our thoughts, we make the world."
– Buddha

Gazing through the clouds at the ocean shimmering far below, Patrick reflected on the striking contrasts of the past three months. He recalled another flight, at the summer's start, on which a fair-skinned boy had sat by a window just like this. He had worn stylish Western clothes then, played video games, and anxiously pondered his first trip out of the country. Awed by the feats of previous generations of Eaton explorers, but convinced he had been born too late to join them, that boy could only guess at what awaited him on the far side of the world.

Patrick glanced down at his lap where his fingers caressed the small jade elephant. On the train ride from Khotan to Beijing, he had discovered the statuette in his backpack. Dad, Ali, and Uri each denied having putting it there. Patrick turned the statuette over in his hands, feeling the edges worn smooth over centuries. Viewed in the sunlight, it seemed to glow with the magic and mystery of exotic Asia. He ran his a finger along the grooved inscription, whose words were too old for Hasan to translate. Looking out the window again, Patrick instinctively touched his lips, which were cracked and scabbed from weeks in the desert. Dad slept in the seat next to him, his hat pulled down over his eyes, revealing only a sun-bleached beard. Patrick smiled and turned back to the window.

Two days earlier he had been sitting cross-legged in the mud-walled home of a Chinese Uyghur – after barely escaping the notorious Taklamakan – and listening to the village elder recount the extraordinary conclusion of Thomas's expedition three-quarters of a century ago. Just a week before that, Patrick had been stunned by the revelation that his own Grandpa – the sweet, absent-minded, old storyteller who lived in a cabin by the lake – had once been a daring spy involved in Cold War intrigues across Central Asia. On top of this, Patrick learned that Ali and Uri not only knew his grandfather – but that, in fact, the three had formed a secret pact to seek the treasure of their fathers!

Of course, all of this came on the heels of a summer spent roaming the Silk Road in the footsteps of his great-grandfather, cracking secret ciphers, braving the decrepit old Dagestan ferry and Soviet-era railcars, engaging in hand-to-hand combat with a double-crossing interpreter, wandering the ghostly ruins of ancient empires, crossing borders and neutral zones, riding camels and hunting for jade, surviving sandstorms, defusing a confrontation with Chinese police, and... the list went on and on.

In contrast, he now sat in the luxurious, air-conditioned cabin of a modern jetliner, cruising along at 30,000 feet, sipping ice-cold soda served by a blonde flight attendant from Switzerland, with a mini-television in the back of the seat facing him. Soon he'd be back home in the United States, snacking from a fridge, mowing the lawn, sleeping in his childhood bed, and getting ready to start his freshman year at Central High. The contrast made Patrick chuckle to himself.

Finally, their fourth flight in twenty-four hours touched down. They were home at last. As they walked through the airport tunnel and into the concourse, Patrick was startled once more by the mob of hectic commuters scurrying this way and that. He winced at the violent jostle of elbows and bags, shrill ring of cell phones, reverberation of the public address system, and flash of televisions and electronic billboard displays. Stepping back into

Western civilization, his senses were overwhelmed by the rumble and roar of the modern-day masses.

When Patrick spotted his mom running toward him, he dropped his bag at his feet so she could wrap her arms around him. For the next several minutes, she cried and kissed him, fussing and fretting, patting and hugging, as he stood dazed but happy.

"Oh, my goodness, Patrick, I missed you so much!" she cried. "Look how big you are! I can't believe I let you out of my sight for an entire summer. I must have been crazy. But, did you have fun? I want to hear all about it. You took plenty of pictures, didn't you? Your skin is so tan! What happened to your clothes? I am so glad you are home!" She continued fawning over him all the way to the baggage claim and then out to the parking garage.

The car ride was like a dream. A gray sky and drizzle greeted them as they pulled out of the garage. It was the first precipitation he had seen all summer, and he marveled at the vibrant shades of green and succulent foliage draping the hills outside. With Mom at the wheel, they entered the highway and wove through the traffic, through the busy tangle of overpasses and construction cones, and past the familiar clutter of car dealerships, fast-food restaurants, outlet stores, and billboards.

The swishing wipers evoked the memory of another rainy car ride Patrick had taken at the start of his summer, after Grandpa's heart attack. It seemed so long ago. He and his mom had hurried to the hospital along this same highway – fraught with fear, sadness and, for Patrick anyway, guilt. Recalling this, it now occurred to Patrick that they were not headed home.

"Where are we going?" he asked.

From the front passenger's seat, his dad turned his head slightly to reply. "We thought we'd swing by the cabin to check on Grandpa. I bet he'd like to see us. What do you think?"

Patrick grinned and nodded. "Yeah, I'd like to see him too." Then, yawning, he turned to the window and fell immediately to sleep.

When Patrick woke, the car was still. His window was open and the birds chirped in the trees outside. Lifting his head, he saw the rain had stopped. A glistening mist hung over the forest clearing, pierced here and there by the silvery rays of sunlight streaming through the canopy of leaves. He knew where he was – he had been here a hundred times before.

"Well, well, my friend. You have returned after all," said a familiar voice from outside his window. Patrick looked up to see Grandpa leaning against the car, cupping a mug in his hands.

"Grandpa!" Patrick fumbled to undo his seatbelt, and then leapt out of the car to hug him.

"Whoa! Look at you!" Grandpa chuckled, wrapping his arms around the boy. "My little adventurer has come home. But you are not so little anymore!"

Patrick beamed. Standing in the serene magnificence of the clearing, Grandpa looked strong – the way Patrick remembered him – and far from the shell of a man he had last seen lying in a hospital bed.

Grandpa gently pushed him to arm's length and sized him up. His twinkling eyes wandered from Patrick's scuffed and weather-beaten shoes to his ragged pants, then to the cotton khalat of the Uyghur, and the desert scarf given to him by Ali. His eyes finally came to rest on the elephant that Patrick clutched by his side. Grandpa smiled and nodded.

"Let's go inside, shall we? We have much to talk about, I think…"

Patrick searched his eyes. How much did Grandpa know about the summer? How much had he known from the very beginning? The old man's face revealed nothing. He merely draped an arm over Patrick's shoulder as they climbed the porch steps to the screen door.

335

Inside, Mom was making tea while Dad was on the phone with Skip. Back to work already... Energy powers the world, and the world never stops. Patrick smiled.

Finding his chair by the fireplace, Grandpa settled into a familiar pose – feet up on the armoire as he methodically stuffed his pipe. Patrick thought he detected a faint grin on his grandfather's face. The master storyteller had always relished Patrick's eagerness for these moments. After a long summer away from his grandson, he seemed especially keen on savoring this tradition.

Humoring the old man, Patrick drifted over to the wall by the fireplace, his hands in his pockets. He looked around the room, somewhat puzzled. The cabin looked different from what he remembered. Perhaps Grandpa had rearranged it, or maybe Patrick was seeing the place through changed eyes. He noticed a pair of framed black-and-white pictures hanging over the mantle. Had they always been there?

Stepping closer, he crinkled his eyes to make out the figures posing together in one of the faded photos. Staring back at him were three dashingly rugged characters, dressed in knee high leather boots, heavy coats, broad rawhide belts stuffed with daggers and pistols, and topped with an assortment of turbans and fur-lined hats. On the left, Patrick recognized his great-grandfather with his classically broad and fearless grin. In the middle of the trio was a bull-necked man with narrow eyes and a handlebar mustache – this was Dmitri, no doubt about it. And on the right stood a man with a long black beard and white skull-cap. He cradled a rifle in the crook of his elbow... Misha.

Patrick shook his head in wonder as his eyes drifted to the second photo below. It, too, showed three figures standing shoulder-to-shoulder. Each held the reins of their camels, their other hands clasping a walking stick, rifle, or leather pouch. Standing on his toes, Patrick squinted to make out their faces. They had thicker hair, broader shoulders, and more chiseled features back then. But their eyes gave them away. Grandpa, Uri, and Ali stood together – their arms linked in camaraderie – framed by the barren mountains of Central Asia in the background.

Patrick hesitated a moment longer, and then went to the couch where his backpack lay. Reaching inside, he fished about until finding his prize. Returning to the fireplace, Patrick reached up and placed the Polaroid photo from Nur Azizi's house on the mantle beneath the others. He turned and smiled at Grandpa who, caught off guard by the gesture, spilled a pinch of tobacco leaves onto his lap. He reached for his glasses on the table beside him and squinted up at the wall, trying to make out the image. Recognizing the faces after a few seconds, he relaxed and slumped back in his chair.

"Okay, my friend," he surrendered. "So you have written your own chapter. Please tell me a story about Turkestan… of the sand and stars, the mountains and rivers, and my old friends there. It has been so long…"

Lingering by the fireplace, Patrick placed one arm on the mantle, prepared to tell a story only his Grandpa could believe or understand. But on second thought he paused, deciding to draw out the suspense just a bit. He blew softly on the tea Mom had brought him, and then took a couple slow sips in playful exaggeration. Recognizing this tactic and enjoying every moment of it, Grandpa laughed and began to gently rock his chair. Satisfied, Patrick smiled and went over to his old chair – the one in which he had sat listening to the old man's stories as a small boy.

Placing his feet on the armoire next to Grandpa's, he cupped the mug in his hands, leaned his head back, and began to tell the story of Patrick Eaton's first adventure to Asia.

THE END

ABOUT THE AUTHOR

Andrew C. Katen is an educator, geopolitical analyst, and geologist. He has taught middle school and college, worked in homeland security, and published and presented on various topics related to geopolitics and risk management. Andrew holds an M.S. in national security studies and B.S. degrees in geology and biology. *Chaturanga* is his first novel.

For more information about *Chaturanga*, email Andrew at akaten@chaturangabook.com. Visit him on Facebook for book updates, as well as geopolitical news and analyses.

www.ingramcontent.com/pod-product-compliance
Lightning Source LLC
Chambersburg PA
CBHW071043250626
47159CB00002B/350